Jayne Ann Krentz, who has also written under the names Amanda Quick and Jayne Castle, has thirty-two *New York Times* bestsellers to her credit. She lives in Seattle.

Other titles by Jayne Ann Krentz:

Light in Shadow
Truth or Dare
Falling Awake
White Lies

Titles by Jayne Ann Krentz writing as Amanda Quick:

The Paid Companion
Wait Until Moonlight
Lie By Moonlight
Second Sight
The River Knows

ALL NIGHT LONG

Jayne Ann Krentz

PIATKUS

Visit the Piatkus website!

Piatkus publishes a wide range of best-selling fiction and non-fiction, including books on health, mind, body & spirit, sex, self-help, cookery, biography and the paranormal.

If you want to:
- read descriptions of our popular titles
- buy our books over the Internet
- take advantage of our special offers
- enter our monthly competition
- learn more about your favourite Piatkus authors

VISIT OUR WEBSITE AT: www.piatkus.co.uk

Copyright © 2005 Jayne Ann Krentz

First published in Great Britain in 2005 by
Piatkus Books Ltd of
5 Windmill Street, London W1T 2JA
email: info@piatkus.co.uk

This edition published 2006

Reprinted 2007

First published in the United States in 2005 by
G.P. Putnam's Sons, a member of Penguin Putnam Inc.

The moral right of the author has been asserted

A catalogue record for this book is available from the British Library

ISBN 978 0 7499 3739 3

Data manipulation by Phoenix Photosetting, Chatham, Kent
www.phoenixphotosetting.co.uk
Printed and bound in Great Britain by
Mackays of Chatham, Chatham, Kent

This one is for Cathie Linz, great writer and great friend

ALL NIGHT LONG

Prologue

Seventeen years earlier . . .

The house at the end of the lane was filled with darkness and night.

That wasn't right, Irene thought. Her parents always left the lights on for her.

"Don't be mad, Irene." Pamela stopped the car in the driveway. The convertible's headlights blazed a short distance into the thick stand of fir trees that loomed beside the house. "It was just a joke, okay? Hey, look, the lights are off inside your place. Your folks are in bed. They'll never know you got home after curfew."

Irene pushed open the car door and scrambled out of the convertible. "They'll know. You've ruined everything."

"So tell them it was my fault," Pamela said carelessly. "I lost track of the time."

"It was my fault. I made the mistake of believing that you really were my friend. I thought I could trust you. My folks only have two rules. No drugs and no driving to the other side of the lake."

"Give me a break. You only broke one rule tonight." In the lights of the dash, Pamela's smile was very bright. "I didn't even have any drugs in the car."

"We weren't supposed to go beyond the town limits, and you know it. You just got your license. Dad says you haven't had enough experience behind the wheel yet."

"I got you home safe and sound, didn't I?"

"That's not the point and you know it. I made a promise to my folks."

"You are such a *good* girl." Disgust and exasperation were thick in Pamela's words. "Don't you get tired of always following the rules?"

Irene took a step back. "Is that what this was all about tonight? You wanted to see if you could make me break the rules? Well, you succeeded, so I hope you're satisfied. This is the last time you and I will do anything together. But that's probably just what you wanted, isn't it? Good night, Pamela."

She turned toward the darkened house, digging into her purse to find her key.

"Irene, wait—"

Irene ignored her. Key in hand she hurried toward the front door. Her parents were going to be furious. They would probably ground her for life or, at the very least, for the rest of the summer.

"Okay, be that way," Pamela called after her. "Go back to your perfect, boring, good girl life and your perfect, boring little family. Next time I pick a best friend I'll choose one who knows how to have fun."

Pamela drove off very quickly. When the convertible's headlights disappeared, Irene found herself alone in the night. She was very conscious of the chill in the air. That was wrong, too, she thought. It was summer. The moon was shining out on the lake. She and Pamela had put the top down on the flashy new sports car this evening. It shouldn't have felt so cold.

Maybe this was what it was like when you discovered that you could not trust someone you thought was a friend.

Morosely she watched to see if a light came on in her parents' bedroom at the side of the house. They must have heard Pamela's car, she thought. Her father, especially, was a light sleeper.

But the house remained dark. She felt a small flicker of relief. If her folks did not wake up tonight, she could put off the inevitable scene until morning. Breakfast would be soon enough to find out that she had been permanently grounded.

She could just barely make out the front porch steps. Her dad had forgotten to turn on the light over the door. That was really weird. He always left that light and the one at the back of the house on all night. It was another one of his rules.

She paused, key in hand. Her parents' bedroom was directly to the right of the entrance. They would almost certainly hear her if she went in through the front door. But if they were still asleep, they might not notice the sound of the back door being opened. Going in through the kitchen would give her a shot at sneaking down the hall to her bedroom without arousing her folks.

Turning away from the front porch steps, she hurried around the side of the house. It was so dark. Too bad she didn't have a flashlight. In the silvery moonlight the small dock and the little boat that her father used for fishing were almost invisible.

She was startled to discover that the light was off over the back porch, too. In the dense shadows, she tripped on the bottom step, stumbled and nearly fell. At the last instant she managed to grab the railing and right herself.

What were the odds that her dad had forgotten to turn on both porch lights? Something was really strange here. Maybe the bulbs had burned out simultaneously.

She fumbled the key into the lock and turned the knob cautiously, trying to open the door without making any noise.

The door resisted her efforts to push it inward. Something heavy seemed to be blocking it from the inside. She shoved harder.

A terrible, stomach-churning smell wafted out through the opening. Had some animals gotten into the house? Her mother would have a fit in the morning.

But a part of her already knew that things were horribly wrong. She started to shiver violently. It was all she could do to move one foot across the threshold and grope for the switch on the wall.

The lights came on, dazzling her for a couple of seconds. Then she saw the blood on the kitchen floor.

She heard someone screaming. In some remote corner of her mind she understood that she was the one who was uttering the high, desperate, frantic cries of grief, horror and denial. But the sound was distant and far away.

She had traveled to some other place, a realm where nothing was the way it was supposed to be; where nothing was normal.

When she returned from the journey, she discovered that her personal, private definition of normal had been altered forever.

Hi, Irene:

I know this e-mail is coming as a huge surprise. Hope you didn't dump it straight into your deleted file when you saw the name of the sender. But I hear you're a reporter now, and reporters are supposed to be curious types so, with luck, you'll read this.

Hard to believe that it's been seventeen years since we last saw each other, isn't it? I realize that, given what happened, you would have been quite happy to go another seventeen years without hearing from me. But I have to talk to you, and I have to do it soon.

This is about the past. What I need to tell you can't be done in an e-mail or over the phone. Trust me, this is as important to you as it is to me.

I've got a few things to take care of before we meet. Come up to the lake on Thursday afternoon. I should have everything ready by then. Give me a call as soon as you get into town.

By the way, I never forgot how much you liked eating orange sherbet and vanilla ice cream together. Funny the things you remember, isn't it?

Your ex–best friend,
Pamela

One

I'll walk you back to your cabin, Miss Stenson," Luke Danner said.

Irene felt the hair stir on the nape of her neck. She paused in the act of fastening her black trench coat. *Should have left earlier,* she thought. *Should have gone back to the cabin while there was still some daylight.*

This was what came of being a news junkie. She'd just had to have her evening fix, and the only television available at the Sunrise on the Lake Lodge was the ancient model in the tiny lobby. She had ended up in the company of the proprietor of the lodge, watching the relentless stream of depressing reports from correspondents around the globe. Earlier she had seen him flip on the No Vacancy sign. That had worried her a bit. There were no signs of any other guests at the lodge.

She tried to think of a reasonable excuse to turn down the offer of an escort. But Luke was already on his feet. He crossed the shabby, well-worn lobby in long, easy strides, heading toward the front desk.

"It's a dark walk to the cabin," he said. "Couple of the lights on the footpath are out."

Another little chill went through her. She'd been dealing with her over-the-top fear of the dark since she was fifteen. But this nervy, atavistic reaction wasn't just the usual twinge of deep dread that she experienced whenever she contemplated the fall of night. It was all mixed up with the edgy, unfamiliar awareness of Luke Danner.

At first glance some people might have been inclined to underestimate him. She would never in a million years make that mistake, she thought. This was a complicated man. Under certain circumstances he would no doubt be a very dangerous man.

He was of medium height with a tough, compact, lean frame and broad shoulders. His features were stark and fiercely hewn. His hazel-green eyes were those of an alchemist who has stared too long and too deeply into the refiner's searing fires.

There was a sprinkling of silver in his closely trimmed dark hair. She suspected that he was within shouting distance of forty. There was no wedding ring on his left hand. Probably divorced, she decided. Interesting men his age had usually been married at least once, and Luke Danner was nothing if not interesting. Make that fascinating.

He'd barely spoken to her over the course of the last hour and a half of all-news-all-the-time television. He'd just sat there beside her, sprawled in one of the massive, ancient armchairs, legs stretched out on the worn rug, and contemplated the unnaturally cheerful reporters and anchors with a calm, stoic air. Something about his attitude suggested that he had already seen the worst the world had to offer and was not particularly impressed with the televised version.

"I'll be fine on the path," she said. She removed a penlight from the pocket of her coat. "I've got a flashlight."

"So do I." Luke ducked briefly out of sight behind the reception desk. When he straightened he held a large, heavy-duty flashlight. In his big, capable hand it looked disconcertingly like a weapon. He eyed her little penlight. Amusement gleamed briefly in his eyes. "Mine's bigger."

Ignore that remark, she told herself, opening the door before he could do it for her.

The bracing night air sent a shiver through her. She knew that it rarely snowed at this elevation. The Ventana Lake resort region was in the mountains, but it was not far from the moderate climes of wine country. Nevertheless, it was still early spring, and it could get very cold after dark in this part of northern California.

Luke whipped a somewhat battered, fleece-lined leather jacket off a coatrack that had been fashioned from a set of deer antlers, and followed her through the door. He did not bother to lock up, she noticed. But then, crime had never been a big problem in the town of Dunsley. She knew for a fact that there had been only two murders here in the past two decades. They had occurred on a summer night seventeen years ago.

She stopped at the edge of the stone-and-log entranceway

of the lodge. It was seven-thirty but it might as well have been midnight. Night hit hard and fast in the heavily wooded shadows of the mountains.

She pulled up the collar of her trench coat and switched on her small flashlight. Luke fired up the giant, commercial-grade torch he had retrieved from under the reception desk.

He was right, she thought wryly, his flashlight was definitely bigger. The wide beam it projected swallowed up whole the narrowly focused rays of her dainty penlight and leaped ahead to rip large chunks out of the dense night.

"Nice flashlight," she said, reluctantly intrigued. No one appreciated a good flashlight more than she did. She considered herself a connoisseur. "What kind is it?"

"Military surplus. Got it on eBay."

"Right." She made a note to check out the military surplus shopping sites online the next time she was in the market for a new flashlight. That wouldn't be long. She upgraded regularly.

Luke descended the three stone steps beside her, moving with a lithe, comfortable ease that told her he certainly had no qualms about facing the night. She got the feeling that very few things scared Luke Danner.

She surveyed the path. "Not just a couple of the path lights out, I see. Looks like none of them are functioning."

"Got some new ones on order down at the hardware store," he said, unconcerned.

"Be wonderful if they got installed by summer, wouldn't it?"

"Is that sarcasm I hear in your voice, Miss Stenson?"

She gave him a brilliant smile. "Heavens, no."

"Just checking. Sometimes you sophisticated folks from out of town are a little too sharp for us locals."

Don't play the small-town rube with me, Luke Danner. I didn't just fall off the back of the turnip truck, myself. True, she didn't know much about him—wasn't sure she wanted to learn more—but she could see the gleam of diamond-hard intelligence in his eyes.

"Something tells me you don't belong in Dunsley any more than I do, Mr. Danner."

"What makes you say that?" he asked, a little too politely.

"Call it a wild, intuitive guess."

"You do that a lot?"

"Do what a lot?"

"Make wild, intuitive guesses?"

She thought about it. "Sometimes."

"Personally, I don't like guesswork," he said. "I prefer facts."

"No offense, but that sounds a bit obsessive."

"Yeah, it does, doesn't it?"

They crunched along the gravel walk that linked the lodge's twelve individual log cabins. Or rather, *she* crunched in her fashionable high-heeled black leather boots. Luke wore running shoes. She couldn't even hear his footsteps although he was right beside her.

Through the trees she caught glimpses of silver on the broad black mirror that was the lake. But the glow of the moon did not penetrate the tall stands of pine and fir that loomed over the grounds of Sunrise on the Lake Lodge. She could hear ghosts whispering in the boughs overhead. Her hand tightened convulsively around the grip of the penlight.

She would never admit it to him, she thought, but she was glad that Luke was with her. Night was never a good time. It would be worse than usual tonight because she was spending it in the town that haunted her dreams. She knew she probably would not sleep until dawn.

The gravel crunching and the eerie sounds of the wind in the trees feathered her nerves. She suddenly wanted to talk; to make casual, reassuring conversation. She needed the comfort of the company of another person. But judging from his earlier silence while they watched the news together, she had a hunch that polite, meaningless, social chitchat was not Luke Danner's thing. Dinner dates were probably a major ordeal for him.

She glanced at the first cabin, the one Luke evidently used as his personal residence. The porch light was on in front but the windows were dark. There were no lights on in any of the other cabins with the glaring exception of the one she had been assigned. Lights blazed in every window of Cabin Number Five as well as on the front and back porches. She had left the place fully illuminated earlier when she decided to make the trek to the lobby and the only available TV.

"It looks like I'm your only guest tonight," she said.

"Off-season."

She reminded herself that the tiny resort communities that ringed Ventana Lake acknowledged only two seasons, off and high. Still it seemed strange that the lodge was so empty.

"Mind if I ask why you turned on the No Vacancy sign?" she asked.

"Don't like to be bothered in the evening," Luke said. "Bad enough having people turn up at all hours during the day wanting to rent a room. A real pain."

"I see." She cleared her throat. "Are you new to the hospitality business?"

"I don't think of it as selling hospitality," he said. "More like a necessity. Someone needs a room for the night, fine, I'll rent one to him. But if the customer can't be bothered to arrive at a reasonable hour, he can damn well drive on around the lake to Kirbyville and find himself a motel there."

"That's certainly one way to run a lodging establishment," she said. "Although maybe not the most profitable approach. When did you take over the lodge?"

"About five months ago."

"What happened to the man who used to run this place?"

She sensed immediately that the question had aroused Luke's curiosity.

"You knew Charlie Gibbs?" he asked neutrally.

She regretted the query. True, she wanted to talk tonight, but the last thing she intended to discuss was her past in this town. Still, she was the one who had invited him down this particular conversational byway.

"I knew Charlie," she said carefully. "But it's been several years since I last saw him. How is he, by the way?"

"Real estate agent who sold the lodge to me said he died last year."

"I'm sorry to hear that."

And she was, she realized. Charlie had been getting on in years when she lived here in town. She was not surprised to learn that he was gone. But the news elicited another of the small, unsettling twinges of loss that she had been experiencing since she arrived a few hours ago.

She had not known Charlie Gibbs well, but, like the monument of a library in the park, he and the dilapidated old lodge had been a feature of the landscape of her youth.

"I'm told business will pick up around here right after Memorial Day," Luke said in a tone that lacked any semblance of enthusiasm. "I hear it runs pretty hot and heavy through Labor Day."

"That's the way it is in summer resort towns." She paused briefly. "You don't sound overly thrilled with the prospect of increased business."

He shrugged. "I like it nice and quiet. Main reason I bought the place. That and the fact that I figured I couldn't go wrong with waterfront property."

"Isn't it a little difficult to make a living with your approach to the business?"

"I get by. Come summer, I'll jack up the rates. Make up for the slow months."

She thought about the SUV parked in front of his cabin. The vehicle was big, expensive and new. Charlie Gibbs had never been able to afford such high-end transportation. Nor had Charlie ever worn a watch like the one Luke was wearing, she reflected. Titanium chronographs that looked as though they could be submerged to a depth of three hundred feet and keep track of several different time zones did not come cheap.

Her curiosity was growing by the second, but she sensed that Luke would not welcome an in-depth discussion of his household finances. She groped for another subject.

"What did you do before you bought the lodge?" she asked.

"Got out of the Marines about six months back," he said. "Tried the corporate world for a while. Things didn't work out."

She could well believe that he had spent time in the military, she thought. It wasn't just the way he held himself, as though he were dressed in a uniform instead of a casual shirt and jeans; rather it was the aura of confidence, authority and command. Alpha male through and through. She knew the type well. Her father had been a Marine before he became a cop.

Luke was the guy who would keep his head and lead you through the smoke and flames to safety when everyone else was running around in a mindless panic. Men like this certainly had their uses, but they were not the easiest sort to live with. Her mother had explained that to her on more than one occasion in tones of great exasperation.

"The lodge must have been in bad shape by the time you bought it," she said. "It was practically falling apart the last time I saw it, and that was quite a while ago."

"Been working on the infrastructure a bit." He looked toward her cabin, perched on the edge of the lake amid a stand of tall trees. "Maybe you didn't notice the little card in the room that suggested you might want to help the management of the

Sunrise on the Lake Lodge save the environment by making sure that all lights were turned off when you left the cabin."

She followed his gaze to Cabin Number Five. It glowed like a football stadium in the middle of a night game.

"I saw the card," she assured him. "But I also noticed that management was driving a very large sports utility vehicle that probably gets less than five miles to the gallon. I naturally assumed, therefore, that the request to conserve energy was merely a devious, hypocritical ploy designed to make guests feel guilty if they didn't help management save a few bucks on the lodge's electricity bill."

"Well, damn. Told Maxine the card wouldn't work. Never pays to be subtle. You want people to obey the rules, I said, you've got to make the rules loud and clear. No two ways about it."

"Who's Maxine?"

"Maxine Boxell. My assistant manager. She's a single mother. Her son, Brady, is going to handle the lodge's boat during the summer. I understand we get a lot of guests who like to go out on the lake at that time of year. Maxine says we can charge a ton of money for a three-hour fishing trip. She's also after me to get another, faster boat that can be used to haul water skiers. I'm holding off on that decision, though. Might encourage too much business."

The name rang a bell. There had been a Maxine who graduated from the local high school in June of the year that the world had shattered. She had been Maxine Spangler then.

"Mind if I ask what brings you here to Dunsley, Miss Stenson?" Luke asked.

"Personal business."

"Personal, huh?"

"Yes." She could do inscrutable, too, she thought.

"What kind of work do you do?" he asked when it became clear that she wasn't going to fall for the not-so-subtle prompt.

What was this about? she wondered. He had barely said two words earlier but now he had suddenly decided to ask some very direct questions.

"I'm a reporter," she said.

"Yeah?" He sounded amused, and a little surprised. "Could have fooled me. Wouldn't have figured you for a member of the media."

"You know, I get that a lot," she said.

"Those high-heeled boots and that snappy coat are real impressive. It's just that you don't look like one of those scrawny airhead beauty pageant dropouts who read the news on TV."

"That would probably be because I work for a newspaper, not a television station or a network," she said dryly.

"Ah, you're with the print media. Different species entirely." He paused a beat. "What paper?"

"The *Glaston Cove Beacon*." She waited for the inevitable response.

"Never heard of it," he said.

Right on cue, she thought.

"I get that a lot, too," she said patiently. "Glaston Cove is a little town over on the coast. The *Beacon* is a small daily, but the owner, who also happens to be the editor and publisher, has recently added an online site where you can download the current edition."

"Hard to think of anything going on here in Dunsley that would draw the attention of a reporter from Glaston Cove."

This was more than polite inquisitiveness, she decided. It was fast becoming an interrogation.

"I told you, I'm here on personal business," she said quietly. "I'm not covering a story."

"Oh, yeah, right. Sorry, I forgot the personal business part."

Like heck he had forgotten it. She smiled a little grimly to herself. He was starting to apply some pressure but it wasn't going to work. She was not about to explain herself to a stranger, especially not one from this particular zip code. After she met with Pamela she would be putting Dunsley in her rearview mirror.

When they reached Cabin Number Five, she was surprised to find herself torn between a sense of relief and a tingle of regret. She took the key out of her pocket and went up the front steps.

"Thanks for the escort," she said.

"No problem." He followed her up the steps, took the key from her fingers and fitted it into the lock. "When I checked you in this afternoon, I think I forgot to mention that there's free coffee and doughnuts in the lobby between seven and ten."

"Really? I'm dumbfounded. You made it clear that the management of the lodge did not believe in offering amenities."

"You were asking about room service, for Pete's sake." He opened the door and surveyed the brightly lit main room of the little cabin. "We don't go in for that kind of thing. But we do have the morning coffee and doughnuts. Assuming we've got guests, that is. Which, thanks to you, we happen to have at the moment."

"Sorry to be such an imposition."

"Yeah, well, guests happen in this business," he observed somewhat dourly.

"That's a very philosophical attitude."

"I know," he said. "I've had to cultivate one since I became an innkeeper. Luckily I've had some training. Anyhow, as I was saying, the doughnuts were Maxine's idea."

"I see."

"I agreed to let her give it a trial run for a month. I don't recommend them, to tell you the truth. They taste like sugar and sawdust. Got a hunch they're a little past their pull dates by the time Maxine picks them up. Can't be one hundred percent positive about that, though, because the Dunsley Market doesn't believe in stamping 'use by' dates on their perishables."

"I should have picked up the makings for breakfast on my way here today."

"You can always drive into town. The Ventana View Café opens at six."

"I'll keep that in mind."

She had to squeeze past him to get into the cabin. The action forced her to brush against his solid, unyielding frame. She could feel the heat coming off him. The tantalizing trace of his clean, male scent sparked another little frisson of awareness through her.

When she turned in the doorway to say good night, she was startled to see that he was studying her with an unnervingly intent expression.

"What?" she asked warily.

"You're serious about breakfast?"

"Yes."

"Most women I know aren't big on breakfast."

She had no intention of explaining that breakfast was one of the small but crucial rituals she employed to maintain a sense of order in her private universe. Breakfast signified the end of night. It was a very important meal. But there was no way she could explain that to him. He would not understand.

The only person who had ever comprehended the vital importance of breakfast was the last of the half dozen therapists she had consulted over the years. Dr. LaBarre had done her gentle best to wean her patient from some of the other slightly obsessive routines that had at one time or another threatened to rule Irene's life. But the good doctor had allowed the breakfast thing to stand on the grounds that it had other virtues.

"Any nutritionist will tell you that breakfast is the most important meal of the day," Irene said. She felt like a complete idiot, the way she always did when she was compelled to explain or cover up her need to stick to a ritual.

To her astonishment, Luke didn't even smile at that. Instead he inclined his head in a very solemn manner.

"Absolutely," he said. "Breakfast is critical."

Was he making fun of her? She couldn't be sure. She drew herself up and took a step back, preparing to shut the door.

"If you don't mind, I need to make a phone call," she said.

"Sure." He moved back a little. "See you in the morning."

She closed the door partway and then hesitated briefly. "I almost forgot. Just so you'll know, I will probably check out tomorrow."

He gave her a hard look. "You booked two nights."

"The second night is a contingency, in case I'm unable to leave on schedule for some reason."

"We don't do contingency bookings here at the Sunrise on the Lake Lodge. We've got a strict twenty-four-hour cancellation policy." He checked his watch. "You're way past the deadline."

"We will discuss your cancellation policy tomorrow after I find out whether or not I'll need to spend another day in Dunsley. Good night, Mr. Danner."

"Good luck with your personal business here in town, Miss Stenson."

"Thanks," she said. "As far as I'm concerned, the sooner it's finished, the better."

His mouth kicked up in an amused smile. "I'm getting the feeling you're not real taken with our picturesque mountain resort community."

"Very observant of you."

"Good night—"

"Don't say it," she warned. "I've heard it before."

"Can't resist." He grinned. "Good night, Irene."

The door made a very satisfying thunk when she closed it in his face. The snick of the bolt sliding into place sounded even better. Very firm. Very final. Luke Danner might be new in Dunsley, but he was, nevertheless, a part of this place that she hated. The last thing she wanted to do was get involved with him.

She went to the window and peeked through the curtains to make sure that he was, indeed, leaving the premises.

Sure enough, he was going down the steps. He raised one hand in casual farewell, letting her know that he was aware that she was watching him.

When she was satisfied that she was alone, she took the phone out of her purse and hit redial. She had lost track of the number of times she had called Pamela's number since arriving in Dunsley that afternoon.

Still no answer.

She ended the call before voice mail picked up. She had lost count of the number of messages she had left today. There was no point leaving another.

Two

Spectacular, haunting, amber-brown eyes lit with intelligence and shadowed with secrets; gleaming dark hair cut with precision to follow the line of her jaw; a sleek, vital, delightfully feminine shape; sexy high-heeled boots and a dashing black trench coat. And the lady did breakfast.

What was wrong with this picture?

He sure as hell was no fashion guru, but he trusted his instincts, Luke thought. Right now his instincts were telling him that Irene Stenson wore the boots and the trench and the attitude the way a man might wear a Kevlar vest—as battle armor.

Who or what was she afraid of?

And what was it with all the lights? He'd checked again a few minutes ago. Cabin Number Five still looked like a bulb factory run amok. He'd only gotten a quick look earlier when he walked her back to the place, but he was sure he'd seen a couple of night-light fixtures plugged into the wall sockets in the front room. Then there was that flashlight she'd pulled out of her pocket.

Scared of the dark, Irene Stenson?

He abandoned the attempt to finish the chapter he had been working on all week and powered down the computer. He couldn't think about The Project tonight. His brain was consumed with the puzzle that was Irene Stenson. Other portions of his anatomy seemed to be equally interested in investigating the matter. He had left Irene in her cabin three hours ago, but he was still restless and vaguely, disturbingly aroused.

He needed to prowl. On nights like this, the really long nights, he usually went for a walk to knock off some of the sharp edges. Afterward he poured himself a medicinal dose of the strong French brandy that he kept in the back of the cupboard to smooth out a few of the remaining rough spots. It was not always an effective routine, but it worked fairly well. Most of the time.

Tonight was different, though. He didn't think a hike along the lake shore and a shot of brandy were going to do the trick.

Maybe everyone in his family was right, maybe he was having some problems getting his act together and maybe things were getting worse, not better, as he had begun to believe. Hell, maybe he was a basket case, just as they all feared.

But one thing he knew was true—he hadn't lost his obsession with dots. Whenever he saw an interesting assortment of the little suckers, he got a bone-deep urge to connect them.

Irene had hit redial on her phone at least five times while she watched the evening news with him. Whoever it was she had come to Dunsley to see had never answered. Something told him that she wasn't going to be able to just sit quietly waiting much longer. She had as good as admitted that she wasn't thrilled to be here and she was looking forward to escaping as soon as her *personal business* was concluded.

The muffled rumble of a car engine emanated from the narrow drive that linked the cabins to the main lodge. Lights flashed on the other side of the curtains, spearing the night briefly before turning toward the main road.

His one and only guest was leaving. Had her phone call finally been answered? Or was she skipping town and her bill here at the lodge?

Automatically, he checked his watch and made a note of the time. Ten twenty-five.

There was not a lot going on at this hour on a weeknight in early spring here in Dunsley, certainly nothing that was likely to lure an out-of-town visitor with obviously sophisticated tastes. The Ventana View Café closed promptly at nine. Harry's Hang-Out, the only bar, generally remained open until midnight, providing there were enough customers, but somehow he didn't think its quaint charms would interest Irene.

He went to the window and watched the twin beams of the snappy yellow compact sweep out onto the main road. She turned left toward town, not right to the highway.

Okay, she wasn't ducking out on the lodge tab. She was definitely off to meet someone. But a lady who was afraid of the dark probably didn't go out alone a lot at this hour unless it was absolutely necessary. Someone or something here in town must be damned important to Irene Stenson.

He had lived in Dunsley for several months. It was a very

small town, a place where nothing out of the ordinary ever happened. Hell, that was the primary reason he had decided to move here. Offhand he could not think of anyone in the community who might scare a woman like Irene, but he was willing to bet that she was afraid of something.

And just why the hell did he care?

He thought about the mix of anxiety and somber determination that had been vibrating in her all evening. He knew the face of raw courage and sheer grit when he saw it. He also knew what it was like to go out into the night to meet the bad guys. You didn't do it alone unless there was no alternative.

Maybe Irene could use some backup.

He fished the keys out of his pocket, grabbed his jacket and went outside to the SUV.

Three

The drive to the Webb house took Irene through the heart of Dunsley's minuscule downtown. The trip proved to be an unsettling experience. So much seemed *familiar*.

It wasn't right, she thought. The place should have changed more than this in the intervening years. She paused at the four-way stop that marked the main intersection. It was as if Dunsley had fallen into a black hole seventeen years ago and remained trapped in a time warp.

True, most of the storefronts had been modernized and repainted. A few of the shops bore new names. But the changes were all superficial. Everything looked uncomfortably the same, if ever so slightly out of phase. Yep, definitely a time-warp thing, she told herself.

There were almost no other cars on the streets at this hour. She tromped on the accelerator, anxious to get to her destination.

The lights were still on in the gravel parking lot outside Harry's Hang-Out. The second H in the faded neon sign still flickered, just as it had seventeen years ago. The small herd of battered pickups and SUVs parked in front was identical to the one that had filled the lot in her youth. Her father had been roused out of bed in the middle of the night on more than one occasion to quell a brawl at Harry's.

She drove past the park and kept going for a short distance. When she reached Woodcrest Trail she made a left and entered the closest thing Dunsley had ever had to an upscale neighborhood.

The houses on Woodcrest Trail sat on large, heavily forested lots that ran down to the water's edge. Only a handful of the homes were owned by local families. Most were summer places that were dark and empty at this time of the year.

She slowed and turned into the narrow lane that led to the Webb house. The windows on this side of the two-story structure were dark, but a light burned over the front door. There was no car parked in the curved drive. The implication was that no one was home, she thought. But Pamela's e-mail had been very clear about the date.

She brought the compact to a halt, switched off the engine and folded her arms on top of the steering wheel, wondering what to do next. The decision to come to Woodcrest Trail after not getting any answers to her phone calls had been an impulse prompted by a growing sense of frustration and anxiety.

Pamela had been expecting her this evening. She should have been here, waiting. Something was wrong.

Irene opened the car door and got out slowly. The chill of the night closed in around her. She gave herself a few seconds to deal with the trickle of fear that darkness always induced. Then she walked quickly to the safety of the well-lit front door and leaned on the bell.

There was no response.

She looked around and saw that the garage door was closed. If her memory was correct, there was a small window on the far side.

She hesitated. It was very dark on the other side of the garage. She fingered the small penlight in her pocket. She needed more firepower, she thought. The flashlight in the glove compartment was larger but not large enough to go up against that kind of heavy night.

She went back to the compact, opened the trunk and selected one of the two industrial-strength flashlights she kept inside. When she hit the switch, the strong beam cut a reassuring swath through the shadows.

Steeling herself, she went back across the drive, rounded the corner of the garage and peered through the grimy glass window. A BMW loomed inside.

Another shivery chill went through her. Someone, presumably Pamela, was here. Why wasn't the person answering the phone or the door?

A faint gleam of light caught her eye. It emanated from the back of the house.

She turned and went slowly toward the glow, feeling a lot like a moth being drawn to a candle flame.

The route took her past the utility room door on the side of the house. She remembered that entrance well. Pamela had kept a key hidden under the steps so she could sneak in and out at night. Not that her father or the housekeeper had ever paid much attention to her comings and goings, Irene thought with a small pang.

At fifteen, she and every other teenager in town had envied Pamela Webb her amazing degree of freedom. But from an adult perspective it was clear that her old friend's much-vaunted independence was the result of parental neglect. Pamela had lost her mother in a boating accident on the lake when she was barely five. Over the years, her father, Ryland Webb, had been consumed with his political career. The result was that Pamela had been abandoned to the care of a series of nannies and housekeepers.

Irene unlatched the gate at the end of the walk and moved into the moonlit garden. The curtains at the floor-to-ceiling windows in the living room were open. The light that she had followed came from a table lamp that had been turned down very low.

Irene aimed the big flashlight through the glass. It came as a shock to realize that she recognized the furniture. Another case of time warp, she decided. Years ago the house had been deco-rated by a professional designer imported from San Francisco. The interior was meant to invoke the ambience of a luxurious ski chalet. Pamela had privately labeled it Outhouse Chic.

She studied the shadowed room carefully and methodically, starting on the left where the massive stone fireplace formed most of the wall. Halfway across the space she saw the over-turned slipper. It lay on the rug at the end of the brown leather sofa. A portion of a bare foot extended slightly off the edge of the cushions.

Irene stilled. Stomach tensing, she moved along the wall of windows until she could aim the beam of the flashlight directly at the front of the sofa.

A woman reclined on the cushions. She was dressed in camel-colored trousers and a blue silk blouse. Her face was turned away from the windows. Blond hair tumbled across the brown leather. One limp arm dangled above the floor.

A cocktail pitcher and an empty martini glass sat on the low wooden coffee table.

"Pamela." Irene pounded on the glass. "Pamela, wake up."

The woman on the sofa did not stir.

Irene seized the handle of the sliding glass door and tugged with all of her strength. The door was locked.

Whirling around, she raced out of the garden, the beam of the flashlight bouncing wildly, and hurried back to the door of the utility room.

Crouching, she felt around beneath the bottom step. Her fingers brushed across a small envelope taped to the underside of the tread.

It took a considerable amount of effort to loosen the aged duct tape, but finally the envelope fell into her hand. She could feel the weight of the key inside. Rising, she ripped open the sealed packet, took out the key and fitted it into the lock.

She opened the door, groped for and found the light switch. The weak bulb in the overhead fixture winked on, revealing decades' worth of boating, fishing and water-skiing gear.

She raced down the shadowed hall into the living room.

"Pamela, it's me, Irene. Wake up."

She stopped beside the sofa and reached down to grip Pamela's shoulder.

The flesh beneath the thin silk blouse was icy cold. There was no doubt as to the identity of the woman. Seventeen years had made remarkably few changes in Pamela's extraordinarily beautiful features. Even in death she was a classic, patrician blonde.

"Dear God, no."

Irene stepped back, swallowing the nausea that threatened to well up inside. Blindly, she reached into her purse for her cell phone.

A figure moved in the darkened hallway that led to the utility room.

She whipped around, clutching the heavy flashlight. The fierce beam fell on Luke. It was all she could do to suppress the scream that threatened to choke her.

"Dead?" Luke asked, moving toward the sofa.

"What are you doing here? Never mind." The questions would have to wait. She punched out 911 with shaking fingers. "She's very cold. Too cold."

He reached down and put his fingers on the woman's throat in a practiced manner. Looking for the pulse, Irene thought. She knew from the way he did it that this was not the first time he had dealt with a body.

"Definitely dead," he said quietly. "Looks like she's been that way for a while."

They both glanced at the empty pitcher on the table. Standing next to it was a small prescription bottle. It, too, was empty.

Irene fought the guilt that clawed through her. "I should have come here earlier."

"Why?" he asked. He went down on his haunches to read the label on the little bottle. "How could you have known?"

"I couldn't, I didn't," she whispered. "But I knew there was something wrong when she never answered the phone."

He studied the body in a meditative way. "She was cold before you even checked in at the lodge this afternoon."

He'd definitely had some experience with the dead, she thought.

The 911 operator spoke sharply into her ear, demanding to know what the problem was.

Irene took a deep breath, pulled herself together and gave the details of the situation as quickly and concisely as possible. It helped to concentrate on the facts.

By the time she ended the call, a strange numbness had settled on her. She fumbled with the phone and nearly dropped it before managing to put it back into her shoulder bag. She could not bring herself to look at the body.

"We don't need to wait in here," Luke said, taking her arm. "Let's go outside."

She did not argue. He steered her back along the hall, into the foyer and out onto the front steps.

"How did you get here?" She looked around the drive. "Where's your car?"

"I left it down the road a ways."

Understanding hit her. "You *followed* me."

"Yeah."

There was no apology in his tone, no hint of awkwardness or embarrassment. Just a simple statement. *Yeah, I followed you. So what?*

Outrage washed through her, dissipating some of the numbness. "Why did you do that? You had no right whatsoever—"

"That woman in there on the sofa," he said, interrupting her short tirade with the calm arrogance of a man accustomed to command. "Is she the person you were trying to get in touch with earlier this evening?"

She clenched her teeth and folded her arms very tightly beneath her breasts. "If you're not going to answer my questions, I see no reason to answer yours."

"Suit yourself, Miss Stenson." He turned his head slightly in the direction of the distant sirens. "But it's obvious you were acquainted with the victim."

Irene hesitated. "We were friends once, a long time ago. I haven't seen her or talked to her in seventeen years."

"I'm sorry," he said, his voice surprisingly gentle, his eyes startlingly bleak. "Suicide is always tough on the people left behind."

"I'm not so sure it was suicide," she said, before stopping to think.

He inclined his head, acknowledging other options. "Could have been an accidental overdose."

She didn't believe that, either, but this time she kept her mouth shut.

"Why did you come here to see her tonight?" Luke asked.

"What's your interest in this?" she countered. "Why did you follow me here?"

A police cruiser turned into the drive before he could respond, assuming that he would have responded, she thought grimly. Harsh lights pulsed in the night. The piercing siren was so loud now that she automatically raised her hands to cover her ears.

The siren stopped suddenly. A uniformed officer got out of the car. He glanced first at Irene and then turned immediately to Luke.

"Got a report of a dead body," he said.

Luke jerked a thumb in the direction of the hallway behind him. "Front room."

The officer peered into the front hall. He did not seem eager to enter the house. Irene realized that he was young. In the course of his short career here in Dunsley, he had probably not encountered a lot of dead bodies.

"Suicide?" the officer asked, looking uneasy.

"Or an OD," Luke said. He glanced at Irene. "At least, that's what it looks like."

The officer nodded but made no move to investigate.

More sirens sounded in the distance. They all looked toward the entrance of the drive. An ambulance and another cruiser were coming toward the house.

"That'll be the chief," the officer said, obviously relieved.

The vehicles halted behind the officer's cruiser. The medics got out of the ambulance and pulled on plastic gloves. Both looked expectantly at Luke.

"Front room," Luke repeated.

Irene sighed. Alpha male, she reminded herself. The kind of guy everyone instinctively turns to for direction in a crisis.

The medics disappeared into the foyer. The young officer followed in their wake, more than willing to let them take the lead.

The door of the second cruiser opened. A big, powerfully built man of about forty climbed out. His light brown hair was thinning on top. The expression on his craggy face was grim.

Unlike Pamela, the intervening years had taken a toll on Sam McPherson, Irene thought.

He gave her a swift once-over. No sign of recognition flickered in his gaze. He turned to Luke, just as the other responders had done.

"Danner," he said. "What are you doing here?"

"Evening, Chief." Luke angled his chin toward Irene. "I'm with Miss Stenson. She's a guest at the inn."

"Stenson?" Sam jerked back around and gave Irene a closer scrutiny. "Irene Stenson?"

She braced herself. "Hello, Sam."

He frowned. "I didn't recognize you. You sure have changed. What are you doing back in town?"

"I came to see Pamela. You're the chief here now?"

"Took over after Bob Thornhill died," he said absently. He

looked through the doorway, a tense, troubled expression creasing his face. "You're sure that's Pamela in there?"

"Yes."

"I was afraid of that." He exhaled deeply, a long, world-weary sigh. "Heard she was in town this week. But when I got the call tonight, I hoped there was some mistake. Thought maybe she'd let one of her city friends use the house for a few days."

"It's Pamela," Irene said.

"Damn." Sam shook his head, mournful but resigned to the inevitable. "You're the one who found her?"

"Yes."

He gave Luke a brief, speculative look and then turned back to her. "How'd that happen?"

"I got into Dunsley very late this afternoon," she said. "I tried to call Pamela several times throughout the evening. There was no answer. I began to get concerned, so I finally decided to come out here to see if she was home."

"Cathy Thomas, the woman who took your call, said you reported booze and pills at the scene?"

"Yes," Irene said. "But—" She started to say that she didn't think Pamela had committed suicide, but Luke gave her a hard look that, much to her annoyance, made her hesitate. By the time she had found her tongue, Sam was speaking again.

"Thought she was doing okay," Sam said quietly. "She was in and out of rehab for a while after college, but in the past few years she seemed to be staying clear of the crap."

"The pill bottle in there has a prescription on it," Luke said.

Sam narrowed his eyes. "Sounds like she was back in therapy again." He moved into the foyer and paused just inside the doorway to look back at Irene. "You going to be in town for a while?"

"I was planning to leave tomorrow," she said, not certain what she would do next.

"I'll want to ask you a few questions in the morning. Routine stuff." He angled his head toward Luke. "You, too, Danner."

"Sure," Luke said.

Irene nodded, not speaking.

"I'll see you both at the station around nine-thirty," Sam said. He vanished into the house.

Luke regarded Irene. "You're not exactly a stranger here in Dunsley, are you?"

"I grew up in this town. I left when I was fifteen."

"First time you've been back?"

"Yes."

He watched her closely in the porch light. "I take it you've got some bad memories of this place."

"What I have are nightmares, Mr. Danner."

She walked across the drive and got into her compact.

It was going to be one of the really long nights, she thought, starting the engine, one of those mini-eternities when none of the usual rituals worked.

Four

When she got back to the brightly lit cabin, she took the travel pouch of tea out of her shoulder bag and went into the tiny alcove kitchenette to boil some water.

The cabins of the Sunrise on the Lake Lodge did not boast many amenities, but they had been designed as long-term-stay accommodations for summer visitors who liked to spend two weeks or a month at a time at the lake. In addition to the minimal cooking facilities, there were place settings for four, a teakettle and a few basic pots and pans.

She thought about Pamela while she waited for the tea to steep. The dark phantoms of memories that were stored in the vault in her mind stirred. Over the years various therapists and well-intentioned counselors had done their level best to help her lay the ghosts to rest, but she knew that only the truth could do that. Unfortunately, the truth had been the one thing denied her.

She took the chipped mug of tea back to the sagging couch and sat down. A heavy engine growled softly in the night. Luke had returned. She looked through the curtains and watched him get out of the SUV and let himself into Cabin Number One. Somehow, it helped knowing that he was in the vicinity.

She sat quietly and thought about the terrible summer of her fifteenth year, the summer when she had become for three short, memorable months, Pamela Webb's best friend. The summer her parents had been murdered.

At a quarter to three in the morning, she made her decision and reached for her phone.

Adeline Grady answered on the sixth or seventh ring.

"You've got Grady," Adeline said in a sleepy voice that had been rendered permanently husky by a daily regimen of expensive whiskey and good cigars. "If this isn't important, Irene, you're fired."

"I've got an exclusive for you, Addy."

Adeline yawned audibly on the other end of the line. "Whatever it is, it had better be a lot bigger than the fight over the proposed dog park at the last city council meeting."

"It is. Senator Ryland Webb's daughter, Pamela, was found dead in the family's summer home on Ventana Lake at—" She glanced at her watch. "Ten forty-five this evening."

"Talk to me, kid." The sleep disappeared miraculously from Adeline's voice, leaving behind an edgy impatience. "What's going on?"

"At the very least, I think I can guarantee that the *Beacon* will be the first paper in the state to break the news of Pamela Webb's mysterious and untimely death."

"Mysterious and untimely?"

"The local authorities are going to call it a probable suicide or an accidental overdose, but I think there's more to it."

"Pamela Webb," Adeline said, sounding thoughtful now. "Is that who you went to Dunsley to see?"

"Yes."

"I didn't realize you knew her."

"It was a long time ago," Irene said.

"Huh." There were some rustling movements on the other end of the line and then the muffled click of what sounded like a light switch. "I seem to recall some rumors about her having done some time in rehab."

Before Adeline had retired and moved to Glaston Cove to take over the *Beacon,* she put in thirty years as a reporter with one of the state's major dailies. Irene was reassured to hear the unmistakable spark of interest and curiosity in her boss's rough voice. There was a story here, she thought. Adeline sensed it, too.

"I'll e-mail you what I've got in a few minutes, okay?" Irene said.

"You're sure this is an exclusive?"

"Trust me, at this point the *Beacon* is the only paper in the entire world that knows Pamela Webb is dead."

"How did we get lucky?" Adeline asked.

"I was the one who found the body."

Adeline whistled softly. "Okay, that qualifies as an exclusive. You'll get your byline and you'll be above the fold. Under most circumstances, the death of a senator's daughter would be nothing more than a private tragedy. But given that Webb is getting ready to make a run for the White House, this is a bigger story."

"One more thing, Addy. Would you ask Jenny or Gail to go to my apartment, pack up some clothes and overnight them to me?"

"Why?"

"Because I'm going to be here in Dunsley for a while."

"Thought you hated that town," Adeline said.

"I do. I'm hanging around because I've got a hunch there's more to this story."

"I can feel lust growing in this old reporter's heart. What's going on?"

"I think Pamela Webb was murdered."

Five

Maxine blew in through the lobby door at nine o'clock, moving like the small whirlwind she was. She was an attractive, high-energy woman in her mid-thirties with blue eyes and a cloud of artificially blond hair that always looked as if it had been whipped up by the rotor blades of a helicopter. She controlled the wild hair with a headband. Luke had discovered over the past few months that she had an endless assortment of bands, each in a different color. Today's was bright pink.

He found her enthusiasm for her job amusing, inexplicable and mildly exhausting.

She kicked the door shut and came to a halt, her arms wrapped around a paper sack that bore the logo of the Dunsley Market, and fixed him with an accusing glare.

"I just came from the market. Everyone's saying that Irene Stenson is back in town and that she's staying right here at the lodge and that the two of you found Pamela Webb's body last night."

Luke leaned on the desk. "The way gossip moves through this town probably ought to be a classified military secret."

"Why didn't you tell me?" Maxine put the sack down on the table she had selected for the morning coffee and doughnut service. "I work here at the lodge, for heaven's sake. I should have been the first to know. Instead I had to hear the news from Edith Harper. Do you have any idea how humiliating that was for me?"

"Irene Stenson phoned in the reservation yesterday morning while you were out running some errands. Checked in late yesterday afternoon after you'd gone home for the day. We didn't find the body until a quarter to eleven last night. What with one thing and another, there hasn't been time to bring you up to speed. Sorry about that."

Maxine whistled softly and slung her coat over one of the antlers of the coatrack. "The whole town is talking. I doubt if there's been this much excitement since the day Irene left all those years ago." She frowned in genuine concern. "How is she, by the way? Finding Pamela like that must have been dreadful. They were best friends for a summer back in high school, you know."

"Just one summer?"

"Pamela was usually only here during the summers. The rest of the time she was away at some fancy boarding school or skiing in the Alps or something. She and Irene made an odd match, to tell you the truth. They couldn't have been more different."

"Maybe that was the appeal."

Maxine pursed her lips, considering the possibility, then shrugged. "Could be. Pamela was the classic wild child. She was into drugs and boys, and her daddy the senator gave her everything she wanted. She always had the newest, trendiest clothes, a flashy sports car the day she turned sixteen, you name it."

"What about Irene Stenson?"

"Just the opposite, like I said. The quiet, studious type. Spent most of her free time in the library. Always had her nose buried in a book. Always polite to adults. Never got into trouble. Never had a date."

"What did her parents do?"

"Her mother, Elizabeth, painted, although I don't think she ever made any money off her art. Her father, Hugh Stenson, was the chief of police here in Dunsley."

"A job that probably didn't provide for unlimited teenage wardrobes, new cars and ski trips."

"You got that right." Maxine scowled at the empty platter on the coffee service table. "You didn't put out any doughnuts for the guests."

"I threw the last batch away yesterday. It was either that or weld them together to make a new anchor for the boat. Besides, there's only one guest at the moment, and something tells me she isn't going to get excited about doughnuts, at least not the kind the Dunsley Market sells."

"It's the principle of the thing. Luckily I picked up a fresh package this morning." Maxine took a box out of the paper sack, ripped it open and began arranging doughnuts on a plastic tray. "It looks inviting to have a few pastries and some freshly brewed coffee available in the mornings. All of the better-class hotels and inns do it."

"I like to think that the Sunrise on the Lake Lodge is in a class by itself," Luke said. "Tell me the rest of the Stenson story."

"Well, as I was saying, for whatever reason, the summer Pamela Webb turned sixteen, she decided to make Irene her best friend." Maxine tipped her head slightly to the side, looking thoughtful. "Maybe you're right. Maybe Pamela liked the contrast she and Irene made. She probably figured that having quiet, unfashionable little Irene in her orbit made her look even more glittery and exciting. At any rate, for about three months they were inseparable. No one understood why Irene's folks allowed her to associate with Pamela, though."

"Pamela was held to be a bad influence, I take it?"

Maxine grimaced. "Worst possible influence. Lot of busybodies took it upon themselves to warn Mr. and Mrs. Stenson that if they didn't keep Irene away from Pamela, she would come to a bad end. It was widely predicted hereabouts that sooner or later sweet little Irene Stenson would fall victim to the evil forces of sex, drugs and rock and roll."

"Ah, the innocent pleasures of youth."

"Yep, the good old days," Maxine agreed. "But for some reason, which no one in town could understand, the Stensons didn't seem to object to the friendship between the two girls. Maybe they liked the idea of Irene hanging out with the daughter of a U.S. senator, although I never thought the Stensons were impressed by that kind of thing."

Luke studied the view of Cabin Number Five through the trees. Most of the lights had been left burning all night. The last time he had checked, sometime after four in the morning, the glow in the bedroom had diminished to a dim, silvery blue. He had concluded that Irene had finally gone to sleep with a night-light in that room.

"Go on with the story," he said. It was going to be bad, he thought. He could feel it in his bones.

"One night Hugh Stenson shot his wife to death in the kitchen of their home. Then he turned the gun on himself."

"Damn." He'd known it would be rough, he reminded himself. "What about Irene?"

"She was out with Pamela Webb that night. When she got home she found the bodies." Maxine paused. "She was only fifteen years old, and she was alone when she walked into the house. Still gives me the creeps just thinking about it after all this time."

He said nothing.

"It was incredibly tragic. Really shook up the community. Later there were rumors that Elizabeth Stenson had been having an affair with someone in Dunsley and that Hugh went crazy mad when he found out."

"Crazy mad?"

Maxine nodded somberly. "There was also a lot of talk about how Hugh had seen some heavy combat during his time in the Marines and that he suffered from that post-trauma thing."

"Post-traumatic stress disorder."

"That's it."

He looked at Cabin Number Five again and saw Irene coming through the trees toward the lobby. She was dressed much as she had been yesterday, in a pair of sleek black trousers and a black pullover. The long black trench coat was unfastened. The hem swirled around the tops of her gleaming black leather boots.

The family history certainly explained the shadows and secrets he had seen in those amazing eyes, he thought.

"Wow." Maxine peered through the window at Irene. "Is that Irene?"

"That's her."

"I never would have recognized her. She looks so . . ."

"What?"

"I don't know," Maxine admitted. "So different, I guess. Not like that poor, brokenhearted girl I remember seeing at the funerals."

"Where did Irene go to live after the deaths of her parents?"

"I'm not sure, to be honest. On the night of the murder-suicide, one of the police officers, a man named Bob Thornhill, took Irene home with him. The next day an elderly aunt arrived to take charge of Irene. We never saw her again after they buried her folks."

"Until now."

Maxine did not take her eyes off Irene. "I can't get over how she's changed. She's so sophisticated-looking. Like I said, she never even dated back in high school."

"Probably dates now," Luke said. "A lot."

He could not imagine any man ignoring that cool, subtle, feminine challenge.

"Who would have guessed she'd turn out so classy and stylish?" Maxine went back to the coffee table and got very busy. "Let's see, she would be about thirty-two now. Still using her own name, too. Sounds like she never married. Or maybe she's divorced and took back her own name."

"She didn't mention a husband," Luke said. He would have remembered that. "No ring, either."

"Wonder why she came back?"

"To see Pamela Webb, apparently."

"Then she goes and finds Pamela's body." Maxine dumped the used coffee grounds into the trash. "I mean, unless you're a cop or something, what are the odds that you would accidentally stumble over *three* dead bodies in your entire life, let alone before you even turn forty? Most people only see bodies at funerals, which isn't the same thing at all."

"You were with your mother when she died."

"Yes, but—" Maxine paused, frowning a little, as though not certain how to explain. "She had been ill for a long time and undergoing hospice care. Her death wasn't sudden or violent or unexpected, if you know what I mean. It was peaceful in an odd way. More like a transition of some kind."

"I understand," Luke said quietly.

She was right, he thought. The violently and the unexpectedly dead looked very different. The living who were unfortu-

nate enough to come upon them without any warning or prep-
aration had no time to process the awful reality in a normal,
careful way.

And some things were too terrible to ever be completely
processed, he thought. You either learned to lock them away or
you went under.

"Poor Irene. It's not as if all three of the bodies she found
were strangers, either." Maxine filled the coffee machine with
fresh water from a jug. "First her parents and now the woman
who was once her best friend."

What *were* the odds? Luke wondered. The question had
plagued him all night and still nagged at him this morning,
a tiny spark that could ignite a forest fire if he didn't stomp
it out.

Dots. They were the bane of his existence. The compulsion
to connect them in order to find patterns was an addiction.

Don't go there, he thought. *You do not need this problem. You've got
enough of your own. You're supposed to be trying to get your life back together.
That's a full-time occupation at the moment.*

Maxine ladled coffee into a paper filter. "After her aunt took
her away, there was a lot of talk around town about how Irene
had probably been traumatized for life. Folks said she would
never be the same after that night when she found her parents
on the kitchen floor. They said she would never really be *normal*,
if you know what I mean."

"Yeah," Luke said softly, "I know what you mean."

Maxine watched Irene with worried eyes. "I overheard Mrs.

Holton telling everyone that finding Pamela's body last night might be too much for poor Irene after what happened in the past. She said it might push her over the edge."

Luke watched Irene walk past the window, heading toward the front door of the lobby. Her face was set and resolute. Not the expression of an unstable woman who was about to go off a cliff, he decided. More like the face of a woman with an agenda.

The door opened. Irene walked into the room, bringing another wave of the crisp morning air with her.

Good morning didn't seem appropriate under the circumstances, Luke thought. He searched for another, more suitable greeting.

"Hey," he said. Who said he couldn't do social repartee?

She smiled a little, but her eyes were wary and watchful. "Hello."

"Get any sleep last night?" he asked.

"Not much. What about you?"

"A little."

So much for small talk, he thought.

"Irene." Maxine grinned at her from across the room. "Remember me? Maxine Spangler. Maxine Boxell, now."

"Maxine." Irene's smile widened. "Luke said you were working here. I thought you were going to leave town after you graduated."

"I did. Went off to community college to study business and accounting. Got a job in the high-tech industry and, wait for it, married Mr. Perfect and had a son." Maxine rolled her eyes.

"But things didn't quite work out. I got laid off. Mr. Perfect left me for his yoga instructor, and then Mom got sick. I came back here with Brady, that's my son, to take care of her."

"How is she doing?"

"She died about six months ago."

"I'm so sorry," Irene said gently.

"Thanks."

"I remember your mother. I liked her. She was a friend to my mother."

"I know," Maxine said.

"You decided to stay on here after your mother died?"

Maxine hesitated. "To tell you the truth, Brady wasn't doing so well in a big city high school. When his dad walked out he sort of fell apart. Grades began to slip. He started to get into trouble."

"I understand."

"What with one thing and another, I decided that maybe he would do better in a small town like Dunsley. He seems to have settled in fairly well. His grades have improved. Also, he's got a couple of good male role models. Sam McPherson lets him ride with him in the police cruiser sometimes and takes him fishing. Luke, here, is teaching him how to maintain the lodge's boat so that he can take the lodge guests fishing on the lake in the summer. Brady's real excited about that."

"I see," Irene said. She gave Luke a long, considering look.

Luke got the feeling that he was being weighed and judged.

"Listen, about Pamela Webb," Maxine continued. "I know it must have been tough on you, finding her the way you did last night." She reached for the coffeepot. "How about a nice hot cup of coffee and a doughnut?"

Maxine was wasting her time, Luke thought. Irene looked like she only drank exotic teas or gourmet coffee made from specially roasted beans that had been freshly ground before brewing. And he was sure that she would hate the doughnuts.

But to his amazement she smiled again at Maxine.

"That sounds great," she said. "Thank you."

Maxine beamed. She handed Irene a mug of coffee and a small napkin with one of the cardboard doughnuts perched on top.

Irene sipped the coffee and nibbled daintily on the lousy doughnut. Her manner suggested that she was savoring both.

Something weird going on here, Luke thought.

"Finding Pamela was certainly a terrible shock," Irene said. "Had she been spending a lot of time here in Dunsley lately?"

What the hell? Luke felt his built-in trouble radar slam straight into the red zone.

"No more than usual," Maxine said, oblivious. "For the past few years she was in the habit of showing up here occasionally on the weekends. She usually had a man with her or a few of her friends from the city. But we didn't see a lot of her."

"Did you know that she was in town?"

"Oh, sure. She was seen driving past the café earlier this week." Maxine glanced at Luke. "Word goes around fast when a member of the Webb family is in town. They're sort of our local royalty, in case you haven't already figured that out."

"I did get that impression after I noticed that the municipal building, the park, the local hospital and the main street in Dunsley are all named Webb."

Maxine laughed. "The Webbs have been connected to Dunsley for four generations."

"The signs on the buildings and the street all honor Victor Webb," Irene explained. "Pamela's grandfather. He's the Webb that built a sporting goods empire several years ago. After he got rich he donated a lot of money to various charities and projects in the local community."

Maxine poured herself some coffee. "You might say that Victor Webb is the town's fairy godfather. A lot of people around here are grateful to him for one reason or another. Isn't that right, Irene?"

Irene nodded. "That's certainly the way it was when I lived here."

"But he doesn't live here," Luke observed.

"Not anymore," Maxine said. "When he founded his chain of stores, he established his headquarters in San Francisco. Later, after he sold the business for megabucks, he retired to Phoenix. We only see him in the fall now when he comes up here to hunt. But he hasn't forgotten Dunsley." Maxine wrinkled her nose. "Can't say the same about his son the senator, though."

"What do you mean?" Luke asked.

"I can answer that one," Irene said around a mouthful of doughnut. "Ryland Webb was always a superambitious politician. He never spent much time here in Dunsley. At least, he didn't when I lived here." She gave Maxine an inquiring look.

"Nothing has changed," Maxine said. She shrugged. "He

shows up occasionally in the fall to go hunting with his father, but that's about it."

Irene took a sip of coffee. "I remember my father saying once that it would not be a good idea to get between Ryland Webb and something that he wanted."

"Can't argue with that," Maxine said. "But I think the real reason folks around here don't feel the same way toward Ryland Webb that they do toward Victor is because the senator never paid much attention to Dunsley after he started winning elections."

"Never brought home the political pork, is that it?" Luke asked.

Maxine waved a hand to indicate the landscape outside the lobby windows. "Look around. You don't see any big federally funded projects going on here in Dunsley, do you? No road construction money. No developments designed to aid the local economy."

"Personally, I consider that part of the charm of the place," Luke said dryly.

Maxine laughed. "Tell that to the town council. The problem here is that we don't have any big, wealthy contributors to help finance Ryland Webb's campaigns so he pretty much ignores us."

"Pamela was involved in Ryland's campaigns, wasn't she?" Irene said to Maxine.

Maxine nodded. "She went to work for her father when she got out of college. She served as his social hostess. He didn't have a wife to help him with all the entertaining that politicians have to do because he never remarried after Pamela's mom died."

Irene looked thoughtful. "But that was about to change, wasn't it? Senator Webb announced his engagement a few weeks ago."

"That's right." Maxine paused, her mug halfway to her lips. "I hadn't thought about it but now that you mention it, Pamela was going to be out of a job soon, wasn't she? A real high-flying job at that. I mean, as Senator Webb's official hostess she was a VIP, herself."

"Yes," Irene said. "She mingled with the movers and shakers, not only in the state, but also back in Washington, D.C."

Maxine's eyes widened. "Do you think that's why she killed herself? She was depressed because she was no longer going to be so important?"

"We don't know that Pamela killed herself," Irene said evenly.

He'd had enough, Luke thought. Time to take control of the situation. He reached into his pocket for the keys to the SUV. "You ready for our little meeting with McPherson? Might as well drive into town together."

Irene pondered the offer briefly and then nodded, as though the decision to get into the same vehicle with him had been a major one.

"All right," she said.

Luke took his jacket off an antler.

"How long are you going to be staying with us, Irene?" Maxine asked.

"Awhile," Irene said.

Luke pulled on the jacket. "She's booked for one more night."

Irene put down her empty mug and tossed the napkin into the trash. "I will probably be extending my stay a bit longer than I originally planned."

Luke looked at her. "How much longer?"

"It all depends." She went to the door and opened it. "We'd better be on our way. Wouldn't want to be late for our meeting with the chief."

"Be back in a while, Maxine," Luke said. He started toward the door.

"Sure." Maxine went around behind the front desk. "Take your time."

Luke followed Irene outside to the SUV, managing, just barely, to get to the passenger door before she could open it.

"Thank you," she said, very polite.

She climbed inside and reached for the seat belt.

He closed the door, went around to the other side and got behind the wheel.

"Mind if I ask what the hell you think you were doing back there?" he said, firing up the engine.

"I beg your pardon?"

"Forget it." He put the heavy vehicle in gear. "Rhetorical question. I already know the answer."

"What are you talking about?"

"You were grilling Maxine."

"I'm not sure what you mean by 'grilling.'"

He smiled humorlessly. "I know a deliberate line of ques-

57

tioning when I hear it. You're trying to do a little investigating on your own, aren't you?"

She slanted him a quick, cautious glance. "Maybe."

"Maxine filled me in on your connection with Pamela Webb. I realize that finding your old friend like that last night was bad. But that doesn't mean there's anything more to her death than the obvious."

She faced straight ahead, watching the narrow strip of pavement that wound toward town.

"What I decide to do is my business," she said quietly.

"Look, I admit I've only been in this town for a few months, but from what I've heard, Sam McPherson is an honest cop. There's no reason to believe he wouldn't conduct a legitimate investigation if he found anything to warrant one."

"There won't be an investigation. Not unless Senator Webb wants it, and I can pretty much guarantee that's not going to happen. Just the opposite, more likely."

"Because he's getting ready to announce a run for the presidency?"

"Exactly. The last thing he'll allow is an investigation into his daughter's death."

He tightened his grip on the wheel. "Judging from some of the local gossip I've heard here in Dunsley, I guess it could get kind of messy."

"For years the Webb family has been able to keep a very tight lid on Pamela's history of drug abuse and her, shall we say, youthful indiscretions. But any serious investigation is bound to dredge up a lot of old stuff that I'm sure Ryland Webb's handlers would just as soon not hit the media fan. It could damage his image as a devoted father."

"He won't be able to escape the media altogether, no matter what he does," Luke pointed out. "A senator's daughter dying of a drug overdose is going to draw some attention from the press."

"Trust me, Webb and his people will be able to control that story. But if it gets out that there's even a remote possibility that Pamela was murdered, it will cause a firestorm."

He exhaled slowly. "Damn. I was afraid that was where you were going with this."

She did not respond, but when he glanced at her he saw that the hand resting on her thigh was curled into a tight little fist.

"Do you really believe that's what happened?" he asked, gentling his tone.

"I don't know. But I intend to find out."

"Have you got any hard evidence to support the idea that someone killed Pamela Webb?"

"None whatsoever," she admitted. "But I'll tell you this much. If I'm right about how Pamela died, then it's very possible that her death is linked to the deaths of my parents seventeen years ago."

"No offense, but you're starting to sound like a conspiracy theorist."

"I know."

"It probably doesn't mean much coming from a stranger," he

said quietly, "but for what it's worth, I'm very sorry for what you went through the night you found your parents. Must have been a god-awful nightmare."

She gave him a curious, half-shuttered look, as though he had surprised her with the simple, utterly inadequate condolences.

"Yes, it was." She hesitated. "Thank you."

He knew better than most that sometimes there was nothing else to say. He concentrated on his driving.

Irene propped one elbow on the side of the door and braced her chin against her hand. "It's true that I don't have any solid evidence to indicate that Pamela might have been murdered. But I do have something."

"What's that?" he asked, deeply wary.

"The summer that Pamela and I spent together as friends, we invented a code phrase that we used to let each other know when something was really important and that it had to be kept a total secret from everyone else."

"So?"

"Pamela used that code in the e-mail note she sent to me asking me to meet her here in Dunsley."

He tightened his hands on the wheel. "No offense, but a teenage code is not a lot to go on."

"It's enough for me," she said.

Six

The center of town was busier than Luke had ever seen it since he had arrived in Dunsley. The parking lot in front of the post office was jammed with trucks, vans and SUVs. He glanced through the windows of the Ventana View Café and saw that every booth was filled.

A long, gleaming black limo occupied three spaces in the parking lot in front of the municipal building that housed the mayor's office, the town council chambers and the police department. Luke pulled into a slot beside the big car and sat quietly for a few seconds, studying the scene.

"Something's missing here," he said.

Irene made a soft little sound of disgust. "Like the major media?"

"Looks like the news of Pamela Webb's death hasn't gone beyond the town limits yet."

"Except for the story in this morning's edition of the *Glaston Cove Beacon*, you mean," she said with grim pride.

"Except for that," he agreed. "But since I doubt that anyone outside of Glaston Cove actually reads the *Beacon*, I think it's safe to say that the story is still very low profile."

Irene unfastened her seat belt. "The *Dunsley Herald* went bankrupt years ago. I doubt if the *Kirbyville Journal* has got the word yet. And you're right about the limited circulation of the *Beacon*." She smiled coolly. "All of which means I've still got an exclusive."

His gut tightened. Disaster loomed.

"You know," he said, choosing his words carefully, "it might be a good idea to talk about how we want to approach this conversation with McPherson. Never hurts to have a strategy."

But he was conversing with himself. Irene was out of the vehicle, slamming the door shut behind her and heading toward the entrance of the municipal building. He saw her reach into her oversized shoulder bag and take out a small device.

A recorder, he thought. As he watched, she slipped it into the pocket of her trench coat.

"And to think that I came to Dunsley for peace and quiet," he said to the empty front seat.

He got out of the SUV, pocketed the keys and went after Irene. He caught up with her just as she strode through the front door of the municipal building.

A short distance beyond the entrance, a tall, distinguished-looking man with a very familiar profile stood talking in low tones to Sam McPherson.

Ryland Webb possessed a full head of the silvered hair that seemed to be a requirement for public office. He also had the face for the job, Luke thought. The combination of rugged, man-of-the-West angularity mixed with just the right touch of old-world aristocrat photographed well.

An attractive, well-groomed woman in her early thirties stood at his side, gripping his hand in a silent gesture of loving support. The fiancée, Luke decided.

On the other side of the lobby, an intense, twitchy man spoke urgently but very softly into a phone. An expensive-looking leather briefcase sat beside one foot.

"Pamela was a deeply troubled woman, as everyone in this town is well aware," Webb said to Sam. He shook his head in a melancholy gesture, the long-suffering, grieving father who has always feared that his daughter would come to a bad end, no matter how hard he worked to save her. "You know as well as I do that she struggled with her inner demons from the time she was a teenager."

"Thought she was doing okay these past few years," Sam said evenly.

"She was seeing a psychiatrist again," Ryland said. "But obviously in the end her illness overwhelmed her."

"It doesn't look like she OD'd on street drugs." Sam frowned. "The bottle we found on the table is a legitimate prescription. I've got a call in to the doctor who wrote it."

Ryland nodded. "That would be Dr. Warren. Worked with Pamela for quite a while. This isn't his fault. I'm sure he never realized that she was planning to kill herself."

The harried-looking man with the briefcase ended his call and hurried toward Ryland.

"Sorry to interrupt, sir, but I just spoke with the people who are handling the funeral arrangements. They picked up your daughter's body at the hospital morgue a few minutes ago and are on their way back to San Francisco. We should be going, too. It won't be much longer before the media gets wind of the tragedy. We need to have a statement ready."

"Yes, of course, Hoyt," Ryland said. "I'll talk to you later, Sam."

"Sure," Sam said.

Irene stepped directly into Ryland's path. "Senator Webb, I'm Irene Stenson. Remember me? I was a friend of Pamela's in the old days here in Dunsley."

Ryland looked startled. But his expression quickly turned warm and polite. "Irene, my dear. Of course I remember you. It has been a very long time. You've certainly changed. I almost didn't recognize you." His expression grew somber. "Sam says you were the one who found Pamela last night."

That was his cue, Luke thought. "She wasn't alone," he said. "I was with her. Luke Danner."

"Danner." Ryland's eyes tightened a little at the corners. "Sam mentioned that the new owner of the lodge was also on the scene." He indicated the woman at his side. "Luke, Irene, allow me to introduce my fiancée, Alexa Douglass."

"How do you do?" Alexa inclined her head in graceful acknowledgment of the introduction. "I'm so sorry that we are meeting under such sad circumstances."

"Excuse me, sir," Hoyt muttered. "We really do have to leave."

"Yes, Hoyt," Ryland said. He looked apologetic. "Irene, Luke, this is my aide, Hoyt Egan. He's in charge of keeping me on schedule. This is a very busy time for me, as I'm sure you're well aware. I've got back-to-back fund-raisers lined up for the next two months. And now I've got Pamela's funeral to worry about."

"Gosh, just think, a fund-raiser and your daughter's funeral in the same time slot," Irene murmured. "Which will it be? Choices, choices."

There was a short, stunned silence. Luke watched every jaw in the room except his own drop so hard it was a wonder they didn't all crack on the floor.

Ryland recovered first. Dismissing Irene, he fixed his attention on Luke. "I'm not entirely clear on why the two of you went to see Pamela last night."

"It's complicated," Luke said.

Irene took the recorder out of her pocket and clipped it to the strap of her shoulder bag. She reached into another pocket and removed a pen and a notepad.

"Senator Webb, I'm with the *Glaston Cove Beacon*. As you may or may not know, we announced your daughter's death in today's edition."

"That's impossible," Hoyt snapped. "None of the media even know about Pamela's death yet."

"I just told you, I'm a reporter," Irene said patiently. "The story ran this morning. You can also find it at the *Beacon*'s online site." She turned back to Ryland. "Can you tell us if there will be an autopsy performed on your daughter to determine cause of death?"

Anger flashed across Ryland's face, but only for a split second. He veiled it almost instantly. "I realize that finding Pamela's body last night must have been a terrible shock for you, Irene. But I must make it clear that I have no intention of discussing the details of my daughter's death with any member of the press, not even you. This is an intensely personal matter as I'm sure you, of all people, understand."

Irene jerked ever so slightly, as though she'd been slapped, but she did not step back. Luke watched her scribble something on her notepad.

"Did Chief McPherson tell you that the reason I'm back in town is because I got an e-mail from Pamela requesting me to meet her here in Dunsley?" she asked.

Ryland was clearly astounded by that information. "Pamela contacted you? What did she want?"

"She didn't say. She just asked me to come here to talk with her."

Ryland swung around to confront Sam. "You didn't tell me about this."

Sam flushed a dark, dull red. "Didn't think it was important."

"Sir," Hoyt interrupted nervously, "we really have to get moving."

Ryland switched his attention back to Irene. "I wasn't aware that you and Pamela were still in contact with each other."

"That e-mail note was the first word I'd had from her in seventeen years," Irene said very steadily. "Naturally I was more than a little surprised to receive it."

"She gave no indication at all why she wanted to talk to you?" Ryland demanded.

"No," Irene said. "But I got the impression that it had something to do with the past."

"What past? Your friendship with her, do you mean?" Ryland grew visibly calmer. "Yes, that does make sense in a way. I expect that she wanted to say good-bye to an old acquaintance. People intent on committing suicide sometimes do that, I'm told."

"Really? Who told you that?" Irene asked, scribbling madly.

"I read it somewhere," Ryland muttered. He eyed the recorder uneasily. "Pamela was being treated for severe, clinical depression," he added, enunciating each word very clearly.

"I don't believe that she contacted me to say good-bye, Senator," Irene said. "I think she may have wanted to discuss the circumstances surrounding the death of my parents, Hugh and Elizabeth Stenson. I'm sure you recall the case."

Ryland stared at her. "What the hell are you talking about?"

Alexa closed her elegantly manicured fingers over his sleeve. "Ryland?"

"It's all right, dear." He pulled himself together. "Years ago there was a terrible tragedy here in Dunsley. A murder-suicide. Irene's parents both died." He raised his voice slightly and spoke directly toward the recorder. "Poor Irene, here, found the bodies. Everyone said she was badly traumatized by the experience and would probably never be quite right again. Don't worry, there is no connection to Pamela's death."

Alexa looked at Irene. "You have my deepest sympathies, Miss Stenson."

"Thank you." Irene did not take her gaze off Ryland. "Sir, don't you agree that there is at least a remote possibility that Pamela's death is connected to what happened all those years ago?"

"No," Ryland said in a thoroughly crushing tone of voice.

Hoyt Egan jerked. He stared at Irene in mounting horror. "What you're implying is impossible, Miss Stenson, absolutely impossible. And if your paper prints any innuendos of that sort, the senator will consult his lawyers."

Ryland gave Irene a hard stare. "You said yourself that you had no contact with Pamela after leaving Dunsley. That means you don't know how unstable she was. Sam says there was nothing at the scene to indicate anything other than an overdose. For the sake of everyone involved, but most of all out of respect for my daughter's memory, I ask that you leave this alone."

Alexa bestowed a kindly smile on Irene. "Rest assured, Miss Stenson, when Ryland returns to Washington he intends to introduce a bill to increase funding for mental health research."

"That certainly makes me feel a lot better," Irene said.

Luke saw her knuckles whiten and knew that she was digging her nails into the leather strap of her purse.

"The senator is a busy man," Hoyt announced. "We can't delay our departure another minute."

He stepped directly in front of Ryland and Alexa and led the way purposefully toward the door.

Ryland paused at the entrance to look back at Irene. "I hope you will remember that you are first and foremost a friend of the family, Miss Stenson."

"I will never forget that Pamela was once my best friend," Irene said.

Uncertainty darkened Ryland's expression. Luke could tell that he was not sure how to take that statement. But Hoyt Egan was on the move again, shepherding his boss through the doorway.

"I've never even heard of the *Glaston Cove Beacon*," Hoyt said to Ryland. "Which means that it is very small-time. Don't worry, it won't be a problem, sir."

The trio went down the steps and got into the limo.

Luke looked at Irene. "Congratulations, I think you just rattled the cage of a U.S. senator."

"For all the good it will do." She shoved her hands into the pockets of her coat. "There isn't going to be an investigation, is there, Sam?"

Sam stirred slightly, as though surprised to learn that anyone had even remembered he was in the room.

"Unless you've got something solid beyond that e-mail note from Pamela asking you to meet her here, I have no reason to push for an investigation," he said quietly.

She smiled coldly. "And every reason not to go there, right?"

Sam's mouth tightened. "You think I'm backing off because I don't want to take on Ryland Webb, don't you?"

Irene winced. "I shouldn't have implied that. But there's no getting around the fact that Webb is a powerful man."

"Webb may be powerful, but he's still a father whose daughter just took her own life, either deliberately or by accident. Your dad once told me that families usually try to keep suicide very quiet. I've dealt with a couple in the past few years, and I can tell you that he was right. It's amazing the lengths folks will go to in order to hush up that kind of thing."

Irene sighed. "I know."

"Far as I'm concerned," Sam said, "unless there's a good reason for thinking otherwise, a family is entitled to keep its secrets."

He looked to Luke, obviously seeking some backup.

Luke shrugged. "Depends on the secrets, I guess. But one thing's for sure, every family's got 'em."

Seven

Forty minutes later, Sam escorted them out the door of the municipal building. Irene was still fuming, but a renewed sense of resolve was setting in. She reminded herself that she had known from the outset that the odds of convincing McPherson to conduct a full-scale investigation were less than zero.

"Give it some time, Irene," Sam said. "I know it wasn't easy, finding her like that. But when the shock wears off, you'll realize that it really was an overdose, not a murder."

"Sure," she said.

Luke said nothing, just took her arm and steered her down the steps to the SUV. He opened the passenger-side door. Irene climbed in swiftly.

Luke got behind the wheel and drove out of the parking lot. Irene could see that every head in the Ventana View Café was turned in the direction of the SUV.

"Pack of ghouls," she whispered.

"Give 'em a break," Luke said quietly. "This is a small town. The death of someone like Pamela Webb, a senator's daughter and former local bad girl, is bound to grab everyone's attention."

She gripped her shoulder bag very tightly in her lap. "They stared at me in exactly the same way at the funerals of my parents."

He gave her a quick, sharp, searching look before returning his attention to the road.

"For what it's worth," he said after a while, "I think McPherson is right. Your friend's death was either an accident or suicide."

"I'm not buying it."

"Yeah, I can see that. Give McPherson his due, though. He's not cooperating in a cover-up. He laid out the facts for you. There's nothing that warrants further investigation."

"There's still that e-mail note she sent to me. How can he ignore that?"

"He didn't ignore it," Luke said patiently. "Like Webb, he thinks that Pamela was planning suicide and going through a process of saying farewell to some of the people in her past."

"Then why didn't she wait until after she had actually said good-bye to me before she killed herself?"

"People who are planning to commit suicide don't follow the same logic that the rest of us do. They're focused on their own pain and suffering. That's all they can grasp."

The too-even way he spoke sent a chill through her.

"You sound as if you've had some personal experience with suicide," she said.

"My mother killed herself when I was six years old."

She closed her eyes briefly against a rush of sadness and sympathy. "Dear God, Luke." She raised her lashes and looked at him. "I'm so sorry."

He nodded once, saying nothing.

"Last night must have been especially bad for you," she said.

"It was my choice to follow you, remember?"

She frowned. "Why *did* you follow me? You still haven't explained that."

His mouth curved faintly. "When I see dots, I feel this overwhelming need to connect them."

"I'm a dot?"

"Uh-huh." He gave her a quick, assessing look and then shook his head, resigned. "You're not going to let it go, are you?"

"Pamela's death? No."

"Mind if I ask why you're so damn sure there's a mystery here? Is it just that e-mail you got from Pamela? Or is there more to it?"

She thought about that. "It's a feeling I've got."

"A feeling."

"Yes."

"A feeling isn't a lot to go on," he said neutrally.

"That's almost funny, considering it's coming from someone who just admitted that he followed me last night because he sensed that I was a dot waiting to be connected to another dot."

"Okay, I'll give you that one," he conceded. "Moving right along, what was your take on Ryland Webb this morning? Think he believes there's more to his daughter's death than pills and booze and wants to cover it up?"

She hesitated. "He certainly doesn't want an investigation, does he?"

"You may not like his reasons, but he does have a few."

"I know." She folded her arms. "I told you, he's an ambitious man, completely focused on his career. He didn't have any time for Pamela seventeen years ago, and he sure doesn't want to waste much time on her now."

"Listen to me, Irene Stenson. If you're thinking of going up against Ryland Webb, you'd better be real sure you've got a big club. Webb is a powerful man."

"Don't you think I know that?"

Luke drove in silence for a while.

"Sam McPherson knew Pamela fairly well, I take it?"

The question caught her by surprise. "They were friends in the old days. I don't know what their relationship has been like these past seventeen years, though."

"Ever have the feeling that he was romantically fixated on her?"

She pondered that for a few seconds. "I certainly never took it that way, and I'm pretty sure Pamela didn't either. Sam was several years older, of course. She was only sixteen. Sam was in his early twenties at the time."

"That's not a big age gap."

"It would have seemed like it in high school." She drummed her fingers on the seat. "But looking back, I think it was the way she treated him that made me assume that there was no romantic link between them."

"How did she treat him?"

"Like a friend, not another potential conquest."

He raised his brows. "Pamela had conquests in those days?"

"Pamela always thought in terms of conquests." She smiled wryly. "What's more, there was never a shortage of males offering themselves up to be conquered. She was beautiful and she had a talent for flirting. Guys fell like flies. But it wasn't just her looks and sex appeal that made her popular."

"She was a Webb."

"You heard Maxine this morning—the family is local royalty."

"Maybe Sam McPherson wanted to be one of her conquests but she ignored him," Luke suggested. "Maybe he developed an unhealthy obsession with her. One of those 'if I can't have her, no one's going to have her' situations."

She shivered a little. "If that was the case, why wait this long to kill her?"

"How the hell should I know? This is your project, not mine. I'm just trying to show you that if you're going to make up a list of potential killers, it could end up being a very long one."

"I'm not so sure about that," she said quietly.

"What's that supposed to mean?"

"Everyone seems to think that Pamela summoned me to Dunsley to say good-bye. But there's no reason to think that in the midst of a severe clinical depression she would have even remembered a girl she only knew well for one summer back in high school. I think she sent me that e-mail because she wanted to tell me something important about the past."

"About the deaths of your parents."

"Yes."

"All right, let's take this logically."

She almost smiled at that. "Translated, that means you're going to try to argue me out of my conclusion."

"Sure. But that's because your conclusion is based on a shaky foundation. What would Pamela know about what happened to your parents? And if she did know something, why would she wait seventeen years to tell you?"

"I don't know the answers to those questions, but I can tell you one thing. Pamela Webb was the last person I saw that night before I . . . found Mom and Dad."

He glanced at her. "The last person?"

"She called me up that afternoon and asked me if I wanted to hang out at her house for a while, get dinner at the café and then go to the movies. Mom said it was okay, provided I made my usual promise."

"What was that?"

"The deal I had with my folks that summer was that if Pamela drank or did drugs while I was with her, I had to leave immediately and come straight home."

"But your parents didn't refuse to let you spend time with her as long as you followed the rules."

"I think Mom felt sorry for Pamela because Ryland ignored her so much. For his part, Dad trusted me to call him to come get me if Pamela started drinking or doing drugs. But she never did either when I was with her."

"Never?"

She shook her head. "Not once. For whatever reason, she really wanted me for a friend. She understood that I would never be allowed to spend time with her again if anything illegal went on. Dad was the chief of police, after all."

"Go on."

"We had dinner at the Ventana View Café and then we went to the movies. Afterward we got into her car. She was supposed to drive me straight back to my house. Dad had another rule, you see. I wasn't allowed to go beyond the town limits with Pamela because she was a new driver who hadn't had a lot of experience behind the wheel. But instead of taking me home, she suddenly turned onto Lakefront Road and headed toward Kirbyville."

"What did you do?"

"At first I thought she was just teasing me. She knew Dad would never let me go anywhere with her again if I violated the rule. When I realized she was serious, I pleaded with her to turn around, but she just laughed and kept driving. I got mad and threatened to jump out of the car. She drove faster. Then I got scared."

"Think she did some drugs without you knowing?"

"I accused her of that. But she said she hadn't used anything.

She was driving too fast for me to bail out of the car, so I did the only thing I could do; I tightened my seat belt and prayed that she would tire of the game and turn around."

"Is that what happened?"

"No. When we reached Kirbyville she had to slow down. I told her that I was going to get out and call my folks to come get me. But she started to cry and then she apologized and told me that she would take me home. I was furious because she had ruined everything. By the time we got back to Dunsley we weren't even speaking to each other. She knew as well as I did that I would never be able to spend time with her again."

"Because you were going to tell your folks what had happened and they would ground you?"

She smiled sadly. "There was no point trying to lie to either of my parents. Pamela knew that as well as I did. In any event, she took me home and dropped me off in the front yard without saying another word. She left before I even got my key out of my pocket. I never saw her again."

She stopped talking because she had gone very cold, the way she always did when she talked about that night. If she kept going she would start to shake.

Luke turned onto the road that led to the lodge.

"No offense," he said after a while, "but it just doesn't seem likely that Pamela would have waited this long to contact you if she knew something important about what happened that evening."

"Maybe she only recently learned some details or some facts that she hadn't known before."

"You're reaching here, admit it." He broke off, jaw hardening. "What the hell?"

She realized that he was looking at a car parked in front of the lobby. A good-looking man in his early twenties leaned casually against one of the stone pillars of the entranceway.

"You've really got a problem with paying customers, don't you?" she said.

"He isn't a paying customer." Luke brought the SUV to a halt beside the other car and shut down the engine. "His name is Jason Danner. He's my youngest brother."

For some reason it came as unexpected news to learn that Luke had a family. Why had she assumed otherwise? Of course he had relatives, she thought. Most people had lots of them. She was the exception to the rule, because after her great-aunt had died a few years ago she had no one left. But that was no reason to assume that everyone else she met was in the same situation.

Still, there was something about Luke that had made her think he was also alone, a sense of distance, perhaps, as if he, too, looked out at the world from another dimension, just as she had learned to do.

She examined Jason through the SUV window, aware of an inexplicable sense of curiosity. There certainly wasn't a great deal of family resemblance, she thought. The two men were very different physically. Jason was not only younger, he was taller and, a picky purist might say, better-looking. Not sexier, though, Irene thought, just handsomer. Big difference.

It occurred to her that, given the obvious age difference between the two and the fact that Luke had said he'd lost his mother when he was six, Jason had to be the offspring of a second marriage. He and Luke were half brothers.

Luke was already out of the SUV. There was a forbidding cast to his face. He was not particularly pleased to see his brother.

"What are you doing here, Jase?" he asked. "I wasn't expecting you."

Jason spread his hands. "Take it easy, Big Brother. Just thought I'd come see how you're doing in the motel business."

He was smiling but it did little to diminish the tension in the air between the two men.

Luke opened Irene's door. "Jason, meet Irene Stenson. She's a guest here at the lodge."

"Hello, Jason." She smiled and got down from the high seat.

Jason nodded, interest flickering in his gaze as he gave her a swift head-to-toe once-over. "Pleased to meet you, Miss Stenson."

The look he was giving her wasn't personal, she thought, more a combination of curiosity and assessment. He was wondering what her relationship was to Luke.

"It's complicated," she said dryly.

Jason blinked, startled. Then he grinned. "It usually is when it involves Luke."

"What are you two talking about?" Luke growled.

"Nothing important," Irene said quickly. "Well, if you'll

excuse me, I'll leave you two to discuss whatever it is you have to discuss."

She gave both men a bright little smile and walked away along the path.

Whatever was going on here, it didn't involve her. It was a family matter.

Eight

Jason lowered himself into one of the porch chairs and drank some of the coffee that Luke had just poured for him. He grimaced.

"You know," he said, "if you invested in one of those high-tech Italian espresso machines you might be able to manufacture coffee that was actually drinkable."

Luke sat down and stacked his heels on the railing. "I don't drink coffee for the taste. I drink it because it's hot and because it helps me to focus."

"Mind if I ask what you're focusing on at the moment?"

Luke looked toward Cabin Number Five. "Irene Stenson."

"Thought so. Correct me if I'm wrong, but I get the feeling that she's not one of your average guests."

"You could say that we sort of bonded last night."

"Boy, howdy, is that what you call it up here in the mountains?"

"Different kind of bond," Luke said. "What Irene and I have is the type of connection that you form when you find a dead body together."

"What?" Jason sputtered on a swallow of coffee.

"Last night Irene went to see an old friend here in Dunsley. Senator Webb's daughter. Found her dead from a bad mix of booze and pills."

"Hang on here." Jason lowered the mug very slowly. "Are you talking about the Senator Ryland Webb who is getting set to make a bid for the White House?"

"Uh-huh."

"His daughter's dead? I didn't hear anything about that on the news."

"You will soon. I understand it was the lead story in the *Glaston Cove Beacon* this morning."

"You know, for some strange reason, I don't get the *Glaston Cove Beacon.* As a matter of fact, I've never even heard of it."

"Neither have a lot of other folks. But it got an exclusive because Irene works for that paper. The news about Pamela Webb will probably hit all the major media this afternoon or tomorrow morning."

Jason frowned uneasily. "Booze and pills?"

"That's what it looked like."

"Suicide?"

Luke studied the lake. "Or an accidental overdose. Hard to be sure."

"Hell of a shock, finding someone like that."

Luke felt his jaw lock. He knew all too well what Jason was really thinking; what everyone else in the family would think when they found out what had happened. For the past six months they had all been growing increasingly worried about him. This business with Pamela Webb's death was only going to alarm them all the more.

"It was a lot harder on Irene," he said quietly. "I never met Pamela Webb while she was alive. But Irene was close friends with her for a time back in high school."

"And you just happened to be with Irene when she found her old friend?"

"Yes."

"How did that come about, if you don't mind my asking?"

"I got curious when I saw her leave the lodge late last night, so I followed her," Luke said.

"Just like that, huh?"

"Yeah."

"You do that a lot?" Jason asked cautiously.

"Do what?"

"Follow your guests around town?"

"No. Mostly I try to avoid the guests as much as possible. Most of them are a damned nuisance."

"But not this one?"

"She's a nuisance, too." Luke drank some more coffee. "But she's different." Time to switch to another topic. "Why did you come up here today, Jase?"

"I told you, just wanted to see how things are going with you."

"Try again."

Jason made an impatient sound and swept out a hand to indicate the cabins and lobby of the Sunrise on the Lake Lodge. "Give me a break. The Old Man is right. You don't belong here. You're no more cut out to run a third-rate motel than I am."

"I'm not cut out to work in the family business, either. Tried that, remember? It didn't go well."

"But that was because it got all mixed up with what was happening between you and Katy at the time," Jason said, very earnest now. "Gordon and the Old Man want you to give it another chance."

"Don't think that would be a good idea," Luke said.

"The Old Man is worried. So is everyone else."

"I know that. There's nothing I can do except keep telling you that I'm okay."

"Mom and the Old Man are convinced that you're sinking into a clinical depression because of what happened when you and Katy went away together."

"I'm not depressed."

"You keep saying that, but no one's buying it."

Luke raised his brows. "It's a philosophical conundrum, isn't it? How do I prove that I'm okay?"

"You could start by making an appointment with Dr. Van Dyke."

"Forget it. Dr. Van Dyke is a very nice lady and no doubt an excellent shrink, but I don't want to talk to her."

"She's an old friend of the family, Luke. It was perfectly natural that Mom and Dad would ask her for advice when they started to worry about you. She's just suggesting that the two of you have a little chat, that's all."

"If I ever decide that I need that kind of help, I'll give her a call."

Jason settled deeper into his chair. "Told the Old Man this was a waste of time."

"It was his idea for you to pay me a visit?"

"He thought maybe I could get through to you."

"Had a feeling that might be it," Luke said. "Consider the message delivered."

"You're coming back for his birthday, aren't you?"

"I'll be there."

"Good. That's important."

"I know," Luke said.

"Be prepared for a sales pitch on the wonderfulness of rejoining the company, though."

"Forewarned is forearmed." Luke started to take another swallow of coffee. The sound of a familiar car engine stopped him. "Damn." He took his heels off the railing and got to his feet. "Now, where the hell is she going?"

Jason watched him, baffled. "Who?"

"Irene." Luke crossed the porch and went down the steps.

"Wait up." Jason launched himself up out of the chair and hurried after Luke. "Where are we going?"

Luke didn't answer. He rounded the side of the cabin, walked into the middle of the narrow lane and came to a halt directly in front of the yellow compact.

Irene was forced to stop. He went to stand at the window on the driver's-side door, braced one hand on the low roof and leaned down to look at her.

She lowered the window and looked at him through the shield of her dark glasses.

"Something wrong?" she asked politely.

"Where are you headed?"

She reached up and removed the glasses with a slow, thoughtful air.

"You know, I've stayed in a wide variety of lodging establishments in my life, but this is the first time I've had to account for my comings and goings to the proprietor."

"We do things a little differently here at the Sunrise on the Lake Lodge."

"I've noticed." She tapped the frames of the glasses against the steering wheel. "Would that be the military way, by any chance?"

"That would be the Marine way, Miss Stenson," Jason offered helpfully. "My brother just got out of the service a few months ago. You'll have to make allowances. He's still adjusting to civilian life."

She nodded once, very crisply, as though the information confirmed some private conclusion she had already reached.

"That explains a lot." She smiled at Jason and then gave Luke a considering look. "It crossed my mind that I owe you something for the considerable amount of inconvenience I caused you last night and this morning."

"That right?" Luke asked.

"I was thinking that maybe I could repay you with an offer of a home-cooked meal this evening."

That was the last thing he had been expecting.

"Boy, howdy," Jason said enthusiastically. "Do you cook, Miss Stenson?"

"I'll have you know that you are looking at the reporter who is single-handedly responsible for selecting every recipe that runs in the Recipe Exchange column of the *Glaston Cove Beacon*."

Jason grinned. "Should I be impressed?"

"You would be more than impressed, you would be stunned speechless if you saw some of the recipes I've rejected. Trust me, you're better off going through life never knowing what some people can do with lime-flavored gelatin and red kidney beans."

"I'll take your word for it," Jason said.

"By the way, you're invited to dinner, too, of course, assuming you're staying overnight?"

"I am now," Jason assured her.

"Excellent. See you both at five-thirty. We'll have drinks before dinner." She turned back to Luke, politely challenging. "If that's okay with you, of course?"

"One of the things they taught us in the Corps was to take advantage of strategic opportunities when they are presented," he said. "We'll be on your doorstep at seventeen-thirty, ma'am."

"I assume that means five-thirty in real time," she said. "Now, if that's settled, I've got a few errands to run."

Luke did not take his hand off the car. "You haven't answered my question. Where are you headed?"

A glint of amusement danced in her amber eyes. "You know, that attitude might work very well in the military. But you may want to rethink it when you're dealing with a paying guest."

"Only two ways to do things, Miss Stenson, the Marine way or the other way."

"For the record, I choose option number two, the other way," she said. "However, in deference to the fact that you will be my guest at dinner tonight, I will be gracious and answer your question. I'm going shopping at the Dunsley Market."

"Shopping?"

"You know, for food and stuff to serve you and your brother?"

"Right. Shopping."

She smiled a little too sweetly. "Care to see my list?"

"Does it include lime gelatin and red kidney beans?"

"Nope."

"Guess I don't have to worry, in that case," he said.

"There's always room to worry, Mr. Danner."

She floored the accelerator. He jerked his fingers off the roof a split second before the compact shot away down the lane.

There was a short silence.

"Boy, howdy," Jason said. "You know, you could lose a hand that way."

Nine

I rene stood at the produce counter of the Dunsley Market, examining the limited selection of lettuce, cucumbers and tomatoes, and pretended not to notice the curious, covert glances of the other shoppers. It wasn't the first time she had been in the middle of a news story here, she thought. But this time around she was an adult, not an emotionally shattered teen.

What's more, after five years of covering the Glaston Cove city council meetings, selecting the Recipe Exchange recipe and profiling local entrepreneurs such as the proprietor of Glaston Cove Seaweed Harvesting, Inc., she was starting to feel like a for-real investigative journalist.

She replayed the conversation she'd conducted with Adeline a short time before.

"Damnit, Irene, you haven't given me anything I can use beyond the vague hints about an ongoing investigation, which, I might add, doesn't seem to be happening, anyway."

"What do you mean? I'm investigating."

"But if the local cops aren't doing zip squat—"

"There's more to this, Addy, I can feel it."

"I know." Adeline exhaled heavily on the other end of the line. "This old reporter's gut is churning, too, and I don't think it's the chili I had at lunch. Too many coincidences here. But promise me you'll be careful. In my considerable experience, politics, sex and dead people make for a real bad mix."

"I'll be careful."

"By the way, Gail and Jenny said they overnighted a week's worth of underwear, pants and shirts. You should have them in the morning. Said to tell you they stuck with basic black so you wouldn't have to worry about mixing and matching. Everything sort of goes together."

"Tell them I said thanks."

The rattle of a shopping cart stopping nearby jerked her out of her reverie.

"Why, if it isn't Irene Stenson. I heard you were back in town."

The speaker had one of those harsh, irritating voices that somehow always manages to rise above the background noise. Irene recognized it instantly although it had been seventeen years since she had last heard Betty Johnson's uniquely grating tones. A searing memory set her heart pounding.

She stood with Aunt Helen in the shadow-drenched vestibule of the Drakenham Mortuary and looked at the crowd in the parking lot. The pouring rain had done nothing to dampen the curiosity of the residents of Dunsley.

"Vultures," she whispered.

"Everyone in town knew your parents and they know you." Helen gripped Irene's hand. *"It was inevitable that they would all come to the service."*

Ben Drakenham, the funeral director, had not been pleased with Helen's choice of cremation for Hugh and Elizabeth Stenson. Irene knew that was because it cost considerably less than the full casket-and-burial arrangement that he preferred to sell.

Her elderly great-aunt had made the decision for reasons other than price, however.

"Headstones in the local cemetery will be lead weight, drawing you back to this time and place, Irene. Your parents would not have wanted that. They would want you to feel free to get on with your life."

She had accepted her aunt's wisdom, but privately she wondered if Helen had made the right choice. Headstones might have served as touchstones, providing her with some tangible links to the past that had been ripped from her.

Every seat in the funeral home's small chapel was filled that cold, rainy day. But Irene was sure that the majority of those present had come to gawk and gossip, not to mourn her parents.

Betty Johnson had made certain to get a ringside seat at the service. Now she and several other people hovered just beyond the front door, waiting to offer their phony condolences and meaningless platitudes.

The car that waited in the drive seemed as distant as the moon.

"Come, Irene," Helen said quietly. *"We will get through this together."*

Irene drew a deep breath and squeezed her aunt's hand very tightly. Together they went down the steps. The crowd parted before them.

Helen acknowledged the expressions of sympathy with a regal nod.
Irene stared straight ahead at the car.

They were only a few feet from the vehicle when she heard Betty
Johnson's voice rising above the hushed murmurs of the crowd.

"Poor little Irene. Bless her heart, she'll never be normal, not after
what happened. . . ."

Irene picked up a head of romaine lettuce with exquisite
care and turned slowly to face the big-haired, sharp-featured
woman behind her.

"Hello, Mrs. Johnson," she said politely.

Betty gave her a superficial smile. "I hardly recognized you.
You look so *different.*"

"So normal, do you mean?"

Betty went blank. "What?"

"Never mind." Irene put the lettuce into the cart and
gripped the handle. "If you'll excuse me, I've got a number of
things to do."

Betty regrouped and tightened her grip on the shopping
cart handle. "Must have been a dreadful shock, finding poor
Pamela Webb the way you did."

With her peripheral vision, Irene watched two other shoppers halt their carts a short distance away. One woman was
making a show of choosing carrots. The other picked through a
pile of baking potatoes as though searching for one made of
solid gold. Both had their heads cocked in a way that indicated
they were listening intently.

"Yes, it was a shock," Irene said. She steered her cart around Betty Johnson.

"I heard that nice Luke Danner was with you when you found the body," Betty said, swinging her cart around in hot pursuit. "You're staying out at the lodge, aren't you?"

"Yes, I am." Irene wheeled the cart around the end of an aisle and plunged between rows of shelves filled with six-packs of beer and bottles of wine.

She chose a modestly priced white wine and then hesitated. Luke looked like the type who preferred beer.

"Someone noticed that you seemed a little upset this morning after you talked to Chief McPherson and Senator Webb," Betty called out behind her.

Irene grabbed a six-pack of beer and kept going. She could hear Betty's cart picking up speed behind her.

"Pamela Webb was a very troubled woman, you know," Betty said. "Always was wild. Why, I remember the time your father found her using drugs along with some of the local kids in one of the boathouses at the old marina. Had to sweep the whole thing under the rug, of course, what with her being Ryland Webb's daughter and all. But everyone in town knew what had happened."

That did it. Irene halted suddenly, let go of the cart handle and stepped quickly to the side.

Betty Johnson was following so closely and at such speed that she was unable to stop in time. Her cart plowed into Irene's with a shuddering clash of steel. Betty staggered under the impact.

Irene smiled politely. "Your memory is a little faulty, Mrs. Johnson. My father didn't do any favors for Ryland Webb."

Betty made a *tut-tut* sound. "Now, dear, everyone knew what Pamela was doing down there at the boathouse."

"The same way everyone knew that your husband was stinking drunk the night he drove his truck into the front window of Tarrant's Hardware store."

Betty stared, stunned. Then her face suffused with outrage. "Ed wasn't drunk. It was an accident."

"You could say that Dad swept that incident under the rug, too, because he didn't arrest Ed, did he? He knew that your husband had just been laid off. He realized that an arrest for drunk driving would have made it very hard for him to find a new job."

"It was an accident, I tell you. Your father understood that."

"An accident." Irene looked around and saw a vaguely familiar face at the end of the aisle. "Like the time Jeff Wilkins and two of his buddies *accidentally* stole Harry Benson's new truck and took it joyriding out on Bell Road."

Annie Wilkins blanched. "How dare you bring up that old incident? It was just a childish prank."

"It was grand theft auto, and you'd better believe that Benson was determined to press charges," Irene said. "But my father convinced him to calm down and back off. Then Dad had a chat with your son and his pals. Gave them a good scare. And guess what? Jeff and his friends avoided getting a rap sheet."

"That happened years ago," Annie said fiercely. "I'll have you know that Jeff is a lawyer now."

"Talk about life's little ironies. I'm sure Dad would have

found that very amusing." Irene turned slowly on her heel, selecting another target from the small crowd. "Let's see, who else benefited from the way my father did his job?"

A shudder went through the small cluster of people poised at the end of the aisle. Two shoppers at the rear abruptly reversed course, trying to escape.

Irene pounced on the woman with fake red hair who was taking a hard left into CAN. FRUITS & VEG.

"Becky Turner, right? I remember you. I also recall the time your daughter got mixed up with that group of summer kids who were causing so much trouble—"

Becky did the deer-in-the-headlights freeze and then lurched toward the checkout counter.

All the shoppers in the vicinity were in motion now, wheeling their carts toward the nearest exit. There was a lot of clanging and clattering, and then an acute silence fell.

For a few seconds Irene thought she was alone in the beer and wine aisle. Then she sensed a presence behind her.

She turned slowly and saw an attractive middle-aged woman watching her with an amused expression.

"Hello, Irene," she said.

"Mrs. Carpenter?"

"Call me Tess. You're not in my classroom anymore. No need to be formal."

Tess Carpenter pushed her cart down the aisle, closing the space between them. For the first time since she had arrived in town, Irene experienced the kind of inner warmth that came with happy memories.

Tess had taught English at Dunsley High. She had enthusiastically encouraged Irene's hunger for reading and her desire to write.

Her honey-colored hair was subtly streaked with blond to hide the gray, and there were some new crinkles at the edges of her eyes, but other than that, Tess seemed to have aged very little.

"Looks like you cleared out the market," Tess said, laughing. "Congratulations. Pamela would have been proud of you. She loved scenes, didn't she?"

"Yes, but only if she was the one causing them."

"That's true." Tess's face softened. "How are you, Irene? Someone said you had become a journalist?"

"I'm with a small paper in a town on the coast. What about you? Still teaching at Dunsley High?"

"Yes. Phil owns the garage now."

Irene smiled. "Dad always said that Phil could work magic when it came to cars."

"Your father was right." Tess surveyed Irene with concern and sympathy. "I heard what happened, obviously. The whole town knows about Pamela. I'm very sorry that you had to be the one to find her."

"The only reason I'm in town is because she wanted to talk to me. After seventeen years of silence she sent me an e-mail saying she had to see me. But we never got the chance to meet."

"Do you really think there's some mystery about her death?"

Irene smiled wryly. "That gossip got around fast."

"This is Dunsley, remember? We don't even need our own paper. News travels at the speed of light."

A woman with a good-natured face and a ponytail came down the aisle.

"Hi, Irene. Sandy Pace. Remember me? I used to be Sandy Warden. I was a year behind you at Dunsley High."

"Hello, Sandy," Irene said. "It's nice to see you again. How have you been?"

"Things are good, thanks. I married Carl Pace right out of high school. We've got two kids now. Carl works construction around the lake. He keeps busy."

"I'm glad," Irene said. "Congratulations on the kids."

"Thanks. They're a handful, and it seems like it takes every dime Carl makes to keep them in clothes, but we're doing fine. We're building a new house."

"That's wonderful, Sandy."

Sandy straightened her shoulders with an air of resolve. "Listen, I couldn't help overhearing what you said back there to Betty Johnson and the others. I just wanted to say that you were right to tell those old biddies off like that."

"I'm afraid that I let them push a few of my buttons."

"I was glad to see you push right back. The truth is, a lot of folks around here have reason to be grateful to your dad. Isn't that right, Tess?"

"Absolutely right," Tess agreed. "It's amazing how short memories can be."

"There were plenty of times when Hugh Stenson handled things quietly so that someone didn't go to jail or end up with a record or was just plain embarrassed to death," Sandy added. "And he knew how to keep secrets, too."

Irene felt a rush of gratitude. "Thank you, Sandy."

"One of those secrets involved my mom and me. My step-dad, Rich Harrell, was mean, real mean. He'd get drunk and slap my mother around, and then he'd start in on me."

"I didn't know that," Irene said. She felt oddly shocked. How could she not have realized what was going on in that household? she wondered.

"'Course you didn't," Sandy said calmly. "I never said a word to anyone. Neither did Mom. She wanted to leave Harrell, but she was afraid he might kill her and me, too. Like I said, she never told a soul, but Chief Stenson somehow figured out what was happening. One day he came to our house and told Harrell to get into his car. They drove off and were gone for a long time. When they came back, I could tell that Harrell was really nervous. He packed a bag and left town that same day. We never saw him after that."

Tess frowned. "Abusive men don't usually disappear so conveniently just because of a conversation with a cop."

"They do if they get real scared," Sandy said. "A few years later we heard that Harrell had gotten drunk, smashed his car into a tree and died. We celebrated, Mom and me. That's when she told me what happened the day Hugh Stenson took him away to have that private chat."

"What was that?" Irene asked.

Sandy's eyes gleamed with remembered satisfaction. "Don't know how he did it, but the chief found out somehow that Harrell had once ripped off a really dangerous man down in San Diego, a guy who laundered money for South American drug lords. Harrell had faked his death after he took the man's cash. Your dad warned Harrell that if he ever came back to Dunsley or if anything suspicious ever happened to me or my mom, he'd make sure the man in San Diego got word that the guy who stole some of his money wasn't really dead."

Irene shivered a little. "I never heard that story."

"Neither did I," Tess said.

Sandy looked at them knowingly. "Like I said, Hugh Stenson kept a lot of this town's dirty little secrets. Took them to his grave."

Ten

S am picked up the clicker and muted the annoying noise
being made by the too-perky, too-perfect woman reading the evening news. He leaned back in the recliner and
closed his eyes.

The crushing guilt closed in on him. He wondered if he
would just stop breathing altogether under the weight of it.
Maybe that wouldn't be the worst thing in the world.

He had been doing okay in the past few years, he thought. It
had taken a lot of work, but he'd finally been able to shove the
guilt into a deep hole and cover it up. Sure he'd had some problems. He'd screwed up his marriage for one thing, but that
didn't exactly make him unique. A lot of people managed that
trick.

On the plus side, he thought he had become a fairly good
cop, the kind of cop that Hugh Stenson would have approved
of. He upheld the law here in Dunsley. He had never accepted
a bribe, not that bribes were a big temptation in a town where

incomes tended to range from modest to low. And he kept people's secrets, just as Stenson had taught him.

Lately he'd even been thinking of trying to resurrect something resembling a social life. Half a dozen times in the past month he'd almost picked up the phone and called her. But always he had hesitated. She was a good woman, a pretty woman, a compassionate woman. The problem was that she considered him a friend. He hadn't been sure how she would react if he tried to turn their friendship into something else.

He looked at the phone on the table beside the chair. One thing was certain, he sure as hell could not call her now. The return of Irene Stenson had changed everything. One look at those haunting eyes and all the guilt that he had buried so carefully had been exhumed from the grave.

He knew that nothing he had accomplished as chief of police could compensate for what he had done seventeen years ago.

Eleven

A thunderous roar of hard rock music blasted out of Cabin Number Six just as Irene handed a bottle of beer to Jason.

"That does it." Luke straightened away from the wall where he had been leaning and set his own beer down on the table. "I knew those guys were going to be a problem when Maxine checked them in this afternoon. Be right back."

He opened the back porch door and went outside.

Irene watched him go down the steps and walk through the trees to the neighboring cabin.

"Always a treat to watch Luke in action," Jason said, teeth flashing in a grin of happy anticipation. He went to stand at the window where he had a better view of the offending cabin. "He's at the door now. I give that music five more seconds, max. One, two, three—"

Silence descended abruptly.

"Make that three seconds," Jason said.

"Your brother does have a way about him," Irene observed.

"A few years in the Marines will do that for you."

"I know." She opened the refrigerator and took out the washed and crisped romaine. "My father was a Marine."

Jason whistled. "So that's it."

"That's what?"

"Why you seem to understand Luke better than most women I know."

She glanced up, startled. "What makes you think I understand him?"

"Something about the way you two communicate, I guess. He gives orders. You ignore him. Seems to work well for both of you." Jason shrugged off the issue. "Need any help with dinner?"

"I think everything's under control, thanks. How long are you staying?"

"I'm going back to Santa Elena tomorrow morning. Got a meeting with a supplier. I just came up here to see how Luke was doing and to make sure he's still planning to come to the Old Man's birthday party."

She opened the oven door. "Who's the Old Man?"

"That's what we all call Dad." He examined the pan she was removing from the oven with acute interest. "Hey, is that corn bread?"

"Yes. Like it?"

"Oh, yeah. But I'm strictly a bush league fan compared to Luke. He loves corn bread. Actually, he loves anything home cooked. I think he ate one too many MREs in the field."

"That would be those instant meals that the military uses?"

"Right." Jason sniffed appreciatively. "What with one thing and another, Luke hasn't had a lot of home-cooked meals since he left to go off to college, and that was a long time ago. He was married for a while once but his ex didn't like to cook. Mostly she specialized in takeout."

"Luke has an ex?" she heard herself say in her best oh-so-casual sort of way. Just a reporter, doing her job. Getting background.

"Don't worry, she's way out of the picture. Been five or six years since they split up. One of those whirlwind things. Lasted about five minutes."

"I see."

"Well, actually, it lasted a little longer than that. They had a couple of months together before Luke was deployed abroad. By the time he got back, it had finally dawned on his bride that there was more to Luke than a good-looking uniform. She concluded that she did not want to be a Marine officer's wife."

"Luke never remarried?"

She knew instantly that she had stepped into forbidden territory. Jason's cheerful, open, easygoing expression was suddenly veiled behind a protective barrier.

"He was engaged for a while six months ago, but—" Jason stopped very suddenly, as if he had said more than he'd intended. "There was a problem. Things didn't work out."

Irene felt the familiar tingle of curiosity stirring deep inside. Some mystery here, she decided. What was it Luke had said about family secrets? *One thing's for sure, every family's got 'em.*

She sprinkled a little coarse salt on the three salmon fillets she had brought home from the Dunsley Market. She had selected the fish from the frozen foods section after recalling her mother's advice on the subject of purchasing fish from the Dunsley Market. *Never buy fresh. No telling how old it is.*

"Where's the big birthday bash to be held?" she asked, trying to reinvigorate the faltering conversation.

"Santa Elena." Jason seemed relieved that she had changed topics. "That's where the family business is."

"What, exactly, is the business?"

Jason raised his brows. "Luke hasn't told you much about himself, has he?"

"Not a lot, no." She took the bottle of inexpensive white that she had purchased earlier out of the refrigerator and set it on the counter. "We've been busy. Haven't had a lot of time for casual conversation."

"Yeah, I guess that's true, all right." Jason studied the bottle of wine she was opening. "But I think it's more likely he doesn't want to talk about the family business these days because the Old Man and his partner are putting a lot of pressure on him to come into it. Ever heard of Elena Creek Vineyards?"

"Well, sure. Anyone who lives in and around wine country has heard of Elena Creek Vineyards. Very classy, upscale wines. They win lots of awards."

"We certainly like to think so," Jason said.

She took another look at the label on the bottle of white. "I'm getting a bad feeling about this."

"Don't worry about the white. Luke and I sure won't."

"Your family owns Elena Creek Vineyards?"

"My dad and his partner, Gordon Foote, founded it about forty years ago. The Old Man was the business brains of the outfit. Gordon was the winemaker. They had a dream and they made it come true. Now they want to pass that dream down to the next generation."

"How does the next generation feel about that?"

Jason smiled wryly. "My brother Hackett and I are on board. So is Katy, Gordon's daughter. In fact, I don't think you could keep the three of us out of the wine business. It's in our blood."

"But not in Luke's?"

"That's what he claims, but the general consensus in the family is that Luke doesn't know what he wants. See, Luke has never really settled into anything for long. Take college, for instance."

"He dropped out?"

"He was doing great. Got his B.A. and got accepted into grad school. We all thought he was on track to enter the academic world."

"What did he study?"

"You'll never believe it." Jason chuckled. "Classical philosophy."

She was momentarily dumbstruck. Then she started to laugh. "You're kidding. It does sort of boggle the mind."

"Don't let that laid-back former-Marine routine fool you. Luke can shoot the academic bull with the best of them. As I was saying, it seemed like he was headed for the ivory-tower world, but the next thing we know, he tells us he's enlisted. It was a real shocker. He was sent off to some sort of new strategy and warfare training program. He actually managed to finish up his Ph.D. in the Corps. But he got deployed. A lot."

"A lot?"

"Things have been busy for the Marines in the past few years."

She chilled. "Yes, I know."

"Anyhow, six months ago he got out. He let the Old Man and Gordon talk him into going to work at the winery."

"I take it that was not a successful career move."

"It was what you might call an unmitigated disaster. Like I said, he also got engaged about the same time and that fell apart, too." Jason swept out a hand. "Now, here he is in Dunsley operating a tumbledown old fishing lodge."

"Let me take a wild guess. The family is deeply concerned."

"There is outright panic in some quarters," Jason admitted. "Personally, I think Luke is just one of those people who take a while to find their thing in life, you know? But the others are afraid he's in a bad downward spiral."

She considered that briefly and shook her head. "I don't think that's it. Just the opposite, I'd say. Luke may be taking a different route, but I think he knows where he's going."

"I'm with you." Jason hesitated. His face grew somber for the first time. "But you can't blame the family for worrying. Luke probably hasn't told you this, but he saw some very rough duty during the last few years."

She thought about what she had glimpsed once or twice behind the iron-clad self-control in Luke's eyes. "I had more or less assumed as much."

"He was very good at what he did. There are some serious

medals tucked away somewhere in a drawer. But that kind of thing exacts a price."

"I know," she said gently.

The tension in Jason's face eased. "Had a hunch you'd probably figured it out. Like I said, the two of you seem to communicate pretty well. Which is a little weird because Luke's not what anyone would call a great communicator." He paused to peer through the window. "Not unless he's giving orders, that is. He's real good at communicating orders."

The door opened abruptly. Luke walked into the kitchen. He came to a halt, looking first at Jason and then at Irene.

"What?" he asked.

Irene smiled serenely. "I just discovered that I'm about to serve what can only be called an extremely unassuming white wine to a couple of men who grew up in a legendary California wine-making family."

"I told her not to worry about it," Jason assured him, "on account of there's corn bread."

"Oh, man," Luke said, looking as if he had just had a religious experience. "Corn bread."

"Your tongue's hanging out," Jason said. "Try not to embarrass the family here."

"What did you tell the guys in the cabin who were playing the loud rock?" Irene asked, popping the cork out of the bottle.

Luke shrugged. "I just reminded them of the lodge's do-not-disturb-your-neighbor policy."

Irene leaned down to check the salmon. "That's all it took to make them lower the volume?"

"I also reminded them that I happen to be one of their neighbors, and I made it clear that if they didn't lower the volume immediately and keep it down I would personally drop each one of them off the dock into the lake."

Jason grinned. "Like I said, Luke communicates orders real well."

"Far be it from me to offer advice to a budding resort operator," Irene said, "but if you're hoping for repeat business, you might want to develop a more diplomatic approach to dealing with your guests."

"Luke joined the Marines, not the foreign service," Jason said. "Different culture entirely."

She took the salmon fillets out from under the broiler. "I've heard that."

Twelve

Luke awoke to darkness. The distant *whap-whap-whap* of a helicopter faded into the night along with the other brittle shards of the dream.

He sat up slowly on the edge of the bed. Sweat plastered his tee shirt to his back and chest. He was wired; preternaturally alert. All of his senses were energized, battle ready.

He knew the sensation all too well. He also knew that the only antidote was to move around, work off some of the adrenaline and force himself to focus on something other than the dream.

It had been a bad one this time. He'd been back in the narrow lanes and dark alleys of an urban landscape that had been ancient before the United States had even been a gleam in the Founders' eyes. There in the shadows he and his men played a deadly game of three-dimensional warfare, one in which the enemy could be anywhere—above, behind, in front or even in a maze of tunnels underground beneath your feet. There was no safe zone, no place where you could relax even for an hour or two and allow your overworked senses to recover. The only way to survive was to stay constantly alert and aware.

Don't go there. Focus on something else. You know the drill. Fill your head with other thoughts.

He punched the little button on the side of his watch to check the time. In the green glow that briefly illuminated the dial he saw that it was ten minutes to one.

He got to his feet but did not turn on the light beside the bed. The last thing he wanted to do was awaken Jason, who was sound asleep on the couch in the front room. He went to the window and twitched the curtain aside.

Cold moonlight gleamed on the lake. The lights were off in the cabin that Maxine had rented to the hard rock aficionados. But every window in Irene's cabin was still ablaze.

He knew exactly what he wanted to do to release some of the excess energy pounding through him. But he was pretty sure that it was against the rules for innkeepers to jump their female guests.

Hell of a dumb profession with rules like that.

He crossed the small space to the battered wooden desk that stood against one wall and powered up the laptop. Maybe doing some work on The Project would help take his mind off the aftereffects of the dream. That had been the whole point of creating The Project, after all. In simplest terms, the strategy was to replace one obsession with another. It sounded good in theory, and many nights it actually worked.

The computer screen winked on and glowed expectantly.

He opened the file and paged through the text until he got to the chapter he had been working on all week.

The soft sound of a small car moving at low speed interrupted his thoughts. He stopped in mid-sentence and listened closely. If the guys in Cabin Number Six were driving into town to look for some excitement, they were going to be sadly disappointed. Harry's Hang-Out was closed by this time.

He waited, but no beams speared the darkness. Whoever was at the wheel was driving toward the main road without lights.

"Damn." He got to his feet and grabbed his jeans off the back of the chair. "There she goes again."

He yanked on the denims, ripped a dark shirt off a hanger, shoved his feet into his running shoes and left the bedroom at a run.

Jason raised his head when he went past the couch.

"Where are you going at this time of night?" he mumbled sleepily.

"Out."

"Right." Jason dropped back down onto the pillow. "Knew when I saw the corn bread that you were a goner."

Thirteen

S he hated the thought of going back into the house, especially at this hour.

Irene stopped in the pool of darkness that drowned the steps outside the utility room and took the key out of the pocket of her trench coat. She had a flashlight with her, but she didn't dare switch it on until she was inside. She had also taken the precaution of leaving her car parked out of sight down the road.

Tonight she did not want to risk being seen anywhere near the Webbs' summer place. What she was about to do probably came under the heading of illegal entry, she thought. Sam McPherson was already unhappy with her. She did not want to give him a reason to try to run her out of town.

A ghostly breeze slithered through the trees. The interior of the house was drenched in night and shadow. Unlike last night, no light burned in the front room.

She unlocked the door, dropped the key into her pocket and

held her breath as she moved into the deep darkness of the utility room. Closing the door very quickly, she removed the small, pencil-slim flashlight and switched it on.

As soon as the narrow beam sliced through the shadows she was able to breathe again.

She moved cautiously into the hall and went toward the staircase that connected the living and dining area to the upper floor. The darkness downstairs seemed especially dense. It took her a moment to realize that someone had drawn the curtains across the floor-to-ceiling widows after Pamela's body had been removed. Sam, probably, she thought. His goal had no doubt been to deter morbid curiosity seekers, but the result was that she did not have to worry about a passerby noticing the thin beam of her flashlight.

It gave her an eerie jolt to realize that everything looked so *House & Garden* normal tonight. Surely there should have been some sense that a person had died here recently. But Pamela's death had not involved overt violence or blood, she reminded herself, just booze and pills.

Booze and pills. One of the classic suicide strategies. What if she was wrong and everyone else was right? What if Pamela really had OD'd, accidentally or otherwise?

Okay, so call me a conspiracy theorist.

She did not linger downstairs. If Pamela had hidden any secrets before she died, they would be in her bedroom.

Over the course of the summer that she and Pamela had been close, she had come to know her friend's bedroom almost as well as her own. She had spent hours upstairs in this house, listening to the latest music, talking about boys and reading an endless array of fashion and celebrity gossip magazines.

She climbed the stairs to the second floor and turned toward the bedroom that Pamela had used when she was a teen. The door was ajar.

That would not have been the case seventeen years ago. Pamela always kept the door closed in those days and with good reason. She'd had a lot of things she wanted to hide from her father and the housekeeper, including birth control pills, condoms and mysterious packets of what she claimed were designer drugs that she had purchased from dealers who hung out around her fancy boarding school.

Pamela had been very proud of the hiding place she had crafted to conceal her treasures—so proud, in fact, that after swearing Irene to eternal secrecy, she had shown it to her.

A trickle of anticipation fluttered through Irene as she moved into the room. It was the memory of Pamela's secret place that had lured her back here tonight. The odds of finding anything in it that might offer an explanation or an insight were slim to vanishing, but it was a place to start.

The curtains and shades had been pulled shut in this room, too. Relieved that she did not have to be overly cautious with the flashlight, she splashed the beam quickly around the space.

Shock drove out the sense of anticipation she had been feeling. A dark, edgy chill of déjà vu roiled her nerves.

Nothing had been changed.

She walked slowly into the room, unnerved. True, the

downstairs had not been redecorated but at least it had always been furnished in an adult manner. Even seventeen years earlier Pamela's pink-and-white bedroom had struck her as somehow too sweet, too innocent, for the sophisticated and worldly Pamela Webb. Tonight the canopied bed with its gossamer clouds of drapery and pink satin pillows seemed downright weird.

Another case of time warp, she thought. It was hard to believe that the room had never been redecorated. Surely Pamela had needed it for her guests on those occasions when she brought friends up to the lake.

Poor Pamela. Had she been so deeply attached to the memories of her girlhood that she could not bear to alter her old bedroom? Somehow that didn't seem Pamela-like. She had been a risk-taker; always excited about the forbidden. And she loved fashion.

But Pamela had been a girl who lost her mother at the age of five, Irene reminded herself. Maybe some part of her had tried to cling to the memories of that shattered bond here in this room.

There was so much that she had never comprehended about Pamela, Irene thought. She did not even know why Pamela had selected her to be her best friend that long-ago summer. At the time she had not questioned her good luck. It had been enough to bask in the reflected glow of Pamela's dangerous, glittery light; enough to pretend that she, too, was a bad girl. But in hindsight, she had often wondered what Pamela had seen in her.

She crossed the room to the fairy-tale bed, selected one of the pink satin pillows and placed it on the nightstand. She propped the flashlight against the pillow so that the beam struck the light switch on the wall.

Reaching into one of her pockets, she took out the screwdriver she had brought with her. Very carefully she inserted the tip into one of the screws that anchored the light switch plate to the wall.

Pamela's words the night she had revealed her secret hiding place floated through her mind as she worked.

"It's such a guy thing, hiding stuff in the wall behind a light switch. No one would think that a girl would do it."

Certainly not the sort of girl who lived in a pink-and-white princess room like this, Irene mused as she removed the second screw.

She put the plate and the screws down on the table and went back to work on the two screws that secured the switch itself. A moment later she was able to pull it away from the wall.

Pulse leaping, she grabbed the flashlight and angled the beam into the outlet box.

Light gleamed on brass. Her breath caught in her throat when she realized that she was looking at a key.

She reached into the outlet box and removed the small find. When she held it up to the light to get a closer look she was disappointed to see that it looked like an ordinary house key.

Why would Pamela keep a spare house key tucked away up here in her secret hiding place?

She dropped the key into a pocket and reached for the light switch plate.

She was tightening the last screw on the plate when she heard the sound of a door opening downstairs.

Her blood turned to ice in her veins.

She was no longer alone in the house.

Fourteen

The almost noiseless plop of the screwdriver falling onto the thick white carpet at her feet broke the trance.

Irene finally remembered to breathe.

In the darkness below, floorboards squeaked. Someone was moving through the house. The intruder was not turning on any lights.

A burglar, she thought. That was the most logical explanation. Some local vandal had decided to see what he could steal from a dead woman's house.

She heard footsteps in the front hall. Whoever was down there was making no attempt to be quiet. She prayed that meant he was not aware that there was someone else in the house. But if he was looking for cash and valuables, he would no doubt make his way upstairs sooner or later.

She had to get out before he found her. People who confronted burglars got killed. She had sometimes wondered if that was what had happened to her parents.

She pushed past the panic that was threatening to clog her throat and tried to concentrate. The only way out of the house from this floor was the staircase, the lower section of which ended in full view of the living and dining area. Whoever was downstairs would surely spot her if she tried to leave via that route.

She realized that the penlight was still blazing. Hastily she switched it off and then worked to fight the inevitable tide of fear that closed in around her together with the darkness.

She went down on her knees and groped for the fallen screwdriver. When her shaking fingers closed around the hard plastic handle she felt an inexplicable rush of adrenaline. The screwdriver wasn't much, but it was all she had in the way of a weapon.

Don't think like that. You're not facing hand-to-hand combat here. You're going to do the smart thing and hide until whoever is down there finishes whatever it is he came here to do.

She had one big advantage, she thought. She knew the layout of the house. Pamela's bedroom was a trap. There was no place to hide.

The good news was that the upstairs was fully carpeted, and whoever was down below was making a fair amount of noise. If she was careful, she could move about up here without alerting him.

She slipped off her loafers. Holding them in one hand, she tiptoed to the doorway of the bedroom.

Under cover of another flurry of footsteps downstairs, she made her way past a guest bedroom and bath.

She paused when she reached the top of the staircase, flattened her back against the wall and risked a peek around the corner.

The narrow beam of a flashlight arced through the shadows at the foot of the stairs, but she could not see the outline of the person wielding it. Talons of fear gripped her insides.

When she heard the ring of shoes on the tile floor of the kitchen, she moved into the master bedroom.

The curtains were open in this room. Moonlight slanted onto the pale carpet through the sliding glass doors. She could see the railing of the deck that overlooked the lake.

The deck was her goal. It formed the roof of the breakfast nook on the first floor. There were no stairs leading down to the ground, but if she could get out without alerting the intruder, she could hide in the shadows of the eaves until he left.

She walked silently across the carpet, trying to time each step with the sound of activity down below.

When she reached the slider, she unlocked it gently and then hesitated.

Something metallic clanged loudly in the vicinity of the kitchen.

She would never get a better opportunity, she decided. She eased the door open and stepped outside onto the deck.

Shutting the slider very softly, she moved into the shadows of the tall storage locker that the Webbs used to protect the deck furniture during the winter.

A moment later light flashed inside the master bedroom. The intruder was already upstairs.

The flashlight beam disappeared almost immediately. The prowler had left the master bedroom and was heading down the hall to Pamela's old room.

She never sensed the presence of the other person on the deck until a man's palm clamped across her mouth. Strong fingers closed around the hand in which she clutched the screwdriver, disarming her with a flick of one powerful wrist.

"It's me," Luke said against her ear. "Don't freak."

Fifteen

It was all she could do not to dissolve into a limp puddle of relief. Too much, she thought. One more shock tonight and she would be a mindless wreck. A body could only take so much adrenaline.

Luke reached around her. He grasped the handle of the door.

It dawned on her that he was going to enter the house and confront the intruder. Another dose of panic hit her over-wrought nervous system.

She grabbed his arm with both hands.

He paused. In the moonlight she saw him turn his head slightly toward her, curious why she was trying to restrain him.

"Are you crazy?" She mouthed the words and yanked harder on his hand.

He put his mouth very close to her ear again. "Stay here."

No. She wanted to scream the word aloud. But men like Luke did not respond to the emotional approach.

"Gun," she whispered, instead, going for the logical angle. *Gun, as in, maybe whoever is in there has one,* she added silently.

Luke patted her on the shoulder in what was no doubt intended to be a reassuring manner. In her considered opinion, it was nothing short of patronizing.

When she refused to let go of his arm, he seemed to get a little annoyed. He pried her fingers away and opened the door very quietly.

The unmistakable odor of kerosene wafted through the opening.

She thought she heard Luke whisper something that sounded a lot like "shit," but she couldn't be sure because he was moving too quickly.

He closed the door, grabbed Irene's arm and hauled her toward the deck railing.

Belatedly she realized what he intended.

She tried to be philosophical about the plan. A few broken bones were going to be a nuisance, but they beat the heck out of the alternative.

"It's okay, I just came up that way," Luke whispered. "Hold on to my wrists. Go over the side. I'll lower you as far as I can. It's all grass and shrubs down there. Soft landing, guaranteed."

"Oh, sure." She looked over the side. The view reminded her of the one time she had mustered the courage to climb up to the high dive board at a swimming pool. She had taken one look at the long drop to the water and immediately climbed right back down. "What about you?"

"Believe me, I'll be right behind you. That bastard is saturating the house with whatever he's using for an accelerant. When he puts the torch to it, this place is going to go up like a bomb. *Move,* woman."

As soon as his powerful hands tightened around her wrists, she took heart. His fingers felt like iron manacles. He would not let her fall.

She scrambled awkwardly over the side and found herself dangling a short distance above the ground. Luke released her. She dropped lightly onto the lawn, stumbled and sat down hard.

That hadn't been so bad, she thought, scrambling to her feet and brushing off her hands.

She looked up just in time to see Luke swing himself over the side of the deck. He hung there for an instant, found the edge of the breakfast nook window frame with one foot and then bounded down to the ground in one easy motion. She realized that it was the window ledge that had made it possible for him to climb up to the deck in the first place. Men and their upper body strength.

He grabbed her hand. "Let's go."

They plunged into the trees.

The muffled roar of a distant freight train shattered the night.

Except that there were no train tracks anywhere near Dunsley, Irene thought.

She did not need the whoosh of the flames or the wave of heat behind her to tell her what had happened. The intruder had ignited a firestorm.

Luke drew her to a halt.

"Stay here," he said. "Got your phone?"

"Yes, but—"

"Call nine-one-one." He turned away.

"For God's sake, where are you going?" she called after him.

"To see if I can find the bastard. He's on foot, same as us. Probably parked out on the road somewhere. Maybe I can catch up with him."

"Luke, for the record, I think that is a very bad idea."

But she was talking to the night. Luke had melted away into the shadows.

Glass exploded. Irene watched, stunned, as the flames engulfed the house with breathtaking speed. She yanked her phone out of her pocket and dialed the emergency number.

Somewhere in the distance an outboard motor roared to life. She knew then that Luke was not going to be able run down the arsonist. The intruder wasn't fleeing toward a car. He had used a boat.

Sixteen

I need a drink." Luke shut the front door of the cabin with a sharp, definitive movement. He slammed the bolt home and headed for the tiny kitchenette. "Got any of that beer left?"

"In the refrigerator." Irene watched him warily, uncertain of his mood. This was the first time he had spoken since they had finished talking to Sam McPherson at the scene of the fire. That conversation had not gone well, in her opinion. Luke's silence in the SUV afterward had not helped. "Look, I'm sorry you got involved in this thing. I never meant—"

"If you say that one more time, I will not be responsible for my actions." He opened the refrigerator, took out a bottle and popped the top. "You know, for the first time in my life I'm starting to believe that there just might be such a thing as bad karma. Nothing else can really explain why I ended up with you for a paying guest here at Sunrise on the Lake Lodge." He took a long pull on the beer, lowered the bottle and looked at her with narrowed eyes. "I mean, what are the odds?"

It dawned on her that he was coldly furious. The unfairness of it all annoyed her. She stood in the middle of the room and folded her arms.

"I didn't ask you to follow me to the Webb house tonight," she said.

"No, you sure as hell did not." He leaned back against the counter, crossed his feet at the ankles and drank more beer. "In fact, you drove out of here with your headlights off in an effort to make sure I didn't see you."

"This isn't your problem."

"Maybe it wasn't in the beginning, but it sure as hell is now." He raised his brows. "You do realize that McPherson is currently contemplating the possibility that you and I are responsible for that fire tonight?"

She swallowed hard. "Yes. But we're the ones who called in the alarm."

"Wouldn't be the first time that an arsonist set a fire, called the fire department and then hung around to watch the excitement."

"I'm aware of that. But Sam has to realize that we have no motive. Neither of us stands to benefit from any insurance policy that the Webbs might have on the place."

"A lot of arsonists don't do it for the insurance money. They're addicted to the thrill of the flames. But that's beside the point in this case. You want to talk motive? Fine. Let's start with me."

She frowned. "You don't have one."

"Exactly." He nodded, as though trying to encourage a slow student. "You, on the other hand, do."

She nearly choked on her outrage. "What on earth are you talking about?"

"It wouldn't take much to make you look like a prime suspect. Everyone in town knows you're obsessing over the idea that Pamela Webb was murdered. You want to force McPherson to conduct a serious investigation, right?"

"Yes, but—"

"Setting fire to the victim's house is certainly one way of getting his attention and ensuring an investigation of some kind."

She was horrified. "That's weak. Very, very weak."

"If you believe that, you're in denial." Luke studied her with a hunter's cold, calculating gaze. "No matter how you slice it, I'm your alibi for that fire tonight and you're mine. Problem is, neither of us has a lot of credibility here in Dunsley. I'm the new guy in town. No one knows much about me. That makes me a natural suspect. But you're in an even worse position because you've got a history around here. McPherson would have to be a really bad cop not to be suspicious of both of us."

She unlinked her arms and threw them wide. "But there was someone else there tonight. We saw him." She hesitated. "Or her."

"McPherson's only got our word on that."

"Okay, you've made your point. You know something? I think I need a drink, too." She marched to the refrigerator, opened it and took out the last bottle of beer. "By the way, I am well aware of the fact that you saved my life tonight." She removed the top of the bottle. "Thank you."

"Huh." He drank more beer.

"True, you scared the living daylights out of me, appearing out of nowhere up there on the deck. But if you hadn't been there, I might not have realized what the intruder was doing until it was too late."

"You were scared? How the hell do you think I felt when I realized you had broken into the Webb house in the middle of the night and that there was someone else inside with you? You want to compare heart palpitations, lady?"

Best to ignore that, she decided.

"You never did tell me why you followed me," she said after a while.

"That should be obvious. I'm renting a cabin to a woman who has a bad tendency to get into trouble in the middle of the night. An innkeeper has to take precautions when he's dealing with guests like you."

"You're really pissed, aren't you?"

"Yeah, I'm really pissed," he growled. "You shouldn't have gone anywhere near that damn house."

"You know, you make it hard to be properly grateful when you take that senior-officer-chewing-out-a-subordinate attitude."

He brooded for a moment.

"Why the hell did you go back there tonight?" he asked.

She leaned against the edge of the sink and contemplated the label on the beer bottle. "You heard what I said to Mc-Pherson. It's been bothering me that Pamela didn't leave a suicide note. Tonight, after you and Jason left after dinner, I got to thinking about it. I still had the utility room key. So I drove out to the house to take a look. The intruder interrupted me while I was searching upstairs."

"I heard what you told McPherson." Luke's mouth twisted humorlessly. "I also know you lied through your teeth."

She felt her face turn hot. "What do you mean?"

"You don't believe Pamela committed suicide, so you didn't go to the Webb house to look for a note. You went looking for something else." He paused a beat and lowered his voice. "What's more, I think you found it."

When in doubt, stall, she thought.

"Out of curiosity, what makes you say that?" she asked.

"Call me psychic."

"I'm no more in the mood for games than you are tonight," she said tightly.

"You and I have spent more serious quality time together in the past couple of days than a lot of married couples do in a year. Let's just say I've learned a few things about you. When I listened to you give your story to McPherson, I got a real solid hunch that you weren't being one hundred percent straight with him."

"We found a dead woman together, escaped from an exploding house fire set by an arsonist and conducted a couple of unpleasant conversations with the local police and a U.S. senator. You've got an odd notion of quality time."

"Probably." He watched her with a relentless expression. "You going to tell me what you found?"

Why not tell him? Unlike Sam McPherson and Ryland Webb, he was at least taking her semi-seriously.

"In the old days Pamela had a hiding place in her bedroom," she said quietly. "A small space behind a light switch plate. That was where she kept the things that she didn't want her father or the housekeeper to find. Not that either of them seemed to care enough to actually look for any of her secrets. At any rate, she showed the hiding place to me and made me promise never to reveal it. I got to thinking about it tonight and decided to take a look."

"Switch plate?" He nodded to himself. "Well, that explains the screwdriver. I wondered where you found it and what you planned to do with it."

"When I heard the intruder enter the house, I realized that the screwdriver was all I had in the way of a weapon." The beer bottle trembled in her fingers. She tightened her grip on it. "In case he found me, you see. I didn't know what else to do."

Very deliberately Luke set down his bottle, removed hers from her shaking fingers and put it on the counter beside his own.

His powerful hands closed around her shoulders.

"It would have made a very good weapon, if you'd needed one," he said. His tone was low and rough but curiously soothing.

She realized that he was trying to comfort her. The temptation to let herself relax against that strong wall of reassurance and understanding was almost overwhelming.

Common sense smashed through her. This was not good,

she thought. She had spent years cultivating the self-control that protected her. Damned if she would fall apart now in front of this man—a man she barely knew, quality time or not.

"The screwdriver wouldn't have been much use against that inferno of a house fire," she said evenly.

He moved his hands upward from her shoulders, cradling her face between his palms. "What did you find in the Webb house tonight?"

She exhaled slowly and reached into the front pocket of her black jeans. "Nothing that looks like a terrifically useful clue. Which is why I didn't mention it to Sam McPherson."

She withdrew the key and held it out to him on her palm.

He lowered his hands from her face and picked up the key.

"Any idea what this opens?" he asked, examining it closely.

She shook her head. "No. Looks like a very ordinary key, doesn't it?"

"Ordinary is right. A key like this could open anything. House, storage locker, toolshed, garage." He frowned a little. "It's a high-quality key, though. The kind you can't get duplicated, at least not at the usual instant key-making places. Someone spent some money to have an expensive piece of hardware installed somewhere."

"There's no way of knowing when Pamela stashed it behind the light switch plate," she said. "For all I know she tucked it away years ago and forgot about it." She hesitated, thinking. "Except—"

"Except what?"

"It looks new, don't you think? It's still bright and shiny. It hasn't had a chance to get scratched or dulled with use. Also, there was a thin coating of dust on the inside of the junction box, but none on the key. Wouldn't you think that if it had been sitting inside that wall for several years it would have collected some dust?"

"Are you sure about the dust inside the box? It was night and you only had a flashlight."

She wanted to tell him that she was absolutely positive. But she had to admit he had a point. She had been working with extremely limited light tonight when she removed the switch plate. In addition, she had been jazzed on adrenaline and anxiety.

"I'll give you that one." She rubbed the nape of her neck with her right hand, trying to ease some of the tension that still gripped her. "I can't swear that there wasn't any dust on the key. If there was some, it was wiped off when I put it into my pocket."

"Tell me again why you didn't show the key to Sam McPherson," he said, his tone a little too neutral.

Her mouth tightened. "Sam cut me some slack tonight because of the past and because half of Dunsley thinks I'm a walking case of post-traumatic stress disorder, even though they aren't sure how to spell it." She broke off when she saw an expression of startled surprise flash across his face. "What?"

"Post-traumatic stress disorder?" he repeated in the same, very even tone.

"That would be the fancy term. The bottom line is that there is a school of thought around here which holds that because of what happened when my parents died, I'm not what you'd call normal."

"Huh. Normal."

"It's a technical term," she said.

"Right. Got it. Go on."

She swung around and paced out of the tiny kitchenette into the living room area. "The point is, although I knew that Sam probably wouldn't throw me in jail because I let myself into the Webb house tonight, I wasn't so sure how he would react if he found out I'd removed that key from Pamela's old hiding place."

"I still don't believe a damn word you're saying."

She stopped and turned to face him. "That's your problem, not mine."

"The hell it is. You have definitely become a very big problem for me. Why didn't you tell McPherson about the key?"

"Okay, okay." She paused. "I have a hunch that Sam is looking for every possible excuse not to conduct an investigation into Pamela's death. I was afraid he would either ignore the key or make it go away. Either way, I'd lose it."

To her surprise, Luke assumed a meditative air. "I'll be damned. You think McPherson is cooperating in a cover-up, don't you?"

"I have to assume that's a possibility." She straightened her shoulders. "I do know for a fact that Senator Webb doesn't want an investigation. I also know that most people in this town are only too happy to fulfill any request that comes from a member of the Webb family."

"I keep hearing that." Luke picked up his beer and drained the bottle. He set the empty on the counter and considered her for a long moment. "People really tell you that you've got post-traumatic stress disorder?"

"That was the diagnosis I got when my aunt put me in counseling for a while after my parents died. Got the same diagnosis from a few other therapists over the years."

"Did the therapy do any good?"

"A little." She cleared her throat. "But it was generally agreed that I would not make any major improvement unless I learned to take a rational, adult view of the facts. I, uh, sort of refused to do that."

"Because you can't or won't accept the facts that were given to you," he said. It wasn't a question.

"I refuse to believe that my father murdered my mother and then took his own life. It violates everything I ever knew or believed about him. The therapists said I won't get any closure until I come to grips with reality."

"What did you tell the therapists?"

"That the only thing that will ever give me anything approaching real closure is the truth." She sighed. "I guess that sounds like your basic obsessed, dysfunctional personality talking, doesn't it?"

"Sure, but I can relate. My family slapped me with the same diagnosis about six months back."

She blinked a couple of times, absorbing that piece of data. "They did?"

He shrugged. "Can't say for sure they're wrong. Got to admit, I'm a little different these days."

The iron ring of quiet certainty in his words shook her. She had never talked intimately to anyone else who had been stuck with the PTSD label, she thought.

"Got a few rituals?" she asked tentatively. "Maybe some private rules that you go out of your way not to break even though you know other people might think you are a little strange?"

"Like leaving the lights on all night?"

She winced. "Yes."

"You bet."

"Get a little moody at times?" she pressed.

"That, too."

"Have bad dreams now and again?"

"Hey, who doesn't?"

"The way I look at it," she said softly, "the line between normal and not-so-normal is a little murky at times."

"On that point I am in complete, one hundred percent agreement." He crossed the short distance that separated them and came to a halt directly in front of her. "Got to say, though, that right now kissing you feels like it would be the most normal, natural thing in the world."

Heat arced through her at his words. The unfamiliar rush of intense sensation startled her. She opened her mouth to explain that this was one of the areas of life in which she had concluded that she was not quite normal.

But she did not get the opportunity to go into an extended

conversation on the subject of her limited arousal capability, because Luke's mouth had already closed over hers and she was suddenly deeply, intensely, stunningly *aroused*.

Electricity danced across nerve endings that had already been set on edge by the effects of too much adrenaline and tension. She wasn't just aroused, she thought, she was ravenous. The hunger was unlike anything she had ever experienced—fierce, exciting and utterly compelling.

Luke muttered something urgent against her mouth and wrapped one hand around the back of her head, anchoring her where he wanted her for the kiss. His other hand flattened against the curve of her waist, locking her lower body snugly against his own. She could feel the shape of him through the denim of his jeans—hard, intense and demanding.

His mouth moved heavily on hers, urging her lips apart. In spite of her excitement, she resisted. The headlong rush into sexual intimacy had caught her off guard. This wasn't her usual slow, boring, cautious routine, she thought.

But Luke used his tongue the way a skillful fencer uses a foil—swift, teasing, provocative strokes that caused her to dig her nails into the back of his shoulders. Instead of making her nervous, she found herself wanting to engage and parry.

Very delicately, feeling enormously adventurous, she nibbled on his lower lip. In response, his fingers slid beneath the bottom edge of her sweater. His hands were warm and strong on her bare skin.

She was channeling lightning now. She wound her arms

around Luke and hung on for dear life. Energy and heat crackled through her all the way to her toes.

Luke's breathing roughened. When she stood on tiptoe and took the lobe of his ear between her teeth, she felt a heavy shudder go through him.

Maybe she wasn't quite as inhibited as she and the depressingly short list of men who had shared her bed had concluded.

Luke raised his head, breaking off the torrid embrace with what seemed to be an extraordinary effort of will.

"I'd better get out of here while I can still walk," he said. "If I wait any longer, I won't be going anywhere for the rest of the night."

It dawned on her that he was the one who was calling a halt. How embarrassing. Another couple of minutes and she would have tripped him and hauled him down onto the floor.

She cleared her throat, aware of the fiery warmth in her face. "We did get a little carried away, didn't we? Probably the aftereffects of all that adrenaline that was pouring through us earlier. I've read that it can really do a number on you. Something about the basic survival instinct kicking in after a close brush with disaster. An elemental need to seek the life force."

"Yeah?" He smiled slowly. "You read up on stuff like that?"

She was beyond embarrassed now. "Well, it's not as if we have what anyone could call a close relationship. For heaven's sake, we hardly know each other."

"You're forgetting about all that quality time I mentioned earlier."

There was something wrong with her center of gravity. Her body kept trying to fall forward, straight back into his arms. To counter the impulse she sat down abruptly on the padded arm of the sofa, crossed one leg over the other and made a heroic effort to look sophisticated and cool. *It was just a kiss, for heaven's sake. Get a grip.*

She tried tilting her chin in what she hoped was a self-possessed manner. "I think we'd better change the subject, don't you?"

"If that's what you want."

"It's for the best. I'm sure we're both going to feel a little awkward about this in the morning."

He glanced at his watch. "Got news for you—it's damn near five A.M. and I don't feel even a little bit awkward."

"You need sleep. We both do."

"Doubt if I'll be able to sleep," he said, remarkably unconcerned. He moved toward the door. "You know, I'm probably going to hate myself for asking, but I'd rather avoid any more late-night surprises. What are you going to do now that the Webb house is in smoking ruins?"

The question stopped her cold.

"I'm not sure," she admitted. "I think the next step is to find out who Pamela employed to take care of the house. It's safe to say she didn't do her own cleaning and dusting. She grew up with housekeepers, after all. I doubt if she would have known how to run a household without one. Besides, she didn't spend much time here in Dunsley. She would have needed someone to keep an eye on the place."

He nodded, as if she had merely confirmed whatever conclusion he had already reached.

"Figured you weren't going to give up," he said.

"I can't. Not yet."

"I know."

He did understand, she thought. He had major doubts about the wisdom of what she was doing, but he understood.

"See you in the morning," Luke said. He opened the door, letting in the cold night air. He moved out onto the porch, stopped and turned. "By the way, you know that little theory of yours, the one about how we almost had hot, sweaty sex on account of we were both running on leftover adrenaline and our primitive survival instincts were kicking in and all that other psychobabble?"

She stiffened warily. "What about it?"

"It's garbage as far as I'm concerned. I've been wanting to have sex with you since the first time I saw you standing there at the front desk, pounding the little silver bell."

He went out into the night and closed the door before she could even begin to get her brain back in gear.

Seventeen

You burned down a house?" Jason started so sharply that the pat of butter he had been in the process of conveying to his plate splashed into his orange juice instead. "I thought you were going over to Irene's cabin for a second helping of corn bread. Or something. You two went out and burned down a house together instead?"

"You know damn well that's not what I meant." Luke shoveled three slices of the French toast he had just finished cooking onto his own plate, carried his breakfast to the table and sat down. "Someone else torched the Webb house. Irene and I just happened to be on the upstairs deck at the time."

"Boy, howdy, wait until the family hears about this." Jason used a fork to fish the butter out of the orange juice. "On the plus side, at least I can report back that you went out on a real date while I was here."

Luke speared a healthy-sized bite of French toast. "I don't think Irene looked at it in quite that spirit."

But she had kissed him good night, he reminded himself.

And it had been a serious, state-of-the-art, top-of-the-line, full-on kiss. In spite of events, he hadn't felt this good in the morning for longer than he cared to contemplate. And it had been only a *kiss*. His brain reeled at the thought of how he would have been feeling today if she had actually invited him into her bed.

"Luke?" Jason waved his fork and snapped his fingers. "Hello? Anybody home in there? Stay with me here, Big Brother. Answer my question."

"What question?"

"About this arson thing. Are we talking potential legal issues? Because if so, we need to let the Old Man and Gordon know what's happening."

"This doesn't involve the family or the business. No one's threatening to arrest me. Yet, at any rate."

"That's certainly reassuring." Jason's expression turned abruptly somber. "You say the house was owned by Senator Ryland Webb?"

"Got a feeling he'll want to keep the arson quiet, the same way he wants to keep his daughter's overdose quiet. He does not want to distract fund-raisers and potential donors."

"Going to be a little difficult to keep the fire under the radar, don't you think?"

"Something tells me that the next time I see Chief McPherson he'll have come up with a perfectly reasonable explanation for ignoring a case of arson that just happened to take place in the home of a woman who had recently OD'd."

He took another bite of French toast, chewed and reached for his orange juice. "Course, McPherson and Webb probably aren't counting on Irene. If anyone can get the arson onto the screen, she will."

"Luke?"

"Yeah?"

"Don't take this wrong, but do you think maybe you should be careful about getting any more involved with Irene Stenson? I mean, I like her a lot. She's really different from anyone else you've ever been with. But there's no getting around the fact that she seems to be contributing heavily to your stress levels."

Luke gave him his war face and ate more French toast.

Jason cleared his throat. "Dr. Van Dyke told Dad that, given your history, it would be a good idea not to subject yourself to too much stress right now."

"Screw Dr. Van Dyke."

Jason grimaced. "I'd rather not. Something about those sensible shoes and those sturdy tweed suits she wears probably. Maybe I just lack imagination, but I don't think I could get past them."

"Go back to Santa Elena and tell everyone to stop worrying about me. I'll see you all at the birthday party."

"What about Irene Stenson?"

"Stressful she may be, but at least she doesn't wear sensible shoes and tweed suits. Or maybe you didn't happen to notice the high-heeled boots and the black trench coat?"

Jason's eyes rolled back in his head. He twitched a little.

"Oh, yeah. Saw the boots. And the black trench, too. You think maybe there's a little whip to go with them?"

"Don't know. But it has become my mission in life to find the answer to that burning question."

Luke was checking in the newlyweds when Irene opened the front door and strode—that was the word for it, he decided, *strode*—into the lobby. One quick, covert survey told him everything he needed to know about her mood. Another black pullover and another pair of black trousers, the black leather boots and the trench. She was in full battle armor again, ready to duel with Dunsley.

She took in the scene at the front desk without saying a word and quietly crossed the room to the coffee service table. Out of the corner of his eye, Luke saw her examine the pot of coffee and the day-old doughnuts that he had put out earlier.

The last thing he wanted right now was to be bothered by paying guests, he thought. He had things to do with Irene Stenson.

He shoved the registration form and a pen in front of the gawky young husband.

"Name, address and driver's license number, Addison," he said. "Full signature at the bottom. Initial the departure date."

The very new Mrs. Addison's eyes widened in alarm. She took a quick step back from the counter, looking as though she thought Luke might vault over it and go for her throat.

Now what? he wondered, striving to hang on to his patience. All he had done was ask her husband to fill out the damn form.

Mr. Addison gulped so hard that Luke saw his Adam's apple move.

"Uh, yes, sir," Addison said. He grabbed the pen and hastily went to work filling out the form.

Across the lobby, Irene paused in the act of removing a tea bag from her purse. She frowned. Luke opted to ignore her.

"All finished, sir." Addison pushed the form back across the counter with obvious relief.

Luke gave the paper a cursory glance, checking to make sure each section had been filled in. "Checkout time is twelve hundred."

Across the room, Irene closed her eyes in a rather pained way.

Addison went blank. "Uh, twelve hundred what, sir?"

"Hours. High noon."

"Yes, sir," Addison said quickly. "Don't worry, we'll leave before noon."

Luke swiped a key off a hook and handed it to Addison. "Cabin Number Ten. There's a list of regs posted on the back of the door. Read 'em."

Addison blinked uneasily. "Regs?"

"Regulations," Luke said, trying to be patient. "No loud disturbances of any kind, no illegal activities, no one who isn't officially registered is allowed to spend the night in the room and so on."

"Right. Sure. I mean, yes, sir." Addison bobbed his head nervously. "No problem. It's just the two of us. Sir."

"You will also find a little card on the nightstand *requesting* that you help the management of this lodge conserve energy. You will treat that request as a regulation. Understood?"

"Yes, sir." Addison cast a quick, urgent glance at his nervous wife. "Janice and me are real big on preserving the environment, aren't we, Janice?"

"Yes," she said, barely audible.

"Glad to hear that," Luke said. "Enjoy your stay in the honeymoon suite."

Addison blinked. "The honeymoon suite?"

Mrs. Addison was clearly astounded. "We got the honeymoon suite?"

"Sure," Luke said. "Why not? You are honeymooners, right? You're not just saying that in order to get the honeymoon suite, are you?"

"No, sir," Mrs. Addison assured him. "We just got married this morning. At the courthouse over in Kirbyville."

Addison looked more uneasy than ever but he stood his ground. "Uh, how much extra is the honeymoon suite?"

Luke leaned on the counter. "For you two? No extra charge. Provided you obey all the regs, of course."

On the other side of the lobby, Irene raised her eyes to the vaulted ceiling.

"Yes, sir. Thank you, sir." Addison grabbed his wife's hand and dragged her toward the door. "Come on, Janice. I got us the honeymoon suite."

"I can't wait until we go back to Kirbyville to tell everyone about this," Janice said, alight with anticipation.

The pair dashed outside.

Luke folded his arms on the counter and watched the young couple through the window. "Honeymooners. Gotta love 'em."

"It looked more like you were trying to scare them," Irene said.

"Why would I do that? Marriage will scare them pretty damn quick. No need for me to speed up the process."

"I'll bet you don't get a lot of repeat business here at Sunrise Lodge, do you?"

He spread his hands. "What did I say?"

"It wasn't what you said, it was how you said it. You talked to that poor young man as though he was a raw recruit in boot camp. He's on his honeymoon, for heaven's sake, and judging by the fact that he and his wife booked a room here, I expect they're on an extremely limited budget."

"Give me a break. All I did was check them into a cabin."

"The honeymoon suite, hmm? I wasn't aware that this lodge had one."

"Management takes the view that if you spend your honeymoon in one of our cabins, said cabin is, by definition, the honeymoon suite."

"I see. Logical."

"Certainly struck me that way," Luke said.

"Nevertheless, you could have been a little more gentle with Mr. and Mrs. Addison."

"All I did was ask them to fill out the damned forms."

"Luke, you made them very nervous."

He went around the end of the counter to pour himself

another cup of coffee. "You know, I'm starting to think that's the biggest problem with the innkeeping business."

"What?"

"The clientele. They're undisciplined, untrained and unpredictable." He watched the Addisons climb into an aging Ford pickup and drive off toward Cabin Number Ten. "Yeah, gotta say, if it weren't for the paying guests, this wouldn't be a bad line of work."

She shook her head. "Where's Jason?"

"He left right after breakfast. Something about a meeting with a supplier later this morning. What are you up to today?"

"I called an old acquaintance here in town, Sandra Pace, and asked her if she knew who has been taking care of the Webb house. Turns out it's Connie Watson, the same woman who cleaned for Pamela and her father all those years ago when I lived here."

"You're going to talk to Watson?"

"Yes." Irene glanced at her watch. "Thought I'd drive out to her place now. I'm hoping to catch her before she leaves for the day."

He exhaled slowly. "Meaning she doesn't know you're coming?"

"I was afraid that if I called her and tried to make an appointment, she might refuse to talk to me. Like a lot of other people in town, Connie has reasons to be loyal to the Webbs."

"I'll go with you."

"That's not necessary, Luke."

"I said I'll go with you."

She looked troubled. "It's probably best if you don't get any more involved in this thing."

"Jason said something along those lines, too."

Shadows deepened in her eyes. "He did? Well, he's right. You live in this town, after all. You've got a business here, although, given the way you're running it, I'm not sure how you're going to make enough to pay the taxes. But that's another issue. The point is, you should try to stay out of this mess. Anything that involves the Webbs is more than a bit dicey here in Dunsley."

"Dicey in Dunsley." He smiled a little. "Got a ring to it."

"I mean it," she said tensely. "I really think you should stay clear of this situation. Obviously your brother feels the same way."

"What you and Jason don't seem to grasp is that it's way too late for all the good advice. I'm already up to my, uh—" He broke off, clearing his throat. "My neck in this thing."

"It's not too late." She set the mug down so hard on the table that tea splashed onto the scarred wooden surface. She grabbed a napkin and hastily blotted up the drops. "You're just being stubborn."

To Luke's relief, the door opened, interrupting Irene in mid-tirade. Maxine breezed into the room.

"Hi, everyone." She peeled off her coat. "I saw a truck in front of Cabin Number Ten. New guests?"

"Pair of honeymooners all the way from Kirbyville," Luke said.

"Really?" Maxine looked thrilled. "We haven't had any

newlyweds here in the whole time I've worked at the lodge. You know, this could be a market niche that we've been overlooking."

"Luke gave them the honeymoon suite," Irene said.

Maxine frowned. "We haven't got one."

"We do now," Luke said. "Cabin Number Ten."

Maxine glowed with enthusiasm. "I know what I'll do, I'll make up a little basket of amenities for them."

"I'd skip the doughnuts if I were you," Luke said.

Eighteen

Connie Watson glared through the screen door. She was a large, big-boned woman with suspicious eyes. She gripped a dish towel in one work-roughened hand. Everything about her from her expression to her body language suggested that she had long ago given up expecting anything good out of life.

"I remember you, Irene," she said. She flicked a quick, uneasy glance at Luke. "And I know who you are, Mr. Danner. What do you two want?"

This wasn't going to be easy, Irene thought. Her hunch this morning had been right. If she had called ahead, Connie would have found an excuse not to be home.

"I want to ask you a few questions about Pamela," she said, keeping her voice as calm and soothing as possible. "I was her friend at one time, remember?"

"Course I remember." Connie wiped her hands on the dish towel. She made no move to open the screen door. "I heard you two found Pamela the other night. Heard you burned down the Webb house, too."

"Someone else set fire to the house," Luke said. "We just happened to be in the neighborhood at the time."

"That's not what folks are saying," Connie muttered.

"It's the truth," Irene said. "For heaven's sake, Connie, do you really think I'd burn down a house?"

"Heard you've been acting a little strange about Pamela's death. Someone told me you've got what they call an *unhealthy fixation* about it, or something like that."

Luke looked at her through the screen. "Who told you that?"

Connie jerked and took a small step back. Then she reached out and hastily locked the screen door. "Doesn't matter. Word's going around town, that's all."

Irene frowned at Luke, silently willing him to shut up. He certainly had a talent for giving orders and intimidating people, but at the moment she needed cooperation from Connie.

Luke raised his brows and shrugged a little, letting her know he had received her message.

She turned back to Connie. "Shortly before she died, Pamela sent me an e-mail telling me that she wanted to meet me here in Dunsley. Do you have any idea what she planned to tell me?"

"No."

"Did she indicate that she was worried or upset?"

"No."

"Did you see her the day she died?"

"No."

This was not going well, Irene thought. She could feel Luke watching her, waiting for her to set him loose so that he could use his own, less polite style of interrogation. She scrolled back through her memory to come up with a new angle.

"Connie, I realize that you feel you owe the Webb family your loyalty, and I agree with you. But you also owe something to my family, don't you?"

Connie crushed the dish towel in one fist. She took another step back. "Maybe I owed something to your pa, but he's dead, God rest his soul."

"Death doesn't cancel all debts," Irene said quietly. "My father is gone, but I'm still here. For the sake of his memory, will you please tell me whatever you can about Pamela's last days here in Dunsley?"

Connie's face crumpled. She gave a vast sigh of weary surrender. "Promise me you won't tell him I talked to you."

"Do you mean Chief McPherson?" Luke asked.

Connie blinked several times, alarmed. "You can't tell him, either. He'd likely go straight to—" She broke off suddenly. "Never mind." She switched her attention back to Irene. "Look, I don't really know anything, and that's the honest truth."

"Just tell me what you do know," Irene said.

"Well, four days before you found her dead, I got a call from Pamela asking me to get the house ready for her. Nothing strange about that. She didn't use the place often, but when she did, she'd call me up and ask me to make sure there was food in the refrigerator and clean sheets on the beds and so on."

"Did you see her after she arrived?"

Connie shook her head quickly. "No. Like I said, I just got things ready and then I left. Someone said they saw her drive through town the next day. Two days later she was dead. That's all I know."

Irene smiled in what she hoped was a reassuring way. "Did she ask you to stock the refrigerator for more than one person?"

Connie frowned. "No."

"So she wasn't expecting anyone else to join her?"

Connie shook her head. "I don't think so. She would have asked me to make sure there were some cocktail crackers and cheese and plenty of booze on hand if she was planning on entertaining some of her fancy city friends."

Irene stilled. "She didn't ask you to buy any liquor?"

"Not this time."

Luke planted one hand against the wall of the house. "There was an empty pitcher and a martini glass on the table when we found her."

Connie made a vague gesture with one hand. "I heard about that. Don't know where she got the booze. Usually she had me pick it up, except for the wine, of course."

"The wine?" Luke repeated carefully.

"She was real picky about her wine. She always brought it with her. But when it came to the hard stuff she had an arrangement with Joe down at the Dunsley Market. He knew what she liked and kept it on hand for her." Connie shrugged. "I reckon she must have brought the martini makings with her from the city this time."

"Liquor keeps well for a long period of time," Irene said. "Pamela could have left a few bottles in the house the last time she was in town."

"No," Connie said with great certainty. "She never left any booze in the house. Everyone around here knew that. She always said it would have been an open invitation to every teen on the lake to break in and steal it. She said she didn't want to be responsible for some local kids getting drunk and driving a car off Lakefront Road into the water. Said it would have been bad for the senator's image."

"How much food did you buy for her?" Irene asked.

"What?" Connie used both hands to twist the dish towel.

"Enough for a couple of days, perhaps? A long weekend?"

"Oh, the food." Connie's grip on the towel lessened slightly. "That was a bit strange, now that I think about it. When she called she said she wanted enough milk and cereal and salad makings and such to last about a week."

"What was strange about that?"

"Usually she just came for a weekend, three days at the most. Can't remember the last time she planned to stay for a whole week. And all by herself, too. She always had a man with her when she showed up in town."

"Always?" Irene repeated carefully.

Connie made a face. "You remember how when Pamela was a teenager, she always had boys hanging around her like bees around a honey pot?"

"Yes."

"Well, some things never change. There was always a man somewhere in the vicinity."

Irene thought about the pink-and-white bedroom. "Where did they sleep?"

Connie looked bewildered. "At the house, of course. Where else would they sleep?"

"I mean, which bedroom in the house?"

"Pamela always used the master bedroom on account of it had the deck and the view of the lake. Her guests used the spare bedrooms. There was one upstairs and one down."

"She didn't put any of her guests into her old bedroom? The one she used when she was growing up?"

"Oh, no," Connie said. "She never let anyone use that room."

"Did she ever tell you why?" Irene asked.

"No." Connie hesitated. "She was a little strange about that room, and that's a fact. Always made it real clear that she wanted it kept exactly as it was. I wasn't even allowed to move the furniture around in there. Guess she was sentimental about it or something."

"Thank you, Connie." Irene stepped back. "I appreciate your patience. You've been very kind to answer my questions."

"That's all you want?" Connie asked, brightening slightly.

"Yes."

"We're square then, me and your family?"

"Yes," Irene said. "Paid in full."

"Wish I could pay them all off that easily," Connie muttered. She started to close the door. But at the last second, she paused, peering through the crack at Irene. Her voice lowered. "You be careful, you hear? There's folks who don't want you asking around about Pamela."

"I don't suppose you'd care to be more specific?" Irene said.

"I always liked you, Irene, and I was real sorry to hear about that post-trauma problem everyone says you've got. Also, I'm truly grateful for what your pa did for my boy. Wayne's been working steady all these years. Got married a while back and has himself a nice little family."

"I'm glad, Connie."

"Like I said, I'm grateful. But I'd take it as a real favor if you didn't come back here again anytime soon."

The door closed with a depressing finality.

Irene walked beside Luke back to the SUV. Neither spoke until they were inside the vehicle.

Irene pulled her notebook out of her shoulder bag. "Okay, let's see what we've got. Pamela ordered in enough food for a week and didn't request any hard liquor, but she supposedly OD's on martinis and pills."

Luke put the SUV in gear and drove off down the narrow road that led away from Connie Watson's small house.

"The quantity of food suggests that she wasn't thinking of killing herself," he agreed. "But it doesn't mean that she didn't OD by accident."

"I know." Irene tapped the tip of the pen against the notebook. "It's the liquor that bothers me the most. It's true, she might have brought it with her this time, but if it was her habit to have Connie stock it along with the other supplies, why alter a long-standing pattern?"

"Good question," Luke admitted. "I've been thinking about the man, though."

"What man?"

"Connie said that when it came to Pamela, there was always a man in the picture."

"But not this time," Irene said slowly.

"At least, not one that Connie knew about."

Irene contemplated that angle. "In the old days, Pamela viewed men as accessories. She always had one or two conveniently on hand to wear whenever she wanted to go out and party. If Connie was right about nothing having changed in that regard, it's a good bet that at the time of her death Pamela had a man available on short notice somewhere."

"If we can find him, he might know what was on her mind during those last few days of her life."

She smiled. "I like the way you think, Danner."

"Gee, thanks. I've always wanted to be admired for my brain." He glanced at her. "What did your father do for Connie Watson's son?"

Irene watched the sunlight and shadows dance on the lake. "Wayne Watson got into some trouble with the law the year after he graduated from high school. Ended up doing time. When he got out nobody around the lake wanted to give him a job. Dad convinced a contractor over in Kirbyville to take him on. Sounds like it worked out well."

Nineteen

From the first time he'd brought the SUV to Carpenter's Garage for a routine oil change and lube job, Luke had admired the place. He knew there were some people who liked walking through art museums and galleries. He took satisfaction from an efficient, functional, well-organized working facility like the garage. Phil Carpenter understood the importance of cleanliness, order and precision.

He paused just inside the entrance and allowed himself a moment to properly appreciate the gleaming, well-lit space. A person could have eaten off the concrete floor, he thought. Every tool and every piece of machinery that was not in use was stowed in its proper place. Stainless steel shone as bright as silver. The two men working beneath an elevated pickup wore clean uniforms emblazoned with the establishment's logo. Luke knew from personal experience that the men's room was equally clean and shiny. There were always plenty of soap and paper towels available.

He started toward the office at the far end of the garage.

A thin, gaunt, hollow-eyed man wielding a mop nodded once as he went past.

Luke returned the greeting.

"How's it going, Tucker?"

"Goin' fine, Mr. Danner."

Tucker Mills's haggard, burned-out expression made it impossible to judge his age. He could have been anywhere between thirty and sixty. His long, lanky hair was sparse and thin and going gray. He operated somewhere at or near the bottom of the social pecking order in Dunsley, surviving on his odd jobs and judicious recon trips to the town dump. Luke had found him to be invaluable when it came to dealing with the myriad maintenance and gardening issues that afflicted the lodge.

Tucker concentrated on pushing the mop head beneath a workbench. He did not encourage familiarity or conversation. It was understood that if you wanted to employ him, you made your needs known in polite terms using short sentences and then you left him alone until it was time to pay for the work. Tucker did not accept checks or credit cards. As far as Luke could tell, Mills had no formal relationship of any kind with a bank or the IRS. He dealt only in cash or goods-in-trade.

Luke kept moving until he reached the office. Phil Carpenter was at his desk, paging methodically through a massive parts catalog. His shaved head blazed as bright as the sun in the glow of the fluorescent lamps.

Phil was built like a brick, but he moved with surprising speed and agility for a man with one prosthetic limb. Luke knew that beneath the long sleeve of Phil's pristine garage uniform there was a globe-and-anchor emblem tattooed on one arm. The missing left leg was the legacy of a land mine explosion. Another war, not my own, Luke thought. But as Connie Watson had observed so insightfully earlier in the day, some things never change.

"Danner." Phil closed the catalog and leaned back in his chair, looking both pleased and curious. He motioned to a chair. "Have a seat. Gotta say, I'm surprised to see you. From what I've heard, you've been right busy lately."

"Things have definitely not been dull." Luke sat down. "How goes the garage business?"

"Not bad. How about the lodging business?"

"Like I told Irene this morning, be a lot more enjoyable if I didn't have to actually deal with the customers."

Phil squinted in a thoughtful manner. "You ever get the sense that maybe you weren't cut out for a career in the hospitality field?"

"Lately people have been asking me that a lot."

"In that case, I won't mention it again." Phil picked up a glass pot full of coffee and poured some of the contents into an unchipped, unscratched white mug. He put the mug down on a small napkin in front of Luke. "Can I assume this is a special occasion?"

"I need some information. Figured this was probably the best place in town to find it."

"It is, indeed." Phil leaned back and laced his fingers behind his head. "Carpenter's Garage is what you might call a regular nexus of the universe." He raised his brows. "This information you're after, would it have anything to do with your new lady friend?"

Luke considered that briefly. "Is that what folks are calling Irene? My new lady friend?"

"The polite ones are starting to refer to her that way, yeah. And the fact that you have not had any other lady friends during the five months you have been living here in Dunsley has only made Irene all the more interesting."

"Is that so?"

"Speculation had begun to circulate that you were, perhaps, not interested in lady friends."

"Huh." Luke tasted the coffee. It was good, just as it always was at Carpenter's Garage.

"Such idle speculation has, however, given way to more in-depth discussion of the unusual nature of the dates that you and Irene Stenson appear to enjoy."

"Unusual?"

"Believe it or not, in this town it's downright rare for two people to spend their evenings finding dead bodies or nearly getting incinerated in house fires. Around here, couples that do not enjoy the bonds of matrimony generally go for a more traditional style of romance. Sex in the backseat of a car, for example."

"Right. Thanks for the tip. I'll have to see what I can do to make things look a bit more normal."

Phil shrugged. "Sometimes normal is hard for guys like us."

"There is that." Luke put the mug down on the little paper napkin so that it wouldn't leave a damp ring on the polished desk. "In the meantime, you can let your loyal patrons know that I will take serious offense if I hear that anyone is referring to Irene in any way that might be deemed impolite."

Phil inclined his head in a sage nod. "Understood." He drank some coffee and lowered his mug. "So what kind of information are you looking for?"

"Irene knew Pamela Webb when they were teens."

"They were close for one summer, as I recall, but that was about it," Phil said. "That was the same summer that Irene's parents died."

"Irene and Pamela didn't see or speak to each other after that summer. Yet for some reason Pamela e-mailed Irene a few days ago, asking her to meet her here in Dunsley. The implication was that she wanted to discuss something important. Even used an old secret code that the two had invented. All in all, that was enough to convince Irene that Pamela's death might not have been a suicide or an accident."

"Heard about Irene's theory," Phil said. "What's your take on it?"

"Let's just say that after watching someone torch the Webb house last night, I find Irene's theory interesting."

"Sam McPherson has put it about that the arson job was probably the work of a vandal, most likely from Kirbyville, a known den of thieves and miscreants."

"Motive?"

Phil unlaced his hands and spread them wide. "That's the beauty of the crime of arson, isn't it? Firebugs are nutcases. Everyone knows they don't need a motive."

"A useful factoid, if ever there was one."

Phil looked thoughtful. "You didn't see the guy?"

Luke shook his head. "Nothing but a shadow. I was too busy getting Irene off that deck before the house went up in flames. All I know is that he got away in a boat." His mouth twisted. "Course I made the escape easy for him because I figured he had come by car. I was heading for the road at the same time he was going in the opposite direction back to the lake."

"Don't blame yourself. Situation like that, you have to make choices."

"Which is a polite euphemism for screwing up."

"Screwing up happens."

Luke extended his legs. "Moving right along, what I came here to ask you is whether you have heard anything about Pamela's latest boyfriend."

"Her latest?"

"Evidently, she was not in the habit of coming to Dunsley on her own."

"True." Phil paused, frowning a little. "But it appears she broke that habit this time. I didn't hear anything about her having a gentleman friend with her on this visit."

"Is it likely that you would have heard?"

"When Pamela was in town, there was always talk. She was a Webb, and the doings of the Webbs have always been of considerable interest to everyone in the community."

"Any possibility that the reason she didn't bring a friend with her this time was because she already had one lined up here in town?"

Phil snorted. "From what I knew of Pamela Webb, I think it's safe to say that there was no man here in Dunsley who would have been able to meet her high standards of elegance and sophistication. Present company excepted, of course."

"Naturally."

"But given that neither of us two classy, sophisticated dudes was dating her, I think it's safe to say that she wasn't fooling around with anyone local. Trust me, word would have circulated like wildfire if she was carrying on with someone from around here."

"It was just a thought."

"Here's another one," Phil said, eyes very steady. "You and Irene are taking on a U.S. senator who, because of his family connections, has this whole town pretty much in his back pocket."

"That thought has crossed my mind more than once."

"Having stated the obvious, I would like to point out that not everyone here is in Webb's pocket," Phil added quietly. "You need anyone to watch your back, feel free to call."

Luke stood. "Thanks."

"*Semper fi*, man."

"*Semper fi*."

Twenty

A quarter of a mile outside town Sam McPherson's cruiser appeared in the SUV's rearview mirror, closing the distance rapidly. This was probably not one of life's astonishing little coincidences, Luke thought. But he waited until McPherson went to the trouble of flashing a few lights before he pulled over to the side of the road and stopped.

He kept his attention on the mirror, watching McPherson's image come toward him. Objects may appear smaller than they really are, he reminded himself, just like it said at the bottom of the mirror. But that didn't mean they couldn't cause trouble.

When McPherson reached the driver's-side door, Luke lowered the window.

"I assume I'm not being stopped for speeding," he said.

Sam planted one hand on the side of the SUV. "Saw you leave the garage. Thought this might be a good chance to talk to you alone."

"That would mean without Irene around, right?"

Sam exhaled heavily. "You're new here, Danner. I think it might be a good idea if I gave you a little background on Irene Stenson."

"Such as?"

"She was always the quiet type. She wasn't exactly shy, but she always seemed real serious, more interested in books than in boys. She had real nice manners. Never got into trouble."

"Not like Pamela, is that what you're trying to say?"

"Don't get me wrong. I liked Pamela. Felt sorry for her. After she hit her teens, though, she went wild. She lost her mother when she was only five, and her dad was always too involved in his next campaign to pay any attention to her. Pamela had problems, no doubt about it. I never understood why the Stensons let Irene run around with her that summer. Talk about one hell of a bad influence."

"You got a point, Sam?"

"I'm getting there. What I'm saying is, Irene wasn't a tough kid. She was a sweet teen who spent most of her spare time in the library. She was absolutely shattered the night her father went crazy and did what he did. Doubt if anyone can ever really recover completely from something like that. But it must have been even harder on a nice, innocent, sheltered girl like Irene."

"You're trying to tell me that she's probably got issues."

"Anyone who went through what she did at the age of fifteen would have issues. I was the first responder that night." Sam looked away toward the water. "When I went into the kitchen she was standing there in the middle of the room, staring at me with those big, terrified eyes. Poor kid had been trying to do CPR on her folks. There wasn't any point. They both must have died instantly."

"Where was Elizabeth Stenson shot?"

"In the head and chest." Sam's jaw flexed a couple of times. "Like she'd been executed, you know?"

"What about Hugh Stenson?"

"After he did her, he put the gun to his own head."

"The side of his head?"

"That's how it looked to me, yeah."

Luke thought about that. "Stenson didn't eat his gun?"

Sam turned his head to look at him. "What?"

"Most men who know something about firearms and who decide to use one to commit suicide put the barrel of the gun into their mouths. Less chance of botching the job and ending up a vegetable that way."

Sam took his hand off the side of the SUV and straightened. "You want to know the damned truth? I can't recall all of the details very clearly. I was shaken up bad. I was twenty-three years old. It was the first time I'd seen anything like that. After Bob Thornhill got there and we put Irene into his car, I went out into the trees and puked my guts out."

"Who wrote up the report for the department's files?"

A great stillness came over Sam. "Bob Thornhill. He was next in line in the department. Took over the chief's job for a while."

"What happened to him?"

"He died about six months later, right after his wife. Heart attack. He went off the road into the lake."

"And suddenly you were the new chief of police in Dunsley."

"I was the only one left on the force."

"I'd like to read the file on the Stenson case."

Sam's mouth tightened. "Not possible."

"You want me to go to the trouble of filing a Freedom of Information Act request?"

Sam exhaled deeply. "It's not possible to get you a copy because there is no file."

"What happened to it?"

Sam's face reddened. "The damned file, along with a lot of others, was accidentally destroyed by a temporary secretary who worked for the department for a while."

"Bullshit."

"It's the truth, damnit. When Thornhill took over the chief's job, the first thing he did was hire some short-term help to clear out the old files. The woman screwed up, okay? It happens."

Luke whistled softly. "No wonder Irene's cooked up a conspiracy theory to explain the killings. She's had plenty of ammunition to work with, hasn't she? No file on the case. The chief who took over after her father dies rather conveniently six months later—"

"Don't drag Bob Thornhill into this. He was a good man who got nothing but a lifetime of bad luck. He spent a year taking care of his wife while she died of cancer, and then the poor guy gets hit with a heart attack, goes off the road and drowns."

"What are the odds, huh?"

"Now look here, Danner," Sam said softly, "you won't be doing Irene any favors by encouraging her in her loony conspiracy theories. Rumor has it she's been diagnosed with that trauma thing that soldiers sometimes get after they've been in combat."

"Where'd you hear that?"

"Not like it's any big secret around here," Sam said. "Look, all I'm saying is that you aren't helping her by feeding her fantasies. In fact, you may get her into some real bad trouble."

"What's that supposed to mean?"

Sam hesitated. "When I told Senator Webb about the fire, the first thing he asked me was whether or not I thought Irene had set it."

This was bad news, Luke thought.

"You told him no, right?" he said evenly.

"I told him I didn't have any suspects yet. But between you and me, Webb figures Irene may have lost it after she found Pamela's body. He's thinking that she torched the house because of some kind of crazy fixation."

"You've got my statement backing up Irene's version of what happened."

"I told the senator that you were there and what you saw," Sam said. "Thing is, like a lot of other people around here, Webb figures you're sleeping with Irene. To his way of thinking that means you're not the most reliable witness. He also pointed out that you're new here in town. No one knows much about you."

"What's the senator planning to do about his burned-out house?"

Sam's expression hardened. "The man's making arrangements to bury his daughter. He doesn't want any more trouble. He just wants to make this whole thing go away."

"Looks like he's using you to make sure that happens," Luke said.

Sam turned a dark, furious shade of red. "What the hell are you saying, Danner?"

"I'm saying it's not your job to make things go away for Senator Webb."

Luke put the SUV in gear and drove back onto the road that led to the lodge.

Twenty-one

They met in the cool, fragrant shadows of the red wine fermentation cellars. Most of the big California wineries had opted for modern steel fermentation tanks for their big reds, but Elena Creek Vineyards had used a lot of oak right from the start. The wood, imported from Europe, added distinctive characteristics not only to the cabernets but to the very air of the cellars.

Jason inhaled deeply, as he always did when he entered the cavernous room. He loved the place. He savored everything about it, from the big vats to the unique smells created in the magical process of fermentation.

"Did he look depressed?" Katy asked anxiously.

"We're talking about Luke," Jason reminded her. "If he was depressed, he sure as heck wouldn't make it obvious. Never knew anyone who could hide his feelings as well as Big Brother. But no, I don't think he was depressed. If you ask me, he's having a very good time up there at Ventana Lake."

Her eyes widened. "A good time?"

Jason smiled. "Yep."

Hackett folded his arms and propped a shoulder against one of the fermentation tanks. "How could he be having a good time? You said he found a dead woman and nearly got incinerated in a house fire."

"Yeah, well, you know Luke," Jason said. "He's got an odd kick to his gallop when it comes to fun."

"Or anything else," Hackett said wearily. "Damn. The Old Man isn't going to like this. Neither is Mom."

"Or Dad, for that matter," Katy said. She rubbed her temples. "They're all so worried about Luke."

"I thought it would make them feel better knowing that he's not sitting around that tumbledown lodge, getting drunk on bad wine and staring at the lake day in and day out," Jason said, going for reasonableness. "Plus he's got a new girlfriend. That should be very reassuring to everyone."

Katy looked at him with an expression of suddenly sharp interest. "Do you think they're sleeping together?"

Hackett was also watching him closely, Jason realized.

"Well?" Hackett demanded.

"Maybe not quite yet," Jason admitted. "Irene arrived at the lodge only a couple of days ago. I got the impression that the first night she and Luke were sort of busy finding the body. The second night there was that business with the arson. Things have been a little hectic up there at the lake."

"And extremely stressful, from the sound of it." Katy sighed. "You know Dr. Van Dyke says that Luke should not be subjected to too much stress."

"I'm just telling you that it's not like Luke and Irene have had a lot of time or opportunity for romance," Jason explained. "But there's definitely something going on between those two. I'm sure of it. When you're in the room with that pair, you can almost hear the sizzle."

Hackett and Katy looked at him with expressions of acute doubt.

"The question," Hackett said, "is whether the sizzle fizzles before it gets to ignition point."

"Okay, so we all know that Luke had that little problem six months ago," Jason said. "I got the distinct impression it's not worrying him much now."

Hackett's jaw tightened. He glanced at Katy and then looked away again very quickly. "He's not likely to talk about that kind of problem to anyone."

"It's a medical issue," Katy said firmly. "He should discuss it with a doctor."

Jason spread his hands. "What everyone in this family can't seem to grasp is that Luke is a little different."

Katy and Hackett exchanged glances again. This time they did a little eye-rolling.

What was it with these two? Jason wondered. On occasion they seemed to be able to communicate telepathically. But most of the time these days they danced around each other like a couple of bad-tempered cats. It wasn't unusual to see them go from shared laughter to edgy irritation in the space of a couple of heartbeats. They argued over everything from the plans to remodel the old tasting room to the design of the new label for the zins.

It hadn't been like that in the old days when they were all growing up together, he recalled. Katy and Hackett had been best friends since forever. It was Hackett who had taken Katy to the senior prom when her date dumped her at the last minute. And it was Katy who had consoled Hackett when his college girlfriend ditched him in favor of his roommate. They'd always had a lot in common. They enjoyed going to the opera together in San Francisco, and they loved sampling new restaurants and the competition's wines.

But something about their relationship had changed dramatically about six months ago. It was almost as if Katy's short engagement to Luke had done something weird to both of them.

"Okay, so we all do grasp the concept of Luke being different," Jason conceded. "But what I'm trying to say is that he's different from the rest of us because he doesn't feel the way we do about the business." He motioned toward the jungle of large vats that surrounded them. "The Old Man and Gordon have got to give up the idea of bringing him into the company. It's not going to happen."

Katy looked thoughtful. "I think they could deal with his refusal to come into the business if they felt assured that he had found something stable and secure for himself. It's the fact that he's so unsettled that's bothering them. They've got visions of him winding up on a street corner in San Francisco, panhandling for spare change."

"For what it's worth, I honestly don't think he's on the edge of flipping out or anything," Jason said. "He'll be at the birthday party. You can see for yourself."

"It isn't us he has to convince," Hackett muttered. "It's Mom and Gordon and the Old Man."

"Okay, that could be a problem," Jason said.

Twenty-two

The sound of Luke's SUV in the drive interrupted Irene just as she was preparing to come up into a full teaser position. Two sharp, demanding knocks a short time later told her that the driver was not in a great mood.

"Come in," she said, holding the V-shaped pose, her legs and arms in the air, toes pointed, balanced on her sitting bones.

Luke opened the door and looked at her. "What the hell are you doing?"

"Pilates exercises." She came out of the movement and rolled to her feet. "I took it up a couple of years ago. It's all about core strength. A lot of dancers use it. It didn't replace leaving the lights on all night long. But it did take the place of needing to check the kitchen sink half a dozen times to make sure the water was turned off every time I left my apartment. That was getting bad."

"Replace one obsessive little habit with another? Yeah, I know all about that theory." He closed the door. "But do us both a favor. Don't let any of the locals see you practice your

Pilates, okay? We don't need to add any more layers of weird-ness to your image."

Definitely not a good mood.

"I find the exercises helpful when I'm trying to clarify my thoughts."

"Getting away from Dunsley for a while would help me clar-ify mine." He walked into the kitchenette. "What do you say we take a drive?"

She watched him open the refrigerator, acting like he owned the place. She reminded herself that he did own it.

"All right," she said, oddly cautious.

He took out a bottle of water and snapped off the top. "Figured we could have dinner in Kirbyville."

It wasn't what anyone would call a romantic invitation, she thought. On the other hand, dinner on the other side of the lake sounded like a lot more fun than the two outings she had recently organized for him.

"Okay," she said. "But first tell me what's wrong."

He settled back against the counter. "For over five months I have been a model citizen here in Dunsley. Not even a speed-ing ticket. Today the chief of police felt it necessary to deliver a warning."

Guilt and dread splashed through her like acid. "Sam McPherson threatened you?"

"It was a little more subtle than that, but yeah, that was the bottom line. Kind of ticked me off, if you want to know the truth, given my exemplary behavior and all."

"Luke, this is all my fault."

"That," he said, tossing his car keys into the air, "has not escaped my notice." He caught the keys and started toward her. "Come on, let's blow this Popsicle stand."

The farther they got from Dunsley, the more relaxed Irene felt. It occurred to her that she had not realized how much stress and tension had been locked up in her muscles since she arrived in town.

Night was falling fast. The waters of the lake were almost black under a dark, heavy sky that promised rain sometime before dawn. She was intimately aware of Luke's presence next to her in the front compartment of the big vehicle.

The road that wound around the long, convoluted border of the lake was a two-lane strip of pavement that twisted and curved in a whimsical fashion. Luke drove it with efficiency and precision but he took his time. She got the impression that he was in no rush to reach their destination.

"I talked to Addy today," she said after a while. "She told me that I shouldn't bother going to San Francisco to cover Pamela's funeral. She said it's bound to be a carefully orchestrated event and that I'd be wasting my time because I won't be able to ask any tough questions."

"She's probably right."

She looked at him. "What did Phil Carpenter have to say?"

"He confirmed what Connie Watson told us. No indication that Pamela had a man with her when she arrived in Dunsley on her last visit."

Irene watched the evening shadows move out of the trees and swallow up the rest of the landscape. "The one thing everyone seems to agree on is that Pamela did not follow her usual routine this time. She had a special reason for traveling to Dunsley, and it wasn't to kill herself."

"She wanted to meet with you."

"Yes."

He chose a restaurant that he had discovered by accident shortly after moving to the lake. The Kirbyville Marina Café was a tad ritzier than most of the other eateries in the vicinity. He hoped Irene would find the fake Italian palazzo atmosphere cozy, maybe even intimate. Like every other establishment in the area, the place was only lightly crowded at this time of year. He had no trouble convincing the hostess to produce a table near the windows.

Irene sat down and looked around curiously. "This is new. It wasn't here when I lived in Dunsley."

Luke opened his menu. "Contrary to popular opinion, some things do change."

She smiled. "Maybe on this side of the lake. Not over in Dunsley, at least not as far as I can tell. It's scary how little that town has changed."

"We came over here to get away from Dunsley for a while. What do you say we talk about something else?"

"Good idea." She gave the menu her full attention. "I think I'll have the sautéed shrimp and the avocado salad."

"I'm going for the spaghetti. Same salad."

"I don't see any Elena Creek Vineyards wines on the list," she said.

"Check out the Rain Creek selections. It's the label Elena Creek Vineyards uses to market some less expensive blends."

"I know that label. I can actually afford Rain Creek wines. I especially like the sauvignon blanc."

"Rain Creek was my brother Hackett's idea. He wanted to go after the mid-range customer, but he had a heck of a time convincing the Old Man and Gordon to buy into the idea. They liked the exclusive image they'd cultivated all these years. So Hackett came up with the idea of using another label. It's worked well."

"What do you think about using another label?"

He shrugged. "Not my problem. I decided long ago that I wasn't going to be an asset to the family business. After I got out of the Marines, I let the Old Man and Gordon talk me into giving it a shot, but it was a disaster."

They gave their orders to the waiter. When the young man left a heavy silence enveloped the table. Irene seemed absorbed in her glass of wine and the view of the night-darkened lake.

Luke wondered if he had made a serious mistake when he suggested that they change the topic of conversation. Maybe she found him hopelessly dull and boring if they weren't discussing the problem in Dunsley. He wondered what she talked about when she was with other men.

"Looks like rain," he said, digging deep for inspiration.

"Mmm, yes."

Dig deeper, pal. You're losing her here.

He reached into the bread basket and selected a breadstick. Inspiration finally struck.

"I have to put in an appearance at the Old Man's birthday celebration tomorrow night," he said. "I could use a sidekick."

She gave him a blank look. "Sidekick?"

"Date," he corrected quickly.

"You need a date to go to a birthday party?"

"Trust me, we're not talking a small family get-together. The Old Man's birthday is a major social event in Santa Elena. Every winemaker in the valley and a lot of people from the town will be there. You'd be doing me a very big favor."

"Sounds like fun," she said. "I'd love to go with you."

He suddenly felt remarkably more cheerful. "Thanks. We'll drive to Santa Elena tomorrow afternoon. The party will run late, so we might as well spend the night at the Santa Elena Inn and return to Dunsley the following morning."

"Just one thing," she said.

"What?"

"Why will I be doing you a big favor?"

He turned the wineglass a little between his fingers, deciding how much to tell her. "I've already explained that my family has been worried about me for the past few months."

"Yes."

"I think that if I show up with you, it will reassure everyone."

"Ah," she said. "Got it. You think that if you arrive at the party with a date, your relatives will think you're moving past the PTSD thing and getting back to normal."

He took a swallow of the wine and slowly lowered the glass. "Unfortunately, it's a bit more complicated than that."

"How much more complicated can it get?"

"Like I said, when I got out of the Marines, everyone was very anxious for me to return to the family fold. What can I say? Seemed like a good idea at the time."

"In other words, you subscribed to the notion of getting back to a normal life. What's wrong with that?"

He looked at her. "Lady, I'm a Marine. I don't just subscribe to notions. Once I decided to go for normal, I committed myself one hundred percent to the mission. I established the goal and devised a strategy for achieving my objective. I then proceeded to execute that strategy using a very precise timetable."

She winced. "Uh-oh."

"Uh-oh is right. Turns out being normal is a little trickier than it looks. One of those nuance things, I guess."

"What happened?"

"Well, I was doing okay for a while," he said judiciously. "Making real progress. Met my first objective just fine. Took the job in the family business. It was boring as hell, of course, but I did it. Went to lots of meetings. Read the company financials. Entertained some clients. But I ran into a little trouble with the second objective."

"Which was?"

"I decided that part of the definition of being normal meant getting married and starting a family."

She watched him with a veiled expression. "Jason said something about an engagement that did not work out?"

"Dad's partner, Gordon Foote, has a daughter. Katy. She's a couple years older than Jason. Her parents were divorced when she was in her teens. She spent most of her time with her father, and that meant she grew up in the wine business, surrounded by Danners. She works in the public relations department. I've known her all of her life."

"You asked Katy to marry you?"

"In hindsight, I can only say that it seemed like a perfectly logical move. Katy seemed to think so, too, because she accepted. The family was thrilled. But something was missing."

"Such as?"

He moved a hand. "Romance. Passion. Sex."

"Sex was missing from your relationship?"

"A few friendly kisses and hugs and that was about it. So, being a trained, strategic thinker, I decided that the problem was too much family. Figured we needed some time to ourselves. Long walks on the beach. Dinners by candlelight. You know the routine."

She looked thoughtful. "Actually, I don't think of romance as a *routine*, exactly."

He ignored the interruption, determined to finish what he had started. "I asked Katy to go away with me for a long weekend at a secluded inn on the coast."

"Something went wrong?"

"Almost immediately, I realized that we had made a major mistake. Katy agreed. We went home and told everyone that we had called off the engagement."

"Sad but not exactly a disaster. Where's the problem?"

"The problem," he said evenly, "is that everyone, including Katy, assumes that the reason I called off the engagement is because I was unable to perform my duties in the bedroom."

Irene stared at him, clearly torn between shock and laughter.

"Oh, dear," she whispered.

"You think being slapped with a diagnosis of PTSD is hard to overcome? Try getting stuck with the Erectile Dysfunction label."

Twenty-three

Luke brought the SUV to a halt in front of Irene's well-lit cabin, switched off the engine and got out.

Irene watched him walk around the front of the vehicle to open her door. Scary anticipation and an unfamiliar excitement fizzed through her. Would he kiss her again tonight?

This was ridiculous. She was acting like a teenager on her first big date. Except that she'd never felt like this on any date in her life, she reminded herself.

The door opened. Before she could negotiate her way out of the front seat, Luke's hands settled around her waist, snug, secure and powerful. He lifted her out and set her lightly on the ground as though she were weightless.

He walked her toward the front porch, not saying a word. The suspense was threatening to steal her breath. He took her key and opened the front door.

"The drive to Santa Elena takes about an hour," he said. "We'll need time to check into the inn, meet the family and get dressed for the big event. What do you say we leave here at fifteen hundred hours?"

She stepped over the threshold and turned to face him. "What is that in real time?"

His mouth kicked up wryly at one corner. "Three o'clock in the afternoon."

She folded her arms and propped one shoulder against the door frame. "Got news for you, we're going to have to leave here a lot earlier than that."

"Why?"

"Because I need to do some shopping. A couple of friends at the paper packed up some clothes and overnighted them to me. But there's nothing in the box that will work for a fancy evening. We'll have to leave around noon, I think. There's bound to be some nice shops in the vicinity of Santa Elena."

"Shopping time, huh?" He nodded agreeably. "Okay, you got it. We'll take off right after lunch. Speaking of food and since we're both into breakfast, can I interest you in my very special French toast tomorrow morning?"

His smile was so slow and so wickedly inviting that she was amazed she did not dissolve into a puddle right there in the cramped little entranceway of the cabin.

A whole bunch of butterflies took flight in her stomach. Was this his way of announcing that he wanted to spend the night? If so, she would have to make a decision. Right now. Oh, Lord, she wasn't ready for this. It was too soon.

"Yes," she heard herself say before she could rationalize her way out of it. "Breakfast sounds good."

Luke nodded, looking satisfied, leaned forward and kissed her lightly on the mouth. He raised his head almost immediately. "My place. Zero seven-thirty. That's plain old seven-thirty A.M. to you."

"Somehow I think I would have figured that out."

And then he was walking away across the porch and down the steps. She stood in the doorway, nonplussed and more than a little chagrined. So much for her making the big decision, she thought.

He paused at the foot of the steps. "Lock your door."

There was a suspicious gleam in his eyes, she decided. He knew full well that he had left her off-balance.

"Okay," she said sweetly, "but I'm not sure why I'm bothering. There certainly doesn't seem to be much of a threat around here tonight."

He grinned. "You never know."

She closed the door and locked it. Eye to the peephole, she watched Luke climb into the SUV.

The vehicle's lights came up, slicing into the darkness. The heavy engine rumbled to life. The SUV moved slowly, ponderously, out of the drive, heading toward Cabin Number One.

Damn. He really was going to leave.

"Son of a—" She broke off, wryly amused by her chaotic reaction to Luke's abrupt departure. She told herself that she ought to feel greatly relieved. It was far too soon to go to bed with a man she barely knew. She had issues that were bound to complicate things, anyway. Sooner or later they always did.

Better to focus on tomorrow night, instead, she decided.

Luke had mentioned staying at an inn. Was he thinking one room or two? Should she shop for a new nightgown tomorrow along with a new dress? And what about her issues?

She turned slowly away from the door, her brain swirling and her senses tingling with the anxiety of anticipation.

The sight of the darkness spilling out of the bedroom hallway did not immediately register.

Her autonomic nervous system, set to a level of hyperawareness seventeen years earlier, responded instantly, however. It flashed into full panic mode before her conscious mind had finished processing the data.

She froze in mid-step and mid-breath, trying to control the fear sparking through her.

The light in the bedroom was off. She knew she had left it on. She always left a light on in every room at night. *Always.*

Maybe the overhead fixture in the other room had burned out.

Get a grip. It's an old cabin. Old wiring. Old bulbs.

Somewhere in the river of darkness that flooded out of the bedroom, a floorboard squeaked.

Twenty-four

What he had glimpsed in those spectacular eyes was feminine disappointment, Luke mused, easing the SUV along the lane back toward his cabin. He was sure of it. Irene had recovered quickly but not quickly enough to conceal her reaction to his oh-so-gentlemanly departure.

She had definitely been willing to do some more fooling around tonight.

Problem is, lady, I'm too old to play games. The next time we get close it's going to be all or nothing, and we both know that tonight is too soon for you.

Strategy was the key, he reminded himself. It was always the key. Unfortunately, strategy exacted its own price. He glanced back at the warmly lit cabin. Maybe he could handle a little fooling around. Sure, it would cost him some sleep.

Don't go there. If you get started tonight, you're not going to be able to stop and you know it. You don't want her having regrets in the morning.

There was something wrong with Cabin Number Five, he thought. It looked different tonight.

The bedroom was dark.

An uneasy sensation whispered through him. He braked to a stop. There had still been some daylight left when they set out for the drive around the lake. Maybe Irene had forgotten to leave the lights on in the bedroom. Or maybe a lamp was out. The least he could do was offer to change it for her. Maxine was always telling him that a strong service orientation was the key to repeat business.

Could he make excuses, or what?

He put the vehicle into reverse.

The front door of the cabin slammed open just as he reached the drive. Irene burst out onto the porch. She vaulted the three steps, spotted the SUV and plunged toward it.

"Luke."

The figure of a man loomed in the doorway of the cabin. He held an object in one hand.

Luke was out of the SUV, moving toward Irene with no conscious memory of having opened the door.

"Someone," she gasped. "Someone inside—"

He grabbed her arm and hauled her around to the far side of the SUV, putting the vehicle's massive bulk between them and the man in the doorway.

He yanked open the passenger-side door and pushed her inside. "Get in and stay down."

She didn't argue.

The intruder moved out of the doorway onto the front porch.

"Miss Stenson, wait," he called in a hoarse, frantic voice. "Didn't mean to scare you."

"What the hell?" Luke moved toward the front of the SUV. "Is that you, Mills?"

Tucker Mills lowered his voice. "It's me, Mr. Danner. I'm surely sorry. I didn't want anyone else to know I was here, y'see."

"It's okay, Tucker. Drop whatever it is you're holding in your hand." Luke kept his tone easy, nonthreatening.

"Sure, Mr. Danner."

Tucker released his grip on the object in his hand. It fell soundlessly to the floor of the porch. Not a gun or a knife, Luke thought.

He went forward swiftly. When he mounted the steps, Tucker stepped back nervously, hands half raised in a pathetic gesture of anxiety and self-defense. "Please, Mr. Danner. I didn't mean any harm. Honest."

Feeling a lot like a thug, Luke glanced down at the object Tucker had dropped. It was a knit cap. He scooped it up and handed it back to Mills.

"What is this all about, Tucker?" he asked quietly.

"Tucker? Tucker Mills?" Irene had scrambled out of the SUV and was walking quickly back toward the cabin.

"Yes, Miss Stenson."

"Good grief, you scared the daylights out of me." She hurried up the steps and stopped beside Luke. She peered intently at Tucker. "What on earth were you doing hiding in my bedroom?"

"I didn't want anyone to see me here." Tucker sounded miserable and very nervous. "You were gone when I got here, so I jimmied the back door. Reckoned it would be better if I waited in the cabin. Less chance of being spotted, that way."

"It's okay, Tucker," Irene said gently. "I understand. Sorry for freaking out like that. I didn't realize it was you."

"I shoulda stayed outside. I know that, Miss Stenson. But I was afraid someone might see me hanging around the back porch. Maybe call the police."

"Let's continue this conversation inside," Luke said.

Irene smiled warmly at Tucker. "I'll make tea."

Ten minutes later Irene set three steaming cups of her specially blended tea on the small kitchen table. She figured it would take a few more hours for her thoroughly rattled nerves to settle down, but at least her pulse was no longer pounding.

Luke had made a circuit of the cabin a few minutes ago, pulling every curtain tightly shut. Now he sat across from Tucker looking grim but amazingly patient and calm. He obviously knew Tucker Mills, Irene thought. He understood that Tucker didn't do well under pressure.

"Start at the beginning, Mills," Luke said.

"Yes, sir." Tucker's expression tightened into a worried knot. It was clear that he was not entirely certain where the beginning was.

"Start anywhere you want," Irene suggested. "Take your time."

"Okay." Tucker shot her a grateful look. "This afternoon, then."

"What about this afternoon?" she asked.

"That's when I saw Mr. Danner, here, in Mr. Carpenter's garage. I was cleaning up the place like I always do in the afternoons. Mr. Danner came in and talked to Mr. Carpenter. I heard him ask about Miss Webb, whether she had a new boyfriend or something like that."

Luke watched Tucker very steadily. "Do you know something about her?"

Tucker gripped his mug in two bony hands. "I do some regular work out at the Webb place, leastways I used to." He paused. "Before the house burned down, I mean. Guess there won't be any more work there now, though."

"Go on," Irene said, fighting to keep her voice even and soothing while everything inside wanted to shout at him to get on with his tale.

"Miss Webb hired me a few years ago to take care of the garden and mow the lawn and check the pipes in winter to make sure they don't freeze up. Things like that."

"Maintenance work," Luke said.

Tucker nodded, pleased by the show of comprehension. "Right. Maintenance. I went there a couple of times a week. I was there the day before you found her. In the morning, I mean."

Irene tensed. "Did you talk to her?"

"Sure. She was always nice to me. Even in the old days. Both of you were, in fact. Neither one of you ever acted like you thought I was a no-account."

Irene was appalled. "You were not a no-account. You always worked for a living. Dad used to say that you were the hardest-working man in town."

Faded sorrow shadowed Tucker's gaunt face. "Chief Stenson treated me with respect. He trusted me. Not a lot of folks do. Oh, sure, they're quick enough to hire me to do odd jobs, but just let something go missing and who do you think gets blamed? Me. But your dad never took those people seriously. Anyhow, that's one of the reasons I came here to see you tonight. Figured I owed something to you because I owed your dad and I was never able to repay him, if you see what I mean."

"Thank you, Tucker," she said.

"What happened on the day before Pamela Webb died?" Luke asked.

Tucker collected himself with a visible effort. "Like I said, I was at the house, working in the garden as usual. Miss Webb was inside."

"Do you know what she was doing?" Luke asked.

"Not for sure. But when she saw me park my truck around back by the dock, she came out to say hello. Then she said something about having to finish some work on the computer and went back inside. A while later a car pulled into the drive."

"What kind of car?" Luke asked.

"It was a real nice car. One of those foreign jobs. Guy behind the wheel didn't see me on account of I was around the side of the house. And like I said, I'd parked the truck in back so I didn't have to carry my tools and equipment too far. Anyhow, I heard the man knock on the front door."

"Did Pamela let him in?" Irene asked.

Tucker bobbed his head. "I could tell she knew him. But she didn't sound real happy to see him. She wanted to know why he was there. Sounded like she was mad at him."

"Did you hear what he said in response?" Irene asked.

"No. But he seemed real angry. She let him in for a few minutes. Not long. Don't know what they talked about, but I could hear him arguing with Miss Webb. I hung around near the utility room door just in case she needed some help getting rid of him. But he finally took off. Drove away real fast. I could tell he was still mad at her."

"Did you get a good look at him?" Luke asked.

"Pretty good."

Irene realized she was holding her breath.

"Did you recognize him?" Luke asked in the same steady, nonthreatening voice.

"That day was the first time I saw him," Tucker said.

Irene swallowed a sigh of disappointment and reminded herself that this was more information than they'd had twenty minutes ago.

"Can you describe him?" Luke asked.

"Sort of medium height. Soft."

"Soft?" she repeated curiously. "Do you mean fat?"

"Not soft that way. I know some real big guys who aren't

soft." Tucker's face pinched into a scowl of deep concentration. "He wasn't fat, but he looked like you could push him over without too much trouble." Tucker looked at Luke. "Not hard like you, Mr. Danner. *Soft*."

"Okay, soft," Irene said. "Go on, Tucker. What else can you tell us about him?"

"Brown hair." Tucker appeared to search his memory. "Fancy clothes. And like I said, that fancy car."

Irene stifled a groan of disappointment. Talk about a generic description, she thought. "Can I assume from the fact that you didn't recognize him that he was not from around here?"

"No, he sure wasn't local. Told you, it was the first time I'd ever seen him." Tucker took a swallow of the hot tea.

They sat in silence for a while. Irene felt her excitement slip away. How would they ever identify Pamela's visitor with such a vague description? she wondered.

Tucker lowered his mug of tea. "Saw him again, though, not long after that."

Irene straightened quickly in her chair. She knew that Luke had also gone on high alert although he did not move so much as a finger.

"When did you see him again?" Luke asked very casually.

"The morning after you found her body."

Irene clutched her mug in both hands. "What was he doing?"

Tucker was befuddled by the question. "Don't know what he was doing, exactly."

"Where was he?" Luke asked.

"Outside the municipal building. He got into that big limo with Senator Webb and that pretty lady they say the senator's going to marry."

Irene looked at Luke, hardly daring to breathe.

"Hoyt Egan," Luke said. "Webb's aide."

Twenty-five

A short time later, Luke stood with Irene on the back porch of the cabin. They watched Tucker Mills shamble off into the darkness of the trees.

"Try not to run away with this." Luke wrapped an arm around Irene's shoulders. She was coiled spring tight, every muscle rigid. "Egan may have had a very good reason for driving up here to see Pamela."

"You heard what Tucker said, they argued."

"I heard. But that doesn't mean that he murdered her." He paused briefly. "Could mean he knows what was on her mind in the last couple of days of her life, though."

"Yes, it does," Irene said eagerly. "Maybe they were lovers. Maybe she had ended the relationship, and Egan didn't take it well."

"It's a possibility," he agreed. "But that's pure speculation at this point. Furthermore, you're trying to prove that Pamela's death was linked to what happened to your folks, right?"

"Yes."

"Got to tell you, it's hard to figure how Egan could fit into any scenario involving the deaths of your parents. He's in his mid-thirties. Not much older than you. He was probably in college at the time. And he's not from around here, anyway. Doesn't seem to be a connection."

"No." Reluctance was a lead weight dragging down the single word.

He felt like a brute stomping on her conspiracy theories, but he told himself that he was doing her a favor, whether she realized it or not.

"Hey." He tucked her closer against his side. "I'm not saying you're going off the deep end here. I was with you the other night when someone torched the Webb house, remember? I agree that something very nasty is going on. I'm just not convinced yet that it has anything to do with the past."

"What's your theory?"

"Given her history of drug use, I'm starting to wonder if maybe Pamela Webb got involved with some very bad guys."

"Oh, jeez." Irene shuddered. "Drug dealers?"

"It's one possibility. Unfortunately there are a lot more."

"Such as?"

He shrugged. "Maybe someone used her addiction to try to blackmail or manipulate her." He hesitated. "Or maybe—"

Irene turned her head very quickly to look at him. "What are you thinking?"

"It occurs to me that a senator's daughter would be a very useful tool for someone who wanted access or inside information. Pamela knew the people her father knew. She entertained his associates. Helped organize his fund-raisers. She rubbed shoulders with some of the most powerful people in the country."

"And she was not just beautiful, she was also sexy," Irene said quietly. "I think it's safe to say she probably slept with some of those important people."

"Which opens up even more really unpleasant scenarios."

"Good Lord," Irene said. "Do you think Pamela was killed and the house torched because she knew too much? That maybe someone was afraid that she would reveal embarrassing or incriminating information?"

"I don't know." He held out one hand, palm up. "At the moment, I'm speculating, just like you."

"But what about that e-mail she sent to me? I keep coming back to that. She must have had some personal reason for contacting me after all these years."

"She probably knew that you had become a reporter," he said, thinking it through. "If she had something to reveal to the media, she may have contacted you because she felt she could trust you."

She wrinkled her nose. "I work for a small-town paper. In Glaston Cove, the biggest story at the moment is the debate over whether or not the city council should approve a new dog park. After all those years of working for her father, Pamela must have had lots of major media connections. I can't see her coming to me if she had some great scandal to reveal."

"Okay, let's assume for the moment that she contacted you because she had a personal reason to do so."

"That personal reason involved information concerning the deaths of my parents." Irene folded her arms very tightly beneath her breasts. "I know it did, Luke. It's the only explanation that makes sense."

"Maybe. Maybe not. But it does look like she might have come to Dunsley to hide out for a while, a week at least."

"Perhaps she felt safe here because of her long-standing connection to the town. She knew everyone, and everyone knew her."

"That may have been the plan, but when you think about it, she was alone and isolated out there at the Webb house. If someone did want to get rid of her, she sure as hell made it easy for him. I would have thought that if she was frightened, she would have wanted someone around her she could trust."

"Unless," Irene said, "she didn't trust anyone she knew. Maybe that's the real reason she got in touch with me. I was someone from her past that she felt she could trust."

"With what?" he asked simply.

"That's what I need to find out."

He said nothing, just tightened his grip on her.

"I can't help but notice that you are no longer trying to argue me out of my conspiracy theory," she said after a while.

"Unfortunately, it's starting to make sense. Probably not a real good sign."

"You think maybe we're both ready for a nice long vacation in a padded room?" she asked.

"On the whole, I'd rather go to Hawaii."

"Me, too." She paused. "But first I need to talk to Hoyt Egan," she said very softly.

"I've been thinking the same thing. Got a plan, if you're interested."

She looked at him. "Tell me."

"The morning after the Old Man's birthday party you and I could drive on into San Francisco and corner Egan. If we take him by surprise, we might get some answers out of him."

"I like your plan." She nodded once, decisively. "I like it a lot."

He smiled a little and turned her in the circle of his arm so that he could see her face. In the glow of the porch light her eyes were deep wells of shadows.

"I'm sorry that Tucker Mills scared you tonight," he said.

"He didn't mean to do it."

"No, but that doesn't change what happened. Are you okay?"

"I'm still a little shaky." She gave a weak, forced laugh. "When I realized that the light was off in the bedroom, I just sort of froze for a few seconds. Talk about a deer in the headlights. When I could move, all I could think about was getting out of the house."

"A real good strategy, under the circumstances."

"I must have looked ridiculous."

"No, you looked scared," he said. "But you were moving, doing the smart thing. Not everyone can function under that kind of fear. Some people stay frozen."

"I was terrified," she whispered.

"I know." He massaged the nape of her neck, trying to loosen some of the taut muscles he found there. "I know."

She closed her eyes after a moment. "That feels very, very good."

He felt some of the tension seep out of her.

"Something I've been meaning to ask you," he said after a moment.

"Mmm?"

"What's with the lights? Why do you leave them on all night long?"

"I suppose you could call it my security system," she said, eyes still closed.

"This may not be the best time to go into the subject, but there are better security measures you can take if you're worried about intruders. A good alarm system, for instance. You saw for yourself tonight that having the cabin fully lit didn't keep Mills from letting himself inside."

Her lashes lifted. He looked into her haunted eyes and went cold to his bones.

"The lights were off in the house that night," she said in a disturbingly steady, dispassionate tone. "I got home late. Long past curfew. I'd violated one of Dad's strictest rules. I allowed Pamela to drive me over to Kirbyville. I didn't want to face my folks any sooner than necessary. When I saw that the lights were off, I thought they'd gone to bed. I went around the back to use the kitchen door."

He remembered what Maxine had told him. *Hugh Stenson*

shot his wife to death in the kitchen of their home. Then he turned the gun on himself.

He gripped Irene's shoulders. "I'm sorry. I shouldn't have asked. You don't have to talk about this. Not now. Not tonight."

She did not appear to hear him. He realized that it was too late. She was in another zone.

"I thought I could sneak into my room, that if I was careful and didn't make any noise or turn on any lights Mom and Dad wouldn't hear me," she said.

He had known it would be bad, he reminded himself. He also knew that there was nothing he could do but hold her while she talked. He tightened his grasp on her shoulders.

"I unlocked the back door, but when I tried to open it, I realized that there was something heavy blocking it. I pushed harder, forcing it open. There was a smell, a terrible stench like nothing I'd ever known. I thought maybe a wild animal had somehow gotten inside the house and ripped into the garbage. But that didn't make sense. Mom and Dad would have heard the commotion."

"Irene," he said softly. "I'm here."

"I couldn't see anything," she continued in the same flat, frighteningly uninflected voice. "It was so dark."

"I know."

"I found the light switch on the wall beside the door. Turned it on." She sucked in a shuddering breath. "And then I could see."

"Irene, hush. That's enough." He cradled her close, rocking her gently. "You don't have to say any more. For God's sake, forgive me. I understand about the lights now."

"It was as if I went into another dimension," she said against the front of his shirt. "I could not deal with being there alone with them, so I went someplace else for a while."

"I know," he stroked her hair. "I've been in that other place, myself."

"Jason implied you were in combat."

"Like I said, another place."

"You've seen how they look, haven't you?"

He knew what she meant. "Yes."

"People you know. People you care about. You've seen what they look like . . . afterward. You know how it is. And you wonder why them and not you."

"The world is different after that," he said. "Things are never, ever the same again. People who haven't been to that other place can never really understand how hard it is for the travelers who return, travelers like us, to pretend that nothing has changed."

She put her arms around him, hugging him fiercely.

They stood there for a long time, holding each other, not talking. After a while he led her indoors. He walked her down the hall to the bedroom and turned on the lights for her.

She pulled a little away from him, putting some distance between them. She gave him a shaky smile and used the back of her sleeve to wipe the moisture from her eyes. "Don't worry, I'll be back to my usual self in the morning."

"Sure," he said. "If it's okay with you, though, I'm going to sleep on your couch tonight."

She blinked and then her eyes widened. "Why do you want to do that?"

"Because you had a bad scare this evening and because I asked you about the past and because you told me. You don't really want to be alone tonight, do you?"

"No," she said.

The stark, painful honesty of the reply hit him hard. She was not used to letting others this close, he thought.

"Neither do I." He opened the tiny hall closet and took out the spare pillow and blanket stored inside. "Mind if I turn down the lights in the front room, though? If it bothers you, I can sleep with my shirt over my eyes."

"No," she said. "As long as I know you're out there, I won't be afraid of the dark."

Twenty-six

An hour and a half later, Irene got up for the second time and embarked on another short trek around the tiny bedroom. Another bad night; another ritual. In the blue glow of the night-light she had installed, she surveyed the rumpled bed and the small chest of drawers. There was barely any room to move in here.

When she was at home, a walk through her well-lit condo to check the locks on windows and doors was the first of a two-part ritual that she used to deal with the midnight jitters. The second part consisted of a spoonful of peanut butter spread between two saltine crackers.

The problem tonight was that she was confined to the bedroom because Luke was sleeping on the couch in the other room. The more she reminded herself that she could not pursue her nighttime routine tonight, the more restless and edgy she felt.

She had to move, she thought. She had to get to the peanut butter and crackers.

She went to the door, cracked it open and peered down the short hall into the darkened front room and kitchen area. There was no sound from the vicinity of the couch. Luke was most likely asleep. If she was very quiet, she might be able to go into the kitchen without waking him. She could get the box of crackers and the jar of peanut butter and take them back to the bedroom.

The package of clothes she had received had not contained a robe. The thought made her hesitate a few more seconds. Then she decided that her cozy, full-length, long-sleeved cotton nightgown would provide ample modesty and coverage if Luke did happen to wake up and see her.

She went toward the front room as stealthily as possible, automatically glancing into the well-lit bath to make certain that the high, frosted-glass window was still securely locked.

When she reached the shadowed living room, she looked toward the couch. Although the lamps were off, there was a fair amount of porch light seeping between the cracks in the curtains. She could make out Luke's sleeping form sprawled on the cushions.

She worked her way cautiously toward the kitchen. When she arrived, she opened the cupboard door as soundlessly as possible and groped inside for the peanut butter jar.

"You going to eat that all by yourself, or are you planning to share?" Luke asked out of the shadows.

She gasped, started violently and nearly lost her grip on the peanut butter. Clutching the jar, she whirled around.

"I thought you were asleep," she said.

"Hard to do that with you prowling around back there in the bedroom."

"Oh. Sorry about that." She took down the box of crackers. "When I can't sleep, I walk. I also eat peanut butter and crackers."

"Personally, I usually go for a long walk and a slug of brandy. But I've got nothing against peanut butter. That works, too."

She looked across the counter at him and nearly dropped the jar a second time.

He wasn't quite naked, but dressed in a pair of white briefs and a black tee shirt, he might as well have been. She saw him reach for something in the shadows. His jeans, she thought. He pulled them on. She heard the metallic slide of the zipper. For some reason it seemed like an excruciatingly erotic little sound.

Be cool, she thought. *Remember to breathe. Look at the positive side, you might not even need the peanut butter to take your mind off your nerves.*

Peanut butter was, however, a good deal safer.

She turned away from the fascinating sight of him, opened the drawer that contained the limited selection of flatware and seized a butter knife.

"Do I get one of those peanut butter crackers?" Luke asked.

She risked another quick glance in his direction and saw that he was coming toward her.

"Uh, sure," she said.

She started to reach for the kitchen light switch but suddenly remembered that, while Luke was now quite decent, she was wearing only a nightgown.

No problem, she thought. She could make peanut butter crackers with her eyes closed.

"You gotta have something to drink with peanut butter." Luke walked around the edge of the counter, heading for the refrigerator. "Otherwise it sticks to the roof of your mouth and gums up your tongue. Scientific fact."

"No, wait," she said quickly.

But it was too late. He already had the refrigerator door open. The fixture inside gave off a shaft of light that illuminated her from head to foot.

Why hadn't she brought along a sexier nightgown? The answer was simple, of course. While she had been careful to pack full fashion battle armor to confront Dunsley and the past, she had expected to spend her nights alone, as was her custom.

Luke glanced at her over his shoulder. She went very still, not knowing what to expect.

What she got was a meltingly slow, breathtakingly sexy, utterly masculine look of appreciation.

Without a word, Luke closed the refrigerator door. He crossed the very short space between them with a single stride and gripped the counter behind her, one arm on either side of her waist. Leaning in close he put his mouth against her ear.

"Told myself I wasn't going to do this tonight," he said. "Clearly I lied."

"This is probably not a good idea," she whispered.

"Got a better one?"

Therein lay the real problem, she thought. She didn't have a better idea. Kissing Luke was far and away the best idea she'd had in years, maybe forever.

She wound her arms slowly around his neck and smiled. "Nope."

He gave a soft, husky groan, and then his mouth closed over hers.

Heat and sparkling energy crackled through her. He made the kiss last a long time, not rushing her. A slow hunger that had nothing whatsoever to do with peanut butter and crackers built inside her, tightening her lower body.

She could kiss him like this for weeks or months at a time, she thought, relaxing into the embrace. The sleek, muscled contours of his back felt wonderful beneath her hands. Experimentally, she slid her palms under his tee shirt and around to the front of his chest. She spread her fingers in the crisp, dark hair she discovered there.

"This," he announced, releasing his grip on the counter to peel off the tee shirt, "is a whole lot better than peanut butter and crackers."

He pulled her close a second time. First she felt his lips on her throat. Her head tipped back. Then she felt his teeth. Thrill after thrill coursed through her. She had been wrong, she thought. She could not go on kissing him like this for weeks or months. If she did, she would suffer unbearable frustration. She needed much more, and she needed it right now.

Obviously he was able to read her mind because the next thing she knew, his warm, strong hands were gliding downward toward the bones that defined the curve of her hips. He flexed his fingers, squeezing gently.

He was so strong. He could break things with those hands. But he wouldn't hurt her. She knew that intuitively in every fiber of her being.

He touched her as though she were made out of silk and moonbeams, making her feel as though she were a rare and magical being, capable of sorcery. She sensed wonder and a deep, clawing need in him. No man had ever made her feel that she could cause him to shudder with desire.

Excitement and a heretofore undiscovered sense of her own feminine power swept through her, a rush of pure, intense sensation that left her dazed and breathless.

She let her hands drift down his sides until her thumbs slid just inside the waistband of his jeans. Slowly she moved her fingers to the front where she could feel the hard, shockingly masculine bulge.

"If I weren't a tough, seasoned journalist, I would probably succumb to an attack of the vapors right about now," she said.

His laugh was rough and sexy. "If it weren't for my rigorous training, I'd probably be doing the same thing."

He scooped her up against his chest. She wrapped her legs around his waist and clung to him. He carried her out of the kitchen, negotiated the narrow hallway with amazing deftness, and put her down on the tumbled bed.

He paused just long enough to get out of his jeans and briefs and remove a small foil packet from the pocket of his pants. He tore off the top of the packet with his teeth.

And then he was coming down on top of her, one leg anchoring her thigh so that she was open to his touch.

He tugged the nightgown up to her waist and higher still until he could pull it off entirely. Out of the corner of her eye she saw the crumpled garment go sailing off into the nearest corner. She didn't see it hit the floor because she was too utterly focused on the looming shape of Luke as he bent his head to her breast.

When he took her nipple between his teeth she heard a soft, breathless sigh of pleasure. It took her a moment to realize that she was the one who had made the sound.

She reached down and enclosed him with her fingers, exploring the length and breadth of him. The fierceness of his erection excited her. She felt him grow even tighter and bigger at her touch.

His hand moved up the inside of her thigh. She did not know whether to urge him to hurry before she lost this glorious pulsing sensation, or if she wanted him to slow down so that it had time to intensify. Decisions, decisions. She was entering uncharted territory. Her trusty vibrator was home in Glaston Cove in a drawer beside her bed.

One long finger slid slowly, deeply into her, stroking, prodding and stretching. Another finger followed. She could feel the slick dampness gathering between her legs.

So far so good. But she knew that without the vibrator this was probably as exciting as it was going to get.

Not bad, though, she told herself. Not bad at all.

Luke did something very interesting with his thumb, startling her out of thoughts of her vibrator. Jolted, her body clenched tightly around his invading fingers.

"Luke?"

"Mmm?" He nuzzled her belly.

"Now," she urged, digging her nails into his shoulders. "Please, yes, *now.*"

He did the thing with his thumb again. "There's no rush."

"Yes, there is." She tried to shake him, but it was like trying to move a large boulder. "You don't understand."

"You're still tight. I don't want to hurt you."

"You won't hurt me." She clutched him harder and moved her hips against his hand. "The thing is, I never get this far without—" She broke off. Don't go there, she thought. Too much information.

"Let's see if we can make you a little wetter first."

He started to move farther down her body, pausing here and there to drop kisses onto her sensitive skin.

He reached the inside of her thigh.

"No, wait," she gasped. "Come back here."

She heard his low, wicked laugh again, and then felt his warm breath and his tongue on her, right there in the place where she usually relied on Big Guy.

It was all she could do to keep herself from screaming.

It was too much. He was taking control, demanding a kind of surrender that she had never been able to give any man. It was unthinkable. She barely knew him. How could she trust him with her most intimate responses?

A moment later the climax rolled through her, as deep and unstoppable as an earthquake.

She was vaguely aware of Luke shifting his weight, sliding heavily between her legs. He pushed himself deliberately into her, stretching her, filling her completely.

She was stunned to feel herself coming again. Luke rode the new tremors with her, pounding hard and fast into her body. His back was slick with perspiration, every muscle rigid.

The ancient bedsprings groaned loudly, rhythmically in protest. The headboard slammed again and again against the wall. Her emotions were in utter, mystifying chaos. She wanted to laugh and was amazed when she felt tears in her eyes. The only thing that mattered was the man in her arms.

It seemed impossible, but Luke's hoarse shout of exultant, triumphant release gave her as much pure, unadulterated pleasure and satisfaction as her own climax.

For a few rare, glittering moments she was not alone.

L uke gradually drifted back to full awareness. He took his time about it, savoring the feel of Irene's body curled alongside his own. Her head was cradled on his arm. She had one palm resting on his chest and one foot wedged tantalizingly, intimately between his legs. He felt her flex her toes a few times as though she liked touching him that way.

A warm, heavy, very bright sensation drifted through him. He could not remember the last time he had felt like this.

Maybe never. He shoved a pillow under his head and smiled into the shadows.

"'Ooh rah," he mumbled.

"I was just thinking the same thing." She folded her arms on his chest and rested her chin on her hands. "I've never actually had that happen with a man."

He went blank for a few seconds. "A woman?"

She smiled and slowly shook her head. "When I'm in the mood, I sometimes get lucky with Big Guy."

"Maybe I shouldn't ask, but just who is Big Guy?"

"My vibrator. But I have to say that the experience has never been anywhere near as intense as what just happened. What I get with Big Guy is more like a good sneeze."

"So, what you're saying is that I'm better than a vibrator and a good sneeze?"

"You are, indeed. Don't let it go to your head."

He grinned. "Be hard not to."

"One of my therapists told me that the reason I couldn't climax with a man was because I had intimacy issues. Something to do with a fear of letting myself get too close emotionally."

"Ever been married?" he asked.

"Right after college, for about a year and a half. My aunt had just died, and I wanted so desperately not to be alone."

He traced the outline of her ear with his finger. "I understand."

"It didn't work out. My fault. My little obsession problems were starting to kick in big time back then. Rick tried to be sympathetic, but given my issues with sex, occasional night-mares and my erratic sleep habits, he just sort of burned out. I was on my third therapist. She suggested meds. When I re-fused to take them, Rick threw up his hands and left. I didn't blame him. It was a relief for both of us when it ended."

"You were in that other zone." He twisted his fingers gently in her hair. "He couldn't reach you."

"And I couldn't reach him. Like I said, it wasn't his fault. I knew I had some work to do before I could be with anyone. I had to get past the past. And I did try. I really did. I've seen three more therapists since the divorce. I finally tried the meds for a while. They helped a little. But I kept coming back to the fact that I wanted answers about what had happened in the past."

"Sometimes we don't get the answers," he said.

"I know." She hesitated. "I suppose that's why I went into journalism. I couldn't get answers in my own life, so I got into a line of work that gives me the ideal excuse to look for answers in other places and other lives."

"I'm not sure it was a good idea for you to come back here to Dunsley, but speaking from a purely selfish point of view, I'm damn glad you did."

She tilted her head a little. "I hated the thought of coming back here, but I think in a way it's been cathartic."

"Even if you don't end up with all the answers?"

"I'm wrestling demons here in Dunsley. I may not subdue them, but—"

"But you're no longer trying to pretend they don't exist."

"Believe it or not, that feels like progress."

When he awoke he was amazed to see the glow of early morning illuminating the world outside the cabin. Irene still slumbered beside him. He knew she had not stirred or felt compelled to leave the bed during the night. He would have sensed such movement.

What amazed and astounded him was that he had slept just as soundly.

Twenty-seven

Hoyt checked his watch in the same nervous, habitual way he did a thousand times a day. The small action never failed to irritate Ryland.

"I've arranged for you to give a short statement to some selected media immediately following the service, sir." Hoyt handed him a folder. "I also canceled the business club luncheon this afternoon and tonight's fund-raiser, but we'll be back on the regular schedule tomorrow."

Ryland opened the folder and read the statement. The request for privacy for a grieving father and the promise to introduce the bill to fund more mental health research was precisely what he had expected.

He closed the folder and looked at Alexa. She sat on the seat across from him, stunning and dramatic in a conservatively cut black suit and veiled hat. She would photograph beautifully today, just as she always did, he thought.

Pamela had been useful in his campaigns in the past few

years, but a presidential candidate required a wife. The voters would never go for an unmarried man in the White House.

"I'll want you beside me when I confront the press this morning," Ryland said to Alexa.

She folded her gloved hands on her lap. "Of course."

He switched his attention back to Hoyt. "Was there any fall-out from the story in the *Glaston Cove Beacon?*"

"Nothing we can't counter easily enough with your state-ment this morning." Hoyt glanced at his watch again. "The *Beacon* did hint at an investigation, but—"

"That's bullshit," Ryland snapped. "McPherson isn't con-ducting an investigation. I made it clear that I didn't want one."

"Yes, sir, I know, but I'm afraid the *Beacon* implied that there were some questions about Pamela's death that were being looked into by the local authorities, or words to that effect." Hoyt glanced at the folder. "The good news is that no one reads that damn rag. It won't be a problem."

"It better not become one," Ryland muttered.

And in all likelihood, it wouldn't, regardless of Irene Stenson's interference, he told himself. Sam McPherson understood that it was his job to keep things quiet.

Nothing like owning an entire town, including the chief of police, he thought. Dunsley was a boring little spot on the map, but he had to admit that occasionally it had its uses.

The limo glided to a halt in front of the funeral chapel. Ryland examined the scene through the heavily tinted windows.

He relaxed when he saw that there were only a small number of media vehicles.

"I don't see any sign of Irene Stenson," Alexa said, sounding relieved. "Everything is going to be fine, Ryland. Stop worrying. As soon as the funeral service is concluded, the press will lose interest in this tragedy."

"I agree," Hoyt said. "Things are under control, sir."

"Your father is here," Alexa said. "He's just going into the chapel."

"Mr. Webb's flight from Phoenix was on time," Hoyt said. "I checked earlier."

Ryland watched his father, distinguished in a gray suit, make his way into the church.

A volatile mix of anger, resentment and, yes, plain old fear churned through him, the same poisonous elixir that he always experienced when Victor Webb was in the vicinity. He could not remember a time when he had not felt the intense pressure to live up to his father's demands and expectations. Nothing was ever good enough for the old bastard.

The sooner Victor went back to Phoenix, the better, Ryland thought. Whatever happened, he had to make certain that the sonofabitch did not discover the blackmail problem. Victor would be furious, and when he was furious, there was hell to pay.

Ryland's fingers clenched around the folder. He had to find the blackmailer and get rid of him before his father found out what was going on. In the meantime he had no choice but to continue making those damned payments into that mysterious offshore account.

One thing was certain. When he did finally succeed in identifying the blackmailer, the extortionist was a dead man. Or a dead woman.

He watched Victor disappear into the chapel. There had been, he reflected, a number of convenient deaths over the years: his wife, the Stensons and now Pamela. Each tragedy had helped him manage a potentially difficult situation. Why not another one?

He was momentarily dazed by his own daring. Get rid of Victor?

For years he had relied not only on the old man's money, but also on Victor's connections and his uncanny ability to assess an opponent's weaknesses. Victor had always been his real campaign manager, the strategist, the power behind the throne.

I'm fifty-three years old, Ryland thought. *I don't need the bastard anymore. I can run my own life.*

He felt as if he were having an epiphany.

Money would not be a problem. He was Victor's sole heir. Besides, Alexa was rich in her own right.

He did not need his father. What a liberating thought.

The door of the limo opened. Ryland assumed an expression that was appropriate for a father who had just lost a troubled daughter to drugs and alcohol and followed Alexa out of the car.

. . .

Victor Webb watched his firstborn son walk slowly, somberly toward the front of the chapel. Anger and a fierce regret clawed at his insides. Years ago he had made a terrible mistake, and now there was no going back.

On the outside, Ryland appeared to be all that a man could want in a son. Victor had showered him with everything required to achieve that goal. He had given Ryland a world-class education, money and connections. Victor knew that his greatest dream, that of founding a powerful dynasty that would last for generations, was on the brink of being realized.

But he also knew now that his worst fears had proven true. In spite of everything he had done to forge his son's character, it was clear that Ryland lacked the strength of will required to overcome the cracks at his core. Deep down inside where it mattered, Ryland was weak.

He had, indeed, made a grave mistake back at the beginning, Victor thought. He had two sons. He had chosen to give everything to the wrong one.

Twenty-eight

I spoke with Dr. Van Dyke yesterday. She informed me that you haven't returned any of her calls." The Old Man looked at Luke across the width of the library. "She says you appear to be refusing to face your issues. You may be in some kind of denial, she says."

Luke came to a halt in front of the hearth and rested one arm on the carved oak mantel. He looked at the shelves full of heavy tomes and scientific papers that surrounded him. Every volume, journal and article in the extensive collection concerned the subject of wine making. Viticulture and enology were matters of great passion for everyone in the family except him.

It wasn't that he had not tried to follow in his father's footsteps. At various times in his life, including six months ago, he had made serious attempts to develop the kind of enthusiasm and all-consuming interest in wine making that drove his father and Gordon Foote and the others. But he had failed. In the end, he had always followed his own path, first into academia, then into the Marines and now into The Project.

He had known from the moment he and Irene arrived at the sprawling complex that housed the Elena Creek Vineyards cellars, wine-tasting facilities and reception rooms that sooner or later his father was going to corner him and raise the subject of Dr. Van Dyke.

He and Jason and Hackett referred to their father as the Old Man, but the term was in respectful recognition of John Danner's status as the eldest male in the family, not a comment on his advanced age.

The Old Man was, in fact, only in his late sixties. He had the hard, ageless face of a hawk, and thanks to a disciplined exercise regimen, some good genes and Vicki's strict attention to his diet, he possessed the physique and stamina of a much younger man.

Dressed in an elegantly tailored tuxedo, as he was tonight, with a glass of very good Elena Creek Vineyards cabernet in his hand, the Old Man looked as if he had been born prosperous, Luke thought. The truth was that he and Gordon Foote had fought their way up every rung of the ladder of success.

"I've been a little busy," Luke said.

John's heavy silver-gray brows bunched together in a watchful frown. "With Irene Stenson?"

"And the lodge," Luke said. He paused a beat. "Also, I'm doing a little writing."

John ignored the reference to the lodge and the writing. "Irene is an interesting woman," he said. "She seems intelligent. Quick. Rather striking."

"I see you noticed the dress," Luke said. "She looks good in it, doesn't she? Must be all that Pilates training."

"The what?"

"Never mind."

John snorted softly. "Jason tells me she's a reporter and that she has a troubled past."

Note to self, Luke thought. *Strangle youngest brother at earliest convenience.*

"Jason used the word 'troubled'?" he asked.

"No," John admitted with obvious reluctance. "But that was the implication."

"What, exactly, did he tell you about Irene?"

"Not a great deal. He seemed taken with her, to be honest. But then he explained that her father killed her mother in a murder-suicide years back and that Irene has cooked up some kind of crazy theory about Senator Webb's daughter having been murdered."

"There are a few murky details surrounding the death of Pamela Webb."

John's eyes sharpened. "I read in the paper that it was an accidental overdose involving meds and alcohol."

"Irene believes there is more to it. I'm inclined to agree."

John's mouth tightened. "I was afraid you were going to say that." He searched Luke's face with a worried expression. "Jason also told me that you were with Irene when she found Pamela Webb's body."

"Yes."

"That had to be very difficult for you, given what happened to your mother when you were a boy."

Luke swallowed some of the intense cabernet. "You've been talking to Dr. Van Dyke too much."

"I think you should talk to her, too."

"Haven't got time right now. Like I said, I'm busy."

John stirred, visibly annoyed. "What's all this about the senator's lake house burning to the ground?"

Luke smiled humorlessly. "Jason did a very good job of filling you in, didn't he? I'll have to speak to him about that."

"Don't blame your brother. I asked the questions. He answered. Look, I know you don't want to admit you might have some issues. No one wants to admit that they've got psychological problems. That goes double for men who have seen combat and probably quadruple for Marines. But Dr. Van Dyke says that PTSD is a wound, just like having shrapnel in a leg. It can fester if it isn't cleaned out."

"I'd like to know how Van Dyke can justify coming up with a diagnosis without ever interviewing the patient."

"That's exactly why she thinks you should make an appointment with her. She wants to get a solid diagnosis. Even though you refuse to talk about it, we all know that you went through some terrible stuff during your last couple of years in the Corps. No one can be exposed to that kind of thing and not be affected."

"I never said it didn't affect me. What I've said is that I'm dealing with it."

"The hell you are. After you got out of the Marines you were unable to adjust to working here at the winery. You failed to establish a normal, intimate relationship with the woman you planned to marry and had to end your engagement—"

"Dad, this isn't a good time."

"Then you take yourself off to the middle of nowhere, buy a third-rate, fleabag motel and get involved with a rather odd woman who appears to be trying to construct a conspiracy theory about the death of the daughter of a U.S. senator. I don't need a degree in psychology or psychiatry to know that doesn't sound exactly normal."

The door opened before Luke could come up with a response.

Gordon Foote walked into the room. He took in the scene with a knowing expression and raised his eyebrows at John.

"Sorry to interrupt," he said. "Should I go back out and come in again?"

"Don't bother," John growled. "You're family. Not the first time you've seen Luke and me go at it."

That was no less than the truth, Luke thought. Gordon had been his father's friend and partner since before Luke was born. The bond between the two men had been forged when they were enthusiastic students in the wine-making program at the University of California at Davis. Together they had built a dream. Elena Creek Vineyards had survived economic recessions, drastic changes in the global marketplace and a number of earthquakes. Today it thrived, thanks to the dedication and effort of these two men.

In many ways the pair could not have been more different. Gordon was the easygoing, genial sort, the kind of man who could walk into a room full of strangers and, within ten minutes, be on a first-name basis with everyone. Women loved to dance with him. Men enjoyed his company. Hostesses knew that the easiest way to ensure a successful party was to make certain that Gordon Foote got an invitation.

Even Gordon's ex-wife was fond of him, although she had left him several years ago during one of the downturns in the wine market. She had assumed, as many in the industry had, that Elena Creek Vineyards was headed for bankruptcy. By the time it became clear that the company was destined to flourish, she had remarried.

Gordon had remained happily single, devoted equally to the business and to his daughter, Katy. As far as Luke could determine, he did not lack for feminine companionship.

Gordon crossed the room to where the open bottle of cabernet stood on a side table. He gave Luke a wry, commiserating look. "Who's winning this one?"

"It's a draw so far." Luke smiled slightly. "Neither of us is giving an inch."

"What else is new?" Gordon raised his glass in a mocking salute. "Don't let me stop the two of you. Always fun to watch the fireworks."

John moved his hand in a let's-change-the-subject motion. "I assume you were sent in here to fetch me?"

"Afraid so." Gordon grinned and rocked on his heels. "The big cake event will commence in fifteen minutes. You've got a few billion candles to blow out, and then you get to take Vicki onto the dance floor for the annual birthday waltz."

John groaned. "I hate the candle part."

Gordon chuckled. "Tradition must be honored. Don't worry, I made sure that there'll be a fire extinguisher nearby."

Luke decided to seize his opportunity. He started toward the door. "I'd better go find my date."

"Last I saw of Miss Stenson, she was outside on the terrace talking to Vicki," Gordon offered helpfully.

"Just the scenario I was hoping to avoid," Luke said.

John scowled. "You can't blame Vicki for being curious about her."

"Your dad's right," Gordon said. Some of his cheerful, bantering air evaporated. Concern took its place. "From what Jason told us about Miss Stenson this evening, she sounds a little unusual, to say the least."

Luke nodded. "Works for me."

He opened the door and let himself out of the room.

Gordon watched guilt and a father's fear coalesce on the face of his old friend. The signs and indications were subtle: the white brackets at the edge of his mouth, the way he gripped the wineglass. Most people would not have noticed. But he and John had known each other for a very long time.

He picked up the bottle, crossed the room and refilled John's glass.

"Take it easy," he said quietly.

"How the hell am I supposed to do that?" John swallowed more wine and lowered the glass. "Luke's in serious trouble. It was bad enough that he fell apart after he and Katy ended their engagement. But now he's involved with a woman who may be in worse shape than he is."

"Maybe you should back off and give him some time and space, John."

John raised stark eyes to look at him. "If I give him too much time and space, I may lose him. Van Dyke says this PTSD thing is unpredictable. There's no telling what might happen if I don't get him into treatment."

Gordon put his hand on John's shoulder. "This is about Sarah, isn't it?"

"Hell, yes, it's about Sarah." John shoved himself up out of his chair and started to pace the room. "He's her son. Van Dyke says that a tendency toward depression and self-destructive behavior can have a strong genetic component. Add to that the trauma of combat and what happened to him the weekend he and Katy went away together, and you've got a very dangerous mix."

"He's your son, too, and he's got your genes. He's not a carbon copy of Sarah."

"I know that." John shoved his hands through his hair. "But I can't take the risk of hoping that he'll pull out of this on his own. Van Dyke says he may be a ticking bomb."

"I know this is hard on you, John. It's hard on me, too. I've known Luke since he was born. You think I'm not worried about him? But he's a grown man, not a boy. You can advise, but you can't force him to seek counseling."

"What am I supposed to do?" John stopped in front of the hearth. "Pretend that he's going to get better on his own? Ignore all the signs the way I did with his mother?"

"You did not ignore Sarah. She was clinically depressed. You are not responsible for the fact that she took her own life."

"Maybe not." John turned around very slowly. "But I don't think I could live with myself if Luke did something like that."

"Luke has always gone his own way. And he can be extremely stubborn." He smiled wearily. "Like I said, he's your son, John."

"I talked to Van Dyke again this afternoon." John's face went stony with renewed resolve. "I told her that Luke would be in town tonight and tomorrow morning. She said there was one more thing we could try. But she needs the cooperation of everyone in the family. That includes you."

"I'm not sure this is a good idea, whatever it is. But you're my friend. You know damn well you don't have to ask me twice to help you."

Twenty-nine

Vicki Danner was a stylish woman with an assured, self-confident manner. Her patrician features showed the long-term benefits of regular professional facials. Of course, Irene thought, the good bones didn't hurt. Dressed in a classic gray sheath, diamonds glittering in her ears and around her throat, she was the picture of expensive, tasteful elegance.

Irene had seen Vicki in action earlier in the evening and knew that John Danner's wife could be incredibly charming. But at the moment, Vicki was not in charm mode. She wanted answers and she intended to get them.

"Are you involved in Luke's new business venture?" Vicki asked with a thin smile.

Irene blanked. "Business venture?"

"The ridiculous little motel he bought in Dunsley."

"Oh, the lodge." Irene took a sip of her sauvignon blanc while she considered her answer. "Hard to think of that as a viable business venture, to tell you the truth. At least not with Luke at the helm. But to answer your question, no, I'm not involved. I'm happy with my job at the *Beacon*. The doughnuts are better."

"I beg your pardon?"

"Forget it."

"How did you meet Luke?" Vicki asked.

"You could say I paid for the introduction."

Vicki frowned.

"I meant I'm a paying guest at the lodge," Irene said hastily.

"This is just a casual relationship, then?"

Irene thought about the kaleidoscopic series of events that had taken place since she first encountered Luke, culminating in the most intense sexual experience of her entire life.

"Not any longer," she said, feeling decidedly more cheerful and relaxed. The wine was working, she thought.

Vicki's smile held no hint of warmth. "When did you find out that Luke's father owns half of the Elena Creek Vineyards?"

"Jason mentioned it when he visited Luke in Dunsley the other day."

"And the next thing we know, Luke is bringing you to a private family gathering. Interesting."

Irene looked through the windows at the large, well-heeled crowd milling around the winery's resplendent main reception room. "Gee, I wouldn't consider that an event with a guest list of a few hundred people qualified as a private family gathering. But I suppose it's all relative, isn't it?"

Vicki looked baffled. "What?"

Irene cleared her throat. "That was supposed to be a clever little play on words. Family gathering? Relative? Get it?"

Vicki glanced past Irene's right shoulder. "Here comes Katy. You two met earlier, I believe."

"Yes." Irene braced herself and turned to smile at the lovely woman gliding toward them across the terrace.

Blond, blue-eyed and dainty, Katy Foote was one of those delicate, ethereal-looking women who made men want to strap on shining armor and go out to slay a few dragons. But within five seconds of meeting her, Irene had decided that she liked her, anyway.

Katy wore a gown of pale azure silk that screamed high-end designer. In a very subtle way, of course.

It dawned on Irene that, dressed in the severely cut little black number that she had managed to find on the marked-down rack in a mall department store that afternoon, she probably looked like the Wicked Witch of Glaston Cove standing next to a dignified queen and a lovely fairy-tale princess.

There's a reason why clothes end up on sale, she reminded herself. It's because no one else wanted them. But she had not been able to justify digging into her hard-earned savings to buy a fabulously expensive gown for the evening, knowing that she would probably never wear the dress again.

"Hello, Katy," Vicki said. "I was just talking to Irene about how she came to meet Luke. She told me that she's staying at his lodge in Dunsley."

"Yes, I know." Katy laughed. "I have to admit, I can't imagine Luke as an innkeeper." She gave Irene an amused look. "Does he issue long lists of rules to his guests?"

At that moment, Irene spotted Luke coming toward her. He was accompanied by his father, Jason and Hackett.

"Let's just say that checkout times are strictly enforced at Sunrise on the Lake Lodge," she said.

She turned to watch the men approach. She had met Hackett and John earlier when she and Luke arrived. She had also had a chance to greet Jason. But this was the first time she had seen all four of the Danner men grouped closely together. Each was impressive in his own right, but taken en masse and dressed in hand-tailored tuxes they were enough to make any woman sit up and take notice.

All three of John Danner's sons had their father's bird-of-prey eyes, but aside from that feature, there was little resemblance. It was obvious that Hackett and Jason owed their good-looking, aristocratic features to Vicki.

The men came to a halt. Irene noticed that Hackett looked first at Katy. The pair exchanged a silent message. Katy's gaze slid away first. Irene thought she saw a melancholy shadow cross her pretty features.

"I can't believe another year has slipped past." John took Vicki's hand and threaded her fingers through his own. He smiled down at her. "Where does the time go?"

"Don't pay any attention to the Old Man," Jason said to Irene. "He says that every year."

"That's because it's true every year." John dropped a light, affectionate kiss on Vicki's cheek. "But at least these damn birthday parties give me an excuse to dance with the most beautiful woman in the world."

Vicki's expression softened. *She loves him,* Irene thought. *And he loves her. Mom and Dad used to look at each other that way.*

"You aren't growing older," Vicki said lightly. "You're just getting more distinguished."

"Could have fooled me," Jason said. He scrutinized his father closely. "Sure looks old."

"Old and sneaky beats young and smart-mouthed every time," John warned.

"There you all are." Gordon Foote hurried across the terrace to take Katy's arm. "The cake is about to be set afire, and the musicians are ready for the waltz. Better get moving, folks."

John, with Vicki by his side, started toward the reception room. But he paused to look back at Luke.

"By the way," he said, "I meant to tell you earlier that Hackett, Jason, Gordon and I have made arrangements for you to join us for breakfast at The Vineyard before you leave town tomorrow. You know the restaurant. It's right across from the inn. They've reserved the private room for us."

Irene tensed. Luke's father had issued the invitation a little too casually, she thought. There was a false quality in the words that set her nerves on edge. She glanced at Luke, curious about his reaction.

"Irene and I had planned to get an early start," he said, evidently oblivious.

"No problem," John assured him. "We'll eat early."

"I think that sounds like an excellent idea," Vicki said with a sudden show of determined enthusiasm. "Katy and I will take Irene to breakfast in the main section of the restaurant while the five of you get together in the private room. It will give you men a chance to spend some quality time together."

"You gotta eat in the morning, anyway," Jason reminded Luke cheerfully. "You know how you are about breakfast."

"Might as well have it with us before you take off," Hackett added.

Luke shrugged. "If you don't mind, Irene?"

"Don't worry about me," she said quickly. Whatever was going on here, it was a family matter. The smart thing to do was stay out of it.

"We'll take good care of her," Vicki assured Luke. "Won't we, Katy?"

"Yes, of course." Katy smiled. "Great idea."

"Thanks," Irene said, feeling her way.

"That's settled, then." John drew Vicki forward again. "Ready, my dear?"

She gripped his arm very tightly. "Yes."

He guided her toward the open French doors. Gordon, Katy, Hackett and Jason followed swiftly.

Irene found herself alone with Luke. Together they watched the small group disappear into the reception room.

"What was that all about?" she asked.

"Damned if I know. Guess I'll find out in the morning. Can't be too bad if it includes breakfast."

"Seriously, Luke."

"Seriously? Got a hunch that tomorrow morning at breakfast I will receive yet another offer I can't refuse to come back to the family business."

She relaxed slightly. "That sounds plausible. Your family is genuinely worried about you, Luke."

"I know, but there's not much I can do about that." He took her hand. "So, what do you say we eat some cake, drink more wine and dance, instead?"

"Sounds like a plan."

Thirty

A long time later Luke followed Irene through the doorway of the inn room. He gave the space a quick, assessing survey. Before leaving earlier, Irene had left lights burning in both the bedroom and the bath. She had also plugged night-lights into two wall sockets, one in each room. He saw her relax ever so subtly when she had satisfied herself that the place was still fully illuminated.

"I thought that went rather well, all things considered," Irene said, sinking down on the edge of the bed. "But I've got some questions for you."

He watched her bend down to unfasten her sexy, black, high-heeled sandals. The intimacy of the situation filled him with a head-spinning heat. This was right, he thought. Coming back here together, watching her undress, it all felt right.

"What kind of questions?" he asked, peeling off the tux jacket.

"For starters, what's going on between Hackett and Katy?"

That stopped him cold. "Hackett and Katy?"

"Is there a problem there?"

"Not that I know of." He stopped in front of the mirror and loosened his tie. "What makes you think there might be?"

She straightened and met his eyes in the mirror. "Something about the way your brother kept watching her all evening. And the way she acted whenever he was close to her. I sensed some tension there."

"Beats me. But I don't think there's anything to worry about. Those two have known each other forever. If there's a problem, they'll work it out."

"I'm sure you're right." She tipped her head slightly and reached up to remove one glittery earring. "None of my business, anyway."

He turned around and went very deliberately toward her. "You're wrong, it is your business."

She was startled. "Why do you say that?"

"You're with me now." He reached down and raised her gently to her feet. "Like it or not, while we're together, you're involved with my family. That gives you a license to comment."

"You're sure?"

"I'm sure."

"Well, then, I think your family is very nice."

"Yeah?" He was amused. "The words that come to my mind are 'interfering,' 'meddling' and 'intrusive.'"

She laughed, "That, too. Guess it's a family thing."

He moved his fingers to the back of the little black dress and slowly lowered the zipper. "Luckily none of the members of my family are around at the moment. So tell me, do you always wear black?"

"No," she said. "Sometimes I wear nothing at all."

"Works for me."

I rene stirred amid the rumpled sheets. The lovemaking had left her feeling boneless, utterly content and curiously calm deep inside. The feeling wouldn't last, she knew, but for now it was enough.

In the glow of the night-light she could see Luke sprawled on his stomach beside her. His face was turned away on the pillow. The white sheet draped carelessly across his lower body. He looked exotic and mysterious and very male lying there beside her, an exciting creature of the night who had materialized out of her most intimate fantasies.

She stroked the sleek contours of his back, enjoying the heat and strength he exuded.

"Are you awake?" she whispered.

"I am now." He rolled onto his back and folded his arms behind his head. "What's the matter? Can't sleep?"

"More questions."

"Let's have 'em."

"I know I shouldn't bring up the subject," she said, "especially at a time like this. All of the advice books say that it's a mistake to talk about previous relationships, especially in bed."

He freed one hand, caught and kissed her fingers.

"This is about Katy, isn't it?" he said.

"Well, I am a little curious," she admitted. "Tonight I could see that the two of you were on friendly terms. There was obviously no animosity between you. In fact, you both seemed quite fond of each other. I just can't help myself, I have to ask. Why didn't things work out between the two of you?"

For a moment she thought he wasn't going to answer. He studied the bedroom ceiling as though searching for inspiration.

"It was my fault," he said finally.

"How is that?"

"I told you that when I got out of the Marines I planned a strategy designed to make me fit into the real world."

She nodded. "You told me that marrying Katy was part of that strategy."

"It took me a while, but it eventually dawned on me that she agreed to marry me because she was too kindhearted and too concerned about me to turn me down."

That gave her pause. "Are you sure about that?"

He exhaled deeply. "Everyone in the family thought the marriage was a terrific idea. They put Katy under a tremendous amount of pressure. I think she was given the clear impression that if she rejected me I might jump off a bridge."

"And you came to this realization in the course of that unfortunate weekend on the coast?"

"I sure did." He paused, looking reflective. "I had that weekend all planned out, same way I had every other element of my strategy planned. Booked the honeymoon suite."

"Oh, my."

"You should have seen the room. It looked like a damned wedding cake. All pale blue and white with lots of gold touches everywhere. The bed was round and there was this stupid lacy thing draped over the top. The bathroom was marble with gold fixtures."

"Gosh. Doesn't sound quite like the honeymoon suite at the Sunrise on the Lake Lodge."

He slanted her a dangerous look. "You want to hear this story or not?"

She drew her knees up and wrapped her arms around them. "I can't wait for the rest. What happened next?"

"I went into the bathroom to get undressed, that's what happened next."

"And?" she prompted.

He cleared his throat. "I looked at myself in the mirror, realized that I was way too old for Katy and had my little epiphany."

She clapped a hand over her mouth to stifle the giggles that were rushing up inside her. "I think I've got the visuals."

"You've heard about the bride who is too nervous to come out of the bathroom on her wedding night?"

"Yes."

"Gotta tell you, it's a heck of a lot less amusing when the one hiding in the bathroom is the groom. Or, in this case, the fiancé."

She buried her face in her hands.

"You're laughing, aren't you?" He sounded grimly resigned. "I knew this would happen."

"I can't help it. I'm sorry. It must have been awful for both of you."

"You've got a warped sense of humor, woman."

She raised her head. "What on earth did you do?"

"What the hell do you think I did? I finally opened the bathroom door and told Katy it wasn't going to work. I got the feeling that she was secretly relieved. But she leaped to the conclusion that the real reason I was ending things was that I had this little physical problem due to my presumed case of PTSD."

"And the conversation went downhill from there?"

"It certainly did."

"You let the impression that you had an erectile dysfunction problem stand?"

He cocked a brow. "That's just it, there wasn't anything standing."

"Oh. Right."

"How was I supposed to prove that I didn't have a problem in that department?"

"I see what you mean."

"I told her that I wasn't ready for an intimate relationship with any woman. Said I needed my space, that I wanted time to get my act together, blah, blah, blah and so on and so forth. She told me she understood, and we agreed to call the whole thing off."

Irene recalled her impressions of Katy that evening. "She doesn't seem to be carrying a torch for you."

"I told you, she was privately very relieved to be off the hook." He sighed. "I should have realized a lot sooner that she was acting out of guilt and concern, but I was too obsessed with my strategy."

She studied him intently. "How do you feel about her?"

"Katy is like a kid sister to me. Actually, that was probably the main problem, come to think of it." He shrugged. "Be that as it may, when we got home and announced that we had called off the engagement, it was clear that something had gone very wrong and that it was my fault. Then I quit my job at the winery, moved to Dunsley and went into the innkeeping business. Next thing I know I'm ducking calls from Dr. Van Dyke."

"Who is she?"

"A shrink who happens to be an old family friend. My father took me to see her a few times in the months following my mother's death. After the weekend disaster, Vicki and the Old Man contacted her and asked her to consult."

"You can't blame your family for jumping to conclusions," Irene said gently.

"Maybe not, but this particular conclusion has proven to be damned irritating."

"Okay, I can understand your point of view."

He smiled slowly, put an arm around her waist and tumbled her down across his chest. "The good news, however, is that I can say with great certainty that at least one of my symptoms has improved since that fiasco in the honeymoon suite."

"I couldn't help but notice." She slid her hand beneath the edge of the sheet and found the hard, satisfyingly rigid length of him with her fingers. "But I suppose it's not exactly the sort of misunderstanding you can clear up in the course of casual conversation with your nearest and dearest, is it?"

"It happens to be the last thing on earth that I want to discuss with my family, a shrink or anyone else, for that matter. As far as I'm concerned, the less said on the subject, the better."

"Got it." She brushed her mouth lightly across his. "What would you like to talk about, instead?"

He eased her onto her back and lightly pinned her wrists above her head. Slowly he lowered his mouth to hers.

"I'll think of something," he said.

Thirty-one

A light rain blanketed the gently rolling landscape that surrounded the picturesque town of Santa Elena the following morning. The vineyards that encircled the community and stretched into the hills beyond were veiled by mist.

It was such a safe, comfortable, self-contained little world, Luke thought, a world he had known from the cradle. Too bad he would never be able to settle into this pleasant realm the way Hackett and Jason had. The wine-making life was a good one, but it required a passion that he could not give it.

But he did have other passions, he thought. Irene was now at the top of the list.

She looked at him from beneath her umbrella. "Something wrong?"

"No. Just thinking."

"About what?"

"That I wasn't cut out to be a winemaker."

"What do you think you were designed to do?"

"Funny you should ask." He draped one arm around her shoulders, surprised to find himself feeling not just protective but possessive. "I seem to be in the process of discovering the answer to that question." He studied the warmly lit windows of The Vineyard restaurant across the street. "Let's go. Time to do breakfast. Forty-five minutes and we're out of there."

"Only forty-five minutes?"

"I want to get on the road as soon as possible." Luke checked his watch. "I'll listen to the new job offer while I eat. I'll turn it down very politely, and you and I will leave."

"Fine by me. But that may be cutting it a bit short as far as your family is concerned."

"I warned the Old Man that I didn't plan to hang around here long this morning. It's an hour's drive into the city. The idea is to catch Hoyt Egan at his apartment this morning, remember?"

Her expression tightened. "I remember."

The Vineyard was surprisingly crowded with early morning breakfast eaters. A young woman dressed in jeans and a white shirt greeted them cheerfully.

"Hi, Brenda," Luke said. "I'd like you to meet Irene Stenson. Irene, this is Brenda Bains. Her father, George, owns this place."

"How do you do?" Irene said.

"Nice to meet you, Miss Stenson." Brenda picked up a menu. "We've been expecting you." She looked at Luke. "Your dad, Mr. Foote and your brothers are waiting for you in the private dining room at the back, Mr. Danner."

"I know the way," Luke said.

"If you'll follow me, Miss Stenson." Brenda turned. "Mrs. Danner and Katy are at a table near the window."

"Thanks," Irene said.

"Forty-five minutes," Luke reminded her.

She gave him an amused look and allowed herself to be led away across the restaurant.

He watched her for a moment, enjoying the sleek, graceful sway of her hips. Then he picked up the day's edition of a San Francisco paper that was lying on the counter and scanned the headlines while he walked toward the rear of the restaurant.

The Webb campaign had done an excellent job of keeping Pamela's death a low-profile event, he noticed. He had to turn to page three before he found a photo of Ryland Webb and Alexa Douglass emerging from a funeral chapel hand in hand. Both were dressed in somber, dignified, well-tailored black.

Behind Ryland and Alexa stood a much older, gray-haired man. The caption identified him as Victor Webb, Pamela's grandfather. This was the Webb Maxine had said everyone liked, Luke reminded himself, the one who had done so much for the people of Dunsley.

He read the short article that accompanied the photo. There was nothing unexpected or startling in it.

. . . Following the private service, Senator Webb met briefly with reporters. He requested that the privacy of his family be respected. He also stated that when he returns to Washington he intends to work for legislation aimed at dealing with mental health and drug addiction issues. "This sort of tragedy has befallen far too many people in this country," he stated. "It is time the government took action. . . ."

Luke stopped in front of the private dining room. He tucked the newspaper under one arm and opened the double doors.

The Old Man, Jason, Hackett and Gordon Foote were seated at the polished wooden table. There was no coffee on the table. No cutlery, plates, napkins or menus, either. Bad sign, Luke thought.

The group at the table looked at him with varying expressions of concern and resolve.

A thin woman stepped out of the small butler's pantry at the side of the room. She was professionally dressed in a tweed suit and sensible shoes. Oversized, black-framed glasses endowed her with an academic air. She fixed Luke with a sincere, kindly but very determined expression.

"Hello, Luke," Dr. Van Dyke said quietly. "It's been a long time."

"Does this mean I don't get breakfast?" Luke asked.

I t's called an intervention," Vicki explained.

Irene choked on a bite of muffin that she had just slathered with butter. "A *what*?"

"An intervention," Katy said hastily. "It's a psychological technique that is used to confront a person who is exhibiting self-destructive behavior patterns. The idea is to force the individual to admit that he has problems and that he needs help."

"I know what an intervention is." Irene swallowed hastily and stared at Katy and Vicki, appalled. "But you don't understand. Luke thinks he's going to get breakfast and an offer of a job this morning."

"Lot of good it would do to ask him to come back to the business," Vicki said. "John tried that approach. It was a disaster."

"Ambushing Luke with a shrink is probably not a real good idea," Irene said uneasily.

Vicki frowned. "Don't be ridiculous. What's taking place in that room isn't an ambush. John and the others are trying to save Luke from himself. This is a last-ditch effort to make him confront his underlying issues."

"We've tried everything else," Katy added. "He refuses to talk about his problems. He won't even admit that he has problems."

"Dr. Van Dyke told John that an intervention was the only option left," Vicki said.

Irene signaled to a hovering waiter. He hurried over.

"Yes, ma'am?"

"I'd like the spinach and feta cheese omelet to go. Would you please ask the cook to rush the order?"

"Of course." He turned to Vicki and Katy. "Ladies? May I take your orders?"

Vicki was disconcerted. "Just coffee for now."

"Same for me," Katy said hurriedly.

"Thank you." The waiter turned to Irene. "I'll make certain that the kitchen receives your request to hurry up the order."

"Thanks," she said.

Vicki waited until the waiter had left and then glowered at Irene. "Why did you ask him to rush your omelet?"

"Because I have a feeling I'm not going to be here very long." Irene stuffed the last bit of muffin into her mouth and smiled at Vicki. "Mind passing the bread basket again?"

Luke, your family and friends arranged this meeting because they are deeply concerned about you," Dr. Van Dyke said. "We all are."

"Got a rule," Luke said. "I never talk about my psychological problems before breakfast." He opened the double doors of the private room.

Behind him, John slammed a fist down on the table. "Damnit, Luke, don't you dare walk out of this room."

"I'm not going anywhere, sir. Not just yet, at least. This is sort of amusing, in a weird kind of way." Luke spotted a harried young man in a white coat in the hall. "Any chance you could find me some coffee and a cup, Bruce?"

"Sure, Mr. Danner. Be right back."

"Thanks."

Luke closed the doors again and turned to look at the others. "Now then, what did you say this ambush was called?"

Jason grimaced. "An intervention. And I would like to go on record as having told everyone present that it wouldn't work."

Hackett leaned back in his chair and shoved his hands into

his pockets. "I said the same thing or words to that effect. I believe 'really stupid idea' was the exact phrase I used."

Luke noticed that the Old Man, Gordon and the obviously intrepid Dr. Van Dyke did not look happy with the direction of the conversation.

"We are all agreed that you need help, Luke," Van Dyke reminded the group.

"She's right," Gordon said heavily. "Luke, you haven't been yourself since you got out of the Marines. You know that."

"You're in a downward spiral, son," John said gravely. "We're trying to stop it before it goes too far. Dr. Van Dyke has a plan."

"Plans are good," Luke said. "I have a few of my own."

A knock interrupted him. He turned back around and opened the doors. Bruce stood there with a tray.

"Coffee and a cup, sir."

"Thanks." Luke took the tray from him.

Bruce looked at the small crowd behind Luke. "Should I bring some more cups?"

"No," Luke said, edging one door closed with the toe of his shoe. "I don't think anyone else here is interested in coffee this morning. They're too busy intervening."

He nudged the other door shut and carried the pot and the cup to the table.

John's face tightened angrily. "I've had enough. You've got problems. Admit it."

Luke poured coffee into the cup. "Everyone has problems."

"Not like yours," Dr. Van Dyke said in a calm, authoritative manner. "Given your history, it is entirely possible that you are suffering from post-traumatic stress disorder with symptoms of anxiety, depression, erectile dysfunction and hypervigilance."

Luke paused with the cup halfway to his mouth. "Hypervigilance?"

"That jumpy, easily startled feeling," Van Dyke explained.

"Right." He nodded. "I drink coffee for that."

Out of the corner of his eye he saw Jason exchange a look with Hackett, who shook his head in silent warning. Gordon's expression tightened. The Old Man seemed to slump a little in his chair.

The others were giving up already, Luke concluded. But Dr. Van Dyke was evidently made of sterner stuff. Oblivious to the changing mood in the room, she plowed onward.

"The best way to approach your issues in a constructive fashion is for you to start therapy immediately," she declared. "Initially we will meet three times a week starting today. In addition, I will prescribe medications to ease your anxiety and depression. There are also meds for your erectile dysfunction problem."

"Good to know." Luke swallowed some coffee.

Irene looked at Vicki. "Mrs. Danner, I understand that, as Luke's mother, you're naturally very worried about him."

"I am not his mother."

"Stepmother, I mean," Irene said quickly.

Vicki's elegantly manicured fingers tightened on the delicate handle of the coffee cup. "Let's get something clear, Irene. I do not know what Luke has told you about our relationship, but I can assure you that he does not consider me to be his mother or stepmother. I am his father's wife."

"Well, yes, certainly, but—"

Vicki sighed. "From day one Luke made it plain that he did not need or want a mother. I will never forget my first impression of him when John introduced us. I swear, that boy was ten years old going on forty."

Katy frowned a little. "Luke is very fond of you, Vicki, you know that."

"He wasn't at the beginning," Vicki said grimly. "At first I made the mistake of trying to take the place of the mother he had lost. But by that point Luke and his father, together with Gordon, had been an all-male team for several years. Luke liked the situation just the way it was." The cup trembled ever so slightly in her fingers. "I've often wondered if I'm the one who drove him out of the family."

Irene took another muffin out of the basket. "What do you mean?"

"Perhaps if I hadn't come into his life, if I hadn't taken so much of his father's attention and then provided him with two younger half brothers, maybe Luke wouldn't have felt compelled to go into academia and then into the Marines." She paused. "And if he hadn't done that, maybe he wouldn't be in the situation he's in today."

"Whoa, wait, stop right there." Irene waved her napkin wildly in front of Vicki's distraught face. "Get a grip, lady. This is Luke we're talking about. He marches to the beat of his own drummer. This is one man who for sure makes his own choices. You are not responsible for him joining the Marines or buying the lodge or anything else he chooses to do."

"John is so very anxious about him," Vicki whispered.

"Luke is okay," Irene said.

Vicki looked at her, seeking reassurance. "Are you sure? Do you think he'll come back to the business?"

Irene considered briefly. "If Elena Creek Vineyards was in serious trouble and if he thought he might be able to help save it, Luke would come back. He knows how much the business means to everyone in the family. Given his sense of loyalty and responsibility, it's safe to say that he would make a rescue attempt if necessary. But otherwise, no. He has his own plans."

"Operating the Sunrise on the Lake Lodge?" Vicki said. "That's ridiculous. Luke is no innkeeper. He belongs at the winery."

Katy looked thoughtful. "You know, Irene has a point. Six months ago, like everyone else, I was focused on trying to help Luke adjust to life here in Santa Elena because I knew that's what Uncle John, Dad and you thought would be best for him. But when I think back, I can see that maybe we were wrong to try to push him into the business and into marriage. Maybe all we were really doing was applying more pressure at a point in his life when that was the last thing he needed."

This time Irene flapped the napkin in Katy's face, instead of Vicki's. "Don't go there, either. There's no call to blame yourselves for urging Luke to join the business, get married and act normal. For a while, that was what he thought he wanted. Trust me, if Luke hadn't been on board with the plan, it wouldn't have gotten as far as it did. Or haven't you noticed that he isn't very easy to manipulate?"

Katy smiled wryly. "None of the males in this family are easily manipulated."

Vicki made a face. "Stubborn and hardheaded, every last one of them."

Irene put the napkin back in her lap. "Luke knows what he's doing." At that moment she caught sight of him making his way across the restaurant toward her. "Oops, gotta go. There's my ride."

"What?" Katy turned and saw Luke. "Uh-oh. I've got a feeling the intervention didn't go well."

Vicki watched Luke with an anxious expression. "Dr. Van Dyke told John that the intervention would last at least an hour and that she hoped to take Luke immediately into a private therapy session afterward."

"Someone should have warned Dr. Van Dyke that Luke usually has his own agenda," Irene said.

Luke reached the table and halted. "Morning, ladies. Nice day for an intervention, isn't it?" He looked at Irene. "Don't know about you, but I've had my fun. Time to leave."

"I was pretty sure you were going to say that." Irene jumped to her feet and seized a fresh napkin. "Hang on a sec."

She spread the napkin on the table, picked up the bread basket and dumped the remaining muffins into the center of the linen square. Working quickly she folded the goodies into the napkin and knotted the ends.

The waiter appeared with a takeout container. "Your omelet, ma'am. There's a plastic knife and fork and some napkins, too."

"Right on time, thanks." Irene took the container from him, grabbed her coat off the back of the chair, slipped the strap of her purse over her shoulder and smiled at Luke. "I'm ready."

"Let's go," he said.

Jason, Hackett, Gordon and John hurried across the restaurant. A woman wearing a tweed suit and shoes that had obviously been designed for comfort, not style, followed in their wake. Dr. Van Dyke, Irene thought.

"Luke, wait," John ordered.

"Sorry, Dad." Luke steered Irene toward the door. "We've got some things to do in the city."

The woman in the tweed suit loomed directly in front of Irene, accusation radiating from her in waves.

"You are enabling his behavior," the woman said quietly.

"Not exactly," Irene said. "Luke pretty much does his own thing."

"I know you want what is best for him. We all do. That's why I'm here."

Irene glanced quickly around at the circle of concerned faces, trying to think of something she could say that would reassure all these people who obviously cared so much about Luke. Inspiration struck.

"If it helps," she said, "I can assure you that there's no need to worry about Luke's erectile dysfunction problems."

"Irene," Luke muttered, "If you don't mind—"

"He's definitely normal in that department," Irene continued quickly, eager to make her point. "Actually, he's a lot bigger than normal."

A great hush had fallen across the entire restaurant. It dawned on her that everyone was staring at her as though mesmerized.

Jason grinned. "Boy, howdy."

Bigger, she thought, had been an unfortunate choice of words.

"I mean *better* than normal," she said quickly.

She could tell immediately that the hasty rephrasing wasn't quite right, either.

"I feel a little faint," she said to Luke.

"That's funny, I feel like I just fell into a pharmaceutical commercial," he said. "I believe this is one of those situations that call for a strategic retreat."

"Yes, please."

He hauled her forcefully toward the door, pausing long enough to collect the umbrella from a wide-eyed Brenda.

A few seconds later Irene found herself outside in the misty rain.

There was a short, freighted silence.

Irene cleared her throat. "I assume you didn't get breakfast or a job offer."

"No."

"Bummer."

"The way I look at it, this day has nowhere to go but up," Luke said.

"Now there's an optimistic, glass-half-full kind of statement."

He ignored that. "What's in the box?"

"Spinach and feta cheese omelet. When I heard about the intervention I had a feeling we might be leaving early. Don't let the rain hit the muffins."

Luke's teeth flashed in a quick grin. "You know, I could have done without the public discussion of my erectile dysfunction issues, but I've got to admit that I do admire a woman who can manage to produce breakfast in a high-stress situation like that."

Thirty-two

The morning fog still clung to the city when Luke wedged the SUV into an empty space at the end of a quiet residential neighborhood. He switched off the engine, folded his arms on the steering wheel and studied the terrain.

The street where Hoyt Egan lived was lined on both sides with modern apartment complexes, the type that were designed to appeal to successful singles and the upwardly mobile. Each building had been given an attractive, Italianate façade. But when he looked past the superficial architectural elements, it was easy to see the basic square boxes behind the artfully sculpted windows and doorways.

"You're sure this is the right address?" Irene asked, opening her door.

"Pulled it off the Internet this morning."

"You're certain that he's home?"

"His office staff was very helpful when I asked about his schedule today."

"What did you do? Promise to make a big contribution to Webb's campaign?"

"There may have been that implication," he admitted.

He climbed out and waited for Irene to join him on the sidewalk. Together they walked toward the entrance to Egan's apartment building. The ornate sign over the elaborately worked wrought-iron gates identified the complex as the Palladium.

Irene stopped, her hands in the pockets of her coat, and looked at the security intercom. "What makes you think he'll see us?"

"Don't worry, Egan will buzz us inside so fast it will make your head spin."

"Why?"

"Pure fear. Works every time."

Her expression transformed into a sunny smile. "Fear of you. Sure, that makes sense."

He was amused. "Don't get me wrong, I appreciate your faith in me, but I can't take the credit. In this case, we're talking fear of bad publicity. Egan is in charge of handling a senator who is on the road to the White House. His job depends on how well he does damage control."

"I get it. We represent potential damage."

"We do, indeed." He punched the intercom button.

An impatient masculine voice, rendered tinny and scratchy by the intercom speaker, answered after only one ring.

"You got apartment three-oh-one," Hoyt said. "Is this a delivery?"

"You could call it that," Luke said. "Luke Danner. I'm with Irene Stenson. Remember us?"

There was an instant of frozen stillness on the other end of the connection.

"What do you want?" Hoyt demanded, voice sharpening.

"To talk to you," Luke said. "If you haven't got time—"

A screechy, buzzing sound interrupted him. Irene turned the handle and pushed open the gate that Hoyt had just unlocked.

"Come on up," Hoyt snapped.

The intercom immediately went dead.

Luke followed Irene through the gate into a small, tiled courtyard decorated with a fountain and a number of plants growing in earthenware pots. They crossed the courtyard and went through two heavy glass doors into a small lobby. There was a door marked MANAGER on one side. It was closed.

Irene started toward the elevator. Luke caught her by the arm.

"Let's use the stairs," he said.

"All right." She slanted him a curious look. "Any particular reason?"

"It's easier to get a feel for the layout of the place that way."

"Why would you want to do that?"

"Old habit," he said. "When you're dealing with people you're fairly sure don't have any reason to like you very much, you can never have enough intelligence."

"Ah, yes," she said with a wise air. "Intel."

"I prefer the term 'intelligence.' Sure, it's a big word for a Marine but now that I've mastered it, I like to use it."

The carpet that covered the third-floor hall hushed the sound of their footsteps, but Hoyt was obviously watching through the peephole because the door of 301 opened abruptly just as Luke raised his hand to knock.

"What's this all about?" Hoyt demanded, letting them into the small, mirrored foyer. "I'm in the middle of preparing for a series of meetings."

He wore an expensive-looking dress shirt and trousers. His shoes were freshly polished. He had not yet put on a tie, but Luke decided he was telling the truth about the meetings.

"We'll keep it short," Luke promised.

"This way." Hoyt angled his head toward the front room of the apartment.

It was obvious at a glance that Hoyt had made no effort to coordinate his interior decor with the Italian influence of the Palladium. In fact, as far as Luke could tell, there was no particular design motif to the space at all, unless Workaholic Political Aide qualified as a decorating style.

Luke counted four lines on the landline phone. Hoyt had another phone clipped to his belt. There was a fax machine in one corner and a copier in another. Most of the walls were covered with newspaper and magazine clippings featuring shots of Webb with various VIPs.

Irene came to a halt in the center of the cluttered living room and shoved her hands into the pockets of her trench coat.

"We want to know what you and Pamela argued about on the day before we found her body," she said.

Hoyt looked at her as though she had just turned into an alien life form before his very eyes. "What the hell are you talking about?"

"We know you went to see her in Dunsley." Luke made his way to the nearest wall and studied a photo of Ryland Webb emerging from a museum. Alexa Douglass and a young girl of about nine accompanied Webb. He glanced back over his shoulder. "We know you quarreled."

Hoyt went rigid. Luke could almost see him running scenarios in his head, deciding how to deal with this unexpected problem.

"You can't prove that," Hoyt said.

"Dunsley is a very small town." Irene smiled thinly. "Did you really think you could visit a member of the town's most high-profile family in the middle of the day and not be seen by someone?"

"No one there knows me or my car," he said automatically. It seemed to dawn on him that might not sound like the remark of an innocent man. "I wasn't trying to sneak around, damnit. All right, it's none of your business, but I did drive up there to talk to her that day. You can't make anything out of that. I sure as hell wasn't anywhere near Dunsley when she OD'd. She was fine when I left her."

"What did you and Pamela argue about?" Irene asked.

Hoyt's jaw flexed. "Why should I tell you?"

Luke looked at him. "Thing is, if you don't tell us why you quarreled with her, we're going to come to our own conclusions and some of those conclusions may wind up in Irene's newspaper. You really want that to happen?"

"You trying to scare me, Danner?"

Luke spread his hands. "Well, sure. Seems like the best way to get answers. Got a better idea?"

Irene scowled. "That's enough, both of you. Hoyt, please, it's important. I need to know what you and Pamela argued about."

"Why? So you can try to pin her death on me? Forget it."

She watched him thoughtfully. "You had an affair with her, didn't you?"

Hoyt hesitated. Once again Luke could see him doing mental calculations.

"We were an item for a while," he said slowly. "No more than a few weeks. It was no secret. What about it?"

"Pamela called it off, didn't she?" Irene said, her voice softening. "When she was a teen, it was always Pamela who ended things. I doubt that she changed much in that regard."

Hoyt's face turned a dull red. For a couple of seconds Luke thought he was going to explode. Instead he seemed to deflate.

"I guess I knew going in that it wouldn't last long," Hoyt said wearily. "Hell, I've worked for Webb for nearly two years. I'd seen Pamela in action. I knew the pattern. But like every other man who got pulled into her orbit, I thought I was different." He shook his head. "She was like a light fixture. When she wanted you, she turned herself on and glowed for you. When she got bored, she turned herself off. Left you standing in the dark wondering what had happened."

"When did she end your relationship?" Irene asked.

"Couple of days before she went to Dunsley." His mouth tightened. "She didn't give me any warning. We attended a fund-raiser together that evening. I took her home thinking that we were going to go to bed. She stopped at the door of her apartment and told me it had been fun but that it was over. Said good night and shut the door in my face. I was stunned, if you want to know the truth."

"What did you do?" Luke asked.

"What does any man do in a situation like that? I came back here and poured myself a large glass of scotch. The next day I tried calling her. There was no answer at her home here in the city. I finally tried the lake house. She answered the phone, but she made it clear she wasn't going to change her mind."

"But you drove up to the lake to see her, anyway," Irene said.

"For all the good it did." Hoyt went to the window and shoved his hands into his pockets. "She told me to go back to San Francisco. Said she had things to do."

"What kind of things?" Irene asked.

Hoyt grunted and turned away toward the window. "I suppose she was doing whatever people do when they plan to commit suicide."

"You think the overdose was intentional, then?" Luke asked. "Not an accident?"

Hoyt shook his head. "How the hell should I know? I'm guessing it was intentional mostly because I can't see Pamela making a mistake of that magnitude with the pills and the booze. She'd been managing her little addiction problem for years. Why screw up now?"

"Did you realize that she might be planning suicide when you left her that day?" Irene asked.

"Of course not." Hoyt scowled. "If I'd had an inkling that she intended to take her own life, I would have done something."

Irene studied him. "Such as?"

Hoyt took one hand out of his pocket and swept it to the side. "I would have called her father, for starters. Webb would have contacted Pamela's doctor. I'm sure they would have worked out a scheme to get Pamela into a private clinic. But I swear I didn't realize that she was in a suicidal state of mind when I left her. I thought she'd grown tired of me and was getting ready to move on to someone else. Like I said, that was her pattern."

Irene's dark brows drew tightly together. "Did you ask her if she was seeing someone new?"

"Sure. She said she wasn't. Said she was taking a little break. That's it. I left and drove back here. Next thing I know, Webb is phoning me at three o'clock in the morning telling me that he's just had a call from the chief of police in Dunsley. He told me that Pamela was dead and that we had to make arrangements to pick up the body, organize a funeral and meet with Chief McPherson." Hoyt gave Irene an accusing glare. "After that I did my job; I focused one hundred percent on trying to keep Pamela's death a private family matter."

Luke studied a photo of Webb and Alexa speaking to the president at a recent fund-raiser. "Whose idea was it to invite Webb's fiancée along on the drive to Dunsley?"

"Alexa insisted on coming with us. She felt that she should be with the senator while he dealt with the loss of his only child. She was right. The press loved her at the funeral."

Luke raised his brows. "The candidate's loyal, supportive fiancée standing by his side while he grieves the tragic death of a deeply troubled daughter."

"Perception is everything in politics, just like it is in real life," Hoyt said dryly.

Luke saw Irene go very still.

"Are you saying that Alexa Douglass isn't genuinely loyal or supportive?" she asked.

Hoyt seemed startled. "Hell, no. Just the opposite. There's nothing Alexa Douglass wants more in the world than for Webb to make a run for the Oval Office. Got a feeling she's already selecting her First Lady wardrobe and making plans to put Emily into one of those fashionable Washington academies where the presidents and diplomats send their kids."

"Emily?" Irene prompted.

"Her daughter," Hoyt explained. "Alexa is a widow."

Irene glanced at the photo on the wall. "Alexa is several years younger than Ryland."

"She's thirty-three, to be exact." Hoyt snorted softly. "But no one seems to care about a little thing like a twenty-year age difference as long as it's the woman who is the younger one, do they?"

"Is it a love match?" Irene asked.

"It's a political match," Hoyt said evenly. "Webb needs a wife if he's going to make it to the White House. The voters aren't likely to go for an unmarried president, now are they?"

"Hadn't thought about it," Irene admitted. "But now that you mention it, I can certainly see that having a spouse would be a huge asset to any politician running for president."

"Alexa is perfect for him. Good family, good schools, no scandals. She's smart and articulate. In addition, her husband left her a very wealthy woman. Also . . ." Hoyt trailed off.

"Also what?" Luke prompted.

"For years Webb's father has been after Ryland to remarry and provide a male heir. It's not exactly a secret that, before he dies, Victor Webb wants a grandson to carry on the family name and legacy. Just between you and me, Alexa was given an intensive physical exam to make certain that she was in excellent reproductive health before the engagement was announced. Also, there's a prenuptial agreement that states she will make every effort to get pregnant within a year of the marriage."

"Talk about pressure," Irene said. "I don't envy Alexa one bit." She paused to glance at one of the photos featuring Douglass. "Alexa is the same age as Pamela was. How did those two get along?"

"At first Pamela treated Alexa the way she did the other women Webb had over the years," Hoyt said. "Which is to say she ignored her. But when Webb announced the engagement, Pamela started taking her damn seriously, I can tell you that."

"What do you mean?" Irene asked.

"Pamela suddenly decided she didn't like Alexa very much. There was gossip that she confronted her in the ladies' room at a fund-raiser a few weeks ago. No one knows what they argued about, but the assumption was that Pamela made it clear she didn't want Alexa marrying her father."

"I wonder if Pamela was jealous of her," Irene said. She walked slowly along one wall, studying the photos. "She was about to lose a great deal. Alexa was set to take over the role that she had played in her father's political life for years. Once married, Alexa will become Webb's hostess and closest adviser. She'll assume the power and social position that Pamela used to enjoy."

Hoyt gave her a pained look. "Who knows what Pamela was thinking? I sure as hell never figured her out."

Ten minutes later Luke got back into the SUV beside Irene. "Well?" he asked, inserting the key into the ignition.

"I don't know what to think," she said. "But it occurs to me that if Pamela and Alexa were feuding, we now have a solid suspect. Alexa appears to be a rather ambitious woman."

"Think she might have gotten rid of Pamela because she believed that Pamela was going to make things difficult for her? Maybe even convince Webb to call off the marriage?"

"It's a possibility," Irene said, studying Hoyt's apartment complex through the windshield.

Luke eased the vehicle away from the curb. "Why burn down the house, though? The arson looks like the work of someone who was trying to get rid of evidence."

"Yes," Irene said. "It does, doesn't it? But what sort of evidence requires torching a house?"

He thought about it for a moment. "The kind that the killer was not able to find but which he suspected was inside the house."

"Something small, maybe."

"Or something very well hidden."

"You know," she said softly, "I don't think we can trust Hoyt Egan."

"I'm with you. He was talking way too fast for a guy who didn't want to talk to us at all."

"We need to learn more about him. I can do some research on the Internet."

Luke turned thoughtful. "I know someone who may be able to get us some deep background on Egan a lot quicker than you or I can working the Internet."

"Who?" she asked.

"Guy I knew in the Marines, Ken Tanaka. He's a private investigator now. He does mostly corporate work but he'll do me a favor."

She thought about that for a while. "Do you have a lot of friends who went through what you went through?"

"Not a lot. A few."

"Do you talk to them about it?"

"Not much."

"Because they know and you know and that's enough," she said.

"Yes."

Thirty-three

Luke showed up on the front step of Cabin Number Five at five-thirty that evening. When Irene opened the door she saw that he was not alone. He had a shaving kit, a small duffel bag and his computer with him.

"Correct me if I'm wrong, but this looks like you're expecting more than dinner this evening," she said, trying for lighthearted banter.

His expression barely flickered, but she thought she could hear a steel door slamming closed somewhere. So much for the lighthearted banter.

"We spent the past two nights together," he said evenly. "Did I get the wrong impression somewhere along the line?"

She looked at him standing there in the doorway and felt as if he were asking her to make a life-altering decision. What was the big deal? They were involved in a highly charged affair fueled largely by the intensity of their recent shared experiences. This relationship probably wouldn't last but while it did,

Luke made her feel like a sex goddess. When was the last time any man had ever made her feel like a sex goddess?

"No." She smiled. "You didn't get the wrong impression."

She stepped back to allow him to enter. The bleak, dark aspect vanished from his face. She sensed the steel door reopening.

Luke moved into the room, looking oddly satisfied, looking like a man who was coming home.

S he awoke much later that night when she felt him slide out of bed. She did not move but opened her eyes in time to see him stealing silently down the hall into the front room of the cabin. He had his jeans in one hand.

When he disappeared she turned to look at the clock on the table. It was two-thirty in the morning.

She gave him a few minutes, time enough to get a snack in the kitchen or use the facilities. He did not return.

She sat up, tossed the covers aside and got to her feet. The man had a right to his secrets, she told herself. But this was downright weird. If he couldn't sleep, she wasn't going to sleep, either. She slid her feet into her slippers and went down the hall.

In the glow of the lamp that she had left burning on the end table she saw Luke sitting on the edge of the couch, his computer open on the coffee table in front of him. His intense expression told her that he was riveted by whatever he was writing on the screen.

"If you're into any late-night Internet chat room hobbies, you'd better tell me now," she said.

He raised his head. For a second or two, she got the distinct feeling that he was surprised to see her standing there. Then he smiled wryly.

"Didn't mean to wake you," he said. "I got a couple of ideas. Wanted to get them down before they faded."

"Ideas about what? The Webb situation?"

"No." He leaned back against the cushions, stretched his legs out under the coffee table and hooked his thumbs in the waist-band of his jeans. "The book I'm trying to write."

"What book?" Curiosity flowered deep inside her. "A novel?"

He hesitated just long enough to make her think he was not accustomed to talking about the book.

"No," he said finally. He studied the glowing computer screen with a basilisk stare. "It's definitely nonfiction. You could call it a textbook or a manual."

"Really? What's your subject?"

"A way of thinking about and formulating strategy."

She moved closer to the coffee table. "Military strategy?"

"Strategy is strategy, regardless of how it is applied. Nobody believes me when I tell them that what saved my team and my own rear on more than one occasion wasn't just my military training, it was that work in philosophy I did before I went into the Marines."

She suddenly understood. "Philosophy didn't teach you what to think, it taught you how to think."

"And war taught me . . . other things. I'm trying to pull lessons from both aspects of those two human endeavors."

"Certainly sounds impressive."

His mouth quirked. "I'm trying to get around that little problem. I don't want people to think the book is too esoteric or arcane."

"Esoteric and arcane. Fancy words. Jason warned me that beneath your laid-back veneer beat the heart of a natural-born scholar. What made you leave the academic world to join the Marines?"

He looked deeply into the computer screen as though searching for the answer to her question. "It's hard to explain. Part of me was drawn to that world. But there was another part of me that felt . . . unfinished. It was as if I needed a counter-balance to my academic side." He shrugged. "Or something."

"You know what you are?"

He raised his brows. "What?"

"A twenty-first-century version of what they used to call a Renaissance man, a scholar-warrior."

"Now who's using the fancy words?"

"And this book of yours," she continued, very sure of herself now, "is an effort to meld both sides of your nature, isn't it? It's your own private version of therapy."

He looked back at the screen. "Dang, woman, you may be on to something here."

She sank down onto the couch beside him. "You came here to Dunsley to find a nice, quiet place in which to write."

"That was the plan."

"Why did you buy the lodge? Don't tell me you need the money because you're not even trying to run it at a profit."

"I'm okay financially. Made a few solid investments over the years." He covered her hand with his own. "As for the lodge, well, you know what they say, you can't go wrong with waterfront property."

"You can in Dunsley. When my aunt sold my parents' house, she got almost nothing out of it."

"Thanks for that cheery piece of data."

"How did you end up as an innkeeper?" she asked.

"I sure as heck didn't intend to go into the hospitality business. The plan was for me to live in one of the cabins and close up the others. But there were a couple of glitches."

"Such as?"

"Maxine and her son, Brady," he said. "And, to some extent, Tucker Mills."

She threaded her fingers through his. "I get it. Maxine is financially dependent on her work here, isn't she?"

"Not like there's a lot of employment options around the lake, especially in the off season. About five minutes after I moved in, it dawned on me that if I closed up the lodge, Maxine and Brady were going to be in serious financial trouble."

"What about Tucker?"

"Tucker probably would have gotten by without the part-time work here because getting by is what he does." Luke hesitated. "But he likes working here. He's used to it. Taking care of the lodge is part of his routine."

"And Tucker needs his routine."

Luke's mouth kicked up again. "Don't we all?"

"For sure. In other words, you didn't close down the lodge because three other people would have been directly affected."

"It's not like the place can't pay for itself. I took a look at the financials and figured that, given enough summer business, the lodge could continue to turn a modest profit. Hell, with Maxine managing it, the place might even turn a *decent* profit."

"Keeping the lodge open was a very generous thing to do, Luke."

"Just seemed like the easiest strategy, all things considered."

"I don't believe that for a moment. You left things the way they were because you felt a responsibility to the people you inherited when you took over. I remember something that Dad once told me."

"What?"

"A good officer always takes care of his people."

She leaned forward and kissed him.

He kissed her back. After a while he closed down the computer and drew her back into the bedroom.

Thirty-four

The call from Ken Tanaka came at seven-thirty the next morning, just as Luke was getting ready to serve his special French toast to Irene.

"I haven't finished examining Hoyt Egan's financial records, but I think you should see what I've got," Ken said. "There's a pattern here. A familiar one. Looks potentially messy."

"Can you e-mail me the information?" Luke asked.

"Don't think that would be a good idea at this juncture," Ken said. "We're talking about bad stuff that may or may not involve the man who might become the next president. I don't want an e-mail trail leading to either you or me just yet. I'd rather discuss it in person. I need to show you some data."

That was Ken, Luke thought, always careful. It was one of the reasons that he had survived in a war zone, and it was no doubt the reason that he had been successful as a private investigator.

Luke looked at his watch. "I can be in the city in a couple of hours."

"I'll be waiting," Ken said.

Luke hung up the phone and went back to shoveling French toast onto a plate. "That was Tanaka. He's found something in Egan's financials that looks interesting. Thinks it might involve Ryland Webb."

Excitement lit her face. "Are we talking political scandal?"

"Maybe."

"A scandal of suitable proportions could explain a murder."

"Calm down." He grated a little orange peel over the toast. "All we've got at the moment are some new dots. I'm going to drive into the city right after we eat. Want to come with me?"

"Yes." She hesitated, obviously torn. "But I think I'll let you deal with your friend. There's something else that I want to do today. We'll get more accomplished if we split up."

Unease trickled through him. "What are you planning to do?"

"Don't look so worried. I'm not going to find any bodies or burn down any houses. Actually, I had a minor brainstorm while I was getting dressed this morning. I was just about to tell you about it when the phone rang."

"What was this brainstorm?" he asked, still wary.

"It involves that key I found in Pamela's secret hiding place the night of the fire." She looked at the plate of French toast, eyes widening with appreciation. "Boy, howdy, as Jason would say. Room service shows up at last."

Thirty-five

The locksmith's name was Herb Porter. He was in his seventies, and he had been in the business for nearly fifty years. He knew locks and keys, and he knew his own work.

"That's one of mine, all right," he announced, examining the key Irene had given him. "First-rate line. Expensive, too. I'm the only locksmith on the lake who handles it. See that little P followed by a number? That's my code."

Irene tried to calm her pounding pulse. She had been prepared for her plan to try to locate the locksmith who had made Pamela's key to hit a dead end. Now that there was a glimmer of hope, adrenaline was spiking through her in heavy jolts.

"Do you remember the person who ordered it?" she asked, forcing herself to speak in a calm, casual tone.

"Sure. Senator Webb's daughter."

Irene clutched the edge of the counter. "She gave you her name?"

"Not at the time. Called herself Marjorie something-or-other and paid cash. I took her for summer people or a weekender. But later, after she killed herself, I recognized her from the picture in the paper." He shook his head. "Real shame about that. She sure was pretty. Dressed nice, too. Looked like she could have been a model or something, you know?"

"Yes, I know." Irene smiled at him, exerting every ounce of self-control that she possessed not to leap onto the glass counter, grab him by the lapels and shake more answers out of him.

Take it easy, she told herself. *Don't rush him. He might stop talking.*

If Pamela had ordered the key from a locksmith located in one of the big towns or cities in the San Francisco Bay area, there would have been very little chance of identifying the shop. But it had occurred to her that there was a very real possibility that the key had been made locally. She had reasoned that if that was the case, it would probably be possible to find the locksmith who had made it. With luck, she might even discover what the key unlocked.

Shortly after nine o'clock, she had set out to drive around the north end of the lake toward Kirbyville, stopping at the two small locksmith shops she passed along the way. She had skipped Dunsley altogether on the theory that if Pamela had something to hide, she would not have taken her business to the town's only full-service locksmith. Dean Crump, the owner of the shop, would have recognized a member of the Webb family immediately.

She had gotten lucky at Porter Lock & Key, located on a quiet, tree-shaded street in Kirbyville.

"When did Miss Webb come in here?" she asked, fighting not to reveal her exploding excitement.

"Let's see." Herb's gaze went to the old-fashioned girlie calendar on the wall. He ruminated for a moment on the buxom redhead dressed in a halter top and short shorts and then nodded to himself. "Few days ago. She was in a real hurry. Said it was important. I scheduled the job for the next day. See? Circled the date in red."

Irene followed his gaze to the calendar. Her pulse slammed into high gear. The date marked with a red pen was the day before Pamela had died.

"She paid you to rekey her house?" She frowned. "There must be some misunderstanding. Pamela didn't install new locks. I used an old key to let myself into the Webb house just a few days ago."

Herb squinted thoughtfully. "You're talkin' about the place over on the other side of the lake, right? The one that burned down the other night?"

"Yes."

"That wasn't the house she hired me to rekey."

Irene held her breath. "It wasn't?"

"Nope. She hired me to redo a place on the other side of town. Located right on the lake. Told me it was a rental. That's why I figured her for weekend or summer people."

Confusion replaced the initial surge of disappointment. Why

on earth had Pamela rented a house on the lake when she already had one?

"I don't suppose you'd give me the address?" she asked, expecting Herb to refuse.

To her amazement, Herb shrugged and hauled out an aging cardboard file. "Don't see any harm in it. Not exactly confidential information now that Miss Webb's dead. No one living there, far as I know." He rummaged through a pile of invoices and worksheets for a moment and then selected one. "Here we go. End of Pine Lane. No number. It's the only house on the road."

Irene felt as though all the air had been sucked out of the room. She had to swallow two or three times before she could speak.

"Pine Lane?" The words emerged in a high, creaky falsetto that she hardly recognized as her own voice. "Are you certain?"

"Yep. I remember it was a mite hard to find. Took a couple of wrong turns before I got to it. Pine Lane is one of those private little gravel-tops that run down to the water off the main road. Dozens of them scattered around the lake. Half aren't even marked."

"Yes, I know," Irene whispered.

He squinted at her, concerned. "Look here, if it's important I can write it down for you."

"No, thanks." She plucked the key from his palm. "That won't be necessary. I appreciate your time, Mr. Porter."

"No problem." Herb leaned his elbows on the grimy glass

counter and shook his head sadly. "Just a real shame about Miss Webb. Why do you suppose a pretty lady like that would take her own life?"

"That," Irene said, "is a very good question."

It took a great deal of concentration, but somehow she made it outside without losing it. She managed to get behind the wheel of the compact and pull out of the tiny parking lot in front of Porter Lock & Key. She drove slowly through town.

When she was beyond the cluster of shops, restaurants and gas stations that made up the heart of Kirbyville, she turned into a small, secluded picnic area and parked. She got out and walked down to the water's edge.

For a long time she simply stood there, gazing at the restless lake. Gradually the shaky sensation and the sick sense of dread began to subside.

When she could think clearly again, she forced herself to confront the question that was screaming and moaning in her brain like a demented ghost.

There was only one house on Pine Lane, at least there had been only one seventeen years earlier. It was the house in which she had been raised, the house in which she had found her parents dead on the kitchen floor.

Thirty-six

S he took the long way back to Dunsley, following the narrow, two-lane road that wound around the rim of the south end of the lake. She told herself that she needed time to think. But she knew, deep inside, that what she was really trying to buy was a little more time before she went back to Dunsley to face the house of blood and darkness that had haunted her dreams for seventeen years.

The big silver SUV with the heavily tinted windows appeared in her rearview mirror just as she started into the most isolated section of the old road. The vehicle came out of the last turn with unnerving speed.

The sight of the silver SUV so close behind her jolted her into a sudden awareness of how slowly she was moving. The absence of other traffic on the road combined with her dark musings had caused her to drift into another zone. She had been driving on autopilot. This was a twisty two-lane road that allowed very few places to pass slow-moving vehicles. Folks got mad when you drove it too slowly. Only tourists made that mistake.

She straightened hastily in the seat and put her foot down more firmly on the accelerator, sending the compact into the next series of turns at a brisk clip. But when she rechecked the mirror she saw that the SUV had not fallen back. It was closing fast.

Whoever he was, she had annoyed him, she thought. He was determined to punish her for the offense of slow driving by pushing her hard. Just what she needed, a short-tempered idiot with a royal case of road rage.

A little chill of fear flickered through her. The section of road on which she was traveling hugged the top of the cliffs. It could be dangerous. Her father had come home on more than one occasion, weary and grim, to report to her mother that one of the locals had gotten drunk and gone through the guardrail into the deep waters of the lake. Several years earlier in her endless, restless, obsessive research into the past, she had learned that Bob Thornhill had suffered his fatal heart attack and gone off the cliffs into the lake near here.

The SUV bore down on her. She tapped the brakes a couple of times in warning. But instead of dropping back, the vehicle accelerated.

Ice formed in her stomach. She was vaguely aware of her, heart. It was thudding heavily in her chest. Fear flowed like acid in her veins. Every survival instinct she possessed was suddenly screaming. The driver of the SUV was trying to scare her, and he was succeeding.

She pressed harder on the accelerator. Her father had taught her to drive on Lakefront Road. Teens raised in urban environments learned to handle the hazards of city streets and freeway on-ramps, but those raised in rural areas learned other skills. It had been seventeen years since she'd driven this stretch, but she reminded herself that the skills you learned early stayed with you. She'd had an excellent teacher, she remembered. Her father had driven the way he did everything else, the Marine Corps way.

She had one big advantage. Her compact clung to the curves like a sports car. The SUV was, at heart, a truck. As it increased speed, it started to take the sharp nips and tucks in the road in an unwieldy fashion.

The problem was the sheer rate of speed at which they were traveling, Irene thought. Sooner or later one of them was going to make a mistake and end up in the lake. The waters were deep in this region. Going over the edge would be tantamount to a death sentence.

She searched her memory for a map of the local landscape. Somewhere up ahead was the entrance to a small, heavily wooded subdivision. Seventeen years ago the real estate venture had not been a roaring success. Only a handful of inexpensive summer homes had been built. With luck, Ventana Estates had been caught in the same time warp that gripped Dunsley.

She heard tires squeal but dared not take her eyes off the road. One miscalculation at this speed would send her straight through the paper-thin metal barrier.

She came out of another sharp turn and saw the faded sign for Ventana Estates. It looked as if no one had ever bothered to repaint it. That boded well for what she had in mind, she told herself.

She had to slow for the turn, but the last hairpin curve had bought her a few seconds of time. The SUV had fallen back in an attempt to regain control.

She hit the brakes hard, spun the steering wheel to the left and stomped on the accelerator. The first portion of road into the failed subdivision had been roughly paved in an attempt to create a more upscale impression on prospective buyers. But she was relieved to note that over the years no one had filled in the gaping potholes.

The SUV's tires howled in protest behind her. The driver from hell was braking hard. The bastard was so mad he was going to pursue her into the subdivision.

Another wave of fear crashed through her. She had been praying that, having chased her off the roadway, the driver of the SUV would be content in his wretched little triumph and continue on along Lakefront Road.

So much for Plan A, as Pamela would have said. Time for Plan B.

She could feel cold sweat under her arms. Everything depended on whether or not the subdivision road had been paved beyond the entrance.

The paved section ended abruptly. The compact lurched and bounced as it made the transition from rough blacktop to even rougher dirt and gravel.

She took her foot off the accelerator and risked a quick glance into the mirror. Like some ravenous beast sensing that its intended prey is tiring, the SUV leaped onto the gravel road to pursue her.

She followed the looping road, letting the SUV get dangerously close. The behemoth filled her rearview mirror now. She envisioned steel jaws opening to devour the compact. The driver was intent on forcing her back onto Lakefront Road.

This was as good as it was going to get, she decided. She tromped hard on the accelerator.

The compact surged forward as though it sensed the fangs hovering close behind. Gravel, pebbles and clods of dirt spurted furiously from beneath the rear tires, creating a driving hailstorm of debris.

She did not have to check the mirrors to see how the SUV had taken the surprise assault. She could hear the heavy, unrelenting rain of hard pings and sharp thuds as the wave of small stones and gravel struck metal and glass. She knew the driver from hell was looking through a windshield that was being pelted by the small meteor shower churned up by the compact's tires.

The SUV hesitated and then fell back. Irene drove faster, following the subdivision's single road toward the exit at the far end.

A moment later the compact bounced and jolted back out onto Lakefront Road. She floored the accelerator. The compact's suspension system was never going to be the same, she thought.

When she dared to glance into the rearview mirror she saw no sign of the SUV. It was still back in Ventana Estates, licking its wounds.

The only consolation was in knowing that the driver of the

SUV was going to pay a price for that display of road rage. The windshield had to be a maze of chips and spiderwebs. In addition, the flying gravel would have caused a lot of damage to the shiny silver finish.

She eased her foot off the accelerator. It was probably not a good idea to drive too fast when you were shaking from head to foot, she thought.

Thirty-seven

H e met with Ken Tanaka in a small café located on a
narrow street off Union Square. Ken claimed that
the little hole-in-the-wall served the best pastries
and baked goods in San Francisco. After a couple of bites of the
croissant he had ordered, Luke concluded that he was right.

Ken slathered butter on his own croissant and angled
his head at the page of handwritten notes he had put in front
of Luke.

"You see why I didn't want an e-mail trail leading to either
one of us?" he said.

"Sure do," Luke agreed.

He contemplated Ken, who was sitting on the other side of
the table. He had never consciously thought about what a private investigator was supposed to look like, but somehow Ken
didn't fit the profile. Then again, Tanaka didn't look like a man
with a degree in forensic accounting, either.

It was easy to underestimate Ken. His quiet, friendly, reassuring manner made people lower their guard. He had been

very good at questioning civilians unlucky enough to be caught in a war zone. More than once he had obtained information from a small boy or a frightened woman that had prevented Luke and the rest of the team from walking into an ambush.

No doubt about it, Ken was good at handling people. But his greatest talent was his almost preternatural instinct for following the money. His firm specialized in corporate security, but Luke knew that the feds came knocking when they wanted Tanaka's expertise to help track drug and terrorist funds.

Luke looked at the notes. "Give me the short answer."

Ken took a bite of the flaky croissant. "In the past four months there have been four large sums of money transferred into an offshore account that I traced back to Hoyt Egan."

"How'd you do that?"

Ken raised one brow. "You don't want to know."

"Right. Go on."

"In my humble opinion, either Egan is taking payoffs from an unknown source for an unknown reason, or he's collecting blackmail. My gut tells me we're looking at a series of extortion payments."

"Big bucks here." Luke drank some coffee. "He's got something on the senator, doesn't he?"

"I'd say that's the most likely scenario under the circumstances. Guy running for president probably has things to hide. But there are other possibilities."

"The fiancée? Alexa Douglass?"

Ken reached for the jam. "I checked around. She and Webb started dating about six months ago. From all accounts, Alexa

Douglass is an ambitious woman who is determined to marry Webb. If Egan discovered something in her past that would cause Webb to call off the wedding, it's conceivable that she might be paying him to keep quiet."

"Egan is playing with matches and probably out of his league. Blackmail is a dangerous line of work." Luke sat back in the booth. "Wonder where Pamela Webb fits into this thing."

"Starting to think she really was murdered?"

"The dots are connecting."

Ken applied more jam to the croissant. "You were always pretty good with dots. What now?"

"I'm going to have to think about that for a while. I need to talk to Irene. This is her mission. I'm just assisting."

Ken smiled. "I'm looking forward to meeting this Irene. She sounds interesting."

"You'll like her."

"Almost forgot." Ken reached inside his hand-tailored jacket. "Here's that key you asked me to get for you."

"I'm suitably impressed." Luke reached across the table to pick up the key "I didn't give you much notice."

Ken managed to appear highly offended. "It's an apartment complex. One bored guy on duty in the manager's office. How hard do you think it was to create a little distraction that made it possible to get into the office and make a duplicate of the master?"

"Not hard, I take it."

Ken did not dignify that with an answer. Instead he picked up a plastic sack he had put on the seat when he first sat down.

"Here's your outfit," he said.

"Appreciate it." Luke took the sack. "You got a look at the apartment complex when you went there to get the key. Any words of advice?"

"Yeah. Don't get caught."

Thirty-eight

I t was midafternoon and the sun was out, but it seemed to Irene that the windows of the house of her nightmares at the end of Pine Lane were just as dark as they had been at midnight seventeen years before.

She halted the compact in the drive and sat quietly for a moment, summoning her courage and fortitude for the task that lay ahead. Walking back into her old home was going to be hard, maybe the hardest thing she had done since she attended the funerals of her parents.

Like every other building in Dunsley, the house looked smaller and more weathered than she remembered, but otherwise disturbingly familiar. Aunt Helen had sold the place as quickly as possible after the tragedy. She had not made much of a profit, because no one in Dunsley wanted to buy a house in which violent death had occurred. The realtor had eventually found an unsuspecting client from San Francisco who acquired it with the goal of turning it into a summer rental.

When she had lived here, the house had been a warm,

golden tan with brown trim, Irene reflected. Somewhere along the line it had been repainted a light gray. The trim around the windows and the front door was black.

It will look different inside, too, she promised herself. *Probably been through several owners. Bound to be new carpet and new furniture. It won't be the same. It can't be the same. I don't think I can take it if it looks the same as it did that night.*

Her breathing was all wrong, quick and shallow. It occurred to her that it might have been a very good idea to wait before she came here, until her nerves had settled down after the road rage incident.

But she dared not put this off any longer. She had to know why Pamela had gone to the trouble of renting and rekeying the house.

She opened the car door and got out before she could talk herself into leaving and coming back some other time. One thing was certain, she thought, taking the key out of the pocket of her trench coat, she was definitely not going in through the kitchen door this time.

She went up the front steps, crossed the porch and inserted the shiny new key into the lock with trembling fingers.

Drawing a deep, centering breath, she opened the door.

Shadows swirled in the hall. Automatically she reached out to flip the light switch on the wall. Another chill went through her when she realized that she remembered exactly where the switch was located.

She closed the door slowly and made herself walk into the living room. The curtains on all the windows were closed. The interior of the room was drenched in gloom, but she could make out the furnishings.

Relief washed through her when she saw that someone had, indeed, redecorated. Her mother's pictures were gone from the walls. The sofa, armchairs and wooden coffee table were generic summer rental, inexpensive and, best of all, unfamiliar.

Keep moving, she ordered herself, *or you won't get through this.* She knew there was, in fact, a very sound reason for hurrying. It would not be a good idea to be caught inside the house. True, it had been her home in her youth, but she had no claim on it now. If someone noticed her car in the drive and called the police, she would have a major problem on her hands. Sam McPherson was definitely not her best friend at the moment. As far as he was concerned, she was still the prime suspect in an arson case. The last thing she needed was for the chief to send one of his men out here to investigate a possible intruder in the house on Pine Lane.

She walked slowly through the shadowed living room into the dining area.

How do you conduct a search when you have no idea what you're looking for? she wondered. *Think about this. If Pamela did intend for you to find the key and if she wanted you to use it, she probably would have made certain that you would recognize whatever it was she wanted you to discover here.*

The wooden chairs and table in the dining room were all new, too. The curtains were closed. That was good, she thought. The last thing she wanted to do was look at the view. It would remind her of all the meals she had eaten in this room, her father seated at one end of the table, her mother opposite, and her in the middle looking straight out at the lake and the old dock.

She pushed aside the memories with the skill and determination born of long practice. Turning, she made herself go to the entrance of the big, old-fashioned kitchen.

At the threshold she was forced to come to a halt. Nausea twisted her stomach. Her breath seemed to be locked inside her lungs. She could not go any farther.

It was all she could do just to make herself look into the room where she had found the bodies. She gave the counters a swift, sweeping glance, saw nothing out of the ordinary and then spun around before she got physically ill.

If the object of her search was in the kitchen, it would have to remain there. She could not bring herself to walk into that space. Surely Pamela would have realized that.

She fled back through the dining room and living room and stopped in the front hall. She knew her labored breathing was caused by incipient panic, not exertion.

Take it easy. You've got to do this logically, or you'll never find whatever it is you're looking for.

She went down the hall to her old bedroom. Dread and certainty gripped her every step of the way.

Like the other rooms, her bedroom, too, had been redone. The colorful posters had been taken down, and the sunny yellow walls that her mother had helped her paint were now a boring shade of beige.

There was a white cardboard box on the bed. On top of the box was a book. She recognized the small volume immediately.

It was a paperback romance novel, one that had been published seventeen years earlier.

Anticipation shuddered through her. She crossed the floor, removed the book and lifted the cover of the white box. Inside was a white dress sealed in clear plastic. At first she thought it was a wedding gown. Then she realized it was too small. A christening gown, perhaps, she decided. There was another object in the box, a video.

She replaced the lid of the box and reached for the paperback novel. The badly faded cover illustration depicted a beautiful blond heroine in the arms of a dashing hero. Both were garbed in romantic nineteenth-century fashions. The edges of the pages were yellowed.

She opened the book to the title page and read the inscription written there.

> *Happy 16th Birthday, Pamela.*
> *You look like the heroine on the cover. I'm sure that one day you'll find your hero.*
> *Love,*
> *Irene*

She tested the weight of the small volume in her hand. Few people would have noticed that the book was a little too heavy for a paperback novel, she thought.

Thirty-nine

I t's too large to be a christening dress." Tess examined the plastic-wrapped gown that Irene had placed on her coffee table. "Maybe it's an old costume that she wore for Halloween or a school play."

Irene turned away from the window and the view of Tess's garden. It had been instinct as much as anything that had led her to bring the dress and the video to her former English teacher. She did not know what to expect from the video, but she had been very certain that she did not want to view it alone. She also knew that she could not wait until Luke returned from his meeting with Ken Tanaka. Tess Carpenter was the only other person in town with whom she felt comfortable enough to share whatever secrets might be revealed.

Student-teacher bonds ran deep. But it wasn't just their old classroom connection that had compelled her to come here. She knew that, in the old days, her mother had considered Tess a friend who could be trusted.

She walked back to stand in front of the coffee table.

"I don't know," she said slowly. "Hard to imagine that Pamela was sentimental about a childhood costume."

Tess frowned in a considering manner. "She didn't show it to you when the two of you were friends that summer?"

"No." Irene studied the dress. "I never saw it."

"But you do recognize the book?"

"Yes. I gave it to her for her birthday." She sank down onto the couch beside Tess. "Thanks for letting me bring these things here."

"No problem." Tess poured coffee for both of them. "I must admit, you've made me very curious. Where do we start?"

"With the novel." Irene looked at the volume, aware of a sad, wistful feeling. "She laughed when she opened her present and saw it. She said that the romance thing wasn't for her. Later she told me that she had found a good use for the book."

"What was that?"

Irene put the novel down on the table, flipped past the title page with its inscription, and turned to Chapter Two.

The rest of the pages following that chapter had been neatly glued together to form a solid block of paper. The center section had been hollowed out to create a small opening that was concealed when the book was closed. Inside was a small key chain–sized object.

"A convenient container in which to carry a supply of drugs, cigarettes or spare condoms," Irene said. "Pamela said every girl should have one."

Tess raised her brows. "You learned a lot from her."

Irene wrinkled her nose. "I was such a complete dork. We

had zilch in common. I never did understand why she wanted to hang around me that summer."

Tess looked at the object she had removed from the book. "What's up with the key chain?"

"It's not a key chain." Irene pulled her laptop closer. "It's a computer data storage device."

"Any idea what's on it?"

"No," Irene said. "But I've got a hunch it's going to be very unpleasant."

Forty

L uke cruised slowly past Hoyt Egan's apartment building, turned the corner and drove two more blocks. He found a space for the SUV on a street where three or four other similar vehicles were parked. Satisfied that his ride didn't stand out in the crowd, he switched off the engine and tried Egan's cell phone and landline one more time. Still no answer.

He reached into the plastic sack and pulled out the cap and windbreaker that Tanaka had supplied. Both articles of clothing bore the logo of a familiar delivery company. There was an outside possibility that Egan was home and not answering his phone for one reason or another. But the odds were good that a busy senator's aide would not ignore his phones.

Luke picked up the empty box he had brought along and got out of the SUV.

The decision to try to take a look at Egan's apartment had formulated at the back of his mind during the drive from Dunsley. Now that there was an indication that Egan was engaged in blackmail, it seemed like an especially good idea. He had no hard evidence on Egan, he reminded himself, as he walked back toward the apartment complex, just that old familiar feeling deep in his gut.

Adrenaline spiked.

There was no one around when he reached the locked gate at the entrance of the complex, but he dialed Egan's number on the entry phone system just in case. When he got no answer, he gave it a few seconds and then palmed the master key and opened the gate, making it look as though he had been buzzed in by a resident.

He went into the lobby, box under one arm, and climbed the stairs to the floor where Egan's apartment was located.

He stepped out into an empty hallway, went down the corridor and knocked gently on Egan's door.

When no one responded, he automatically tried the door before inserting the duplicate master key.

The knob twisted easily in his hand.

Another jolt of adrenaline shot through him. Guys like Egan, guys with heavy responsibilities and lots of important senatorial secrets probably didn't forget to lock their doors when they left their apartments.

He opened the door. The stench that wafted out of the room brought back memories and nightmares.

He didn't need the sight of Egan's body lying facedown on the blood-soaked carpet to know that death had arrived here first.

Forty-one

The message on the computer screen chilled Irene to the bone. She could almost hear Pamela's voice in the words that she and Tess were reading.

If you found these files, Irene, then it looks like Plan A failed. This is Plan B. By the way, if you're not Irene, screw you. The rest of these files are seriously encrypted and will automatically be fatally scrambled if the wrong code is used.

Irene, if this is you, you know the magic words. Here's the big clue: You are the only person on the planet other than me who knows them. Eternal secrecy, remember?

"Think she's telling the truth about the files being destroyed if I use the wrong words?" Irene asked.

Tess studied the screen with a worried expression. "Depends on what kind of encryption program she used, I suppose. But Phil says that, even with a good system, it would be next to impossible to completely delete all traces of the files."

"Probably take a real expert to recover them, though. The average person certainly wouldn't be able to salvage anything." Irene poised her fingers over the keyboard. "Here goes."

She typed in *orange vanilla*.

"That's it?" Tess asked. "That's the supersecret code?"

"Hey, we were teenagers, remember? Seemed like a great secret code at the time."

The screen went blank. Irene froze, appalled.

"Wrong code?" Tess asked nervously.

"I can't think of anything else. If that wasn't it, I've just destroyed all the data Pamela stored on the computer."

A list of files appeared. There were four of them.

Irene started to breathe again. "Might as well start with the one labeled Number One."

She opened the file.

"A film clip," Tess said. She leaned forward to get a better look.

Pamela appeared on the screen. She was sitting on the sofa in the Webb summer house.

"Oh, jeez." Another eerie chill whispered through Irene. "This is going to be very, very weird."

Tess watched the screen, her unease clear in her strained features. "You can say that again. Look at the date on the film clip. She made this the day before she died."

"The day the Pine Lane house was rekeyed," Irene said.

Pamela was dressed in a pair of dark trousers and a snug pullover that revealed a lot of cleavage. She had a glass of wine in one hand. Her smile was cool and sophisticated, but her eyes were shadowed.

"Hi, Irene. Long time no see. Sadly, if you're looking at this it means I lost my nerve and decided I couldn't face you, after all. You obviously got a second e-mail note from me telling you where to find the spare key to your folks' house."

"I never got that e-mail, because she never sent it," Irene said. "She didn't lose her nerve, she was murdered."

"I'm probably sitting on a nice, sunny island somewhere in the Caribbean right now, downing those drinks they serve with those tacky little umbrellas. Sorry about that. I'd hoped I'd have the guts to tell you the truth in person. But then, I've never been real big on doing the right thing or telling the truth. I'm more the self-indulgent type, as we all know."

On the screen, Pamela paused to take a sip of wine.

"She's drinking wine, not martinis," Irene said.

Pamela put down the wineglass and continued speaking into the camera.

"I've thought about you a lot over the years, Irene. You probably won't believe it, but you were the closest thing I ever had to a real friend. I'll try not to get too sappy about it, though. This is true confession time. I'll come straight to the point.

"I know you never really believed that your dad killed your mother and took his own life. Guess what? You were right. You want to know who was responsible? Me."

Irene stared at the screen. "What is she talking about? That's impossible. I was with her that night. There's no way she could have shot my parents."

"Hush." Tess touched her arm. "Listen."

"No, I didn't pull the trigger, but I might as well have. Because what happened that night was my fault."

Pamela tucked one long leg under herself and reached for more wine.

"But first you'll have to watch the next film clip. Better warn you, it is definitely not PG."

The scene of Pamela on the sofa winked out. Another living room setting appeared.

"The interior designer who did that place must have had a previous career as a wedding cake decorator," Tess observed.

"Or else he specialized in bedrooms for little girls," Irene said, studying the scene.

The room was a pink-and-white fantasyland. Pink velvet draperies, white carpet and furniture upholstered in pink satin created a fairy-tale feeling. But there was something off about it, Irene decided. This was going to be one of the old, dark, truly frightening fairy tales, she thought, not a modern, cleaned-up, politically correct version.

"No dolls," she said.

Tess looked at her. "Dolls?"

"It looks like a girl's bedroom except there are no dolls or tea sets, stuffed animals or children's books. None of the trappings that you'd expect to see in a real child's bedroom."

"Like I said, the guy who did the place probably did wedding cakes on the side."

Irene examined the image more closely. "There's something old-world about the room, don't you think?"

"What do you mean?"

"Forget the fairy-tale color scheme. Look at the scale of the place and those windows. Early nineteenth century, I think. See those crown moldings? They're not reproductions. It looks like an old house that you might see somewhere in Europe."

Tess nodded slowly. "Now that you mention it, yes, it does."

Before Irene could make any more comments, a man walked into view. There was no audio with the clip. The figure moved in unnatural silence.

At first it was only possible to see him from the waist down because of the camera angle. Then he lowered himself onto one of the pink chairs. The change of position brought his face into clear view.

"Ryland Webb," Irene whispered.

"What in the world is going on here?" Tess said.

Webb settled back into the chair, hitched up his elegantly tailored trousers and cocked one ankle over his knee. Everything about his pose suggested ease and familiarity. He had been in this room before.

He looked at someone off camera, smiled and made a comment. A moment later a drink was placed in his hand by a woman dressed in a black skirt, severe white blouse and starched white apron. It was impossible to see the maid's face.

The toe of Webb's gleaming shoe bounced a little. Irene got the impression that he was looking forward to whatever was about to happen. She sensed suppressed excitement in him. There was a sheen of sweat on his brow. As she watched, he loosened his tie and focused his attention on a point across the pink-and-white room that was just out of the camera's view.

Irene's cell phone rang, jarring her so badly that she jumped a good three inches. She did not take her eyes off the screen as she punched the key to take the call.

"Irene?" Luke's voice carried the hard, no-compromise edge of command.

"What's wrong?" she asked instantly.

"Hoyt Egan is dead."

"Dead?"

Tess's head came around very fast, an alarmed, questioning expression on her face.

"Who's dead?" she asked.

Irene held up a hand to silence her so that she could hear Luke.

"I found him a short while ago," Luke said. "Someone hit his head very hard and very often with a heavy, blunt object. The cops are here now. They're going on the assumption that Egan interrupted a burglary in progress."

"Dear heaven." Stunned, she tried to gather her wits. She looked at Tess. "Hoyt Egan, Webb's aide. He's dead." She turned her attention back to the phone. "Wait a second, Luke. What do you mean, you found him? Where are you now?"

"In the hallway outside his apartment. The cops have set up a crime scene. I'm calling because I'm not going to be able to get away for a couple of hours, at least. The detective in charge has made that real clear. He wants to talk to me."

"Of course he does. You're the one who found the body. Why on earth did you go to Egan's apartment?"

"Call it a whim," Luke said dryly. "Look, I'll give you the whole story when I get home. Meanwhile, I don't want you there alone at the lodge."

"I'm not at the lodge," Irene said automatically. "I'm at Tess Carpenter's house."

"What are you doing there?" he asked sharply.

"At the moment we're viewing some computer files that Pamela left for me to find."

"What files? Where did you get them?"

"She stashed them in my old bedroom at the house where I lived with my parents here in town."

"You went there?" Luke paused. "Alone?"

"I'll explain later. The important part is what I found. Some of the files are film clips. We're watching one now. It shows Senator Webb in this really odd pink-and-white room. He doesn't seem to know that he's on camera."

"What the hell is he doing?"

"At the moment, he's sitting on a chair with a drink in his

hand. But it looks like he's waiting for someone else to come into the room."

"Irene, pay attention," Luke said. "I called Phil Carpenter just before I called you. He's headed out to the lodge. I'm going to call him back and tell him where you are."

"Why?"

"I want him to keep you company until I get back to Dunsley."

"I don't understand."

Tess was watching her with an expression of total confusion now.

"Didn't you hear what I just told you?" Luke said. "Someone murdered Hoyt Egan."

"A burglar."

"That's what the detective suggested. Me, I'm not taking any chances, given your theory about Pamela Webb's death."

Irene swallowed hard. "Got it."

At that moment a girl walked into the pink-and-white fairy-tale room. She appeared to be no more than ten or eleven years of age, blond and delicate.

"She looks like a flower girl at a wedding," Tess said softly.

The girl was dressed in a floor-length white satin gown. A gossamer veil clouded her features. She came to a halt a few steps away from Webb.

Irene went cold. She felt the phone start to slip from her suddenly nerveless fingers and hastily tightened her grip.

"Not the flower girl," she whispered. "She's the bride."

Tess paled. "Oh, my God. You're right."

"Irene?" Luke's voice crackled roughly. "Are you okay?"

"It's the film clip," she said. "There's a young girl dressed as a bride. And Webb. I can't believe it. No. I *can* believe it. That's what's so awful."

"I've got to call Phil. As soon as I get in touch with him, I'll call you right back."

"Okay." She was vaguely aware of Luke's cutting the connection, but she could not take her eyes off the screen.

Webb rose from the pink chair. The bulge of his erection was clearly visible, tenting the fabric of his trousers. He reached out, took the child bride's hand and said something to her, his manner a mockery of gallant behavior. The girl did not respond in any visible way. Irene assumed that she was in some sort of trance that had been induced by either the psychological trauma of the situation, drugs or both.

Webb tugged the girl toward the door. She trailed after him listlessly, the train of her miniature white gown dragging forlornly across the carpet behind her.

The film clip went dark. A second later a new scene appeared. The setting was a frilly pink-and-white wedding-cake bedroom. It was obvious from the limited range of the camera's view and the lowered lighting that this clip had also been shot clandestinely. The child bride stood statue-still next to the bed, clutching her bouquet.

Webb walked into view. He was nude, his middle-aged body soft and sagging and obscene without the camouflage of his expertly tailored clothes. He reached out to raise the wedding veil that covered the child's face.

"I can't watch any more of this," Irene said. She spun away from the scene before she got physically ill.

"Neither can I." Tess lowered the screen of the computer.

Irene's phone sounded.

"Luke?"

"Phil's on his way," Luke said. "What's happening in that film clip?"

Irene looked out the window at the dark expanse of the lake. "I think we just found out why Pamela was murdered."

Forty-two

P amela looked into the camera. She was still sitting on the sofa, the glass of wine in her hand. A mocking smile curved her mouth, but her eyes were as cold as northern seas.

"That was taken on Daddy's last trip out of the country. Pretty sick stuff, isn't it? Got to give Hoyt Egan some credit. He accompanied Daddy on some of the foreign junkets and figured out what was going on. He bribed one of the brothel employees to make that video. Thing is, until I discovered a few weeks ago that Hoyt Egan was blackmailing my father with that video, I had convinced myself that Daddy wasn't doing little girls anymore. Turns out he'd just taken his business out of the country. Talk about denial, hmm?"

Irene clutched the cell phone. "Can you hear this, Luke?"

"I can hear it," he said softly. "Webb is a pedophile, and he's getting set to run for president. You're right, what you're looking at is a hell of a motive for murder—a couple of them, in fact."

"Pamela and Hoyt Egan."

"I've got to call Tanaka," Luke said. "I want him to find out where Webb is right now. Once I know the sonofabitch isn't anywhere near Dunsley, I'll feel a little better. Meanwhile, make sure Tess's doors are locked."

Tess was close enough to hear Luke's voice coming out of the small phone. She was already on her feet. "I'll take care of it."

"I'll be there as soon as I can get away from here," Luke said. "Don't let anyone in except Phil."

"Understood," Irene said.

Luke cut the connection.

Tess hurried back into the living room and sat down on the couch. "We're all secure, as Phil would say."

On-screen, Pamela lowered her wineglass.

"You'll see from the charge card expenses and flight records that I've included in one of the other files that Daddy's done a lot of traveling abroad in the past few years. Southeast Asia used to be his favorite destination. Lots of kiddie brothels there.

"But there are plenty of similar operations in other parts of the world. Last year Daddy found the one in Europe that you just saw on the film clip. It's his favorite these days. I included the address for you, Irene. I know reporters like lots of details."

Tess looked at Irene. "This is devastating stuff. Ryland Webb's campaign will go down in flames when this hits the media."

Irene did not take her eyes off the screen. "Yes."

"If you got this far, Irene, you've probably already figured out that I want you to be the one to go public with the news about Daddy's little hobby. I owe you that much, at least."

"She knew you had become a reporter," Tess said thoughtfully. "She kept track of you over the years."

"Evidently."

On-screen, Pamela leaned back into the corner of the sofa and stretched out one long leg.

"But before you break the big story, I have to tell you what really happened to your parents. I said I was responsible for their deaths, and that's the simple truth. You see, at some point that summer, your mom began to suspect that I had been abused."

"Webb raped his own daughter," Tess said, face tight with anger.

"You may have wondered why your mom would never let you stay overnight at my house when Daddy was in town that summer. She needn't have worried, though. Daddy was no longer coming into my room in the middle of the night in those days. I was too old at sixteen. He liked me better when I was younger. It started when I was ten, you know. Stopped when I was about thirteen."

"Poor Pamela," Irene whispered. The weight of a great sadness pressed down upon her. "I never knew. She always seemed so incredibly sophisticated and cool and worldly."

"I pretended that nothing had ever happened, of course. That's what kids do in those situations. They keep the secret, sometimes even from themselves. I never even told any of the therapists I saw over the years. I can't explain how it works. I think they call it compartmentalizing. I read somewhere that it's a survival mechanism or something. Whatever, I was real good at it."

"I wonder how Mom found out," Irene said.

"Your mother was a very intuitive person, Irene. She started talking to me that summer, asking me questions. At first I blew her off. But then, one day I suddenly got the urge to let her discover the truth. Didn't have the guts to do it in person, of course. But I knew where Daddy kept his favorite video, the one he had made of the two of us."

Irene went very still. "She gave that video to my mother, who would have told Dad."

"Who, in turn, would have done something very serious about it," Tess concluded quietly.

Irene drew a deep breath. "Yes."

On-screen, Pamela was gazing very intently into the camera.

"*I arranged for your mother to find the video. That same evening I made sure that you were with me. I couldn't stand the suspense of not knowing what was going to happen, you see. I didn't want to be alone.*"

"She wouldn't take me home." Irene laced her fingers very tightly together in her lap. "Kept me out past curfew. Made me drive all the way to Kirbyville with her. I was so angry. I knew my parents would be furious."

"*I thought I had it all planned out, Irene. But I made a terrible, terrible mistake. I can't really explain why I did it, except to say that, having made the first move to share my secret with your mother, I could no longer pretend the secret didn't exist, if you see what I mean. All of a sudden, it was boiling up inside me. So that afternoon, before I picked you up to go to the movies, I told someone I thought I could trust about the video and what I had done with it.*

"*Later, after I heard what happened to your folks, I realized that person must have called Daddy in San Francisco.*"

"Only a couple of hours away," Tess whispered.

"Ryland Webb knows how to handle a gun," Irene said. "He goes hunting every year with his father."

Pamela blinked a couple of times. Irene got the impression that she was trying to get rid of tears.

"*You'll never be able to prove that Daddy killed your parents, of course. I'm very sorry about that, Irene. But we both know that too*

much time has passed. Any hard evidence that might have existed dis-
appeared long ago."

A key turned in a lock. Irene and Tess both started.

The door opened. Phil loomed in the entrance, a small duffel bag in one hand. He looked very reassuring, Irene thought.

"I hear Luke wants me to keep you company until he gets
back to Dunsley, Irene." Phil closed the door and locked it.
"What's going on?"

"You'll never believe this." Tess scooted closer to Irene to
make room for him on the couch. "Take a look."

Pamela was talking again.

*". . . It's too late to get justice for your parents, Irene. But you can
make sure that my father never gets to the White House. You can destroy him. Don't worry, this time I didn't make the mistake that I made
last time. I didn't tell the person I confided in the night your parents
were murdered. You'll be safe until you get the story into print. After
that, it won't matter, will it?"*

Pamela paused again, reaching out to refill her wineglass.

*"Well, I think that's about it. Oh, except for the little wedding
dress, of course. I wore it for Daddy. He never knew that I kept it all
these years. Probably forgotten all about it. Don't unwrap it. Let a
DNA testing lab do that. Mustn't tamper with the evidence.*

*"I was able to duplicate the video and the film clips and the travel
records, but there was no way to copy the dress. I had intended to give*

it to you when I spoke with you. But after thinking about it for a while, I've decided to leave it with the duplicate set of evidence that I'm going to put in your old house here in Dunsley. Just a precaution. It will be safe there, regardless of whether or not I lose my nerve. As soon as I finish this video recording, I'll take everything over to Pine Lane and put it in your old bedroom.

"By the way, I rented the house under another name from the real estate firm in San Francisco that manages it. No one here in Dunsley knows that I've got any connection to the place.

"Good-bye, Irene. I wish I had the courage to face you with all this. But I'm not surprised that in the end I decided to avoid our meeting in Dunsley. I'm very good when it comes to practicing the fine art of denial."

The screen went dark.

For a long moment, no one spoke.

Phil whistled softly. "Looks like your theory was right, Irene. Someone killed her."

"Ryland Webb," Tess said. "It must have been him. He murdered his own daughter. It's unbelievable."

"No, it isn't," Irene said fiercely. "He was quite capable of raping her. Why would a monster like that stop there?"

"After he killed her, he must have taken the copy of the old video and Pamela's computer, which contained one set of the files of evidence," Tess said. "He probably thought he had everything. But he obviously never realized she had made a copy of the evidence and left it for you to find in Pine Lane."

"Wonder how he cracked the password code to access the files on Pamela's computer?" Phil said.

Irene shrugged. "Maybe he didn't. But he must have realized that there was damning information on it. Perhaps he simply tossed it into the lake."

Phil nodded. "Wouldn't be surprised if he torched the house just to make sure there was no other evidence left that could come back to haunt him."

Irene looked at the white box. "Or maybe he somehow found out about the little wedding dress."

"But he couldn't find it," Tess added thoughtfully. "So he burned down the whole house hoping to get rid of it."

Energy snapped through Irene. She reached for her phone. "I've got to call my boss."

Before she could punch out Adeline's number, the small phone chortled in her hand.

"Hello?"

"Looks like we've got some breathing room," Luke said. "Tanaka just located Ryland Webb. He's at his office in San Francisco, in a meeting with some heavy-hitter campaign contributors. He's got a fund-raiser tomorrow evening, so he probably won't be leaving town anytime soon. Stay with Phil and Tess until I get there."

"I'll be waiting."

When he hung up, she made the call to Adeline Grady. While she waited for Addy to answer, she watched Phil unzip the small duffel bag. He did not remove the contents. It wasn't necessary. From where she was sitting she could see light gleam dully on the barrel of a gun. It came as no surprise to discover that Phil owned one. This was Dunsley, after all, a genuine slice of rural California. There was probably a gun in every house in town. But the realization that Phil had come armed today sent an odd chill through her. Luke was definitely worried, she thought.

"About time you checked in, Irene," Addy said. "Talk to me."

"I've got the story that is going to make the *Glaston Cove Beacon* the most famous newspaper in the state within forty-eight hours. But we need to make some plans."

Sometime after eight o'clock that night, Irene heard Luke's SUV pull into the drive of the Carpenter house.

"There he is," she announced to Tess and Phil. "About time he got here." She tossed her cards down onto the table and jumped to her feet.

Phil and Tess exchanged amused expressions as they gathered up the cards. It dawned on Irene that she was acting like a lover or a wife who has been waiting impatiently for her man to come back to her after a lengthy absence in foreign climes.

You've only known him for a few days, she lectured herself sternly. *Try to be cool here.*

But she flung open the door with a sense of expectation and spiraling relief. Luke stood there, looking hard and cold-eyed and a little bleak.

"I was about to call you again to find out where you were," she said.

"Long drive," he said. "Long day. You okay?"

"Yes," she said. "Oh, heck with being cool."

She launched herself against his chest. He seemed startled but he recovered instantly. His arms closed tightly around her.

"Ready to go home?" he asked.

"Yes."

Forty-three

I can't believe you went to that house alone." Luke crossed the small living room of the cabin with long, restless strides, tossing his jacket over the back of a chair along the way. He went into the tiny kitchenette. "You should have waited until I got back."

"Once I knew the key fit the locks on those doors, I didn't have much choice," Irene said quietly. She folded her arms tightly around herself and watched him take a bottle of water out of the refrigerator. "I couldn't put it off. I had to know."

He looked at her. "Must have been bad."

"Someone had redecorated. New carpet, paint and furnishings." She hesitated. "I couldn't bring myself to walk into the kitchen, though."

"No surprise there." He drank some of the water and then set the bottle down on the counter. His eyes were steady and knowing. "Are you okay with what you found out today?"

"I'm not sure how I feel," she admitted. "I've known for so long that there had to be an answer. Now that I've got it I feel a little—" She broke off, groping for the right word. "Disoriented or something."

She fell silent, unable to think of anything else to say. The first rush of savage satisfaction that she had experienced when she heard the truth from Pamela's own lips had faded, leaving behind an odd sense of disconnect. She had her answers, she thought. Why was she feeling so unsettled?

"Answers aren't everything," Luke said, as if he had read her mind. "You need time to process them."

She nodded. "I think you're right."

"You shouldn't have gone to that house alone."

"You're repeating yourself."

"Probably because I'm pissed and I'm trying to process my anger. That's how men deal with emotions, didn't you know? We either get mad or we have sex."

She frowned. "Why are you mad at me?"

"Because someone else got killed today." His eyes darkened. "All I could think about on the way back here was that you and Tess were sitting there with enough evidence to destroy a U.S. senator and that said senator was obviously willing to murder people to keep his secrets."

"So you're angry because you were worried, is that what you're saying?"

"It's not that simple, damnit." He walked toward her. "We haven't had a lot of time together, but I thought we were involved in a relationship. This isn't just a fling or a one-night stand." He stopped in front of her. "Or is it?"

"No."

"I admit I'm not the world's leading expert on relationships, but it was my understanding that people in our situation are supposed to talk to each other. You should have waited until I got back here before you went to that house today."

"I'm used to doing things on my own, Luke."

"I know that. But you're not alone anymore." He gripped her shoulders. "Try to remember that, okay?"

She realized that she was about to burst into tears. "I think I'm going to cry. This is crazy."

"No, you're just processing." He pulled her hard against his chest. "Go ahead and cry."

She pressed her face into his shirt. "I thought men got nervous around crying females."

"I'm a Marine, remember? We're trained to handle anything."

She started to laugh and then, to her shock, she was sobbing. Great racking, gushing, cleansing sobs poured forth from the very core of her being.

She could not fight it, so she abandoned herself to the storm. Luke held her tight until it was over.

Afterward he made her a cup of tea. She sat with him at the little table looking out at the lake, aware that something inside her was now calm.

"Better?" he asked.

She realized she could smile again. "Yes."

· · · ·

I rene was in bed when he got out of the shower. Luke stopped in the doorway, one hand securing the knot of the towel wrapped around his waist. He took in the sight of her propped against the pillows.

Waiting for him, he thought. Urgent need unfurled inside him. Within the space of a couple of heartbeats, he went from being exhausted to fully aroused.

This was not a good time, he thought. Between that visit to her nightmare house and Pamela's message from beyond the grave, Irene had gone through some very heavy stuff today.

He reminded himself that he was in control. He was *always* in control.

He took two steps toward the bed and then stopped a second time.

"Luke?" Her brows drew together in concern. "Is something wrong?"

"I should probably use the couch," he said, aware, even as he said it, that he wanted her to argue with him.

"Why?"

"I'm feeling a little restless. Might be a while before I can get to sleep. You've had a tough day. You need your rest."

She looked pointedly down at the bulge in the towel. When she raised her head, her expression had turned sultry and knowing.

"I think what you need is a sleeping aid," she said. She smiled slowly. "Lucky for you, I've got just the thing."

Delight and anticipation burned through him.

"Does it involve batteries?" he asked.

Her laughter danced and sparkled in the room. "Come here and find out."

He switched off the bedside light and released his grip on the towel. But when he got into bed and started to lower his mouth to hers, she planted one hand flat against his chest, stopping him.

He raised his brows. "Something wrong?"

"I told you I'm going to help you get to sleep, remember?"

"Sleep is the last thing on my mind at the moment."

"Let's just see if you're still saying that after I'm finished with you."

She pushed firmly against his chest. He hesitated and then rolled obligingly onto his back. She came down on top of him, soft and warm and smelling of exotic seas and flowers that have no name.

He folded his hands behind his head, enjoying the seduction. "Now what?"

She did not answer. Instead her hand slid down across his belly. When she reached her goal and encircled him with her fingers, he felt everything inside him clench with eagerness.

"That works," he said.

"I noticed."

And then she found him with her mouth, and he thought he would shatter. He unfolded his arms and caught her head between his hands.

"You might want to go easy there," he managed.

She looked up at him through her tumbled hair. "Thought Marines never did things the easy way."

"Exception to every rule."

"Not in your case." Her tongue tripped lightly along the length of his erection.

He groaned, squeezing his eyes against the hot pleasure.

She released him to glide up his overheated body. He opened his eyes and watched, riveted, as she settled herself astride and took him deep inside. She was so tight, so hot and so very wet.

Sensation pounded through him. He wasn't going to be able to last much longer, he realized. He could feel his climax thundering down on him like a runaway train. He gripped her waist, intending to reverse their positions.

"No," she said, flattening her palms on his chest. "You don't have to be in control every time. Just let go."

"You're not there yet."

"We'll worry about me next time."

"No." He knew he was dampening the sheets with his perspiration. "I want you with me."

"I'm here. I'm not going anywhere."

The soft promise in her words sent him over the edge. Suddenly he was flying.

A long time later, he came back to his senses. The room smelled of sex and satisfaction.

"No wonder you look so good in black trench coats and

leather boots." He contemplated the shadowy ceiling. "Remind me to get you a little whip for your birthday. It would sort of complete the outfit, you know?"

She stretched languidly and cuddled closer. "I don't think my high school guidance counselor ever mentioned that becoming a dominatrix might be a good career path for me."

"Goes to show those high school guidance counselors don't know everything."

"True, but I'm sure they do their best." She levered herself up onto her elbow and regarded him with a smug smile. "Enjoy yourself, Marine?"

"'Ooh rah." He tumbled her back down across his chest and contemplated her with a sense of certainty. "I don't think I'm ever going to get enough of you."

She looked pleased. "That sounds nice. Are you going to be able to sleep now?"

"Are you kidding? After that experience it's a wonder I'm not comatose."

"It has been a very long day, hasn't it?" She yawned.

"For both of us." He sobered as events flooded back into his head. "My personal issues aside, that was a clever idea you had, checking out the locksmith over in Kirbyville."

"Adeline Grady trains her reporters to follow up on the details." She made a face. "I almost got into a serious accident on the way back, though."

He levered himself up on his elbows. "What are you talking about?"

"I was so busy thinking about the key and what it might mean, that I wasn't paying attention to my driving. I was moving very slowly on that curvy section of road along the south end of the lake. Some jerk in a big SUV came up behind me and got really pissed off."

He felt the all-too familiar prickle of awareness. "What happened?"

"I think he sort of lost it, to tell you the truth. Major road rage. He came up really hard and fast behind me. He was probably just trying to scare me to death, but a part of me wondered if maybe he was so angry he wanted to force me off the road into the lake."

He jackknifed to a full sitting position. "The hell he did."

"I decided that the best thing I could do was get off the road, so I turned into that old subdivision at the end of the lake."

"Ventana Estates?"

"The idiot followed me."

"You are scaring the living daylights out of me."

"Have to admit, I was a little tense myself at the time." She shivered. "But that old road through the subdivision was still covered in gravel, just as I remembered. What's more, it hasn't been maintained very well. It's a real mess."

"I know. I drove through Ventana Estates shortly after I moved to Dunsley just to check it out."

"A little local recon, hmm?"

"Tell me the rest of it."

Her smile faded. "I did the only thing I could think of. I stomped on the accelerator as soon as I realized the SUV wasn't going to back off. Believe me, he got a windshield full of gravel and rocks."

"That," he said, thinking about it, "was a very good maneuver."

"I could hear the rocks and pebbles hitting the SUV. I'm pretty sure I did some serious damage to the windshield and the finish on the hood and front fenders."

"He didn't follow you out of the subdivision?"

"No. I had my eyes glued to my rearview mirror all the way home. Never saw him again."

"Did you get a good look at the SUV?"

She shook her head. "Not really. He came up behind me very suddenly. I was so rattled that it was all I could do to concentrate on my driving."

"What color?"

"Silvery gray, like yours and a few hundred others in the area. It was one of the larger models with tinted windows. But that's all I noticed."

"License plate?"

"Are you kidding? I never even got a glimpse of it."

He sat quietly for a moment.

"Luke?"

"Yeah?"

"You're thinking that maybe it was more than a case of simple road rage, aren't you?"

"I'm thinking that's a real possibility," he said, forcing all emotion out of his voice. "Both Pamela Webb and Hoyt Egan are dead. If you had gone off the road into the lake today people would be talking about your unfortunate accident tonight. And Senator Ryland Webb could rest a little easier, knowing that the woman his daughter had contacted just before she died was gone."

"That bastard isn't going to rest easy for the rest of his life if I have anything to say about it," she vowed. "Tomorrow night at the fund-raiser I'm going to nail his hide to the wall. The story will break in the *Glaston Cove Beacon* the next morning and Webb's career will be in smoking ruins within hours."

Forty-four

The following evening Irene stood with Luke, Adeline Grady and Duncan Penn, the *Glaston Cove Beacon*'s one and only photographer, in the shadow of a potted palm. Together they surveyed the crowded hotel ballroom.

"Very slick," Luke said. He was dressed in a suit and tie, and he carried a laptop under one arm. "No one even blinked when we walked through the door."

"That's because all they saw were our press credentials," Irene said. "How did you get them, anyway, Addy?"

Adeline, short, round and magnificent in a stoplight-red pantsuit, rocked on her heels and looked smug. "Some of the easiest things to get in the entire universe are press credentials for a political fund-raiser. The campaign officials want the media to attend." She waved in the direction of the buffet table. "Why do you think they put out all the good grazing food?"

"Not a bad spread, either," Duncan said. Young, thin and slight of build, he looked as if the weight of the cameras draped around his neck might cause him to topple over. He examined the canapés, sliced cheeses and small sandwiches heaped on the small plate in his hand. "I'd give the Webb campaign a seven out of ten for the buffet. Maybe an eight."

Irene looked at Adeline. "I wouldn't have thought that the *Glaston Cove Beacon* was particularly popular with the Webb campaign people, given that we broke the story of Pamela's death."

Adeline downed some champagne and lowered the glass. "There may have been a slight misunderstanding regarding the exact name of the paper when I phoned to request the credentials."

Luke studied the plastic-encased card slung around his neck. "That would probably explain why our paperwork says that we're with the *Beacon Hill Banner.*"

"A temporary miscommunication, which I am only too happy to correct." Adeline reached into her tote bag, withdrew four press cards and handed them around. "Here are your replacement credentials."

"Misunderstandings happen," Luke said, removing the *Beacon Hill Banner* card from the plastic holder.

"They do, indeed," Adeline agreed. She looked at Duncan. "I'll hold that plate for you while you exchange the cards."

"Thanks." Duncan gave her his heavily laden plate and busied himself with the process of removing and replacing the press cards.

Adeline ate one of the sandwiches and immediately helped herself to another.

Irene exchanged her credentials and went back to surveying

the room. "No one here seems to be mourning the death of Hoyt Egan."

Adeline shrugged and selected another tidbit from Duncan's plate. "Webb's new campaign manager released a statement earlier today. Called Egan's death a terrible tragedy and said it clearly demonstrates that it is time to get tough on crime and that Ryland Webb has a plan to do just that."

"Heard that before," Duncan said. He finished fiddling with his credentials and reached to take back his plate. An alarmed scowl widened his eyes. "Hey, that's my food, boss."

"Oh, is it?" Unperturbed, Adeline seized one last cocktail sausage and then handed over the plate.

Luke looked at Irene. "How does it feel to be a big-time investigative journalist?"

"Adrenaline city," she confessed. "Don't usually get this jazzed when I cover the Glaston Cove city council meetings or choose the recipe of the week."

Addy rubbed her hands together. "You aren't the only one who is in high gear tonight, kiddo. Got to admit this story of yours feels big, very, very big."

Irene reached into her handbag, took out the little recorder and clipped it to the shoulder strap. She switched it on to make certain that it was working. "These gadgets have a bad habit of failing just when you're about to start an interview. Cameras ready, Duncan?"

"Ready and waiting." Duncan gazed longingly at the buffet table. "Do I have time to refill my plate?"

Irene saw commotion in a doorway at the back of the room.

Webb appeared. Alexa Douglass was at his side. A short, anxious-looking man hovered in the background. Hoyt Egan's replacement, no doubt.

"Forget the food, Duncan," she said. "Webb just arrived."

A keen expression lit Adeline's face. "Here we go, boys and girls."

Irene stepped out from behind the palm, notebook in hand. "Follow me."

"The two scariest words in the English language," Luke said dryly.

She paid no attention. She concentrated on forging a path through the crowd. Ryland Webb was surrounded by a group of well-wishers and potential contributors, but his height made it possible to keep him in view.

Alexa Douglass spotted Irene first. Surprise and then a frown of alarm flashed across her face. She suppressed both reactions quickly beneath a polite smile and then whispered something to Ryland.

His head swiveled as he searched the crowd. When he saw Irene and her companions, he spoke urgently to his new aide.

The short man hurried forward, obviously intent on intercepting her.

"Miss Stenson?" The aide planted himself directly in front of her. "I'm afraid I'm going to have to ask you to leave." He glanced at Luke, Adeline and Duncan. "You and your friends."

"I have some questions for the senator," Irene said.

"He's not giving interviews tonight. He's entertaining his guests."

"Tell Senator Webb that I am in possession of a video that was recently shot on location in Europe," Irene said. "Make it clear that the story about that particular junket and several others to the same destination is set to appear in tomorrow's edition of the *Glaston Cove Beacon*. Ask him if he would care to comment."

The aide's face creased with bewilderment. He glanced back over his shoulder at Webb, who had turned his back on the small group.

"Better not make this decision on your own, son," Adeline advised the aide. "This is big."

The short man dithered briefly.

"Wait here," he said.

He spun around and worked his way back through the throng to where Ryland stood surrounded by people. Irene watched him deliver the message in low-voiced tones.

Ryland jerked as though he had been tapped by a cattle prod. He turned slowly to look at Irene. She had to hand it to him, she thought, his expression was well schooled, giving nothing away. But she could see raw fury burning in his eyes.

"If looks could kill," Adeline murmured, "I think we'd all be smoking cinders about now."

"Oh, man, he looks pissed, all right." Duncan sounded remarkably cheerful. He took aim with a video camera. "This'll be great for the online site."

Ryland said something to the aide and to Alexa. Then he started toward Irene.

"Showtime," Irene said softly. She stepped forward to meet

him, raising her voice. "Senator Webb, what can you tell us about your last trip to Europe?"

"Not here." Ryland glared at Luke, Adeline and Duncan. He angled his head toward a hallway. "I'll speak to you all in private."

He moved off through the crowd, not waiting for an answer. Irene followed quickly, aware that the others were close behind her. She checked the recorder clipped to her shoulder bag one last time. Duncan selected another camera.

Ryland strode swiftly down a hall and turned into a small conference room. Irene, Luke, Adeline and Duncan trooped in behind him. He slammed the door shut and whirled to confront Irene.

"What the hell do you think you're doing?" he demanded in a voice that vibrated with rage.

"Senator Webb, the *Glaston Cove Beacon* is in possession of some computer files containing evidence and videos that appear to show you in the act of raping an underage girl in a European brothel," Irene said. "Do you have a comment?"

"You stupid bitch, how dare you suggest anything of the kind? I've never raped anyone in my life." Ryland turned a dark shade of red. "If you've got film, I guarantee you, it's fake. If you go public with it, I will see that you and your damned newspaper are ruined. Do you hear me? I'll destroy you." He looked at the others. "All of you."

Irene nodded at Luke. "Show him what we've got."

Luke set the computer on a table, raised the lid and powered up the machine. Ryland watched with an expression of gathering horror.

"You can't do this," he said. "Do you realize who you're dealing with? I can make your lives a living hell."

Adeline gave him a sunny smile. "I love threats. They make great quotes. Is that recorder working, Irene?"

"Yes, boss."

Ryland stared, face working, at the little device clipped to Irene's shoulder bag. "Stop it. Stop it right now."

"My paper is also in possession of a video recording made by your daughter, Pamela," Irene continued, scribbling rapidly in her notebook. "On it, she states that you are a pedophile and that you abused her when she was a girl."

"That's a lie." Ryland fisted his hands and took a step toward her. "I've told you, my daughter was mentally disturbed. If you print that garbage, I swear I'll—"

Luke moved up close behind Irene. "No threatening the reporter."

Ryland rounded on him. "You're a fool to get involved in this, Danner."

"Not like I had anything more interesting to do," Luke said.

Irene heard one of Duncan's cameras whir. She made some more quick notes and then looked up.

"Pamela knew that you would attempt to portray the videos as frauds, so she also supplied copies of travel records and credit card statements that verify that you made several trips to the city in which that particular brothel is located. My paper is prepared to fly me to Europe to investigate."

Out of the corner of her eye she saw Adeline blink at that outrageous statement.

"I'll sue your paper right into the ground," Ryland said. "Those trips were made for legitimate reasons. Trade issues." On-screen, Pamela started to talk. Ryland went still, as though hypnotized. "Shut it down. Do you hear me? Shut it down."

Adeline followed his gaze to the screen. "FYI, we made several copies of those computer files, Senator. Didn't want to take any chances."

Ryland turned on her. "My lawyers are going to tear all of you limb from limb."

Duncan's video camera whirred some more, catching what Irene knew would be a compelling scene of Ryland leaning over the much shorter Adeline in an extremely intimidating fashion while he made his threat.

Ryland realized what was happening and jumped back.

"Pamela also implicates you in the death of Hugh and Elizabeth Stenson seventeen years ago," Irene continued. "Care to comment?"

"I had nothing to do with their deaths. Everyone knows your father was a nutcase. He killed your mother and then committed suicide." Ryland seemed to regain some of his composure. "Obviously you are just as crazy as he was, Miss Stenson."

"What about the recent murder of your aide, Hoyt Egan?" Irene said. "Pamela claims that he's the one who filmed you having sex in that European brothel and that he was using the videos to blackmail you. Any comment?"

"I've got a comment, all right," Ryland said tightly. "This whole thing is nothing but a setup. You're trying to take me down because you think I killed your parents. You're a delusional woman who has concocted a load of bullshit with the help of a digital camera and a computer. Well, I won't let you do it. Do you hear me? I won't let you ruin me and everything I've achieved. This country needs me."

The door opened behind him. Alexa Douglass walked into the room and stopped short. "What is going on here?"

"These people are out to destroy me any way they can," Ryland said fiercely. "You won't believe the lies they're threatening to print. I have to call my lawyers immediately. They'll put a stop to this."

But Alexa was gazing at the computer screen, mystified.

"That's you, Ryland," she said. "What on earth?"

"It's a digitized fake," he told her. "Don't believe anything you see."

On the screen Ryland had accepted the drink. The little bride entered. Ryland rose and took her hand.

The scene shifted to the bedroom. Ryland appeared, naked.

"Dear God," Alexa whispered, clearly stunned. "I didn't believe her. She tried to tell me, but I didn't believe her."

Ryland took her hand. "Pamela lied, dear. Whatever she told you about me was false. She was very, very disturbed. You know that."

"Not Pamela." Alexa yanked her hand out of his. "My daughter, Emily. She told me a few weeks ago that you tried to touch her in what she called a bad way. I thought she was making up a story because she doesn't want a new daddy. But she was telling the truth, wasn't she?"

"I'm going to be Emily's father," Ryland said, gravely

authoritative now. "It's only natural that I would want to be affectionate. I'm trying to bond with her."

"Obviously Emily has a better understanding of what you were trying to do than I did," Alexa said, dazed and shaken. She put her hand to her stomach. "I'm going to be ill. I've got to get out of here. I must find Emily. I've got to talk to her, tell her I understand and that I won't let you touch her again. How could I have been so blind?"

She flew to the door, wrenched it open and fled the room.

Ryland swung back to face Irene. His rage had turned ice cold.

"I'll see that you pay for this," he said. "You have absolutely no solid evidence. No one is going to pay attention to doctored videos."

"I think they will, but just in case, I've got something else you might want to see." Irene reached into her purse and took out the packet of photos that Duncan had made earlier in the day. She scattered the pictures on the table. "Pamela wanted to be very certain that I had enough evidence to make her accusations stick. In addition to the computer files, she also left me this miniature wedding dress costume preserved in a plastic wrapper. Care to comment?"

Ryland glanced at the photos. At first he appeared baffled. Then recognition struck. His jaw sagged. He went pale.

"Where did you get that dress?" he demanded, hoarse with fear and fury.

"Pamela saved it," Irene said. "She states that you forced her to wear that gown on several occasions when she was a girl. She says you got a kick out of raping her when she was dressed like that."

"You can't prove anything, do you hear me?" Ryland snarled. "Not one damned thing."

"Pamela also states on the video that any reasonably good lab will find DNA evidence all over the skirts of that dress."

Ryland uttered an inarticulate roar and leaped toward her, both hands outstretched.

Instinctively she fell back, vaguely aware of the sound of Duncan's video camera in action. All she could see was the rage on Ryland's face as he came toward her.

And then Luke was suddenly between her and Ryland, moving so quickly she wasn't sure what had happened until she saw Webb stretched out flat on his back on the floor.

Luke stood over him. "I told you, no threatening the reporter."

"I want my lawyer," Ryland said, strangely composed now. "I'm going to ruin each and every one of you."

Forty-five

Two days later Irene sat in a booth next to Luke in the Ventana View Café. Tess and Phil faced them from the opposite side. The remains of four platters of pancakes littered the table.

Irene was aware of the curious eyes that surrounded them. The café had filled up with remarkable speed shortly after she and the others had been seen entering the establishment.

"You did it, Irene." Tess picked up the copy of the previous day's edition of the *Glaston Cove Beacon* that Adeline had sent via overnight delivery. She waved it like a banner. "You brought down Senator Ryland Webb. I heard on the news this morning that there are rumors that he'll officially call off his campaign by the end of the week. Not only did you crush his chances of getting into the Oval Office, it's safe to say that his odds of being reelected to the Senate again in this state are less than zero."

Irene looked at the headlines splashed across the *Beacon*. She had already viewed them on the online edition of the paper, but there was something very satisfying about seeing them in print.

WEBB CAMPAIGN HIT BY ALLEGATIONS
OF SEX WITH MINORS

The scandal was in full sail. All of the major dailies in the state, including those from San Francisco, Los Angeles and San Diego, were rushing to jump on the story, but they were still playing catch-up. Two had announced that they were launching independent investigations of their own. The radio and television talk shows were in a frenzy. New evidence of Ryland Webb's murky sexual past was pouring in hourly. Adeline had phoned three times to gloat over the number of hits at the *Beacon*'s online Web site.

"At least this time the politician's loyal little woman isn't going to stand by her man." Tess indicated the photo that Duncan Penn had shot of Alexa Douglass. It showed her getting out of a limo with her daughter in front of an elegant San Francisco town house. The caption read *Douglass ends engagement to Webb.*

"Webb is definitely dead meat," Phil said. "And Irene is the one who brought him down."

Irene looked at the three of them, gratitude and affection so thick in her throat she was afraid she might burst into tears. "I couldn't have done it without the help of all of you. I don't know how to thank you."

Luke grinned. "Guess that makes us all junior cub reporters. Who knew we had the talent? Here I thought I'd be stuck on the innkeeping career track for the rest of my natural life."

Irene picked up her coffee mug. "I just wish I could have

found a way to force Ryland Webb to confess to the murders. He killed four people that we know of—my parents, Pamela and Hoyt Egan. And he's going to walk."

"Maybe not," Luke said. "It's true that the cops probably won't be able to prove that he killed your folks and Pamela, but they may be able to link him to the death of Hoyt Egan. They've got a strong motive, after all."

"Blackmail," Phil said. "Yeah, that definitely works as a motive. Now that they know what to look for, the cops may get lucky and turn up some solid evidence in that case."

Tess leaned back in the booth, a worried frown shadowing her face. "There's one thing that I'm not sure I understand here."

Luke speared a wedge of the uneaten portion of the stack of pancakes on Irene's plate. "What's that?"

"Why did Pamela decide to expose her father after all these years?" Tess asked. "She kept the secret for so long. Why go public now?"

"She had been in therapy," Phil reminded her. "Maybe something happened in those sessions that pushed her into going public."

Irene looked at the newspaper on the table. A sense of absolute certainty welled up inside her.

"It wasn't the therapy," she said quietly. She pointed to the photo of Alexa Douglass and her daughter. "There's the reason. Little Emily Douglass. Pamela realized that her father was about to acquire another child bride. She could keep her own family secret, but in the end she could not stand by and allow history to repeat itself."

Forty-six

I rene tossed the pen onto the table and studied the latest version of the time line. Frustration churned in her stomach. No matter how she tried to connect the dots, she could not come up with a reasonable way to put Ryland Webb anywhere near Dunsley on the day of Pamela's death.

She had been so certain that when she sat down with all the facts she would find something in addition to a motive that she could give to the police to tie Webb to the murder. But thus far she had come up empty-handed.

There had to be a connection, she thought. It was inconceivable that Pamela had died because of an accidental overdose.

She got up and went into Luke's small, orderly kitchenette to pour herself more tea. It was the fourth time she had gotten out of the chair in the past forty minutes. She had already wandered into the kitchen area three times, twice to refill her mug, once to check the refrigerator to see what she needed to buy for dinner.

Mug in hand, she went out the back door of the cabin, propped one hip against the porch railing and contemplated the placid surface of the lake. The view from this cabin was slightly different from the one she'd had while residing in Cabin Number Five. From here she could see more of the lake.

She had promised Adeline another local-color piece to feed to the maw of the wire services and to keep the hits coming at the Web site. The new deadline was looming, but she had been unable to concentrate on the story. Instead, her brain insisted on returning to the problem of Pamela's death. Maybe this intense fixation was the true definition of a conspiracy theorist, she thought.

A chill went through her. Maybe all the therapists over the years had been right when they tried to convince her that she was obsessing on her own fictional version of events because she could not deal with reality.

No, don't go there, she ordered herself. *You're a reporter. Try sticking with the dots. Better yet, try coming up with some new ones.*

She watched a battered pickup pull into the drive and park near the lobby. Tucker Mills got out and removed a rake and a large broom from the back of the vehicle. Maxine emerged to greet him, radiating animation and enthusiasm.

The Sunrise on the Lake Lodge was enjoying a rush of out-of-season business due to an influx of members of the media who had arrived in Dunsley to get background on the big story. Appalled at the prospect of so many unanticipated paying guests, Luke had abandoned the front desk altogether, leaving everything in Maxine's hands.

Once in command, Maxine had risen to the challenge immediately. Her first act had been to quadruple the rack rates. After renting up all of the available space, she had politely but firmly suggested that Irene move into Luke's cabin, thereby freeing up another room. An hour ago Maxine had dispatched Luke into Dunsley to pick up fresh supplies of toilet paper, coffee and doughnuts. Irene knew that he had been grateful for the excuse to escape.

The small media frenzy would not last long, Irene reflected, but while it did, the lodge was flourishing.

She took another swallow of tea and thought some more about previously unconsidered dots. Shards of one of her old nightmares flickered through her head.

It occurred to her that she was one of the dots.

I'm sorry Irene didn't come with you," Tess said. She poured freshly made lemonade into Luke's glass and sat down in one of the living room chairs. "I have all sorts of questions for her."

"She's working on another piece for the *Beacon*." Luke downed half the contents of his glass, savoring the tangy taste. "Adeline is leaning on her for more local stuff. The Ryland Webb story is getting deeper and wider by the hour."

Tess chuckled. "Who would have thought that quiet little Irene would have turned out to be a fiery investigative journalist?"

"She's a woman on a mission," Luke said. "I'm supposed to

be on one, too. I put Maxine in charge of the lodge, and the next thing I know, she's issuing orders. She sent me out to scour the local terrain for toilet paper. Personally, I don't see any reason why the guests can't supply their own, but Maxine feels differently."

Tess laughed. "I'll bet she's enjoying herself out there at the lodge."

"She's making money, that's for sure. At any rate, on the way into town I got to thinking that you might be able to help me clear up one question that's been bothering me."

Tess's intelligent face lit with interest. "What do you want to know?"

"The name of the person Pamela confided in the day Irene's parents died."

Tess's enthusiasm faded abruptly. "You're talking about the individual who called Ryland Webb and warned him about what Pamela had done?"

"Any ideas?"

Tess sighed. "Phil and I talked about it. We came up with one possibility, but neither of us believes that there's any point pursuing it. I'm sure the person we're thinking of did what he thought was the right thing, never guessing where it would lead."

"How the hell could he believe that calling Webb was the right thing?"

Tess pondered the view outside her window for a moment and then turned back to face him. Her expression was very steady.

"First, I'd better give you some local history," she said. "Phil and I were born and raised in this town. One way or another we've experienced the effects of three generations of Webbs."

"I'm listening."

"My mother told me a story once. It was about a girl named Milly, whom she knew in high school here in Dunsley. Evidently Milly was quite a beauty. The summer she graduated Victor Webb gave her a job as a receptionist in his company's headquarters in San Francisco. She was thrilled. She took off for the bright lights of the big city without a backward glance. My mother and her friends were incredibly envious of her good fortune."

"I sense a bad outcome here."

"You sense right. A year and a half after she left Dunsley, Milly returned with a baby boy. She raised him here. She was a single mother living in a small town where jobs have always been scarce, but she and her boy never seemed to lack for a nice roof over their heads and decent clothes."

"Did she work?"

"Occasionally, but mostly just to keep busy, I think. As I said, she didn't appear to need the money."

"Where did the cash come from?"

Tess reached for the lemonade pitcher. "Milly told everyone that she'd had an affair with a man who was killed in a car accident before he could marry her, but that he left her something in his will. She stuck to that story until the day she died, although my mother and her friends never really believed it."

"Milly's dead?"

Tess nodded. "Cancer. But her son still lives here in town. And if the old rumors were right, Victor Webb is his father."

"That would make Ryland Webb his brother."

"Yes."

The houses in the heavily wooded subdivision were not the most upscale in town, but they were solidly middle class. The vehicles in the paved driveways were of recent vintage. Luke saw gardens and lawns but no front porches. This was a neighborhood of backyard decks and patios.

He left the SUV at the corner and walked back to the police cruiser that was parked in front of a closed garage. The window was conveniently lowered on the driver's side. A garage door opener was clipped to the visor.

He reached inside the vehicle and depressed the button. The garage door rumbled open in response. A heavy, silver SUV was parked inside.

Luke went forward to take a closer look. The finish on the front of the vehicle was badly dinged and chipped in several places. Myriad spiderweb cracks marred the windshield.

He heard the front door of the house open.

"What the hell are you doing in my garage, Danner?" Sam McPherson called out from the top of the steps.

Luke went to stand in the garage opening. "Out of curiosity, were you just trying to scare Irene to death the other day when you chased her on Lakefront Road, or did you intend to kill her?"

Sam came down the steps. "I don't know what the hell you're talking about."

"That SUV looks like it went through a bad hailstorm."

Sam scowled. "Some kids stole it. Took it joyriding. I haven't had a chance to take it in to Carpenter's garage."

"How long have you been doing favors for your older brother, Sam?"

Sam looked as if he'd been punched in the gut. "What?"

"We're going to talk. Either we do it out here where your neighbors can watch, or we go inside and do this in private. Your choice."

"Why should I talk to you?"

"Because I know you're Ryland Webb's half brother. I figure it was you who called him seventeen years ago to warn him that Pamela had given the video to Elizabeth Stenson. Did he ask you to burn down the Webb house the other night? Or did he drive up here to do the job himself?"

"I don't know what you're talking about," Sam rasped, unnerved now. "Get out of here."

"Must have been hard watching your brother get the benefits of being a legitimate Webb all these years. Ryland was the golden boy, wasn't he? The local crown prince. You never told anyone that you had just as much Webb blood in your veins as he did. Why was that, Sam? Was it because Victor Webb paid your mother to keep the secret, and after she was gone you felt you had to do the same?"

Sam made fists of both hands. "Shut up."

"You seem to do okay on a small-town police chief's salary." Luke angled his head toward the garage. "Nice new car. House in a good neighborhood."

"I don't have to listen to this."

"Yeah, you do have to listen, Sam." Luke started toward him. "Because the way I figure it, you're an accessory to at least three murders, maybe four. I'm not sure about Hoyt Egan yet. It's possible that your brother handled that one all by himself."

"You can't prove anything."

"That's what your brother keeps saying. But you'll notice that he's going down in flames. Won't be long before he breaks. If you didn't help him commit any of the murders, you'd better be prepared to prove it."

"I don't have to prove a damn thing," Sam said.

"You're wrong. You'd better prove to me that you didn't try to force Irene off the road into the lake the other day, or I'm going to take you apart."

Sam's face worked. "For God's sake, man, I didn't try to kill her. Why the hell would I do a thing like that?"

"Maybe because Ryland Webb asked you to do it?"

Sam's eyes hardened. "I don't take orders from Ryland Webb, damn you."

"Pamela trusted you, didn't she? You were her uncle, after all. Not like she had a lot of close family to turn to. The day she gave the video to Elizabeth Stenson, she confided in you. She told you that Ryland had abused her for years and that the secret was about to come out. But instead of honoring your niece's trust, you called your brother and warned him about what was going to happen."

"No, damn you, I didn't call Ryland."

"Did you kill them yourself, McPherson?"

"No." Sam looked as if he were drowning in a sea of anguish. "God help me, I didn't believe Pamela that day. I thought she made up the story about being abused because she wanted to get back at Ryland for sending her away to boarding school. I didn't know what was on that video she gave to Elizabeth Stenson, but I was afraid that Pamela was about to create a lot of trouble for herself and the family. So I did the only thing I could think of."

All the dots were connected now. Ice sleeted through Luke's veins.

"You didn't call Ryland," Luke said. "You called your father, Victor Webb."

Forty-seven

I t took more courage than she had ever dreamed she possessed to walk into the ghastly kitchen. Pushing through the invisible veil of the old nightmare aroused a wave of nausea and terror so powerful she had to cling to one of the counters to keep from falling.

Fighting the vertigo, she looked down at the floor. *Oh, God, the floor.* It was the same imitation white stone tile that her mother had chosen for the room on the grounds that it would be easy to clean. The kitchen had been repainted over the years, but no one had replaced the tile.

Easy to clean.

Don't think about the blood. You are not going to be sick. You can't be sick. You came here to look at the evidence. This is a crime scene, and you were the first witness. You are also a journalist. Do your job. Step back and take another look.

She straightened and studied the sunny kitchen. Very slowly she unlocked the vault in her mind and dragged the nightmares out into the light of day.

She took her notepad and pen out of her handbag. Then she forced herself to cross the kitchen, open the back door and walk out onto the small porch. She closed the door behind her and stood still for a moment, bracing herself.

The plan was a simple one. She would retrace her movements that night, recalling as many of the dreadful details as possible to see if she could come up with anything that might serve to link Ryland Webb to the murders of her parents. Even the smallest sliver of memory or evidence might be enough to pressure Webb into a confession.

Taking a deep breath, she checked the time on her watch and reopened the door. Moving slowly, she stepped back into the kitchen. The nightmarish images she had worked so hard to hide in the vault smashed through her.

Panic and anguish screamed in her head. It took everything she had to get the emotions under control. So much for the theory that facing your fears rendered them less awful, she thought.

She made herself take her time, reliving it all in as much detail as possible from the first chilling realization that the door was partially blocked by some heavy object, to the moment when she managed to punch in the emergency number on the telephone.

At first it was disconcerting, even disturbing, to discover that, although the images stored in the vault were shattering and intense, there were very few of them.

Then again, that made sense, she reflected. All the psych articles she had read over the years pointed out that when an individual was thrust into the center of a traumatic event, the deluge of adrenaline and shock created a very narrow range of focus. It was a survival mechanism, she thought. You can't deal with everything that comes rushing at you in that sort of situation, so you tune out the nonessential elements and concentrate on what you need to do in order to keep going.

Nevertheless, when she rechecked her watch a short time later, she was stunned to realize how little time had passed between the moment she had discovered the bodies and when she made the call that brought Sam McPherson to the front door. Not long at all, she thought. At the time it had seemed an eternity.

She made herself examine the kitchen counters, trying to recall if there had been any dishes or cooking utensils out when she got home that night. It seemed to her that the countertops had been clean. Did that indicate that the killer had arrived after dinner and the dishes had been done? Or had he come before her mother had even started the evening meal?

It was hopeless. She wasn't going to get any answers from the kitchen. What else did she remember about that night?

There had been a great deal of confusion, she thought. She recalled Sam's horrified expression when he had seen the bodies. He had been shaking when he called Bob Thornhill.

When Thornhill arrived, he and Sam had taken her outside to one of the cruisers, bundled her into the passenger seat and wrapped a blanket around her shoulders. Later Thornhill took her home to his house for what remained of that terrible night.

She recalled sitting huddled on the bed in the Thornhills' spare bedroom until dawn, the soft, relentless hiss of Gladys Thornhill's oxygen machine a sad pulse beat in the darkness.

The phone had rung just as the sky began to turn a dull gray over the lake. Bob Thornhill came out of the bedroom and trudged down the hall to answer it.

Irene rubbed her temples, struggling to recall more details. She knew she could not possibly remember every word of the conversation, and several of her therapists had warned her about the danger of inventing memories of that night. Still, some of the truth was there.

Think like a good reporter, not a frightened teen.

The low-voiced, one-sided discussion she had overheard never seemed important before. But in light of what had happened in the past few days, it took on new meaning. For the first time she tried to reconstruct it as accurately as possible.

". . . Yes, sir, she's with us. Pretty much what you'd expect, sir. She's in shock. Hasn't said hardly a word. . . . No, I asked her that, and it's clear that she got home too late to see any of it, thank God. Judging from the condition of the bodies, I'd say it went down at least a couple of hours or more before the poor kid walked in the back door."

There had been a long pause, during which Thornhill listened to the person on the other end of the phone.

"Not much doubt about it. Hugh Stenson went crazy, shot Elizabeth and then turned the gun on himself. Terrible, terrible thing."

Another pause.

"Yes, sir," Thornhill said. *"I called the aunt. She'll be here tomorrow."*

There had been a few more soft-spoken words, and then Thornhill hung up and made his way back down the hall to his dying wife.

"Who was that?" Gladys Thornhill mumbled.

"Webb."

"What did he want?"

"He was worried about the girl. Called to see how she was getting on."

"At four-thirty in the morning?" Gladys asked.

"He said he had just heard the news."

"What did he want, Bob?"

"I told you, he was concerned about the Stenson girl. Asked if there was anything he could do."

"I know him." Bitter resignation laced Gladys's words. "Sooner or later, he always wants something. Someday he'll make you pay for what he's doing for me, mark my words."

"Try to get some sleep."

Irene shuddered. In light of what she now knew, it was obvious that Webb had called Bob Thornhill that night to make sure the daughter of his victims had not seen or heard anything that might implicate him as the killer. Perhaps Thornhill had unwittingly saved her life when he assured Webb she had not come home for at least two hours after the deaths and that she was in a state of complete shock.

She let herself out the kitchen door and made her way to the edge of the lake. Stepping onto the old wooden dock, she went to stand at the far end. She studied the surface of the lake the way her father had done when he wanted to think things over.

"I know him. Sooner or later, he always wants something. Someday he'll make you pay for what he's doing for me, mark my words."

There had been a disturbing intimacy about the way Gladys spoke, she thought. True, she had lived in Dunsley all her life. She certainly knew Ryland Webb. But Ryland had been many years younger than Gladys Thornhill, a different generation altogether. It was odd that she had spoken of him in such a resentful, knowing way.

"I know him."

A cold thrill of comprehension whispered through Irene.

In her shocked and dazed condition on the night of the murders, she had assumed that Ryland was the one who called the Thornhills that night. He was the father of her best friend that summer. It had seemed natural that he would call to check on her. But what if it had been Victor Webb who phoned?

Gladys and Victor Webb had been contemporaries. The two had no doubt gone to school together before Victor left Dunsley to make his fortune. Everyone in town knew that Victor Webb had paid Gladys's medical bills during the last year of her life.

The dots were connecting so quickly now that she could barely keep up with them.

Her cell phone rang, jarring her out of the trance of concentration into which she had plunged. She jumped a little and then quickly opened her handbag, half turning.

She saw him then. He had come from the shadows at the side of the house. He had a gun in his hand.

"Don't answer that," Victor Webb said. "Take the phone out very slowly and drop it into the water."

Her first, disoriented reaction was that he looked so *normal*. He was dressed in a black-and-tan golf shirt, a khaki windbreaker and a pair of light-colored golf slacks. He looked as though he had just come off a fairway.

Somewhere in the back of her mind was the knowledge that she ought to be terrified, but all she could feel in that moment was a rage that was so red and so powerful, it swamped every other emotion.

"I said drop the damned phone into the water," Victor barked. "Do it now, you stupid bitch. You're just like your damned parents, nothing but trouble."

Slowly she reached into the bag. With shaking fingers she fumbled around a bit and eventually managed to extract the phone. She tossed the device over the side of the dock. There was a small splash, and then it disappeared beneath the surface.

"You were the one," she whispered, barely able to speak through her fury. "You murdered them all—my parents, Hoyt Egan and Pamela. How could you kill your own granddaughter?"

Victor snorted. "Odds are good that she wasn't my granddaughter. Her mother was a tramp who slept with anything in pants. She suckered Ryland into marriage when my boy was barely twenty. Didn't take me long to figure out that he had married a woman who was going to be a millstone around his neck. I tried to get him to dump her."

"But he didn't," Irene said tightly. "Because of Pamela."

"He was obsessed with that child from the get-go. Never did I understand it until I found out he had a thing for young girls."

"You killed Pamela's mother, too, didn't you? Everyone thinks she died in a boating accident out on the lake, but I'll bet you arranged it. Why didn't you get rid of Pamela at the same time?"

"I gave it some thought," Victor admitted. "But Pamela was almost five by then. Ryland was running his first campaign, and the kid looked great in the press releases. The media and the public loved her. After her mother died, voters went crazy for the image of Ryland as the young, noble, committed father, grieving the loss of his beloved wife and determined to raise his daughter on his own."

"But when Pamela hit her teens, she started to become a liability, didn't she? Ryland no longer found her sexually interesting, so he stashed her in a boarding school most of the time."

"In her teens Pamela discovered drugs," Victor said, disgusted. "She also found out she could manipulate any male who happened to be in her vicinity. The school kept her out of the public eye for the most part. I was concerned that she might prove to be a problem after she graduated, though. I started to make some plans."

"Instead, after she graduated, she made herself useful in Ryland's campaigns again."

"What can I say?" Victor shrugged. "She was her mother's daughter all the way to her little round heels. Pamela was a whore at heart, but she was our whore and she was damned good at what she did. She was willing to sleep with Ryland's rivals, enemies and anyone else, male or female, who had information that we could use. She enjoyed her role as a spy. It made her feel powerful to know that she was a critical part of the campaign strategy and that Ryland had come to depend on her. I think it gave her a sense of vengeance. The silly creature probably felt like she was in control of her father at last. But I was always the one who ran the show, right from the get-go."

"You talk as if Ryland's success was your own."

"It is mine." Anger twisted Victor's face. "I made my son what he is today."

"A disgraced pedophile who won't even be able to run for dogcatcher?"

"You've ruined everything," Victor said, voice thickening with rage. "My son was on his way to the White House until you came along. The White House, damn you. He was going to be president. My grandsons would have followed in his footsteps."

"Don't know about the grandsons," Irene said. "Ryland prefers little girls, doesn't he?"

"Shut up. Ryland promised me sons. It was in the prenuptial agreement he signed with Alexa Douglass. It was spelled out that she would produce a male heir within two years with the help of in vitro fertilization if necessary or else accept a quiet divorce. The fact that she had already produced one child meant that she was fertile."

"You saw Alexa Douglass's daughter as evidence of her fertility, but your pervert son saw her as a target for future abuse.

Pamela's the one who pulled the plug on your plans, not me. She did what she had to do to save Alexa's daughter, and you killed her in an effort to silence her."

"I should have gotten rid of you seventeen years ago," Victor said. "If you had been in the house the night I did your parents, I would have taken care of you, too. Unfortunately, you weren't there when I arrived. I didn't want to risk hanging around for what might have been hours waiting for you, so I left. Later, it was obvious you knew nothing about the video or who had shot your parents, so I decided not to worry about you. To tell you the truth, Irene, I damned near forgot about you over the years. Obviously that was a mistake on my part."

"How did you find out that Pamela planned to go public with the accusations against Ryland?"

Victor gave her a thin, humorless smile. "She called me the day before she planned to meet you."

"Of course," Irene whispered, suddenly understanding. "She knew that what she was going to do would rip the family apart. She felt she owed you, the head of the clan, some advance notice and maybe an explanation."

"I tried to talk her out of it, but it was clear that she had made up her mind. So I came up here to Dunsley to take care of things."

"She opened the door to you, didn't she?"

Victor snorted. "No, as a matter of fact, I let myself into the house very late that night. She was asleep in bed. I injected her with a lethal dose of a certain pharmaceutical. She woke up and struggled for a few seconds, but the drug works fast."

"And then you set the stage to make it appear that she had OD'd. When did you find out about the little wedding dress?"

His face worked in remembered fury. "The drug worked a little too fast. She laughed at me at the very end. She actually *laughed*. Told me I'd never find the wedding dress that Ryland had made her wear, said it was on the video and that it had DNA evidence all over it. I looked for it that night, but I couldn't find it."

"Later when you watched the video, you realized that the dress was potentially a huge problem. You had to get rid of it. So you went back the next night and burned down the house in hopes of destroying it."

"It never occurred to me that Pamela might have hidden the dress off-site," he admitted.

"How did you find out that Hoyt Egan was blackmailing Ryland?"

He shrugged. "When Pamela called me to tell me what she intended to do, I demanded to know how she could be sure that Ryland was still screwing little girls. She said she had pictures that had been taken on some of Ryland's foreign junkets. She told me they had been taken by Egan. He accompanied Ryland on several of those trips. Somewhere along the line he figured out what Ryland was doing on the side. That's the problem with aides. There's a tendency to let them get too close to the center of power. Ryland got careless."

"What did you do the night you killed my parents? Ambush them?"

"In a manner of speaking. I used a boat that night, too, just as I did the night I got rid of Pamela and again when I torched the house. Tied up at the dock behind your parents' place and went to the back door. Your folks had finished dinner and were sitting in the living room, talking about the video they had just watched."

"I don't understand. They were killed in the kitchen."

"They both came into the kitchen when they heard me knock on the back door. They recognized me, naturally, and let me in. I told them I'd heard about the video and explained how shocked I was to discover that Ryland had a little problem."

"A little problem?" Irene stared at him. "Your son is a monster. So are you, for that matter. Talk about bad genes."

Victor ignored that. "I told your folks that I had made plans to put Ryland into a psychiatric hospital for treatment. Asked them to keep the whole business quiet for everyone's sake. But Hugh looked out at the dock and my boat. I could see that he was starting to get suspicious, wondering why I had come by way of the lake. I had my gun inside my coat. It was the same make and model that he carried on the job. He wasn't wearing his gun in the house, of course. I moved up right beside him and shot him before he had a chance to turn around. Your mother screamed and launched herself straight at me like some kind of wild animal. I shot her, too. It was all over in an instant."

Rage-induced adrenaline flowed through Irene. She wanted to do what her mother had done and fling herself on Victor Webb. She yearned to slash him to pieces with her nails. But she knew that if she rushed him, he would cut her down before she got close enough to claw his face.

She flicked a disgusted glance at the gun in his hand. "Do you really think that killing me will fix things? There's no way Ryland's career can be salvaged."

"Don't you think I'm aware of that? Thanks to you, I've lost one son. But I've got another and I've got a plan."

"Freeze, Webb."

Luke's command had the strobe-like effect of lightning on the lake at midnight. For an instant everything and everyone, including Victor Webb, went utterly still.

Luke emerged from the shadows at the side of the house, moving with the lethal grace of a predator who has had plenty of experience bringing down prey.

He had a gun in his hand.

Sam McPherson followed close behind him, a pistol in one fist.

Webb snapped out of his startled trance. He turned his head and saw the two men approaching.

"You're both fools," he said. "Shoot me and you'll hit Irene."

He was right, Irene realized. Victor stood directly in front of her on the narrow dock. Once the bullets started flying, it would be a miracle if she wasn't hit.

"Give it up, Webb," Luke said, moving slowly toward the dock. "This thing is over. We all know that."

"It's over when I say it's over, Danner."

Victor suddenly lunged toward Irene, reaching out to seize her by the arm. She realized that he intended to use her as a shield and a hostage.

She dropped her shoulder bag onto the dock and threw herself backward off the dock. The last thing she saw before she hit the water was Victor Webb bringing his gun to bear on Luke.

She landed with a heavy splash and sank quickly. The cold waters closed over her, muffling the roar of the shots.

Her first instinct was to swim away from the vicinity of the dock. She went as far as she could underwater, hugging the shoreline. The weight of her coat and boots tugged at her, threatening to pull her deeper.

When she could hold her breath no longer, she surfaced, gasping for air, and turned to look back. Luke stood at the end of the dock, searching the water for her. Behind him Sam McPherson crouched beside Victor Webb, who lay crumpled on the boards.

Luke spotted her and raised a hand.

"You okay?" he called.

"Yes." She got to her feet and staggered out of the shallow water. The crisp air struck like a knife, plastering her cold, wet garments around her.

Luke came toward her, peeling off his windbreaker. When he got close, he yanked off her soaking trench coat and wrapped the light jacket around her.

"You gave me one hell of a scare," he muttered, dragging her against his warm, hard frame. "When you didn't answer your phone a few minutes ago, I went a little crazy."

"Oh, God, Luke, I have never been so glad to see anyone in my life." She clung to him. "Is Webb dead?"

"Not yet." His arm around her, he guided her back to where Sam was using his own shirt as a makeshift bandage to staunch the blood flowing from Webb's midsection.

"Just called the aid car," Sam said tonelessly.

"Are you both all right?" Irene asked, surveying Luke and Sam in turn.

Before either man could answer, Victor Webb groaned and opened his eyes. He squinted up at Sam, evidently trying to bring him into focus.

"Son," he said in a grating whisper.

"Ryland isn't here," Sam responded without a flicker of emotion.

"You're my son. You know that. Listen to me. What happened here will come down to our word against theirs." Victor glanced at Luke and Irene and grimaced with pain and hatred. "They're outsiders, and you're the law here in Dunsley. And I'm Victor Webb. The locals will believe whatever we tell them."

"Sorry, but that's not how it's going to be," Sam said. He got slowly to his feet.

"You're family, damn you." Victor broke off, coughing blood. "When the chips are down, family takes care of its own."

"I am taking care of my own," Sam said quietly. "I'm arresting the man who murdered my niece."

"Pamela was a cheap little tramp. Listen to me, Sam, I've got a plan. You're going to take Ryland's place. You'll have to start small, naturally. A state office to begin with, but we can build you fast. No one outside Dunsley knows that you're a Webb.

You'll be the heroic small-town chief of police who helped take down a U.S. senator. The voters will love you. But first you've got to help me clean up this mess."

"What I've got to do is my job. If Bob Thornhill had done his all those years ago, Pamela would still be alive." Sam took a card out of his back pocket. "You have the right to remain silent—"

"Shut up, you ungrateful bastard," Victor screamed. "My word is the one everyone will believe. I'm Victor Webb."

"You're right, Mr. Webb." Irene picked up her handbag, reached inside and took out the recorder she had turned on when she pretended to fumble for her phone. "Your word is good enough to take to the bank around here."

She switched on the recorder. There was no mistaking Webb's harsh, angry voice coming from the machine.

"... *If you had been in the house the night I did your parents, I would have taken care of you, too....*"

Forty-eight

That evening, after a late dinner, they went out onto the back porch of the cabin and stood looking at the lake. The air was chilled and clear, and the moon cast a cold white light across the dark water.

Irene pulled the collar of her coat up around her neck and leaned into Luke, seeking his heat. He put his arm around her shoulders and held her tightly against his side.

"When they take that bullet out of Victor Webb, they're going to discover that it came from your gun, aren't they?" she asked.

"Yes," he said. He didn't offer anything else.

"Did Sam fire his weapon?"

"No." He was quiet for a moment. "It would have been a damn tough thing to do, firing a gun at your own father."

"Even if he was a murderous sonofabitch."

"Even if," he agreed.

She shivered. "I'm glad you were with Sam this afternoon, or I probably wouldn't be here now."

"Don't think about what might have happened. Think about what really did happen."

She wrapped her arms around his waist. "What happened was that you saved my life."

"I had a lot of help from you." He bent his head and brushed his lips across her forehead. "If you hadn't jumped off the dock into the lake—"

She tightened her arms around him. "Don't think about what might have happened."

"Okay, so much for discussing the past." He turned her so that he could see her face. "Got any objection to talking about future possibilities?"

Joy bloomed through her. "No."

"I'm thinking of selling the lodge."

"Where will you go?"

"I've heard Glaston Cove is a nice town. Got an active city council and a dandy little newspaper."

"Picturesque, too. Perched on the cliffs overlooking a small, charming bay. It's just the place for a writer, if you ask me."

He eased his fingers through her hair. "I told you, I fell in love with you the day you walked into the lobby and asked if there was any room service available."

"I thought you said you wanted to have sex with me the first time you saw me."

"That, too."

A deep sense of rightness warmed her all the way to her bones. "As I recall, you informed me that the goal of the management of the Sunset on the Lake Lodge was to provide guests with a genuinely rustic experience. No room service, no TV, no pool, no workout facilities."

He stopped her by putting his fingertips on her lips. "But you have to admit that management did provide certain other amenities that are not typically available even at the finer, five-star establishments."

She smiled and kissed him lightly on his mouth. "This is true."

"Management stands ready to continue providing said amenities."

"Even though management is selling the property?"

"Yes."

"How long do you think management would care to go on providing those amenities?"

"For the rest of our lives," Luke said quietly. Absolute conviction rang in the words. "I know I'm rushing you, sweetheart, but I feel like I've been looking for you for a very, very long time. I love you. I will always love you. I've never been more certain of anything in my life. And I sure don't want to waste another minute."

"You aren't the only one who has been searching for a future," she said. "I love you, Luke Danner."

His mouth came down on hers, sure and true and right.

A long time later she stirred beside him in the cozy bed. "You really are going to sell the lodge?"

"Yes."

"Might be tough to find a buyer for this place, especially at this time of year."

"Already got a buyer."

"Really? Who?"

"Maxine."

"Luke, that's a lovely idea. But she can't possibly afford it."

He turned over on the pillow and gathered her close. "We'll work something out."

Forty-nine

S eventeen years ago, I spent a lot of time convincing myself that there was no link between that damned phone
call that I made to Victor Webb and the murders of your
parents, Irene," Sam said wearily. "Did a pretty good job of
it, too."

Luke turned away from the view outside Sam's office window to watch Irene's reaction. He wasn't surprised when he
saw the look of mingled sadness and compassion on her face.

It had been two days since Victor Webb was taken to the
hospital that he had financed years earlier and placed under
guard. In those forty-eight hours Irene had changed in some
subtle ways. It was as if she no longer viewed the town of
Dunsley through a dark lens, he decided. Much of the cautious
reserve with which she had treated most of the locals had
dissipated.

Maybe there was something to that old adage about the
truth setting you free. Or maybe, in this case, the truth had

simply made it possible for Irene to give the past a proper burial.

"I understand, Sam," she said gently.

McPherson folded his hands very deliberately on top of his desk. "Later, when the rumors started up about your mom having had an affair with someone in town, I told myself that might have been enough to push your dad over the edge. I knew that you and Elizabeth were the two most important things in the world to him."

"Victor Webb must have been the one who planted those rumors," Irene said. "It would have been easy enough for him to do, given his connections in this region."

Sam nodded. "Got to admit that I had a bad time for a while after I found out that the file on the case had been destroyed. I think I knew, deep in my gut, that Bob Thornhill had engineered that little so-called accident."

"As a favor to Victor Webb," Irene said.

"It wasn't a favor." Luke went to stand behind her. He put his hands on her shoulders. "He saw it as repaying a debt. Like so many other people in this town, he owed Victor Webb. Webb had paid for his wife's medications."

Sam exhaled heavily. "Hell, even if I had tried to reopen the case after I took over this job, I would have been looking at the wrong member of the family. When I did allow myself to speculate on who might have killed the Stensons, I always assumed the most likely suspect was Ryland."

"But it was Victor you called that night," Luke reminded him.

"Thing is, I never figured him for the killer." Sam unfolded his hands and spread them wide. His eyes were bleak. "He never acknowledged me, but he was my dad."

"Yes," Irene said.

Sam scrubbed his face once with his right hand. "I considered the possibility that after I called Victor, he turned around and called Ryland to confront him about the accusation of incest. There was some logic to that. I thought it was possible that Ryland had, in turn, rushed up here to Dunsley to get rid of the Stensons before the scandal broke. But that was as far as I got with my theories. Like I said, I just didn't want to go there."

Luke looked at him. "I'll bet Bob Thornhill wasn't eager to go there, either."

"No," Sam admitted. "He was my new boss, and he had a lot of years of experience. I was twenty-three years old, and that was the first killing I'd ever seen. When Thornhill announced that it was a murder-suicide and closed the case, I was more than willing to go along."

"As the new chief of police, Thornhill had no problem shutting down the investigation," Irene said.

"It wasn't like there was anyone in town who was going to argue that there was an unknown killer running loose in Dunsley," Sam agreed.

Irene studied him. "You called Victor because you were sure that Pamela was lying about the abuse, didn't you?"

Sam nodded. "I just couldn't believe it. I knew Pamela was angry at Ryland because he'd forced her to go to that boarding school. I thought she was trying to punish him so she invented the tale about the incest."

"What about the video? Did you think she faked it?"

"I didn't know what was on that video. She wouldn't tell me. She just kept saying it was bad. I wondered if maybe she'd caught Ryland having sex with someone from Dunsley or something along those lines. I was still pretty naive in those days. Just couldn't believe that my older brother had abused his daughter. So, yeah, I called Victor."

"What did he tell you?" Irene asked.

"He said he'd take care of things, the way he always did when there was a problem in the family. He reminded me of how he had always taken care of my mother." Sam closed his eyes for a few seconds. Then he looked straight at Irene. "He was in his office at the San Francisco store that day. Just a couple of hours away."

There was a short, heavy silence. Luke squeezed Irene's shoulders to reassure her and then went back to the window.

"He used an inflatable boat with an outboard motor each time he came to Dunsley to kill," he said quietly. "Launched it in some deserted section of the lake. That way there was no risk that anyone would see him entering or leaving Dunsley. Probably didn't worry at all about being seen when he murdered Hoyt Egan, though. No one at the apartment complex would have recognized him. Hoyt would have opened the door to him."

"Just as my parents did," Irene said.

"I'm betting that he used drugs to kill Pamela's mother all those years ago," Sam said grimly. "When he decided to get rid of Pamela, he was forced to act quickly. He must have concluded that it would be easiest to use the same method. After all, he had already done the research."

The certainty in Sam's voice caused Luke to turn around. "You found some evidence?"

Sam's mouth thinned. "I discovered an empty syringe in the glove compartment of my SUV this morning. Sent it off to a lab to run some tests on it. Expect they'll find traces of whatever Victor used to kill Pamela."

Irene's brows rose. "Speaking of your SUV, what reason did Victor Webb give you when he borrowed it?"

"He didn't exactly knock on my door and ask permission to take it," Sam said evenly. "He stole it while I was here in my office. I got a call from the chief of police over in Kirbyville saying he'd found the vehicle abandoned out near the old Ventana Estates subdivision site. We both figured some kids had taken it joyriding."

"Victor must have been desperate to use your vehicle to try to get rid of me," Irene said. "It meant he had to take the risk of slipping into town and stealing the SUV out of your garage without being seen."

"Not that much risk involved." Sam shrugged. "He probably used the old logging trail that runs through the forest behind my subdivision. Remember, he hunted around here all of his life. He knows the terrain as well as he knows his own face in the mirror."

"Still, it seems odd that he used your SUV," Irene insisted. "Why not his own vehicle? Or a rental? And why did he leave the syringe in your glove compartment?"

"Because he knew that things were starting to fray," Luke said quietly. "Victor realized that there was a growing risk that the situation would get out of control. If that happened, he wanted to be sure that there was a convenient fall guy."

Irene's face tightened with dismay. She looked at Sam.

"You," she whispered.

"Me," Sam agreed. "He was setting me up. Just in case."

None of them spoke for a while.

Eventually Sam fixed Irene with his world-weary look. "Your dad knew about the gossip that I was Victor Webb's son. He talked to me about it once."

"When was that?" Irene asked.

"One night when he found me pursuing my favorite hobby, getting drunk at Harry's Hang-Out. That was just after Mom had died. I wasn't handling things very well. He shoved me into his cruiser and took me for a ride. Talked to me."

"What did he say?" Irene asked.

"He told me that in the end it doesn't matter who your father is. He said sooner or later, every man has to take responsibility for inventing himself, has to decide just what kind of man he wants to be. A week later he offered me a job with the department on the condition that I never came to work drunk and never drank on duty. I promised him I wouldn't. I know it doesn't mean much to you, Irene, but I kept my word to him all these years."

"It does mean something." Irene reached across the desk and touched his hand. "It would have been important to Dad, so it's important to me." She rose and looped the strap of her handbag over her shoulder. "You know, I have a very clear memory of the evening that Dad told Mom over dinner that he had given you the job. He said you had what it took to be a good cop."

Sam frowned. "Hugh Stenson said that?"

"Yes." She smiled. "You know, my father was an excellent judge of character."

Sam looked at her the way a man looks at the doctor who has just told him the lab tests came back benign.

"Thanks," he said, his voice very husky. "Thanks."

He sat at his desk for a long time after they had left. It was as if he had been living inside a cage all of his life, Sam thought. But Irene had just opened the door. All he had to do was walk through it.

Still, like any creature faced with a sudden twist of fortune, he hesitated, giving himself time to adjust to the idea of moving into a slightly altered universe.

When he thought he was ready, he opened a drawer, removed the slender volume that was the Dunsley phone book and flipped through the pages until he found the listing.

He punched in the number with short, stabbing motions.

She answered on the first ring.

"This is Sam," he said. "Sam McPherson."

"Oh, hello, Sam." She sounded surprised but not displeased.

"I was just wondering if you would like to have dinner with me some night this week," he said, bracing himself for rejection. "Maybe go over to Kirbyville. If you can get away, that is. If you're not doing something else. I mean, I realize that you're really busy these days."

"Why, Sam, I'd love to have dinner with you," Maxine said.

Fifty

"Heard that bastard Victor Webb died from complications following surgery," Hackett said.

"No loss, as far as I'm concerned." Luke sat sprawled in a chair in Hackett's office, elbows propped on the arms, fingertips together. "The man murdered in cold blood at least five people that we know of. Wouldn't be surprised if there was another victim, too."

"Who?"

"Bob Thornhill, the man who took Irene's father's place as chief of police for a few months. The circumstances of his death are more than a little suspicious. Got a hunch Webb killed him after he was sure all of the evidence and records relating to the deaths of the Stensons had been destroyed."

"Used him and then got rid of him." Hackett shook his head. "Victor Webb must have been a complete sociopath."

"I'm just thanking my lucky stars he didn't realize that Irene would be a problem until it was too late. It was still one damn close call. If she hadn't told Maxine and Tucker Mills where she was going that afternoon when Webb cornered her at the house on Pine Lane—"

"But she did tell them," Hackett interrupted evenly. "And you saved her. Don't waste your time thinking about possibilities that didn't happen."

Luke smiled. "Hey, you know, that's good advice. I believe I'll take it. Thanks."

"You're welcome. Now what's this I hear about selling the lodge?"

"I'm signing the papers tomorrow."

Hackett's brows knitted together in a troubled frown. "Why? Don't get me wrong, no one in the family figured you'd last long in the hospitality industry, but this seems like a rather sudden decision."

"Another one of my unpredictable little turns, you mean?" Luke nodded. "Guess it looks that way. But truth is, the lodge was never meant to be more than a temporary arrangement. I just needed a quiet place where I could work on my book for a few months."

Hackett looked bewildered. "You're writing a book?"

"Been working on it for a while. Another month and it will be finished."

Hackett flattened both hands on the desk. "Why the hell didn't you tell anyone?"

"Well, I did mention to the Old Man that I was doing a little writing."

"'Doing a little writing' is not the same as writing a book, for crying out loud."

"Cut me some slack, here. Everyone in the family assumes that I'm having problems adjusting to the real world. No offense, but I didn't think it would be smart to give you all more ammunition for thinking I was becoming downright eccentric." Luke shrugged. "Besides, I didn't know if I was going to be able to finish the damned thing. Got the end in sight now, though."

Hackett turned abruptly curious. "Have you sold it?"

"Not yet. But I've got an agent who likes the first few chapters and thinks she can peddle it if the rest of the book holds up."

Hackett pondered that for a while. "So, why are you moving away from Dunsley?"

"Among other things, it turns out the place wasn't quite as quiet as I had anticipated. Thought I'd try another town."

"What other town?"

"Glaston Cove."

Understanding lit Hackett's eyes. He started to smile. "This is about Irene, isn't it?"

"It is all about Irene."

"You know something? I think she's going to be very good for you. Maybe just what you need."

"That's sort of how I'm looking at it," Luke said. "By the way, while we're on the subject of my little idiosyncrasies, I would like to clarify what appears to be a serious misunderstanding of what, exactly, happened the weekend that Katy and I went away together."

Hackett stopped smiling. "I heard that nothing happened because of, uh, your problem."

"That's half true."

"Only half?" Hackett looked wary.

"Nothing happened. But the real reason nothing happened was that Katy and I came to our senses and realized that, although we will always be very fond of each other, we are never going to be in love."

"She had a crush on you when she was a teenager."

"That's all it was, a crush. Lasted about five seconds, as I recall. Hell, I'm too old for her, and she's way too young for me."

"She agreed to marry you," Hackett said evenly.

"Don't blame me for that. It was your fault."

"My fault?"

"Yours and the Old Man's and everyone else's in the family. Katy went along with the engagement because you and the others put the mother of all guilt trips on her. You convinced her that I was an emotional basket case and that I might crack under the slightest bit of pressure. She was terrified that if she rejected me, I might follow the same path that my mother took."

Hackett was appalled. "I swear, we never meant to make her think that she would be responsible if you did something like that."

"Yeah, well, that was how it went down. Guess it falls into the no-good-deed-goes-unpunished category."

"Well, damn." Hackett sagged a little, as though he had taken a body blow. Then he straightened. "You really aren't in love with Katy?"

Luke gripped the arms of the chair and pushed himself to his feet. "No. And she is definitely not in love with me."

"Wait a second. If you weren't in love with her, why the hell did you ask her to marry you in the first place?"

Luke walked to the door. "Getting married was part of my strategy. It was one of the things I thought I needed to do to feel normal again."

He opened the door.

Hackett was on his feet, circling his desk. "Luke, wait."

Luke looked back at him, smiling slightly. "It's okay, Hack. Turns out I had the wrong objective. The trick to dealing with real life is to accept the fact that sometimes things never go all the way back to normal."

He went out into the carpeted hall and closed the door.

Hackett stood perfectly still for a few seconds, savoring the incredible sensation that was sweeping through him. He felt as if he had just been released from the weight of an ocean that had been crushing him for the past few months.

He lunged for the door, flung it open and went swiftly down the hall to Public Relations.

Jason came around the corner, a half-eaten wedge of pizza in one hand. "What's up?"

Hackett did not break his stride. "I'm going to try to get a date. Wish me luck."

Jason grinned. "This sounds like fun. Can I watch?"

"Go eat your pizza."

He went through the open door of Public Relations. Katy was seated at her desk, talking on the phone. Her eyes widened a little when she saw him.

"I'll get right back to you, Mr. Perkins," she said quickly. She hung up and looked at Hackett. "What's wrong?"

"Nothing is wrong today." He reached down and hauled her up out of the chair. "Today is a perfect day."

She laughed, confused but delighted. "How is it perfect?"

"Luke just told me that he is not in love with you. He said he never was in love with you and you are not in love with him, and that is the real reason nothing happened that weekend when the two of you went away together."

She went still. "He said all that?"

"Yes. Can you confirm?"

She swallowed hard. "I can definitely confirm that I am not in love with him."

"He also assured me that in spite of the Old Man's and Dr. Van Dyke's fears, he is not in the slightest danger of doing himself any harm. You know what? I believe him. Luke can be stubborn and difficult and unpredictable, but he has never lied to me in my entire life."

"Good point," Jason said around a mouthful of pizza. "Maybe we should have listened when he kept telling us not to worry about him."

Katy glowed with hope. "Does this mean we don't have to be concerned about Luke anymore?"

"Luke can take care of himself," Hackett said. "What's more, if he does run into trouble, he's got someone he can call on for backup now."

"I'm guessing that would be Irene," Jason said.

"You guess right." Hackett did not take his eyes off Katy. He knew that his whole future was hanging in the balance. "Will you have dinner with me tonight? Someplace very private. Just the two of us."

She put her arms around his neck. Her smile lit up the room. "I would like that very much. I've even got a great idea where we can go."

"I am open to suggestion."

"My place," she said.

"Like I said, this is a perfect day."

He pulled her close and kissed her.

"Boy, howdy, this sure explains a few things," Jason said. "Obviously, what we had here was a major breakdown in communications between the executive suite and the PR department. Glad we got that straightened out. If you'll excuse me, I'm going to get another slice of pizza."

Hackett ignored him. So did Katy.

Epilogue

You know," Irene said, "I think your father actually looks younger this year than he did last year on his birthday."

She looked across the crowded room to where John and Vicki stood with Gordon, talking to some guests. Luke followed her gaze, amused.

"Probably because he's no longer worrying about me," he said. "I hear stress can really age you."

"I thought he looked pleased when he came to our wedding, but tonight he seems even happier."

Luke grinned. "That's because he's looking forward to his first grandchild. Expect he's already making plans to bring the kid into the business."

Instinctively she touched her very pregnant shape, mildly astonished that she wasn't glowing as brightly as one of her own flashlights. "I think John and Gordon will have more than one grandchild to work on soon. Katy told me that she and Hackett intend to start a family right away."

"Boy, howdy," Jason said, coming up beside her. "At this rate, there are going to be little rug rats all over the place."

"Your turn next, little brother," Luke said.

"All in due time," Jason said, munching on a canapé. "Life is like making good wine. You don't want to rush it, or you'll miss all the nuances."

"Wow," Luke said. "Listen to Mr. Philosopher."

Jason grinned. "I thought that was pretty good, myself. Speaking of academic stuff, when does your book get released?"

"Next month," Irene said before Luke could respond. She was barely able to restrain her excitement. "The publishers say that advance orders have been very good. They think that *Strategic Thinking, Lessons from Philosophy and War* will not only find an audience among people who read military and business books, but may even cross over into the general market."

Hackett and Katy appeared out of the crowd.

"Nice going," Hackett said. "Looks like you've found another career for yourself."

"It lacks some of the zest of the innkeeping business," Luke said, "but I think it suits me better. The best part about the job is that I get to work at home."

"Which is good," Irene added, "because he is going to make an excellent father."

Jason nodded with an air of great seriousness. "Sure glad you got past your little ED issue, Big Brother."

"You know," Luke said, looking both dangerous and thoughtful, "with all the new offspring on the way in this family, you can probably be replaced one of these days."

Irene and Katy dissolved into laughter. Luke, Hackett and Jason exchanged grins.

On the other side of the room John, Gordon and Vicki turned their heads to look. Irene could see the satisfaction and pride radiating from the two men. Vicki gave her a warm, knowing smile and winked before she turned back to her guests.

Joy, bright and full of promise, flooded through Irene. Luke tugged her closer, his arm around her waist.

"What are you thinking?" he asked.

"I'm thinking that this is how it feels to have a family. That with a love like ours and a family like this one, we can handle whatever comes along in the future."

He smiled, looking satisfied and certain. "Talk about your astonishing coincidences. I was just thinking the very same thing."

Light in Shadow

Jayne Ann Krentz

New York Times **bestselling author Jayne Ann Krentz welcomes you to Whispering Springs, Arizona, where, for the right price, anyone can buy a new identity and get a fresh start. But as Zoe Luce is about to learn, no one can truly escape.**

Zoe Luce is a successful interior designer who's developed an unusual career speciality – helping recently divorced clients redesign their homes, to enable them to forget the past and start afresh. But Zoe knows that some things can't be covered up with a coat of paint. And when she senses that one of her clients may be hiding a dark secret, she enlists private investigator Ethan Truax to find the truth.

Working together, they start to unravel the mystery, but Ethan's investigative skills start to backfire on Zoe: she never wanted to let him find out about her former life; she never wanted to reveal her powerful, inexplicable gift for sensing the history hidden within a house's walls; and she never wanted him to know that "Zoe Luce" doesn't really exist.

But now, Ethan may be her only hope, as just when Zoe started to dream of a normal life and think about the future, her own past starts to shadow her every step – because the people she's been running from are getting close to finding her. . .

Praise for Jayne Ann Krentz and *Light In Shadow*:

'Hearts will flutter. Spines will tingle.' *People Magazine*

'If Krentz's newest thriller doesn't send your pulse racing, dial your cardiologist's number. Krentz's storytelling shines with authenticity and dramatic intensity. . .Tightly written and packed with twists and shockers at every turn, this top-notch thriller keeps readers on the edge of their seats' *Publishers Weekly*

Truth or Dare

Jayne Ann Krentz

Zoe is an interior designer with a unique sense of style. But even more uncanny is her sense of what's going on under the surface, the secrets a house can hold.

At the moment, though, Zoe is more concerned about what's going on in her own house in Whispering Springs, Arizona, where she lives with her new husband, private investigator Ethan Truax.

But newlywed life is suddenly interrupted when a shadowy figure from Zoe's past shows up in Whispering Springs, and her closest friend is put at terrible risk. For Zoe and Arcadia Ames share a shocking secret. And as they seek to protect the truth, they must join together, and with Ethan's help, accept a very dangerous dare...

Falling Awake

Jayne Ann Krentz

Isabel Wright spends her days at the Belvedere Centre for Sleep Research analysing the dreams of others. It's satisfying, lucrative work, but it can be emotionally draining at times. Especially when one of her anonymous subjects, known only as Client Number Two, captures her imagination through his compelling dream narratives.

Client Number Two's real name is Ellis Cutler. A loner who learned long ago not to let anyone get too close, he works for a highly classified government agency with an interest in the potential value of lucid dreaming.

When they meet in the flesh, the dream becomes real enough to touch. And a waking nightmare begins. For a suspicious hit-and-run leads them into a perilous web of passion, betrayal and murder, and forces them to walk the razor-thin line between dreams and reality. . .

The Paid Companion

Amanda Quick

Adam Hardesty has a serious problem. The secrets of his past are in danger of being exposed, and in the course of investigating his would-be blackmailer, he discovers the dead body of a prominent psychic. To make matters worse, her house has been torn apart, and the diary containing Adam's secrets is missing.

His only lead is a list of the psychic's last visitors – the people who came to her house for a sitting on the night of her death. The most likely suspect is a woman named Mrs. Caroline Fordyce, whom he confronts in her parlour, only to discover an inconvenient attraction to the beautiful young widow.

Alarmed by Adam's insinuations and questions, Caroline concludes that she must conduct her own investigation into this strange matter. If she can discover the true killer, Adam will have no reason to expose her connection to the dead psychic, which would cause a scandal she and her aunts could ill-afford. Besides, her life has been boringly uncomplicated for too long, and the exciting tension she feels around Adam presents a welcome alternative to her mundane daily routine. But as Caroline and Adam journey deeper into the shadowy world of psychics, mediums and con artists, they find that the only ones they can count on are each other. . .

Praise for Amanda Quick and *The Paid Companion*:

'Amanda Quick is one of the hottest writers in romance today . . . Her heroines are always women you'd love to know, and her heroes are dashing guys you'd love to love . . .' *USA Today*

'What fun! This action-packed tale, brimming with witty characters, vivid historical detail, and tautly woven intrigue kept me guessing until the very end. I loved the book and can't wait to brag to my mother that I've already read the latest Amanda Quick.' Lisa Gardner

Wait Until Midnight

Amanda Quick

Adam Hardesty has a serious problem: a diary containing his family's darkest secrets has been stolen and, in the course of investigating his would-be blackmailer, he discovers the dead body of a prominent psychic.

His only lead is a list of the psychic's last visitors. The most likely suspect is a young woman named Mrs. Caroline Fordyce, whom he confronts in her parlour only to discover an inconvenient attraction to this beautiful young widow. But Caroline has secrets of her own and will do anything to avoid another scandal, even if it means journeying deeper into the shadowy world of psychics, mediums and con artists, to help the enigmatic Mr Hardesty catch a killer.

Praise for Amanda Quick:

'I love this author!' IRIS JOHANSEN

Lie By Moonlight

Amanda Quick

During an investigation into a woman's death, gentleman thief turned private inquiry agent Ambrose Wells finds himself at Aldwick Castle – and in the middle of chaos. The building is in flames. Men are dead. And a woman and four young girls are fleeing on horseback.

A confirmed loner, Ambrose nevertheless finds himself taking Miss Concordia Glade and her young charges under his wing. With their lives at risk, he insists they must remain in hiding until he is able to unravel the truth behind their recent imprisonment at the castle.

Concordia has never met anyone like Ambrose Wells before. He is bold, clever, and inscrutable – even to the perceptive gaze of a professional teacher such as herself. He is also her only hope to protect her pupils from the unscrupulous men who are after them – powerful, shadowy figures who will stop at nothing to get what they want.

A Victorian Romance

'Amanda Quick is one of the hottest writers in romance today . . .'
USA Today